A VERY ACCIDENTAL LOVE STORY

Claudia Carroll was born in Dublin, where she still lives and works as a full-time writer.

CLAUDIA CARROLL

A Very Accidental Love Story

AVON

This novel is entirely a work of fiction.
The names, characters and incidents portrayed in it are
the work of the author's imagination. Any resemblance to
actual persons, living or dead, events or localities is
entirely coincidental.

AVON
A division of HarperCollins*Publishers*
77–85 Fulham Palace Road,
London W6 8JB

www.harpercollins.co.uk

A Paperback Original 2012
1

A catalogue record for this book is
available from the British Library

ISBN-13: 978-1-84756-272-2

Set in Minion by Palimpsest Book Production Limited,
Falkirk, Stirlingshire

Printed and bound in Great Britain by
Clays Ltd, St Ives plc

Acknowledgements

As always, huge and heartfelt thanks to Marianne Gunn O'Connor, or as she's known in my house, Marianne; Miracle Worker Extraordinaire. Thanks for working so tirelessly and for being such a constant source of inspiration and encouragement. An agent this amazing doesn't rightfully deserve the title 'loveliest woman you could ever possibly meet,' but she *is*, she really is.

Thanks to Pat Lynch, for keeping the show on the road. Pat, I honestly don't know what any of us would do without your calm, friendly voice down the other end of the phone!

Very special thanks to the wonderful Claire Bord. Claire, I really hope you know what an absolute pleasure it is to work with you, the kind of editor any author would gladly give their eye teeth for. Thank you for all the incredible hard work you put into this book and for your wonderful thoughts and suggestions which, as always, were pitch-perfect. Already looking forward to working with you on the new one!

Huge thanks to all the ladies at HarperCollins Avon, or the 'A' team as I call them. You're all amazing and it's a pure pleasure to work alongside you all, although somehow it never feels like work! Very special thanks to Caroline Ridding, Claire Power, Sammia Rafique, Keshini Naidoo and Helen Bolton. And a huge big thank you to the ever-patient Sam Hancock who works so hard on our digital campaigns, websites and newsletters. Looking forward to seeing you all very soon!

Harper Collins are lucky enough to have two of the hardest working people in the business based here in Dublin, who do so much and who make our lives so much easier. A very warm thank you to the legendary powerhouse that is Moira Reilly and also to Tony Purdue, who works so hard, he'd nearly put you to shame.

As always, massive thanks to the lovely Vicki Satlow in Milan, who daily performs miracles in selling translation rights. Vicki, you're a wonder and I only wish we got to see you in Ireland that bit more often. But I'll continue to nag at you!

This book is about a newspaper editor and when I was researching it I was cheeky enough to approach Geraldine Kennedy, then editor of the *Irish Times*, with all the blithe confidence of the gobshite. Here's the problem you see, everyone thinks you're telling lies when you ring them up and say, 'no really! I'm researching a book! Honest!) But with Geraldine, did I hit the jackpot or what? Instead of politely showing me the door, she was extraordinarily generous with her time and really went out of her way to give me insights into the workings of a scarily massive paper like that. Huge thanks again for everything Geraldine, and I wish you well in this exciting new phase of your life.

Very special thanks to my family, Mum and Dad and to my gorgeous gang of buddies, who've been in my life for decades now. (Yes, we are all VERY old, *scarily* old . . . . . .)

When I first got published way back in 2004, I had the real pleasure of meeting a whole new group of friends, female writers one and all, who've been so welcoming and so incredibly supportive from day one. I'm so grateful to have you all in my life and on a personal note, can I just say that I've dedicated this book to one of those very special writer buddies I've been lucky enough to meet along the way.

This one's for Anita Notaro.

For Anita Notaro, with love.

Watch your thoughts, for they become words,
Watch your words, for they become actions,
Watch your actions, for they become habits,
Watch your habits, for they become character,
Watch your character, for it becomes your destiny.

Anonymous

Prologue

They say no man is an island, but Eloise Elliot was.

Not that this particularly bothered her most of the time, but tonight was different.

It was her thirtieth birthday, and, bar a few stragglers from the accounts department who'd famously go to the opening of a fridge door if they thought they might scab a free drink out of it, no one had turned up.

No one.

Not a single one of the Board of Directors she worked so slavishly for; nor any of her senior editorial team, colleagues she'd known and worked shoulder-to-shoulder with for the past seven gruelling years. Not even the few – the very few – co-workers who, if she didn't exactly think of them as friends, at least didn't physically hurl furniture at her as she passed them by.

And so this was it. This was how Eloise Elliot came to mark her thirtieth year: upstairs in *The Daily Post's* conference room, surrounded by a few mangy-looking helium balloons and trays of dismal egg and watercress sandwiches that were already curling up at the edges, making faux-polite small talk with a bunch of semi-strangers. All of whom, for the record, then cried off early, pleading early starts the next day and in all likelihood only dying to get out of there the minute the free gargle ran out.

'Sure you wouldn't like a vol-au-vent?' Eloise asked a smiley-faced blonde girl, whose name she hadn't quite caught. 'Go on, look, there's loads left. You can't leave now, look at all this grub! You've got to help me get rid of at least some of it.'

'Emm,' Blonde Girl said uncertainly, glancing at the others for support, 'well . . . I'd love to stay, but . . . I've got this really early meeting in the morning.'

'Mini vegetarian frittata then?' said Eloise, wafting an untouched tray under her nose. Like this might make a difference.

'I'm so sorry, I really have to go . . .'

'Yeah . . . me too, it's so late,' said her pal, a tall modelly-looking one who Eloise vaguely recognised from seeing in the staff canteen a few times.

'Go on, just have a slice of birthday cake before you go. You know you want to!' Eloise offered, trying her best to keep the slightly hysterical note out of her voice. And not succeeding very well.

'Can't, I'm afraid. I live miles away and if I miss my bus . . .'

'How about yourself?' Eloise said to a new intern, whose name she thought might be Susan, as she thrust a plateful of vanilla sponge gateaux at her.

'Oh . . . ehh . . . thanks so much,' Susan answered politely, the only one to look even slightly sympathetic, 'but you see, I really do need to make tracks as well, been a really long day . . .'

Lost cause, Eloise thought. Waste of her time even asking them to stay. Instead she stood and watched the three of them clatter out the door and on towards the lift bank in their too-high heels, getting giddier by the minute it seemed, the further they were away from her.

So this was it, she thought, this was the start of a brand-new decade for her. And so far, it was her worst nightmare come true.

She hadn't even wanted a party in the first place – no time, thanks very much – but then Eloise was famous for rarely socialising with anyone unless it was a) work related, b) would involve making several important new business contacts or c) there was just no possible way out of it. Even then, she'd be the last to arrive, the first to leave and would impatiently nurse a glass of still water for the hour or so that she was there, all while checking emails on her iPhone approximately every ten minutes or so.

Oh sure, she'd put in an appearance at the staff Christmas party mainly because she didn't really have a choice after all, she was the boss and even she knew how crap it would look if she didn't. But by and large, she was her own best friend and perfectly happy to be so. She was an island and islands are rarely bothered about popularity. Which at that particular moment in time, as she sat all alone on an empty desk beside rows and rows of untouched wineglasses, was probably just as well.

Absent-mindedly, she started to play with the string hanging off the end of a gaudy pink 'Congratulations!' helium balloon anchored beside her and for the first time in years, allowed herself a rare moment of introspection.

Welcome to my life, she thought. Thirty years of age and utterly alone. No friends, no 'significant other', no office colleagues who, perish the thought, might actually want to spend some non-work-related time with her – no one.

When it came down to it, she was basically living the life of a nun on a six-figure salary.

Sure she had family, but she saw them so rarely, they barely even figured. Her darling dad had passed away years ago and her mother now lived in Marbella with a duplex, a perma-tan and a worrying habit of drinking during the day. But although they'd have a weekly chat on the phone and in spite of countless invitations to 'jump on a plane and come and get some sun for yourself,' Eloise really only got to see her mum once a year, when she'd fly home for Christmas. If work permitted even that much. Last Christmas Day, a story had unexpectedly broken in the Middle East and Eloise ended up having to rush back to the *Post* to cover it.

She had a younger sister too, Helen, but she'd upped sticks and moved down to Cork a few years back. Besides, it was unspoken between the sisters, but deep down each knew they'd next to nothing in common. They saw each other rarely, spoke even less and even that was just for form's sake, little more.

In fairness, most of the time, Eloise didn't particularly miss having friends, mainly because how can you miss what you never really had in the first place? Dating right the way back to primary school, when she continually came top of her class, the other kids, viciously cruel as small kids usually are, would ostracise her and call her a freak, mainly because no one wanted to be pals with the girl who constantly badgered the teacher about their homework load being insufficient and unchallenging.

Eloise read at Junior Cert level by the age of four, was declared a member of Mensa at five and by nine, had composed a violin concerto to accompany the senior school's production of *Romeo and Juliet*.

For God's sake, even the teachers were a bit scared of her.

And so unsurprisingly, she grew up being utterly self-reliant and not really needing other people, thanks very much. Totally married to her job; in fact, she *was* the job. Youngest senior editor the *Post* had ever had, by the way, with all the stress ulcers to prove it, and in the space of a few short years she had not only trebled their circulation but completely turned their readership around, *a la* Tina Brown. First at her desk every morning, last to leave at night; this is not a woman who did down time, friends, family or socialising, ever. Sorry, no time.

Small wonder people didn't warm to her. She had a clatter of various nicknames behind her back among sub-ordinates at her office, none of which stuck, mainly because the very phrase 'Eloise Elliot wants to see you in her office, now,' delivered just like that, unfrilled and straight up, was pretty much enough to terrify any poor unfortunate who worked for her into white-faced, trembling, silence.

And now on this of all nights, Eloise was suddenly seeing the rest of her whole life stretching right out in front of her. Seeing it as vividly as if she'd already lived it. Clear as crystal, she could see herself at forty, then at fifty, then right up all the way to retirement age, still editing the paper, still working eighteen-hour days, and still alone.

Pretending to celebrate a day she didn't particularly care about, while a handful of strangers looked at her the way everyone seemed to look at her these days; with a mixture of pity and terror.

Sometimes we don't recognise the most significant moments of our lives till they've long passed, but not Eloise. Hard to believe that miserable night would change the whole course of her carefully ordered existence, and yet that's exactly how it would pan out.

Years later, she'd look back and pinpoint this as the precise moment when heaven whispered in her ear and when she suddenly knew what needed to be done to kill this life, to fix this problem. Because to someone with Eloise's keen mathematical brain, that was all this was; a problem to be solved, like a simple maths equation.

And make no mistake: solve it, she would.

So with that same dazzling clarity that you only ever get on rare, road-to-Damascus moments in life, Eloise Elliot rubbed sore, red eyes, took a deep breath and made one of the lightning-quick, clear-headed decisions for which she'd become legendary.

It was time to take action.

PART ONE

ELOISE

THREE YEARS LATER

Chapter One

Not today. Just please not today. I can't tell you how I so do NOT need this today.

It's barely five thirty in the morning and already my whole life seems to be spiralling dangerously out of all control, something that's happening with all-too alarming frequency these days. For starters, while I'm trying to slip out the door at the crack of dawn (nothing unusual there, this is when I have to leave for work every morning), Elka, my Polish nanny, picks today of all shagging days to have an out-and-out meltdown.

There I am, sneaking downstairs in my bare feet, trying not to wake anyone, already running late for the early morning news briefing. Never, ever a good start to the day. Next thing, madam stomps out of her bedroom, still in her dressing gown, not so much asking, as demanding, to have a 'queek word with you.'

'Emm . . . yes, of course, Elka,' I say, instantly smelling trouble and deliberately keeping my voice down to a low hiss, so as not to disturb Lily.

Lily, by the way, is my little girl; almost three years old now and the light of this exhausted, knackered-to-her-very-bone-marrow mummy's life.

13

'Is everything OK?' I ask politely, biting my tongue and bracing myself for the answer. Elka is the one nanny we've had who Lily adores and behaves beautifully for, and for her part, Elka herself genuinely seems fond of her too.

'I neeeeed to speak with you, and this crazy hour of morning is only time I am seeing you all this week,' she tells me in her still-rubbishy English, in spite of the small fortune I've forked out on audio books and private lessons for her over the past few months.

Please don't tell me you're about to leave. Please for the love of God, don't let another one leave . . .

'Go ahead, Elka,' I manage to say calmly, but with bowels clenched, only dreading what's going to come out of her mouth next.

'In my contract, it say that you am paying me to look after Lily,' she says crisply, arms folded, ponytail swishing back, nostrils flaring. 'But you must understand me when I tell to you, this mean during *reasoning* hours.'

'I think you might mean *reasonable* hours,' I tell her. 'Can I ask you what's suddenly brought all this on?'

'You have huge nerve to ask that of me!'

'Shhh! Can you keep it down please? You'll wake Lily.'

'I have many, many problem with the hours you expect me to be working. None of the other nannies who am my friends work as long days as I must.'

'But Elka, your hours are hardly long. At least, not compared with mine, they're not . . .'

'Look at time now! Five thirty a.m.! And already you are going to office, which mean I am in care of Lily. You meant to be home at seven in the night times so I can have free time for me, and you never are. Ever!'

Okay, I'm momentarily silenced here. Because actually,

the girl does have a point. Technically I'm supposed to be home at seven-ish in the evening so she can clock off, but . . . well, for the past while, it's been a tiny bit later than that. Like eleven p.m. Or even midnight.

'All other nannies have evenings free! They am all meeting for coffee and beer and movies. All having good time in Ireland! All have boyfriends and days off and nights out! But never me! No fun for me, ever. I tell you I am sick of it, have enough! Is total crap!'

'Shhh! Elka, please will you keep your voice down,' I stage whisper at her, but madam's having none of it. Instead she's whipped herself up into a right frenzy and there's no stopping her now.

'No, you must be listening to me. Because you am working late, I must too. It's too much and I want to quit!'

'I hear what you're saying and I completely understand but can I also remind you that this is the nature of my job?' I tell her as soothingly as I can, knowing full well she has me backed into a corner now. Because if she walks out on me . . . Oh dear God, it just doesn't bear thinking about.

'And if you don't like the schedule I have to work Elka, well . . . I'm really sorry but there's absolutely nothing I can do about it. Believe me, I don't like working such long hours, any more than you do. So if you're looking for someone to blame, then take it up with . . . Eurozone leaders and the global economic meltdown. Or . . . blame the Arab Spring in the Middle East, which is hardly my fault, now is it?'

'I no understand . . . you must use little words for me!'

I take another deep breath.

'I'm so sorry Elka,' I tell her as calmly as I can, given that I should have been out the door ten minutes ago and

15

even though the day has barely started, I'm now already well behind schedule, 'but if there's a big news story, the editor has to be there to oversee it. That's my life. News doesn't take time off and therefore neither can I. Editors at the *Post* don't sit around. In fairness, I did make this perfectly clear to you when I hired you. Plus, can I point out that I pay you far and above the rates all your other nanny pals are earning? But of course,' I tack on brightly, hoping against hope that this might just work, 'if it's a question of giving you yet another salary increase, I'd be perfectly happy to discuss it with you later.'

No, not even that sways her though. In fact, I might as well be talking to the back of my hand.

'You work too long days and it no good for Lily, as well as no good for me,' she lobs in, a cheap shot if ever there was one. The old emotional guilt-card thrown at a busy working mother.

'She miss her mama so much when you not here. All the time she ask me, when is Mama coming home?'

'Come on Elka, that is blatantly ridiculous and deeply hurtful . . .'

'Even at the weekend time, when you should be with her, you am still in the office. Always, always working.'

Now that bloody stung, and just as this conversation was heating up, temporarily stuns me into silence. I mean, yes, of course I wish I could spend twenty-four hours a day with Lily, I mean, who wouldn't? But how can I possibly?

I get a lightning-quick flashback to the first year she was born, when somehow, I seemed to manage just fine; got to spend whole weekends with her, even managed to get home relatively early most nights. I can do this, I thought;

I can have the best of both worlds. I can be Superwoman. I had my whole work/life balance sussed back then and can honestly say it was the happiest time of my life. By far.

But then the recession hit hard and the staff cutbacks started and that was the end of that. Suddenly I was expected to do the work of three people for the same money or else get out, that was it. Well, it was worse than Sophie's bleeding Choice. Because much as I love and adore the ground Lily walks on, work is a hugely important part of my life too and if these are my new working hours, then bar resigning, there's not a whole lot I can do about it.

In brutal moments of introspection, I just know I'm someone who'd go off her head in less than a week without a full-time career to nourish my soul. Sure, parenthood is a huge high, but then so is my job. *Peppa Pig* and *Barney* videos could never possibly give me the same buzz. So, if it's not too much to ask, can't I just have both? I mean, plenty of other women do, don't they?

But I have at least established clear boundaries with the office and made it perfectly clear to everyone that my Sundays with Lily are sacrosanct. The one day out of an otherwise mental week when I get to read her stories and make pancakes with her, then maybe take her to a Disney movie, or else to feed the ducks in the park. You know, spoil her rotten. Be a proper mummy.

Mind you, ever since the most recent staff culling started, I reluctantly have to admit that Elka might have a point and that even Sacred Sunday Mummy Time seems to have been seriously curtailed lately. Last week for instance; I'd made Lily her breakfast, played imaginary tea parties with her small army of dolls and was just about to take her to the toystore for a *very* special treat, when I got a call to get

17

into the office ASAP. There was an emergency news conference about a breaking story developing in Afghanistan, so
what else could I do? I had to be there, simple as that. Goes
with the job.

And I may not let it show, but I love my little Lily so
much that it physically aches to be away from her for any
length of time, never mind for the eighteen-hour days I'm
practically expected to put in right now. For God's sake,
don't I have enough guilt of my own to deal with at being
apart from her, without having it flung into my face by
someone who I'm employing? And at premium rates too,
I might add?

'Tell you what, I have a suggestion Elka,' I say, evenly
and deliberately locking my voice into its lowest register,
which I've learned is absolutely the best way to deal with
any confrontational situation. And I should know, having
been through more than a fair few in my time. 'Is it too
much to ask that you just get on with your job, let me get
on with mine and then this evening when I'm home from
work, we can discuss this calmly, at a more appropriate
time. Come on now, what do you say to that?'

But madam's in no mood to listen to reason.

'I say to all the other nannies, you have no husband, you
have no boyfriend, no man, instead you are married to
your work.'

And . . . bam.

'Excuse me, *what* did you just say?'

'. . . all other children I know each has each mother and
father, but not Lily. She only have mother. So the mother
need to be here for her more. Much, much more.'

Okay, now that feels exactly the same as a hard wallop
across the cheek and hurts so much it momentarily stuns

me. So of course, the second I come to, I snap right back at her, the way I seem to snap at everyone these days. But there you go, that's what deep, ongoing exhaustion and off-the-scale stress levels will do to you.

'Elka, I made it perfectly clear to you from day one that I was a single parent,' I tell her crisply. 'I don't have a problem with it and neither does Lily, but if this is some kind of issue for you, you really should have said so before now.'

'Single parent need to spend more time with kids, not less.'

Okay, so now I'm fuming, feeling like smoke is physically puffing out of my ears, cartoon-like. Because she's hit my weak spot square-on, with all the accuracy of an aircraft bomber. Yes, I'm a lone parent and yes, there can be huge disadvantages to that. But deal with it, is my attitude.

The subject of Lily's father is one that's not up for discussion. Not now, not ever.

And when I think of the amount of money I pay Elka every month – and all for what? So she can stand here, pass judgement on my life and make me feel about two inches tall? So she can spend all day playing with a little girl who's not even three years old? Does she think that I wouldn't jump at the chance to stay home all day and be a full-time mum? Doesn't she realise how it's like a stab in the chest every time I have to kiss Lily's little strawberry-blonde head of curls goodbye? Or, worst of all, when I have to listen to the innumerable voice messages she leaves on my phone when I'm at work, in her angelic little baby voice, all with the same unvarying theme? 'I miss you Mama. When are you coming home?' There are times when all I want to do is hug her and hold her and tell her not to bother growing up, it's not worth all the hassle. Just stay like this, stay my little girl forever.

Doesn't anyone realise how gutted I am that I seem to be missing out on so much of her? Missed her taking her first baby steps, missed her saying her first words . . . I'm never there, I'm either in a meeting or writing an editorial or chairing a news conference; always, always, working. And of course I went into single parenthood with both eyes open; I knew massive life changes would be involved. Which is why I hired a live-in nanny, plus two back-up child-minders in case of emergencies. Hired them – and then subsequently had to accept all their resignations, one by one like ducks in a row, for exactly the same reasons Elka is now citing.

But come on, in my defence, how was I supposed to know with all the redundancies at work in the past two years that my workload would effectively double? Anyway, I think, furious with exhaustion now, what does Elka think I'm putting in all these ungodly hours for anyway? Only to keep myself sane, while giving my little girl the best life that I possibly can. Hardly my fault that I can't be in two places at once – not with the hours I'm expected to put in, and certainly not with my contract up for renewal in six months. Not now. Apart from everything else I have to worry about, now there's trouble afoot at work, you see, though it's not normally something I articulate out loud.

Trouble by the name of Seth Coleman, managing editor of the *Post*.

Ah, Seth Coleman. Where do I begin? He hasn't even been in the job that long; he was headhunted from *The Sunday Press* when his predecessor at the *Post* left. Who by the way was a gorgeous, preppy, easy-going guy I strongly suspect I drove out of there and who I now miss more than my right hand. His official reason for quitting was for 'work/life balance', and to be perfectly honest, who could blame him?

Anyway, when pressed officially as to my opinion of Seth, I smile curtly and acknowledge his fine leadership qualities and firm grasp of the newspaper business, always adding that he's never anything else than a consummate professional, at all times, always.

But when I'm standing in the shower, which is about the only place I get any kind of private time to myself these days, I will name-call Seth Coleman as the sleaziest, most hypocritical b**locks on the face of the planet, with a thin, slimy, greasy head of hair, and pockmarked, boiled-red skin, whose total absence of neck gives him more than a passing resemblance to Barney Rubble. Oh, and with an ego the approximate size of Saturn's fifty-seven moons. Represents just about every trait that I despise in the male sex and even manages to discover a few new ones along the way. Patronising to my face, but behind my back, I know right well that he's deeply resentful of working for a woman. And with my seven-year contract up for renewal in the next few months, even the dogs on the street seem to know that his greedy eye is now firmly focused on the big prize.

A classically mean-spirited man, he's also someone who keeps a mental tally of all my losses in work, diligently measuring all my shortcomings, rather than any of my gains. For starters, he's been busily spreading rumour after rumour about me and they've all filtered back; that I'm slipping, that ever since I had Lily I'm not the firebrand I once was, that I'm not living and breathing the job like I used to. And I know, just know without being told, that he's just biding his time, waiting for me to crack, and so therefore I can't.

So I do what I have to do. Go into work and act the part of the bossiest boss that the world of big bossy business could ask for. Do exactly what I'm programmed to do. And it's tough and getting tougher by the day, even though my job defines me; it's who I am and not for one second could I consider doing something less stressful.

But having said all that, the brightest part of my day isn't when I sign off on the next issue of the *Post*, it's seeing the little strawberry-blonde head of an almost-three-year-old sleeping like an angel when I get home, cuddled up in her bed with her favourite teddy bear beside her. And I'll gaze at her adorably freckled pink little angel's face and whisper to her that I love her so, so much and that one day we'll have proper time to be together.

Then I do what I always do; collapse into bed and try to lock away the guilt that feels like heartburn every time I realise the one single thing that has the power to kill me on the inside; the only time I seem to see my baby girl these days is when she's sleeping.

But back to Elka, still spitting fire and venom at me on the upstairs landing.

'Lily is beautiful little girl,' she spews, 'and I will be sad to say goodbye to her, but the hours you make me work are crazy. Crazy! And they making me crazy too!'

'Really sorry about this,' I'm forced to interrupt, unable to take much more, But 'I'm going to be late for work. Could we please discuss this later?'

'I not finished! I know my entitlements too. My other friends tell me you must give me P45 with full salary entitlements paid up front before I leave.'

22

Interesting, I think wryly, grabbing my car keys. Elka's grasp of English is so weak she can barely get by in the supermarket and yet her vocabulary freely encompasses quite scarily impressive phrases like 'P45 with full salary entitlements paid up front'?

'Elka,' I tell her, as briskly as I can, given that I'm now running so late it doesn't bear thinking about. 'Can I just point out that it's not as if you have to take care of Lily all day, every day? She's only just started in pre-school and is there till early afternoon every day, which gives you a good five-hour break, plus it's not like you're expected to do housework on top of everything else. I've a cleaning lady, a gardener and a handyman, who between them pretty much do everything that needs doing around here, so you'll forgive me for thinking that you actually have it pretty easy compared to some.'

Like oooh . . . me for starters.

But the snarling harridan stands firm, arms folded, eyes slitted, ponytail swished defiantly back over her shoulders.

'You not listening to me. I am handing you in my notice and I want to be gone by the end of the week. I'm veeeery sorry, but that's final.'

It's all I can do to nod curtly, resisting the temptation to wham the hall door behind me, and get into my car as calmly as I can, above all trying not to let her see how much she's knocked me for six.

Stopped at traffic lights on Leeson St. on the way to work, I have to pull the car over when I realise that out of nowhere, there's a hot hole in the pit of my stomach and suddenly I have an urgent need to cry. And now here it comes, my daily anxiety attack – jeez, I could nearly set a clock by its arrival. So out they come, messy, uncontrollable,

23

dry, hiccupping tears of frustration and tiredness that I never allow myself, born from not having paused for breath in . . . Oh . . . about seven years now. Can't help it. It's like my heart is aching with a pain that's completely indescribable.

Christ alive, not even six a.m. in the shagging morning and already I'm filled with a darkness that's almost unbearable at the thoughts of the day ahead. To my knowledge, I've never actually had a heart attack, but I swear, it couldn't possibly feel much worse than this.

Because I have never felt so torn in my whole life. Not just between work and home; that I could deal with, that wouldn't be a problem. Trouble is my job isn't just one big job, it's also about nine hundred and ninety-nine small jobs that go with the one big job, so instead of feeling pulled in two directions, I'm being pulled in around a thousand. And frankly there are times when I just don't know how much longer this can continue.

'Oh what the hell is wrong with me?' I say aloud, starting to get panicky as I fish round the bottom of my handbag for a Kleenex. Can this really be me, Eloise Elliot, acting like such a complete milksop? Time was when I would work this exact same schedule and it barely knocked a feather out of me. Time was if I happened to drive past a woman on her own sobbing her heart out in a parked car at dawn, I'd look at her pityingly and assume she was having some kind of breakdown and clearly needed professional help. Time was when I used to think that I'd somehow been born without tear ducts.

But that girl only existed B.L. – before Lily – and now in her place is a shadow of the old Eloise Elliot, a woman filled with darkness who's expected to do the work of a dozen people and never ever crack, all the while eaten up with guilt like I've never known. And why? Because a little girl who's nearly three will come home from pre-school later on today, full of stories and chat that her mummy will never get to hear.

And now, on top of everything else, I'm nannyless. Yet *again*.

The six a.m. news comes on the car radio and I know this bout of unforgivable self-indulgence is over and it's time to go and face into another day. So I make a huge effort to compose myself, knock back a large gulpful of Rescue Remedy (an editor's best friend), pat a bit of concealer round my puffy, red-raw eyes and with shaking hands, drive on. I'm already a good fifteen minutes behind schedule so I put my foot to the floor to try and make up the time. If I dared to arrive in late, word would spread that something was up and rule one of survival in my job is simple; never let anyone see a chink in the armour for any reason, ever. They're like a pack of barracudas in my office, I swear they can physically smell the fear.

Calmly as I can, I make a mental note to find another childcare agency and leave a voicemail message for Rachel, my assistant, telling her to start setting up interviews as soon as she gets in. Easier said than done, given that the last agency I went to fired me about two years ago. Which stung more than a bit too. But I managed not to let it show. You just can't in my game, not for one second.

Anyway, by six fifteen a.m. I'm racing upstairs from the underground car park of the *Post's* offices on Tara St., the only bit of exercise I ever seem to have time for these days, what with all the extra work that I'm now expected to do for pretty much the same money I was making three years ago. Which by the way, is a fairly standard change in the newspaper industry now, ever since the recession hit in a big way and our sales took a sharp decline. I.e. yet another stress-inducing source of sleepless nights, if you're the editor and your contract is up for renewal later on in the financial year.

Particularly if you happen to be answerable to a board of directors who are all male, with a collective average age of about sixty-five. The T. Rexes, I call them; they're like dinosaurs from a bygone era, representative of a time when all you could hear in the newsroom was the furious clacking sound of clunky metal typewriters. The days when senior editors swaggered in drunk after big, boozy lunches, where they'd all quaff cognac, wining and dining advertisers on fat expense accounts, then roll back to the office late in the afternoon pissed as farts and no one would so much as bat an eyelid.

A whole other age ago, during the glory days of the newspaper industry. And right now, frankly there are times when I feel like all I'm doing is fighting a brave rearguard action trying to sustain what I worry is turning into more and more of a twilight industry, with the internet now leading the field as the gutteriest gutter press out there. More and more each day, I'm starting to feel that my job is like trying to steer an oil tanker through a minefield and that it's only a matter of time before the whole industry is declared as extinct as the dinosaur.

It's as though the board of directors feel that survival is a form of success and as far as I'm concerned, that's just not enough, not in this climate. Their old-fashioned attitude is that the *Post* is a bastion of tradition that holds up the sky, and while that may have been the case at one time, it sure as hell isn't now. Times have changed and we either evolve or we die, simple as that.

What's worse though is that redundancy is now in the air again. I can smell it sharp as you like; it's hanging round every office corner, it's in the stale, recycled air we're breathing. And I know, just know without being told, that it's only a matter of time before there's yet another staff culling, another round of people being asked to exactly the same job, except for far less money, on a three-day week.

Oh God, I think, suddenly sickened just by the very thought that I have colleagues I pass on corridors each and every day whose days here are numbered and what's worse, that I'm the only thing standing between them and a dole queue. Or more precisely, me and the amount of sales volume I can continue to generate for the paper. They may not know it, but they're dependent on me and me alone for their job survival, and the pressure is at times overwhelming.

I quicken my pace, puffing and panting to make up time, thinking *must try harder*. Don't know how I'm going to do it, but I'm just going to have to find more hours in the day, somehow. Because if it kills me, no one is going to lose their job, not on my watch. Not if I can help it.

Oh God, half of me wonders if I've got room for another stress ulcer.

My office is all the way up on the fourth floor, a gorgeous, airy, spacious room with floor-to-ceiling windows that look down onto all the briskness and business of Tara St. below me. Not that I've ever got a spare second to enjoy the view, that is. Or indeed, to luxuriate in the early-morning stillness, a few precious hours before the phones start hopping and things really get pressurised round here.

27

And every single morning of my life when I flash my pass at the security doors and stride across the main open-plan office to get to my inner sanctum, there waiting for me on the wall above my desk is a giant portrait of one Douglas Merriman, our founder and first editor. Who by the way, would have sat in the very same office now occupied by me, all of a hundred and fifty years ago. He's a heavily bearded geezer who looks exactly like Tolstoy, and when I feel those stern Victorian round owl glasses glaring down at me, I look back up at him, thinking the same thought that I do every single day since I took this job.

Bastard. You never had to work in a digital age, with email and mobiles to connect you to the office even on a Sunday at two a.m. did you? You never had to compete with twenty-four hour news channels or try to sell papers in the middle of the worse economic slump since the Great Depression, did you?

I'm just flipping open my briefcase and whipping out my initial draft of notes on today's edition, always how we kick off the day round here: with a thorough going over of this morning's early edition; where we scored, where we could have done better, where there's vast room for improvement, that kind of thing. All department heads are required to be here for this, which means about a dozen people sitting round the conference room in total, ranging from political affairs, to foreign, to sports and culture.

Next thing, without even bothering to knock, Seth Coleman's lean, slimy, Basil Rathbone-esque form is filling my office door. Looking like he always does, like he was dressed by his mammy. Funny, but for the longest time I assumed he was gay but still in the closet; no straight man would ever wear trousers that sharply ironed, for starters. But then a few years back, he made a bizarre and badly misjudged pass at me at the Christmas party. I remember looking at him in blank astonishment that he'd somehow misread my deep loathing of him for in-your-face lust and it now lives on forevermore in the comedy quadrant of my brain.

'Morning Eloise. So what's keeping you? In exactly one minute, you're going to be late.'

Like this is an episode of *24*, and I'm Jack Bauer.

'Everyone's already waiting for you in the boardroom, you know,' he says in his nasal whine, slicking his hair back, even though there must be a half-pound of grease already holding it there. 'All department heads, present and correct. Hope there's nothing wrong with you, is there? Not like you to sail this dangerously close to unpunctuality.'

I say nothing, nod curtly and smile though gritted teeth.

'So have you thought any more about my offer to escort you to the directors' weekend this year? It's just round the corner you know.'

A brief, unspoken thought filters between us, him mentally spelling it out to me: 'and let's face it, I'm the best offer you're going to get'.

I totally ignore it, hide my annoyance behind a sheet of A4 paper, then briskly brush past him, ready to start the day.

And just when I think things can't get possibly get any worse, *da-daaa*, they do. *Course* they do. What else did I expect? It's already past two in the afternoon and I'm back in the conference room, feeling like I've never left it, chairing our first meeting about the mock-up of tomorrow's paper.

This, by the way, is where we sit around and thrash out the overall shape of the news, what the lead item should be on the front page, what stories are developing and need to be closely monitored over the next few hours, what feature and opinion pieces should be placed where. Everyone's here at my insistence, the political editor, foreign, financial, regional, culture, the whole lot of them, all pitching their stories and vying for the maximum coverage possible, with a front page slot the absolute Holy Grail.

Ordinarily I get a huge buzz out of this meeting; tempers tend to flare, passions run high – something I freely encourage – and it's always exhilarating to hear each editor push their stories and battle to get the maximum number of column inches allowed. We're a bit like a debating club, minus the alcohol, but bear in mind the department heads here are about as vocal, argumentative and aggressive a bunch as you'd care to fight in a bar-room brawl on a Friday night. For some reason though, I just don't seem to be on the ball this afternoon.

Can't concentrate, can't focus. Impossible to after what's unfolded since this day from hell began, and certainly not given what's happening in my personal life outside of these four walls. Oh sure, no doubt about it, by about eight this morning I was supremely confident that I'd have a replacement for Elka before the day was out; someone far more suitable, I even went so far as to think smugly. Someone, let's just say, a bit less moody and demanding, who understood what it was like to work for a busy, professional single parent.

By ten-thirty, when I'd clocked a look at the first few candidates for the job, admittedly I was taken aback, but still reasonably sure that it was just a matter of trawling through the dross before I hit on my perfect Mary Poppins. Candidate numbers one and two were just a bit of a blip, no more that that. Just a simple matter of doing a little bit more weeding, that was all, with absolutely no call for panic whatsoever.

By eleven forty-five, yes, okay . . . so the mood had shifted a bit and now I was starting to get tetchy, unable to figure out why in the name of God it was so bloody difficult to fill a perfectly simple job in the throes of an economic meltdown, but I still held onto a sliver of hope that so far I'd just been unlucky and it was simply a matter of hanging in there till the perfect nanny calmly strolled into my life. To stay.

And right now at two in the afternoon, after the last and final disastrous interview, there's no other way to describe it: I'm in a blind bleeding panic. About a dozen voices are bickering for all they're worth, clamouring for my attention across the boardroom, while I sit at the top of the table, looking and acting like I'm listening intently; but actually, I'm a million miles away.

Because now I know. It's finally official. I'm on the brink of a crisis.

I Have. No. Childcare. As of the end of this week, I have no one to help me; not a single soul. And what in the name of God am I going to do then? Take Lily into work with me and stick her into a playpen in the middle of my office, hoping no one will notice? Yeah, right, some hope. If I were to even think about doing that, I might as well tie a large neon sign around my neck saying, 'Have finally cracked up, kindly fire me ASAP as Seth Coleman is only chomping at the bit waiting to take over anyway'.

The more I dwell on the problem, the more my mouth begins to feel dry; and although I'm desperately trying not to let it show, I know that tiny beads of worry sweat are forming on my forehead, as my heart palpitates with anxiety. I hear nervous rattling and realise it's my ring off the desk in front of me, so I snap open a bottle of water and try to focus on the length of my inhale and exhale, desperately trying to stay in the game. Because if I am in the throes of a full-blown panic attack, no one in this room can ever know about it. Try as I might though, the same sickening thought keeps playing like a loop in my head, over and over again, and there's just no getting away from it.

Every available nanny out there is completely unhireable, I'm in the middle of the biggest crisis I've had since having Lily, there is no one, absolutely NO ONE out there to help me and what in the name of arse am I supposed to do now?

Earlier today, Rachel, my long-suffering assistant, managed to trawl through the few childcare agencies that I haven't been blacklisted from as of yet and scraped together a grand total of four nannies for me to interview. Yes, that's right, *four.* We're in the middle of the deepest recession since the Dark Ages, no one is spending a red cent, property values have dropped so much that people's homes have fallen back to the prices they would have been in Viking times and above all . . . There are NO JOBS.

And yet here I am, fully poised to pay top dollar plus bribe money to someone who'll take care of a child who's almost three years old, and move into a perfectly comfortable home in Rathgar, with their own bedroom and ensuite to boot. Not exactly a demanding gig; it's not brain surgery, it's not like running a global corporation, all I'm looking for is some reasonable, responsible person who'll make sure a little girl eats up her vegetables, gets to pre school on time, takes her naps when she's supposed to and doesn't spend the entire afternoon watching CBeebies on telly . . .

and can I find anyone to fill the vacancy? No, not a solitary soul.

It beggars belief. Three interviews in total today and each and every one has been an unmitigated disaster. You want to see the standard – and I really wish I were joking, but some of these people would make Mel Gibson look employable. And so now, there's no getting around it; as of the end of this week when Elka buggers off, I can't get anyone to take care of Lily for me. I have no one. *No one.*

And believe me, I've done everything. I've swallowed my pride and called Elka, offering to double her salary and negotiate more time off if she'll only reconsider, but no joy; she's had enough of the job and wants out, simple as that. In desperation, I even thought of calling on my sister Helen, but know without even bothering to ask that it's not a runner.

Being brutally honest, I have to admit that Helen and I have little in common and have never really been all that close, so she's hardly someone I can expect to come to my rescue in my hour of need. Besides, since I had Lily, Helen's gone and met a guy called Darren who runs a small seaside B&B in Cobh and within an alarmingly short space of time, she upped sticks and announced she was moving down the country to work side by side with him. Packed everything in for him; her job in a call centre, her brand-new flat, the lot. But then that's my sister for you; she's always struck me as someone who panic-dated, panic-settled and is now living with the consequences . . . in Cobh, miles and miles away from her old friends and her old life.

Total insanity, I thought at the time, and I still continue to think it. And although I've only met Darren a handful of times at Christmas dinners, or else on the rare occasions when they both come to Dublin and drop in to visit me and Lily, I can't help wondering if Helen is actually happy living with him, two hundred miles away in a tiny remote village. But then, keeping up to date on what's happening in each other's lives is tough and apart from the odd 'Hi, great to hear from you, but can I call you back? I'm running into a meeting' type chat, we never seem to really get a chance to catch up properly.

And no, I still haven't taken Lily down to Cobh to visit, in spite of all the child's entreaties and in spite of the fact that she adores her auntie, because how could I possibly leave work? Every now and then Helen will email, mainly either to vaguely moan for a little bit about Darren or else, in a roundabout way, to ask for a lend of money; it seems people in the hotel business are even more savagely affected by the economic downturn than the rest of us. And I always oblige and fire off a cheque and never ask for it back, and she'll gratefully accept, then send bright, breezy emails inviting Lily and me down for a freebie weekend anytime we want. Which is a nice thought and much appreciated, but come on . . . me? Get a whole entire weekend off? Saturday AND Sunday? One day after the other? Are you kidding me?

That aside though, I know Helen's up to her tonsils with trying to make ends meet at the B&B *à la* Sibyl Fawlty anyway, so I'm sure she's quite enough on her plate without me landing Lily on top of her too. Plus, no matter how desperate I was and no matter how much money I paid Helen to take care of her till I got sorted, it would mean I'd never get to see my little girl at all, wouldn't it? And frankly the snatched glimpses of her slumbering little head first thing every morning and last thing at night are about the only thing keeping me sane after the daily grind I'm expected to get through. The one dangling carrot in my life that somehow makes the rest of it all that bit more bearable.

'Barack Obama's re-election campaign has just GOT to get a page one tomorrow, Eloise,' Robbie Turner is thundering on, interrupting my incessant stream of worrying. Robbie is the *Post's* chain-smoking, gravelly-voiced chief political editor; a likeable guy, young but never youthful looking, he just streels round the office night and day looking as washed out and baggy-eyed as the rest of us. But then, because of the time differences involved in covering any foreign story, the political editor is expected to put in hours almost as ridiculous as I do myself. The general rule of thumb is that if I'm here till the night editor takes over at eleven p.m., chances are I'll catch a glimpse of Robbie's thick, prematurely white shock of hair and John Lennon glasses still at his desk, bashing out a first draft of a story breaking in the Middle East while the rest of the Western world snoozes peacefully on.

So I happen to know that Robbie rarely gets any time off to be with his own young and growing family and to his credit, it's something he's never once complained about. I may not let it show, but I'm genuinely fond of him; as I've told the Board of Directors on many occasions, Robbie is someone who does consistent good work in the face of pressure that would drive a lesser personality straight to the nearest home for the bewildered.

The only slight downside in these meetings is that Robbie's sole weak spot tends to come to the fore; his unhealthy obsession with Barack Obama, to the point that the running joke in the office is that he's actually a tiny bit in love with him. I'm not kidding, he eats, drinks, sleeps and breathes Barack Obama and the highlight of his life to date was getting to shake the hand of The Mighty One when he visited Ireland. True, there were about four hundred other people in the room with him at the time, but Robbie still managed to wangle past the secret service and touch the hem of the garment of the Chosen One, so to speak. All while making it sound like they'd shared an intimate one-on-one meeting, just the two of them chatting about the re-election campaign over a nice cuppa and a plate of Hobnobs. He even had a photo of said momentous event taken and turned it into his personalised Christmas card last year.

'Eloise, you have to listen to me,' Robbie's insisting, getting red-faced now as his voice rises to be heard about the clamour. He doesn't lose his cool often, but when he does, it's almost like watching a cartoon: eyes popping, red veins bulging out of the side of his neck, white hair nearly standing up straight on the top of his head, the whole works.

'This is getting to be too big a story just to tuck away on page three in world news beside David Cameron making a speech about landmine victims in Angola, like we did yesterday.' He has to almost shout to be heard above the racket in the room. 'The primaries are in full swing, the election proper is only round the corner and it's high time it got the front page! Can I remind you that it's page one on every US national daily and has been for weeks now? So why are we lagging behind US coverage, when we need to keep pace with this story!'

Robbie might sound narky and aggressive, but I know he's not; this is just how he comes across and I know him well enough to know it's not bolshiness on his part, it's purely because he cares so much.

Sign of a good political editor.

On and on he goes, enthusiastically firing off statistics about Democratic versus GOP expenditure on the President's re-election, to heated shouts of 'ahh, not this again! Give it a rest, will you?' from the rest of the room, while a few hacks start humming a sarcastic chorus of *The Star Spangled Banner*.

Next thing, Seth Coleman sits back, arms folded, and throws in his two cents' worth.

'Yes, we're all aware there's an election coming up in the US, thanks for that Robbie,' he spits dryly, with his lizardy unblinking eyes focused on me. 'As ever, your fundamental grasp of the obvious is overwhelmingly helpful. Can we please move on to some actual hard news?'

And although I'm nodding, giving the outward appearance of being focused and interested in the game, the truth is . . . to my shame I'm actually miles away, utterly and totally absorbed in my own worries. I may look like I'm listening but all I can really hear is the sound of the blood singing in my ears as my pulse rate feels like it's soaring well up into triple figures.

Then, dimly in the background, like a kind of accompanying soundtrack to all my stressing and fretting, our Northern correspondent, Ruth O'Connell manages to successfully shout Robbie down, take up the intellectual cudgels and is now aggressively pitching a two thousand word story on a car bomb that went off in Newry last night, injuring a high ranking senior sergeant in the PSNI.

Ruth's from Belfast, thin and wiry with severe jet-black bobbed hair and the whitest skin you ever saw, which kind of gives her the look of Louise Brooks, except with muscles. Even her teeth, which are irregular and uneven, seem to strike an attitude. She wears skinny little trouser suits like they're a uniform, always in varying shades of black or grey, and has exactly the same washed-out, bleary-eyed look on her pale, gaunt face as the rest of us.

Ruth's also a terrific sub-editor, feisty and like a dog with a bone when she's on the verge of a breaking story, always with an uncanny sixth sense for what will be next week's big lead. On the down side though, she's a bit too fond of the sound of her own strident voice and tends to try and dominate these meetings, pushing her own agenda with the aggressive tactic of simply yelling down the rest of the room. At the best of times I'm always glad to have her here because, hard as it is to believe, she and I are the only two women in the room. But I'm even more so today; her banging on about Catholic versus Protestant attitudes to joining the PSNI and the resultant socio-economic effect on whole communities gives me space to think a bit more clearly about the disastrous interviews I had to suffer through earlier.

Ohgodohgodohgod. Where do I start? Maybe by asking Rachel if she's accidentally rung up a theatrical agency and told them I was holding open auditions for 'third thug from the left' in some TV cop show? Maybe then I'd be able to understand the parade of headcases I had to deal with. And to think that these people were actually vetted and approved by a nanny agency? It's just beyond comprehension.

Candidate number one sauntered in earlier this morning, ten minutes late and wearing a tracksuit with a tight leather jacket over it, with – and I wish I were joking here – the words *Mega Revenge* written in flames across the back of

38

it. Oh and if that wasn't enough, she had a pierced nose and eyebrow with a black tattoo all down the side of her hand. I caught a glimpse of her in the reception area outside my office and that was frankly enough. The very sight of this one was enough to make my bowels wither and I knew Lily would take one look at her then either start crying, or else innocently ask me who was the scary lady and why did she have an earring coming out of her nose? Not a runner. So I called Rachel in and told her in no uncertain terms to get rid of her. And that if she wouldn't leave, then to threaten her with security.

Hot on her heels was candidate number two, who tip-toed pale and shaking into my office, stinking of cigarette smoke. No CV, no experience, nothing. Her boyfriend had just left her, she immediately told me, and now she not only had nowhere to live, but absolutely no reason to live either. 'So, what have you been doing for the past few years?' I asked, anxious to get off the subject of her private life. I've been a patient in the John of God's, she told me, suffering from bipolar manic depression. But according to her, the good news was she was officially off suicide watch and fully prepared to mind my child for forty euro an hour. I was half afraid she'd throw herself out of the window if I told her there and then that she wasn't exactly what I was looking for, so I gave her the more cowardly 'don't call me, I'll call you' line, and gently shooed her out of there ASAP.

This is what should be on the front page, the complete and utter lack of childcare for busy working parents, I find myself silently ranting while Ruth thunders on. Now she's rolling up her sleeves – always a bad sign with her, means a row is never too far off – and spouting on about a recent survey indicating the tiny minority of Catholics who now

39

are fully paid-up members of the PSNI and the general unfairness of it all and how it's setting the whole peace process back a full decade.

That's another thing about Ruth; she's superb at what she does, but never in your life have you come across anyone carrying as many chips on their shoulders.

Anyway, Kian O'Sullivan, sports editor, former Irish rugby international and something of a lust object among just about every female P.A. up and down the building (who I happened to know have collectively nicknamed him Don Draper), playfully fires a rolled-up ball of paper over at her. Then in no uncertain terms he tells her to shut up and demands to know why sports always gets considered last on anyone's list of priorities when we're blocking out tomorrow's paper.

'Because people only really care about sports results on a Sunday after all the Saturday games, you gobshite,' growls Robbie in his twenty-fags-a-day voice, but coming from him that could be deemed a term of affection.

'Seriously Eloise, you have GOT to listen to me on this!' Ruth is almost screeching to be heard over the racket, waving a fistful of notes in front of her, like that's going to catch my attention. 'It's front page stuff and if we don't run with it, make no mistake, *The Chronicle* will and then it'll be my head on the block, won't it?' On and on she spews, thumping her fist off the table in angry frustration now.

Meanwhile out of the corner of my eye, I'm dimly aware of everyone looking to me, waiting on me to call the lot of them to order, like some overly strict school headmistress whose class has sensed that she's a bit distracted and is now all acting up accordingly.

'Eloise?' says Seth Coleman from directly across the table,

de-latticing his fingers, slicking back the lank, greasy hair and giving me one of his unblinking, lizard-like stares. Very disconcerting, if you're not used to him. 'We really do need to wrap this up. *Tempus fugit.*'

I hide my irritation and point out that we haven't heard from our finance editor yet, throwing the floor open to Jack Dundon, a bespectacled, grey-haired, grey-skinned, softly spoken guy with a background as an award-winning economist; someone who rarely shines at these meetings, but who'll consistently come up trumps and turn out impeccably researched stories written in language readers can grasp, unlike those on some of our rivals' finance pages, that you'd nearly need a Harvard master's in finance to get your head around.

He draws the air of experience deep into his lungs and addresses the now silent room. The European Central Bank have announced an interest rate hike of half a per cent, is his calm opener, which mightn't exactly be the sexiest lead story at the table, but it'll affect hundreds of thousands of mortgage holders and so therefore it has massive bite. On and on he goes, giving me the freedom to let my thoughts take me back to my more pressing concerns and back to about noon today, when in sauntered a slightly more promising candidate for the job of nanny/lifesaver.

But when I say 'slightly more promising', all I mean is she was young, reasonably well groomed and at least had the courtesy to turn up for the interview appropriately dressed, even if her eye make-up did happen to be the exact colour of bright yellow hazardous waste. Trouble was, she had precious little experience in childcare and when I asked her why her CV only had one reference on it, her answer was that she was really an out-of-work actress and thought this would be a nice little earner until her big break arrived.

'I mean, it's only minding a kid, isn't it? Besides, I've loads of nieces and nephews and I know I'm well able to handle it,' she coolly informs me. 'And the reference I have is good, my auntie went to load of trouble to write it for me. Oh, but by the way,' she added, hammering a further nail into her own coffin, 'if my agent rings about an audition, then I'll need time off. Plus I don't work evenings after seven p.m. or weekends. And I should probably tell you that I already have my holidays booked for the first two weeks in June, I'm going to Spain with my boyfriend, so that's out as well. I assume that's all OK with you?'

It's not often I'm at a loss for words, but on this occasion I was. I didn't answer, couldn't. Just sat there staring at her in disbelief thinking, 'next!'

And the *piece de resistance*? Just after lunch (which in my case is rarely more than a cereal bar wolfed down at my desk between phone calls, and that's if I'm *very* lucky), Rachel buzzes into my office to say the final candidate the agency have available to start work is now waiting patiently at reception. I stride out of my office to greet her, praying, just praying that this one will look not unlike Julie Andrews in *Mary Poppins*, act like a firm but kindly Angela Lansbury in *Bedknobs and Broomsticks* and keep perfect law and order in my house when I'm not there as strictly as Emma Thompson in *Nanny McPhee*.

Initial reaction was positive and for once, my stomach didn't sink at the sight of what was waiting beside Rachel's desk for me. Mrs. Adele Patterson was sixty-something, with a grey perm so tight it looked like someone had accidentally poured a tin of baked beans over her head, wearing a coat that looked like it was made out of the same uphol-stery they use on bus seats and laden down with two Marks and Spencers grocery bags. But she was the only candidate who actually looked like an actual proper nanny, wise and calm and experienced, someone you'd unhesitatingly trust your child with. Plus she at least looked me unflinchingly straight in the eye, doing me the courtesy of coming straight to the point.

'I don't work in other people's houses,' she told me straight up in a no-nonsense style that I at least respected, even if what she'd just said made me break out in an anxiety sweat. 'You're welcome to leave your daughter, Lily isn't it? Well, you can drop her to my house at nine in the morning, no earlier, and I'm strict about collection time too, no later than six o'clock in the evening please. That's quite a long enough day for any child, believe me. And for me too, I might add. I'm not getting any younger, you know.'

'Mrs. Patterson, I'm afraid . . . Well, the thing is that's going to be a problem. What I need, you see is . . . Well, let's just say that there might be the odd evening – just the occasional one, that's all . . . when I could possibly get delayed getting home from work, so I really am looking for someone who's prepared to live in, at my house, which is very comfortable, by the way . . . It's in Rathgar,' I tack on hopefully, like this'll make a difference.

'Makes no difference to me if you live in the penthouse suite of the Four Seasons, love,' she snapped back, sounding shell-shocked at the very suggestion and getting pinker in the face by the minute.

'Well, I would be paying premium rates, of course, and we can always negotiate a day off for you . . .' I exaggerated, astonished at the sheer brazenness of my lie.

43

Day off? I think. Elka got one day off in the past year and that was on Christmas Day. And even at that, she still had to take Lily for a few hours in the afternoon while I dashed into the office to check the layout for the Stephen's Day edition of the *Post*.

But my back is to the wall here, and short of Mrs. Patterson producing references that implicate her in the massacre of a school full of small children, she's hired.

'Then I'm very sorry to waste your time, Miss Elliot, but I'm afraid this is just not going to work out, simple as that. You see, I take care of my two grandchildren at home as well, so either your little girl can stay with me daytimes only, with collection strictly no later than six p.m., or that's it. I'm not here to bargain with you or to offer you any other alternative. And what's more, I'm going to have to leave now: as it is, I had to ask a neighbour to look after the other children for me so I could get into town to meet you.'

OK, it was at this point that I got desperate, not even able to conceal the pleading in my tone. This woman was my last hope and I couldn't, just couldn't let her walk out the door.

'Mrs. Patterson, as you can see, my job here doesn't exactly allow me to work regular nine to five hours, but if you'll just hear me out about moving into my home, only for a short time you understand, I'd be happy to pay you far, far more than the agency rates.'

I look at her pleadingly, silently begging her to say yes.

'Lily's such a good girl,' I tack on for good measure, 'she's very well behaved, everyone says so and minding her really is a doddle . . . '

'It's a no, I'm afraid,' Mrs. Patterson replied crisply. 'There's no way that I'd just abandon my own husband

and grandchildren to move into a stranger's house, no matter what you paid me. You must understand that there are some things in life that are far, far more important than any job or any amount of money, like family, for one,' she said, looking pointedly at me.

Then, picking up her handbag and groceries and tossing me a curt nod, she showed herself out of my office and back towards reception. Leaving me feeling like I'd just been cut and dried and left to hang out for dead on a line.

Back to the meeting and it seems Seth Coleman, with his barracuda-like instincts, is onto me.

'Earth to Eloise? Are you with us or what?' he says, rapping a pen with bony fingers impatiently off a pile of folders in front of him. 'We really need to move on this. Some of us have work to do, you know.'

I'm suddenly aware that all eyes are locked on me and that I'm in danger of losing control of the room. It's gone quiet, scarily quiet; people are coughing and looking in my direction, anxious to get out of here. Which means it's now over to me and I'm going to have to make it at least look like I'm on the ball.

'Fine, thank you Seth,' I manage to say, crisply as I can. 'In that case, the mock-up of tomorrow's front page is this. Firstly, we lead with the ECB interest rate hike.'

Cut to groans and moans from the rest of the table, which I have no choice but to swat aside.

'Jack, you're on the story and I'll need hard copy on my desk by four p.m. at the latest. Second lead is Northern, Ruth, but no more than five hundred words on page one, with an opinion piece in domestic, on page four.'

'Page FOUR? That is so unfair!' Ruth yells disappointedly, but again, I override her.

Sorry, but in this gig you learn very quickly how to prioritise.

'As for the US primaries, they'll stay in Foreign on pages four and five until one month before the election proper and that's final,' I say to frosty looks from Robbie Turner, which I instantly tune out.

'This story may be front page in the States Robbie, but we're not living in Washington, now are we? The lead US story we go with on page three is Obama's statement that he's not ruling out seeking to overthrow rebels in Afghanistan, in spite of the phased withdrawal. There's a press conference on the situation from the White House at five o'clock Eastern time, which is going to mean a late night for you Robbie; that'll be eleven tonight our time and I'll need full copy for the night editor before the late edition hits the presses.'

A deep heartfelt sigh from Robbie, who's worked late pretty much every night for the past few months and who has probably forgotten what his kids even look like by now. I feel a sudden flash of sympathy at the sight of his exhausted, washed-out face, but I rise above it and move on. Because I have to. Yes, I know, he never gets to see his kids, but then I never get to see Lily either, do I? And it's not like I'm asking him to do anything I'm not doing myself.

So on I steamroll, undeterred.

'Also, make a note that I want an opinion piece on Irish Life and Permanent and how it may be sold off as a result of bank stress tests. Seth? Get Miriam Douglas onto it, seven hundred words. Regional, I want to lead with that car crash in Kerry that killed three kids over the weekend, plus photos too. Find out their ages, talk to the school friends and if you can, get the families to talk too. That's our big human interest story and I want it to be gut-wrenching. Also, I need six hundred words on the search for those two missing teenagers, latest updates in one hour, please. We need recent photos of both of them, get Derek Maguire onto it right away. There's a press release on its way here and as soon as it lands I want to see it. Courts page, I want three hundred words on how in the name of God a convicted drug dealer got out on appeal yesterday, no photos of him looking shifty with a hood over his head though, too clichéd. To similar to what the *Independent* will run with, so get me a better shot than that. World news, we open with Japan scrapping four of its stricken reactors, and follow up with an update on the Greek situation, six hundred words each, photos for both, quarter page. But I want to see the proofs first, so Seth you need to tell the picture desk that's non-negotiable. Mock-ups no later than four p.m. sharp and thank you all for your time.'

And there it is, the old familiar buzz I get from doing what I do best. Feeding me like an adrenaline rush.

Filthy looks all round at me, but there you go. Sometimes you need to have a spine of steel in this job.

Class dismissed. And onto the next problem.

It's coming up to three o'clock in the afternoon, and as usual, I'm multi-tasking. Or triple-tasking, to be more precise. I'm in my office checking through the rough drafts of tomorrow's advertising pages while at the same time trying to type out a rough draft for tomorrow's editorial, both of which I might add are now *well* behind schedule. And on top of all that, I'm simultaneously holding a meeting with Marc Robinson, editor of the paper's Arts and Culture section, a magazine-formatted supplement which comes with our Saturday issue, but which is put to bed the previous Monday. Which is today. Which is why Marc is in my office now, arguing and bickering with me. The way absolutely everyone seems to argue and bicker with me these days.

'I'm really putting my foot down on this Eloise,' he's saying, pacing up and down while throwing me the odd scorching look for added dramatic effect. 'You have to trust me. I absolutely, categorically refuse to give the Culture cover to a kids' Disney movie . . . not when Wim Wenders has a new art-house film out. It insults our reader and it's just . . . just plain degrading. May I remind you, it's called the Culture section, not the commercial section, you know. We're trying to be out-there and edgy. And that bloody kids' film has all the cutting edge appeal of . . . of Val Doonican sitting in his rocking chair and wearing a woolly jumper.'

Marc, as you see, is a passionate movie lover in his early thirties and even manages to look exactly like a European art-house director should, with a clever, lugubrious face, eccentric hair and let's just say *difficult* glasses. It's also received wisdom round here that he's official holder of the title Dossiest Job Ever. He's forever annoying everyone else by pootling off to art-house cinemas in the middle of the day to review obscure, subtitled films badly dubbed from Finnish, then writing three page dossiers on directors I've never heard of. Which it's my job to then edit down and try to make a bit more, let's just say, reader-friendly.

I, on the other hand, am in a constant push-pull battle with him to reflect cultural choices that our readers might, perish the thought, have actually heard of. Basically, that's anathema to someone like Marc, who considers a movie seen by more than a dozen people to be an over-hyped, commercialised Hollywood sell-out. But then Marc is someone who regularly claims that Paul McCartney's *Maxwell's Silver Hammer* is the greatest offence ever perpetrated on mankind, in the history of the planet. Even worse than Cromwell.

'Too bad Marc,' I tell him firmly, while at the same time tapping out an editorial about the health service on the computer screen in front of me. 'It's coming up to the Easter holidays, parents with kids need to know what family movies are opening and the Disney Pixar one will be a blockbuster. Sorry, but you'll have to swallow your art-house pride and just get commercial once in a while.'

'Eloise, please don't take this personally, but what in the name of God would you know about culture? You never go out anywhere.'

I look up at him in dull surprise; it's not often anyone makes comments about my private life and even though it's true, I don't particularly like hearing it. Mind you Marc and I go back a long way – we were at college together – so in his defence, he knows he has the liberty to use that kind of shorthand with me.

What he doesn't know though, is that the board of directors is seriously concerned at the overheads his department are running and that when the axe falls, which it inevitably will, mark my words the Culture section is certain to be in line for a good pruning. And Marc, who's been here as long as I have and who's being paid what management consider a highly inflated salary, could well be first for the chop.

Marc's a good writer, I've pleaded with them in the past, with a large and ever-growing cult following. Readers buy our Saturday edition just to read his columns and reviews. Which, frankly, is the main reason he's lasted as long as he has in the job. But the hard, cold reality is that unless he wises up and stops being such a cultural snob, he could well be in trouble.

And so the only reason I'm being as hard on him as I am, is because I just don't want him to lose his gig. Not on my watch.

'Oh, I support the arts alright,' I smile quickly back at him. 'I'll write the cheques, I just haven't time to see anything. And just on a point of order, you try sneaking off to a movie at the weekends in my job and then see how fast you're propelled to the back of a dole queue. Disney gets the cover, Marc, and that's final.'

Then out of the blue, my internal phone rings, sending an ice-cold chill right up my spinal cord. Never, ever a good sign. I tell Marc I have to take it, and he skulks off, knowing he's been beaten. This time.

Okay, the internal phone ringing usually only means one thing.

Oh Christ alive, no. Please don't let this be happening . . . Not today.

But no two ways about it, the nightmare is real. The chairman's assistant is on the phone, summoning me upstairs to a meeting of the board of directors – the T. Rexes – right this minute. This rarely happens on the spur of the moment like this and it doesn't take Einstein to figure out why they've convened this meeting at such short notice.

The online issue of the *Post*. Can't possibly be anything else. I know it's a matter of huge concern for the board and the last time I bumped into Sir Gavin Hume, our esteemed chairman since the year dot, he as good as told me it was a matter requiring their immediate attention. That it's costing too much and is effectively losing readers.

And here's me in a severely weakened position, because it was my brainchild and I've effectively staked my reputation on it. So I whip out a bulging file of notes I've been working on about the online edition and mentally steel myself for the grilling that lies ahead.

Anyway, I'm just clickety-clacking out of my office to get the lift to the boardroom on the top floor, when Rachel, my assistant, stops me in my tracks.

'Eloise?' she says standing up behind her desk and looking petrified. 'Thank God I caught you. There's a phone call for you. And it's urgent.'

Odd, it strikes me: Rachel looking so terrified about whoever's on the phone. Mainly because every single phone call that comes for me is urgent; there's always some emergency. Frankly, the day that someone leaves a message for me saying, 'Oh tell her it's not that important, no rush at all in getting back to me' is the day hell will freeze over.

Plus, Rachel is normally the epitome of glacial blonde coolness under pressure, which is not only why I hired her, but it's the main reason why she's survived so many staff cullings round here. She's around my own age and the human equivalent of half a Xanax tablet; always chilled, always in control, never loses her head; in short, the perfect assistant for someone like me.

But right now, she's thrusting a phone at me, looking ghostly pale, ashen-faced and like she needs to be treated for deep shock.

'Trust me, you need to take this call.'

'I'm on my way to the boardroom!' I almost hiss at her impatiently, not meaning to be rude, but come on . . . surely Rachel of all people knows that when the board of directors calls, you drop everything and go running?

It's non-negotiable.

'I'm sorry Rachel, but you'll just have to tell whoever's on the phone that they'll have to wait till I call them back.'

'Eloise, you *have* to listen to me. Please try to stay calm, but . . . it's about your little girl.'

Chapter Two

And the day from hell rolls relentlessly on.

I'm now sitting in a poky little waiting room outside the principal's office at the Embassy Pre-School, where Lily has been a pupil for about three weeks now. The emergency call came through from the principal, one Miss Pettifer, to say I needed to get here urgently – but as soon she'd reassured me that Lily was neither sick nor had been in an accident but was safely at home with her nanny, I calmly told her that I was on my way to a board meeting and it was a bad time for me to talk. Elka, I told her in no uncertain terms, would call her ASAP and troubleshoot whatever storm in a teacup was going on. So I'd just get her to do what she was being paid to do, while I obeyed the royal command to haul my arse up to the T. Rexes in the boardroom above, right away.

But Miss Pettifer was having none of it.

'I'm terribly sorry if there's any inconvenience Miss Elliot,' she told me in no uncertain terms, 'but I'm afraid this is a matter for the parent and the parent alone, which I can't simply delegate out to a childminder. I realise that you're a busy woman but I can assure you, I am too. Now, we close for the day in just under an hour's time and as this matter is of some significance, I strongly suggest that you come in here immediately. Surely you agree that the welfare of your child is more important than any board meeting?'

No more information forthcoming about what in the name of God could be so pressing anyway, or why the antics of a little girl now had her principal acting like the child had tried to set fire to the place or else gone into her pre-school brandishing a shotgun. And if Lily's okay and not sick or anything, then what in the name of God could it possibly be?

'Ah, Miss Elliot, please come in; so sorry to have kept you waiting.'

I look up from where I'm impatiently perched in the waiting room and there she is, the famous Miss Pettifer. We've never actually met before; a few months ago, when I stuck my head in the door to vet the place and see if I could enrol Lily as a pupil, I was dealing with her assistant and of course, ever since then, Elka brings her to and from pre-school. So apart from writing humongously inflated cheques for their services, to my shame I've next to nothing to do with the place. Or with Miss Pettifer, who's now holding out an outstretched hand and beckoning me into her tiny little office, decorated with dozens of kids' class photos and cute little drawings done in coloured pencil dotted all around the brightly painted walls.

She's early fifties, I'd say, holding middle age tenuously at bay, with more than a touch of the Aunt Agathas from P.G. Wodehouse about her; grizzly grey hair that looks like it could be used for scouring pans tied back in a no-nonsense bun, clipped speech and dressed like she's about to referee a hockey match any minute. Stern and stentorian; I instantly get an image of her parading up and down past a line of toddlers inspecting their finger paintings and checking for runny noses. A bit like the Queen doing a meet and greet on a visit to a toilet roll factory.

She invites me to sit down on a coloured plastic chair opposite her desk, which immediately wrongfoots me; normally it's me on the far side of a desk, the one who's about to initiate a meeting and take charge.

'Miss Elliot, may I call you Eloise?'

I nod mutely, thinking, please for the love of God, just cut to the jugular and tell me what this is all about. No time for preambles here. No time for anything.

Mercifully, she's a woman who seems not to believe in sugar-coating things and comes straight to the point.

'Eloise, I'm afraid we've been having problems with Lily, which I strongly feel you need to be made aware of. And so, it's my duty as principal here to ask you, let's just say a few *personal* questions.'

Okay, now I'm staring dumbly back at her, thinking, ehhh . . . What exactly can a little girl who's not even three years old have got up to that merits the bleeding Spanish Inquisition?

'Fire away,' I manage to say, calmly as I can, given that the mobile on my knee is switched to silent and hasn't stopped flashing up missed calls from the office ever since I got here.

Miss Pettifer instantly cuts across my stream of worry.

'Eloise, I'm afraid I need to be perfectly frank with you here. You're a single mum, I know, and a very hardworking one at that. You single-handedly carry out an incredibly demanding job. I'm an avid reader of the *Post* every day, you know, and greatly admire your editorials . . .'

I nod mechanically, pathetically grateful for the bone she's just thrown me.

'But leaving your career aside, being a single parent is probably the toughest job in the whole world. May I ask if you have help of any kind? Apart from your nanny, do you have family support? Your parents, perhaps?'

'No, I'm afraid not.'

'Because you know there are any number of wonderful one-parent support groups locally that I'd be more than happy to recommend to you . . .'

One-parent support groups? I find myself looking at her numbly. What does this one think I am anyway, on welfare?

'I feel they might help you to cope with a lot of the demands laid on any busy working single mum. They could help. You see, I have some most unwelcome news to tell you, I'm sorry to say. A problem for us, which sadly could represent an even bigger problem for you.'

Involuntarily, I throw a look of pure panic across the desk at her.

Tell me, just tell me quickly before I pass out with worry . . .

'There was a deeply regrettable incident earlier here today, which is why I've had to call you in.'

Okay, now I'm on the edge of my seat, palms sweating, breathing jaggedly, bracing myself for what's coming next. 'What happened?'

'Lily, I'm afraid to say, got into a heated row with Tim O'Connor, another little boy here in pre-school. There were tears, there was screaming, and worst of all, Lily resorted to smacking him until he cried . . .'

'She *WHAT*? Are you sure?'

'I wouldn't have called you in here if I weren't,' she says, looking evenly at me.

'But that's outrageous! Lily has never behaved like that before!'

I'm on the verge of spluttering indignantly at her that I'd surely know all about it if she did, but then, with a sudden, sharp stab of guilt have to remind myself . . . How exactly *would* I know? These days, when do I ever get to see or spend quality time with the poor child anyway, barring our precious Sundays together? The only way I know if there's trouble at home is if Elka tells me, and lately Elka's been telling me nothing, just whinging about how late I work and how there are no KitKats in the fridge and how we're out of Cheerios. And these days I've been working so late, even she mostly communicates with me via Post-it notes stuck on the door of the microwave.

So instead of opening my mouth, I sit quiet and listen to the sound of the blood whooshing through my brain while Miss Pettifer relentlessly goes on and on.

'. . . Which of course is behaviour we simply can't put up with. We have a strict policy of zero tolerance, you see, with any kind of unruly behaviour. We expect children to attend having already been taught the rudiments of basic manners and social skills around others.'

'But . . . *why* did Lily smack him? Do you have any idea what the row was about?'

'Ahh, you see that's where it becomes delicate and personal. And believe me when I say I hope this doesn't cause you any offence, but it was over the question of Lily's father.'

Suddenly, after all my panic and stress and shock . . . I find myself without a single word to say. And now there's silence. Horrible, awkward, bum-clenching silence.

'You're rearing Lily on your own and believe me, I know

how difficult that can be, Eloise,' Miss Pettifer says to me, sounding almost gentle now, which, in the state I'm in, I'm oddly grateful for, 'but may I ask you a very personal question?'

I nod mutely.

'Do you have any contact at all with Lily's dad?'

Lily's dad.

Oh shit and double shit. I can't believe she just asked me that. And worse, is now looking expectantly back at me, waiting on an answer.

'Well, not exactly . . .' is the best I can manage, totally thrown at being caught on the hop like this.

'It's just that, in years to come, it's highly likely that Lily will want to know more about him and to spend time with him too. Which is only right and fair, of course. In an ideal world, children should grow up knowing each of their parents, even if they happen to live in a single parent family. They have a right to know both parents equally well, regardless of circumstances. We have several other children here who all come from wonderful one-parent families and although they may not live with Mum and Dad, they at least have regular contact with each. Unlike Lily, I'm afraid.'

I've absolutely no answer to that so I just stare back at her, as calmly as I can.

'I'm so sorry to have to persist, Eloise, and I appreciate that this is uncomfortable, but it's your daughter I'm thinking of and so I really do need to ask you these questions. You see, even if you have no dealings whatsoever with this man, he still is the child's father and as such he does have rights.'

'Yes . . . I know that, but you see . . .'

And the best of luck finishing that sentence, I think to myself.

'I know you must feel very strongly about not allowing him access to Lily, and undoubtedly you have your own personal reasons for this, but really, I've seen all this happen more times than you can possibly imagine in the past and I can assure you it's inevitable. Remember, if he wants to see her, he can easily go to the family law courts and request visitation rights and no judge in the land would deny that to any father. Trust me, you don't want to have to deal with Lily when she becomes a teenager accusing you of never allowing her to see her dad. It just wouldn't be right, not to mention it's completely unhealthy for her. I know it's none of my business, but I would beg you to take my advice; build bridges with this man, no matter how difficult it is for you. Because mark my words, if you don't, the day will come when Lily *will*.'

'No she won't.'

She looks over the desk at me in dull surprise, probably unused to being contradicted.

'Excuse me?'

'What I mean is, Lily won't be able to track down her father.'

'I'm afraid I'm not with you.'

'She won't be able to find out who he is or where he is, because I couldn't even tell you that myself. I was never in a relationship with him. That is, I don't know his name or where he is or . . . In fact the truth is . . . I don't know anything about him at all.'

Then I suddenly backpedal and have an urge to clamp my hand over my mouth, realising that makes me sound like some spray-tanned, bleach-headed tarts who got up the duff after a one night stand with a bloke whose name they now can't even remember.

And now Miss Pettifer is peering curiously at me over the rims of her glasses, and I can practically read her thoughts. God almighty, never would have had this one down as someone who'd be a bit of a goer of a Friday night on the town, after a few shots of vodka and Red Bull. Hard to imagine Miss Prissy newspaper editor in a pair of leather trousers and a cropped-top bra, falling drunk out of some nightclub at five a.m., draped round some unknown fella she's only just met and is about to drag home for a quickie one night stand.

'And no, I promise, it's not what you're thinking either,' I tell her with a heartfelt sigh, knowing I can't circle around this any longer.

The time has come for the truth.

Hard to blurt it out though; this is not something I ever talk about, barely even think about most of the time. Aside from my family, no one really knows the truth, the whole truth and nothing but, which is exactly how I like to keep it.

But seeing Miss Pettifer looking expectantly at me, waiting for my answer, I know I've no choice but to tell her.

'I had Lily by artificial insemination.'

I try my best to say it evenly and without embarrassment. For God's sake, haven't I been putting up with all sorts of rumours and sly stories circulating round the office about Lily's parentage, ever since the day I first announced my pregnancy? All widely exaggerated and laughably wide of the mark.

Because the truth was this; almost three years ago now, dating right back to that dismal night when I turned thirty,

I made one life altering decision. Not to rush into marriage, or find a significant other to share my life with and take away the loneliness; I didn't mind being on my own and was never particularly bothered about being single. Unlike a lot of my contemporaries at work, I was never emotionally double-parked and in a mad, tearing rush to meet someone. Singledom held out no threat for me whatsoever.

As far as I was concerned, the road to love was far too full of potholes and roadblocks to be even worth the hassle. And on the rare occasions when I did date, I'd pretty much been able to see the end of every single love affair right from its very beginning. I was someone who actively preferred my own company to that of any guy brave enough to ask me out, and who didn't want the mess of relationships, thanks; that was my sister Helen's department and not mine. In fact, my heart was so untroubled by emotion that it might as well have had a big 'do not disturb' sign permanently hanging from it.

I'd dated in the past, of course, and like everyone else could boast of having my heart smashed to smithereens back in college by 'the one that got away'. Who's married with two kids now and who recently rang me up out of the blue, saying he'd just been made redundant then asking me for a job. In spite of no experience whatsoever in the paper business; this guy was a chemical engineer. Mortifying, for us both, on so many levels. And certainly before I had Lily, from time to time I'd go out on the odd date. But they always seemed to me to end up like a job interview where no one ever got hired. My overall verdict on my chances of ever finding a life partner? Meh.

No, it wasn't that I was ever lonely . . . Besides, how could anyone who worked a sixteen-hour day ever call themselves lonely? But dating back to that night of my miserable, pathetic thirtieth birthday, I was filled with a dark and inexplicable horror of ending up alone. Because there's a world of difference between the epic loneliness I was so frightened of and being alone, as I was terrifyingly beginning to see.

And that's when I absolutely knew for certain. Whatever else the future might hold for me, and even though there were times when I felt crushed under the sheer weight of it, there was one thing that I didn't want the chance to miss out on, and that was to become a mother. That was without a doubt, the one, personal thing that I wanted out of life for myself more than anything else. A child of my own. No head space for the inconvenience of a man in my life, thank you very much, I just wanted a baby, full stop. And once I'd made the decision, it was like a tight iron band had been lifted from round my heart. No question about it, this wasn't just the right thing to do, it was the *only* thing.

And okay, so I might not exactly have had close female friends to confide in – or indeed, any mates at all – but believe me, I'd heard enough horror stories circulating round the office to know precisely the best plan of action open to someone like me. I'd overheard bloodcurdling tales told in whispered conversations by the watercoolers, heart-rending sagas about women who'd had kids with partners who suddenly became ex-partners and then spent years dragging the mother of their child through the family law courts demanding access rights. Which always and inevitably seemed to be granted.

Overnight access seemed to be the first step, followed by

62

weekend access . . . Quite enough to send a shiver down my spine. Shared parentage, I just knew, would never be an option for someone like me, so instead I just went for the next preferable option.

Namely, a sperm bank, where I was successfully inseminated and successfully managed to conceive on my very first go, astonishing just about everyone at the clinic. To this day I can still remember my mother quipping at the time that even my ovaries, like the rest of me, were high-performing and anxious to get on with it.

And now here she was, my little Lily Elizabeth Emily, representing the one single personal thing I actively wanted out of life for myself and for no one else. And not for one second do I ever regret the decision I made. Lily's the single best thing ever to have happened to me and as far as I'm concerned, let people gossip about who her dad is all they shagging well like. Because she's my soulmate, the real love of my life. Lily's my reason for running home every night and our precious Sundays together are what I live for, the highlight of my whole week.

There's a long, long pause as Miss Pettifer digests this, nodding thoughtfully.

'I see. Well, thank you for telling me. And does Lily know this?'

'Well, no . . . But then she's not even three yet. Hardly an appropriate conversation to have with the child, is it?'

'You might just be very surprised at what they're able to understand at that age. The regrettable incident which happened here earlier being a case in point. Miss Simpson was doing a little exercise with the class where each child had to tell the others what they'd all done at the weekend.

So of course, they all spoke about going to visit grand-parents with Mum and Dad, or else going to feed the ducks in the park, again with either Mum or Dad. Miss Simpson told me that Lily became agitated at all the other children talking so openly about their fathers. The poor child didn't seem to understand what was going on. Then things became exacerbated when Tim O'Connor quite rudely accused Lily of not having any dad at all and asked her why; was it because her dad was dead?'

'And what did Lily say back to him?' I ask in a tiny voice, throat completely dried up now, dreading the answer.

'From what I can gather, Lily stoutly told him that yes she did have a dad and that one day he'd come for her. This is when Tim provoked her, calling her a liar and saying that everyone else in class had a dad, bar her. So then Lily lashed out at him; kicking, screaming, punching, the whole works. It really was the most awful scene and deeply distressing for the other children to witness. Now in Lily's defence, Tim's behaviour was also completely out of line. He absolutely should not have carried on the way he did, but believe me, his parents have been notified about this incident as well. Bad behaviour of any kind isn't tolerated here.'

I'm too dazed by what I've just heard to even bring myself to answer her. The words Lily used keep floating back to me. That she did have a dad and that one day he'll come for her. Is that really what's been going through her little mind?

And for how long, I wonder?

Suddenly I'm now finding it hard to breathe, my chest is that tight and constrained. This actually feels like taking a bullet. The same sharp, sudden, hot, searing flash of deep, flesh-ripping pain.

Because never before has Lily even asked me about her father; not once, ever. Maybe because she's been so shielded ever since she was born, always at home or else with a nanny; it's only since she began at pre-school that she must suddenly be aware that other kids have two parents coming in to drop them off and then collect them later on. Something that she so obviously doesn't. And what does my little girl have instead? A mother she only sees properly one day a week and Elka, one in a steady stream of nannies, who's now about to desert her in just a few days' time.

I do have a dad and one day he'll come for me.

I can almost hear her little singsong, baby voice saying that, proudly, defiantly and the blow it gives me right to the solar plexus is physically making me nauseous.

I knew, of course I knew, that one day I'd have to have the awkward chat with her, that I'd have to tell her why I'm a single mum by choice – I just had no idea that it would creep up on me this fast. And how exactly do I explain to an innocent little child that I never even met her father? That he's in fact some nameless, faceless Petri dish in an industrial estate out in Sandyford? All I know about him really is the basics; his height, eye colour, hair colour, occupation and IQ. That's it. And worst of all, that he's never going to come for her, because how can he? He doesn't even know of her existence. Or of mine.

Christ alive, what chance has the poor kid got? No father and, judging by the not-too-difficult-to-read subtext of what Miss Pettifer's telling me, an absentee mother to boot. I look across the desk at her and can almost see a cartoon thought bubble coming out of her brain saying that there are probably undiscovered terrorist cells in the mountains of Afghanistan more nurturing that I am.

The worry swirls round my brain now, dull and nauseating, over and over again. No getting away from it, I am
a horrible parent whose child doesn't even know the truth
about her own parentage. A child, to my shame, that I
barely see at all. And now my Lily, my little strawberry-
blonde angel, is acting like Damien from *The Omen* and
taking pot shots at her little classmates for accusing her of
not having a dad . . . Oh God, now the guilt feels exactly
like heartburn.

I'm just wiping away tiny beads of worry-sweat,
wondering how in hell I'm going to fix this, when Miss
Pettifer cuts into my thoughts as if there's more – worse
– to come.

'So you see why I had to call you in Eloise.'

'Yes, of course I do, and thank you for letting me
know . . .'

With jelly legs, I make to get out of my chair, but she
holds her palm up to stop me.

'And there's something else too,' Miss Pettifer says.

I look dumbly up at her, dreading the next sentence. But
she must realise the deep, nightmarish turmoil I'm in and
second guesses me, actually coming round from behind
her desk and perching right beside me, taking my hand
and speaking to me quite kindly.

'Come on Eloise, I know all of this has been awful for
you to hear. It was difficult for me to tell you too, though
I wouldn't have been doing either you or Lily any favours
if I hadn't. But you have to believe me when I say that
you're not a bad mother. You've just been run off your
feet, that's all. And essentially, Lily is an adorable little girl
who we're all very fond of. Just remember though, these
precious years with your child are very fleeting and will all

be over in a blink. Before you know it, she'll be an independent little lady who won't need you any more. So please, before it's too late, take this advice from me. Explain to her about her father. She's crying out to know why her life is different from the other children's and I know that once you do, you'll never regret it. Otherwise, when she's older, she might track him down for herself and possibly even end up resenting you for not being more open on the subject with her before.'

I look up at her, pathetically grateful to her for not making me feel any worse than I already do.

Miss Pettifer stands herself up straight, mercifully indicating that our meeting is over, and instantly resumes her straight-backed, sergeant major pose. I manage to stand up beside her and am just scooping my handbag off the floor with trembling hands . . . And then, just when I think I can take no more, comes the killer blow.

'But you do understand that naturally you and I must put Lily and what's best for her first. As you know, we're completely full up here, with a very long waiting list; I was only able to squeeze her in at all because you were so very insistent.'

I nod, remembering that I practically had to donate a spare kidney just to get them to take Lily on in the first place. And even then, I could only get her in on a monthly trial basis.

'However, it's a strong principle of mine that if a child isn't happy or for any reason doesn't settle in with us, then the parent really should look elsewhere. Of course, perhaps in time we many look into taking her back here . . .'

'What do you . . . Hang on; did you just say taking her *back*?' I splutter, confused.

'But you have to understand that, with regret, we just don't feel that at the moment it's working out for Lily here as a pupil. It's your daughter I'm thinking of, you must understand. So I wish you and Lily all the very best in future, Eloise. But I'm afraid you have to understand that at this point in time, I'll have to offer her place to another child.'

Ten minutes later, I swing my car into the driveway outside my house, blatantly ignoring the flashing of my mobile as yet another angry missed call comes through and remains unanswered. I glance down at the phone; thirty-five missed calls is the total to date and twenty-eight voice messages, all from the office. And that's not even counting the number of emails that have landed in my inbox. Christ, I think impatiently, I've barely been out of the place an hour and now they're acting like the whole building is about to blow up any second?

But on the principle that I might as well be hung for a sheep as a lamb, I make an executive decision to ignore each and every one of their so-called urgent calls. I'll think of something to tell them all when I get back. I'll improvise wildly, I'll fib shamelessly, but I'll wriggle my way out of it somehow. I'll plead my hitherto impeccable record if I have do, I'll stay there till two in the morning to make up the time . . . But there's something else, something far more important I need to do first.

And so, for the first time in the best part of a decade, I'm actually home during daylight hours, pulling my car through the gates and parking in the tiny, gravelled driveway. I bought this house not long after I was made editor, thinking that I'd get to actually spend a reasonably decent amount of time in it, poor misguided gobshite that I was back then. It's a neat, terraced little Edwardian redbrick in lovely, leafy Rathgar, two storeys over a basement, with a study that I never go into (no time, I'm only ever really in this house to sleep), a pretty, landscaped garden at the back that I'm never in (ditto) with a sunny little patio area that I once dreamt of sitting outside having a civilised breakfast in.

Breakfast? Who, may I ask, has time for breakfast? I'm doing well if I get to stuff a banana into my face while driving to work at dawn – and that's on a good day when I'm not driving and having to hold a meeting over the phone at the same time.

Then there's a lovely, sash-windowed, high-ceilinged dining room that I never entertain in. *Entertain? Are you kidding me? When, exactly?* Not only that, but I forked out a small fortune for a stunning Victorian dining table and chairs that comfortably seats twelve and to date, has only ever been used once. I'll never forget it; for a mortifying attempt at a dinner party that I gave as a housewarming, where the guest list included a few of the T. Rexes and their wives, plus one or two from the office, that, if not actual friends, were at least people who seemed not to actually despise me. And of course in the end, it was one of those awful, excruciating nights where no one really had a non-work related thing to say to anyone else and where everyone started asking me for the name of a good local taxi company . . . at half ten. Anyway like I say, I'm rarely home before the wee small hours and as I trip up the stone steps to the front door, stick my key into the lock and kick my way inside, the first thing I'm instantly hit by is the sheer state of the place. Now, I fork out good money for a cleaning lady to come in every morning, but never in a million years would you think it if you saw the manky hellhole I'm looking at right now. My jaw physically dangles open with the sheer astonishment of it.

A box with a half-eaten pizza in it lies plonked on the bottom of the stairs, like someone was eating it there, then decided they'd something better to do and just abandoned it and walked off. Meanwhile, a big pile of washing lies abandoned outside the living room door, with loose, dirty knickers strewn all round it, none of which are mine and certainly not Lily's either. Then just as a stale stench hits me I realise I'm standing beside two stuffed-to-the-brim black binliners just inside the hall door, miles away from the outside bin where, judging by the stink off them, they should have been dumped hours ago.

Not unlike the *Marie Celeste*, there's no one in sight. No one hears me, no one knows the boss has unexpectedly come home on a stealth mission. Slowly I make my way down the hallway, to the soundtrack of Adele's *Someone Like You* blasting out loud and clear from the very top of the house.

Elka.

But I let that slide for the moment and on I go, on what's now become something of an evidence-gathering mission, down the elegant cream-carpeted staircase at the very back of the hall that leads down to the basement. I've converted the whole downstairs area into one supersized family room, kitchen at one end opening out onto the patio, family room at the other. Which, needless to say, I neither cook in, eat in, nor get to see my family in, but there you go.

I see Lily before she sees me. She's all alone, plonked on a bright pink bean bag in the family room right in front of the TV, still in her little pinafore that she wears to pre-school and twisting one of her strawberry-blonde ringlets round a pudgy finger, with the same pasty, expressionless face of someone who's been listlessly watching telly for God knows how long. And as ever, I almost well up at the sight of this precious bundle that's mine, all mine.

In a million years though, you would never put Lily down as my daughter, nor me as her mother. Because she and I are absolutely, one hundred per cent, nothing alike; in fact, there's not the slightest scrap of a single physical resemblance between us. Whereas my build is wiry and lean, Lily is chunky and cuddly, with thick strawberry blonde, almost reddish, curly locks and bright blue eyes, in total contrast to my thin, dark hair and black eyes. Then, whereas my skin is grey and pasty looking most of the time, Lily has freckles all over her full little round face; cuteness personified.

I neither look nor have ever felt particularly Irish, ever once in my life. My skin doesn't go bright red after thirty seconds of sun exposure (mainly because when am I ever in the sun?), nor do I drink Guinness (eughhhhh . . .), enjoy GAA (oh please . . . do I look like a culchie?), vote Fianna Fail or go to Mass (perish the thought). But looking at Lily, with her reddish curls, freckles and plump, potato-fed little body with chunky white legs, there's no nationality that the child could possibly be, other than Irish.

In fact, she and I are so physically unalike that way back in the early days when I could snatch a bit of time to take her for strolls outside in her buggy, no one ever assumed she was my daughter. 'What a gorgeous little girl,' people would tell me as I'd swell up with maternal pride. 'Who are you babysitting for?'

A box full of expensive educational toys from the Early Learning Centre – toys that Elka is supposed to be playing with alongside her – lies untouched and ignored, while Lily gazes listlessly at the screen ahead of her. The same TV which I explicitly told Elka was barred and banned during daylight hours in this house.

My heart physically twists in my ribcage at the sight in front of me.

Lily looks tired, bored, neglected; enough to make any mother want to crawl into a hole and die quietly of guilt before social services come to take the child away. But instead, a white-hot anger starts out as a swell inside my chest, then spreads over my body till my fingers tingle with pure, undiluted rage. Now ordinarily, I have a good, clear brain that can be relied on to filter the emotion out of anger, but not here and certainly not now.

I shell out a fortune for Elka to take proper care of Lily during the day; she's *supposed* to take her out for walks and fresh air, she's *supposed* to take her to the park to feed the ducks or else stay home with her, keeping her engaged, amused and entertained at all times, always. She's meant to be working on Lily's reading with her and developing her vocabulary, while feeding her healthy, organic food and most importantly of all, never ever letting the child out of her sight. And if she looks as washed out and tired as she does right now, then Elka is under strict instructions to put her down for an afternoon nap; pretty much the only time she's ever allowed to leave the child alone.

But that's not all. What's making me physically see stars in front of my eyes with near-blinding rage is that this is

72

what Elka has been *telling* me she's been doing all day, every day with Lily.

On my father's grave, I will strangle that lying, conniving, over-paid and under-employed little chancer when I get my hands on her; I will physically do harm to her. Right now I'm in danger of crippling her.

Sweet Jesus, if social services saw this, they'd take one look and throw away the key.

'Mama!'

Suddenly Lily looks up and my heart almost breaks at the sight of her little pink face lighting up with pure, undiluted joy as soon as she sees me. A second later, I've scooped her up in my arms, marvelling at how heavy she's got and clinging to her so tightly that I think I might squeeze the air out of her tiny lungs.

'Mama, you home!' She squeals delightedly and buries her tiny white freckly face into my shoulder, fat little arms tight locked round my neck.

'Yes, I'm home bunny . . .'

Then suddenly, her expression changes in a nanosecond, from pure joy to shifty, shame-faced guilt.

'Is it 'cos I was naughty in pwe-school?'

I pull her down on the sofa beside the TV and sit down beside her, arm still tight around her.

'Well, partly pet.'

'I HATE pwe-school. NEVER going back. I'm never going back and you can't make me!'

And seeing how her expression goes from remorseful to thunderous with such sudden ferocity makes me almost want to laugh. She's folded her arms now and jutted out her bottom lip and is glaring at me defiantly, heels dug in.

Did she get that stubborn streak from me? Is that the only characteristic of mine she did inherit? I think, guilt suddenly magnified tenfold.

'Now Lily, you know I'm not going to make you do anything you don't want to do, love . . .'

'Miss Pettyfour is mean and I hate her too but the one I really HATE more than vegetables, more even than bwoccolli is . . .'

'. . . Let me guess . . . A little boy in pre-school called Tim O'Connor. Would that be right, love?' I say softly.

An angry, furious nod, then suddenly she starts to wriggle awkwardly beside me, like she knows what's coming next and is physically trying to get out of it. Such, it would seem, is the cognitive reasoning process of a small child; run away from the confrontation and it'll just go away all by itself.

'You know Lily,' I tell her, gently pulling her back then folding my arms around her so she can't toddle off. 'I've just been to see Miss Pettifer and she told me all about what happened.'

The blue saucer eyes look worriedly back up at me, like a little puppy that's just weed on the carpet, and knows right well it's in trouble and there's no backing out of it.

'So honey, would you like to tell me your side of it? Don't worry, Mama's not angry,' I tack on, pulling a stray, scraggy red hair back off her freckly face and biding my time, waiting for her answer.

'Tim said I had no daddy,' she eventually tells me sheepishly. 'He said every other kid had a dad 'cept me. He said all I had was a mummy and a minder who collected me. So I smacked him and he cried and cried and then Miss Pettyfour made me go on the naughty step till bweak time . . .'

'Lily,' I say gently, 'you know it's very wrong to smack anyone, especially other children?'

A small, guilty nod.

'I'm sowwy Mama.'

'I know you are bunny.'

'Won't do it again.'

'There's a good girl.'

Then the little arms fold defiantly and the chin thrusts out.

'But I'm still never going back to smelly pwre-school. EVER. 'Kay?'

'That's absolutely fine. No one, and especially not me, is going to make you do anything you don't want to.'

She thinks for a second, then seems happy enough with this. So now that she's not in trouble any more, she flashes me a gap-toothed smile and snuggles tight into me, warm and heavy and woozy with sleep, smelling of milk and plasticine.

I let her cuddle tightly into me as my thoughts race. Because how best to bring up that other, far more delicate subject? Her earlier words, the ones Miss Pettifer quoted back to me, are swirling round my brain now.

I do have a dad and one day he'll come for me.

How in the name of arse am I supposed to explain this to a small child?

'Lily?' I begin slowly, gently.

'Mmmmm?' she says, sounding groggy now after all the drama in her little day, her sleepy, heavy head buried deep under my arm.

'You know all families are different, don't you? Some families have a mum and dad, whereas some just have a dad and then there are families like us, where the mummy is the one in charge.'

75

And just like that, she's bright-eyed, alert and awake again.

'But I DO have a dad. I DO. All kids do. Tim says you can't be born unless you have a mummy *an'* a daddy.'

Shit. Deep breath, try again. Try better.

'Well, that's true, but only up to a point.'

'What's uppa point mean?'

'It means that some families have a dad who lives with them, and that's fine. But plenty of families, like us, don't live with their dad and that's fine too.'

'But where *is* my dad? Where'd he go? Did someone bold steal him?' She's looking intently at me now, little freckly face now frowning with worry.

'He mus' be *somewhere* Mama!'

'Of course he's somewhere love, but the point is, we don't know where and we don't need to know.'

'Is he hiding? Like in a game? Is he playing hide and seek with us, Mama?'

Bugger. I'm making a right pig's ear of this.

'No pet, you see he doesn't exactly know that we're here. But then, that's not really important, because we don't need him, do we? We're fine without him, aren't we?'

'But *where did he go* Mama?' she pleads, looking dangerously close to tears now. 'Why doesn't he come to see me? It is 'cos I was naughty?'

My almost-three-year old looks at me with puzzled, monkey eyes, desperately wanting answers that her mother can't give. Please, please, please, I find myself absently praying to a God I don't believe in, send me the right words to explain this inexplicable situation to the tiny, precious bundle that's cradled in my arms, looking up at me with absolute trust in my judgement. Please, just once, please

Allah, Buddha, Santa, anyone up there who's listening, steer me through this icky conversation in a way she can grasp.

Another deep breath.

'OK Lily, let me put it to you this way. Before you were born, I wanted you so, so badly, that I had to go to a very special hospital to get you. And they planted you in my tummy and nine months later, out you came. Tiny and perfect and so good you rarely cried, ever.'

'So . . .' she says, frowning, concentrating hard and scrunching up her tiny, freckly nose 'did you pick my daddy out when you were in the 'pecial hospital? Did you meet him there?'

Not for the first time, I'm totally taken aback at just how bright the child is; at the fact that she can grasp something so vague and inexplicable. With great pride, I cuddle her closer and she slips her thumb in her mouth, plump little arms locked tight round my waist.

'No darling, I never met your dad either. Sometimes mummies don't need to, you see. And that's OK you know. mums and dads don't always need to know each other or even be friends, just so mummies can get babies.'

A long silence as she tried to digest this.

And then it comes.

'But . . . but I wanna see him Mama. I wan' him to be my fwiend. I wanna *see* him. I wan' him to play with me and give me piggy back rides and . . . and . . . I want my dad to take me to the park and the movies, like the other dads in pwe-school all do. Can we just find him and say . . . Hello?'

'Sweetheart . . . I don't think that's going to be possible . . .'

Now her face is getting pinker and the bottom lip is dangerously close to wobbling, a red-light warning sign that tired, cranky, exhausted tears aren't too far off.

'Mama PLEASE! Is it 'cos I was bold in playgwoup?'

'No, of course not . . .'

'I only want to meet him, that's all! And I'll be a good lickle girl. I pwomise!'

I sigh deeply. One the one hand, you should never make a promise to a child you can't keep and on the other hand, there's every chance she'll have clean forgotten all about this by morning. But most of all, I never again want to see this level of disappointment in my daughter's big saucery blue eyes. Again.

'All right pet. I'll try my very best.'

I'm rewarded with a toothy smile, then, as only small kids can, she puts the whole thing clean out of her little head, sticks her thumb in her mouth and cuddles back in tight to me, her worries banished as though they never were and all set for her afternoon snooze. I pull a cashmere throw off the back of the sofa and wrap it round her, tucking it tight in around her pudgy little legs and gently settling her down for her nap.

Then, just as I'm about to ease myself off the sofa without waking her, I hear the sound of footsteps click-clacking down the back stairs.

Ooooh, this'll be good.

I stand up, arms folded, calmly waiting. The element of surprise, I feel, being the essential element here.

And sure enough, in trots Elka, wearing my silk dressing gown and with a sea-green facepack on her that looks suspiciously like the Crème de la Mer one sitting on my dressing table.

She nearly leaps six feet in the air when she sees me, standing nice and composed by my slumbering daughter, waiting like a praying mantis for her.

'Eloise!' she says, in her clipped, over-articulated English. 'What are you doing back home? I did not expect you for a long time . . .'

'You handed in your notice this morning, remember?' I say coolly, voice even, fixing her with a steady, measured stare. One I save up for special occasions in the office, if I really need to terrify the bejaysus out of someone. Rarely fails me. Been known to reduce grown men to tears on occasion.

'Eh . . . Of course I do . . .'

'Well, I've got wonderful news for you, Elka. You can leave even earlier than you thought. Like – how about right now? And what's more, you can take your manky laundry strewn across my hallway and your abandoned, half eaten pizza with you. Oh and by the way? I'd strongly suggest you don't come looking to me for a reference. Trust me, it would be a really, really bad idea.'

In the end, of all people, my sister Helen ends up being my saviour, my messiah in this hour of need. In total and utter desperation, I put out not so much a distress flare as an SOS to her, and to my astonishment and eternal gratitude, she tells me not to panic, that she'll be on the next train up to Dublin from Cork.

Miracle. It's a bloody miracle. I feel huge gratitude, mixed with a pang of sharp guilt when I think of how dismissively I've treated her over the years. And now, here she is, in my hour of need, dropping everything and running just to give me a dig out.

Hours later, while I'm still at home dealing with the massive backlog of phone calls and replying to all my emails from the office, while simultaneously seeing off Madam Elka, my nagging conscience won't let up on me.

Would I have done the same for Helen?

The answer's obvious. Not a bleeding snowball's chance.

Bad mother, bad sister . . . Soul searching is something I rarely have the luxury of spare time to indulge in, but somehow there's just no avoiding it today.

And then there's little Lily, snoozing peacefully on the sofa, clinging to her battered and almost threadbare comfort blankie, worn out after all the high-octane drama of her day.

She'll forget all about that other matter, I think smugly to myself, feeling a cool, tigerish joy flood over me at the happy sight of Elka finally getting her arse out of here in a taxi. She'll wake up shortly, all refreshed and happy after her nap and the whole notion of her father will all have been banished right out of her little head, as though it never was.

I continue to think that as I tidy the spare room to get it ready for Helen. I still think it when Lily wakes up, beams to see me still in the house, then immediately waddles upstairs to her bedroom.

She's ages in there, and in between firing off an email to Seth Coleman and putting a clean duvet cover on the spare bed, I suddenly realise the child is gone suspiciously quiet, so I stick my head round her bedroom door to do a lightning quick check on her.

'Look at me Mama!' she squeals excitedly as soon as she sees me, twirling round in the outfit she's just changed into. A pink leotard and a matching fluffy tutu with bits of diamanté all over it, along with sparkly little pumps in . . . what else? Bubblegum pink.

'You look lovely sweetheart,' I tell her distractedly. 'Now come on downstairs, I want you to have some dinner.'

'NO! I HATE dinner! And I'm playing dwess up!'

'Later, you can play dress up later. Is this so you can wear something pretty for Auntie Helen?'

'NO Mama!' she yells at me, stomping her foot in a gesture that a silent movie actress would shudder to use. 'This is what I'm going to wear when we go to meet my daddy. Like you pwomised. Wemember? You *pwomised!*'

With that, the mobile tucked into my suit pocket rang out loud and clear. And this time, I never even bothered checking to see who it was.

Chapter Three

Pay absolutely no attention to this, I tell Helen as soon as she's settled in and used to us all. Lily's just developed a bee in her bonnet about the whole idea of having a dad and maybe even getting to meet him, nothing more. But she'll pretty soon forget all about it; wait and see. All we need to do is starve the whole thing of oxygen. Simple as that. Not unlike my strategy with her whenever she's stomping her feet and demanding whole dessert spoonfuls of Nutella on top of her toast for her breakfast on our Sundays together; I just blatantly ignore it, distract her by dangling some kind of toy in her face and in no time, all her little demands disappear as though they never were.

Such are the vagaries of being almost three years old it seems; you're cursed with the short-term memory of a fruit fly. What was bringing on hysterics two seconds ago is banished instantly at the sight of anything pink and glittery dangled in front of your face. Complete doddle.

I continue to believe that the whole 'when am I meeting my daddy?' issue has finally been put to bed right up to the following weekend which, in spite of my best efforts, is the next window of peace I get from work, so I can spend a bit of time at home.

I race home on Friday night so I can give Lily her bath and put her to bed, aching to do some mother/daughter bonding with her, but to my dismay I find out I'm already too late.

Helen's waiting up for me, watching TV while texting away on her phone downstairs in the family room, wearing an oversized dressing gown and a mansize pair of fleecy socks, sofa-lising. (New buzzword dreamt up by Marc, from Arts and Culture. A bastardisation of words to describe the act of socialising whilst your bum is glued to the sofa. Marc, as you see, is very fond of his word mash-ups.)

She doesn't hear me slip into the kitchen at the far end of the room and looking at her from this distance all I can think is . . . so much about Helen has changed over the years and yet so much has stayed exactly the same. She's gained weight, but she's lucky, it happens to suit her. Fills her face out and makes her look even younger. She still has the same even temperament and insuppressibly sunny good humour, the exact same general Pollyanna, glass-half-full outlook on life, at all times, always. Just like an air hostess, smiling through her pretty, even white teeth and unfailingly polite, even when living under the same roof as a termagant like me.

She and I don't look even remotely alike. Helen is bright-eyed and fair-haired, with a sunny, sparkly, outgoing personality to match; not so much a glass-half-full person, as a Waterford crystal, limited edition glass, half full of rare, vintage champagne. Then there's me; small, dark, unsmiling, with deathly, Morticia Addams-pale skin that's the bane of my life and a permanently hollow, sunken-eyed look about me, which, in spite of the most expensive face creams money will buy, still seems to be permanently etched in.

Helen's adopted you see, something which always left me with the lifelong sensation that I somehow wasn't good enough for my parents, which was why they felt the need to go out shopping for another daughter, as I'd seen it at the time. It had hurt me as a little girl, hurt me far more deeply then I ever let on, and to this day remains a searingly vivid memory, one that still has the power to sting even now, from a safe distance of decades. Coming home from primary school to be told by Dad that there was a 'surprise' waiting for me in the good front room. Course I was all excited at first, then bitterly disappointed to discover nothing other than my battered old cot with a new baby sleeping in it. I'd thought at the very least that I was getting a new home computer or a maths set. Something useful.

As time went on though, I realised the truth; that Mum and Dad had just brought home what appeared to the five-year-old me to be an improved version of what a little daughter should be. One who grew up to be pretty and blonde who lisped and giggled and wore pink and got invited everywhere. And although they'd die rather than admit it, one who they both clearly preferred; to this day, I can still hear the three of them happily laughing and messing about while watching some TV programme together night after night, like a proper family. All while I sat all alone upstairs in my room, getting ahead on the next day's homework and trying to choke back hot, furious tears at being so blatantly excluded. Five years old was a young age to learn all about rejection, and yet that's exactly what I had to do.

Course years later, after several gin and tonics, my mother has told me that this actually wasn't the case at all; that she and Dad were if anything just utterly exhausted and worn out by all the various demands involved in rearing a child genius – the special tutorial classes, the constant IQ tests, the violin/cello/clarinet lessons, the way I never seemed to need sleep for more than a few hours, instead reading book after book throughout the long, lonely nights.

According to Mum, they could deal with all that though; what worried them was always hearing that other kids in my class were organising birthday parties for their friends, trips to the movies or else days out to the zoo, none of which I ever seemed to be invited to. But once they adopted little Helen, all that changed for them; because this, thank God, was a more normal child, one who failed maths tests and struggled with her reading, but who was bubbly and friendly and perennially popular; forever getting invited out on play dates and sleepovers with all the other kids in her class. The complete polar opposite to me, in other words.

And now here we are, living under the same roof together, for the first time since we were teenagers. Except now, instead of feeling old pangs of childhood jealousy towards her, all I can think is, this girl really must be some kind of walking saint. I can't describe just how hugely grateful I am to her for doing this and for putting up with me, when not many would. Grateful to her for dropping everything to help me out in my hour of need, though I did insist on paying her far more than I ever paid Elka, stressing that this was just a temporary measure till I found someone more permanent. (Not an easy task, given that I've been blacklisted by just about every nanny agency in town.)

'Hi, I'm home. So where's Lily?' I ask, still breathless from the mad dash to get back to see her and knowing full well what the answer will be. The house is way too quiet, for starters; course she's already in bed.

'Asleep hours ago,' Helen smiles sweetly up at me from

where she's sprawled out in front of the TV, eating Haagen-Dazs straight from the tub. 'Oh you should have seen her in the bath! She was so adorable! We had the BEST fun. Then she got into her little pink sleeper suit and insisted on me reading *Sleeping Beauty* to her . . . You know that's her number one story now? And her new thing is that as soon as I've told it to her, she has to tell it back to me. She's completely word perfect, her memory is just incredible you know, almost photographic, just like yours . . .'

Helen happily chatters on while I stand rooted to the spot, fixing her with a borehole stare. No, I did not know *Sleeping Beauty* was now Lily's favourite story. Or that she likes to tell it back to you as soon as you're finished. I knew none of this; how could I? The one night I can get away from work relatively early to see her, I'm already too late.

'I really wanted to do all that with her,' I tell Helen, as a flood of disappointment suddenly makes me irrationally snappy. 'Just once, just for tonight. I nearly crashed the car I rushed home that fast, I had to spin a pile of stories even just to get away this early . . .'

'But it's half eight at night!' Helen insists. 'The poor little thing was exhausted. We'd been to the park earlier today you see, to feed the ducks and the weather was so fine, we stayed there much longer than I'd planned. Then we came back here and had dinner, and of course by then, she was practically falling asleep into her spaghetti hoops. So what else was I to do?'

I give a long, defeated sigh and tell her it's okay, it's not her fault. I was just looking forward to seeing my little girl, that's all. But she knows me of old and knows only too well when to pay no attention to me when I'm ratty from sleep deprivation, so she quickly goes back to her TV show.

'By the way, Sean called for you today,' she calls over to me cheerily from the sofa as I tear open the post from the island in the centre of the kitchen.

'Who the hell is Sean?'

'Oh you know Sean, he's the FedEx guy. Left a package on the hall table for you. He says he's been delivering to you for years. Such a sweet guy; do you know he has a daughter exactly Lily's age with another one on the way?'

Vintage Helen, getting pally with all around her, entrancing everyone she meets with her natural charm and old-fashioned niceness. In the space of a few days, she's also befriended the cleaning lady over big, bonding mugs of tea and whinges about the respective men in their lives, not to mention the gardener, who she's now on first name terms with as well. Whereas the sum total of my knowledge about the cleaner is that her first name is Mary and that she has the permanently disappointed look about her of a woman whose husband left her for someone younger, but not before transferring all his assets into an offshore account. Wait and see though, I bet before the month is out Helen will end up going out on a drunken girlie night in Temple Bar with the cleaner and it wouldn't surprise me a bit if she ended getting invited to the gardener's house for a Sunday roast.

Not that I'm holding any of this against her, it's just a constant daily reminder of our sibling relationship; I'm permanently cast in the role of bad cop against her perennially popular good cop. I'm the green-faced Wicked Witch of the West to her Glinda, the Good Witch in the meringue dress that everyone loves and gravitates towards and wants to hang around with. This was our central casting as kids and this, it would seem, is how we still are.

Then there's the fact that she seems to be in constant and daily contact with our mother and feels the need to tell me this all the time. Now every family has someone like Helen; the glue person. The one who tries their level best to keep each one in check and fully informed about everyone else, no matter how much indifference and how many shrugged shoulders they come across. Since she moved in, Helen's forever passing on little titbits of news, like, 'Guess what? Mum's just gone and bought a lovely new patio set for her back garden. The wooden one she had just fell apart after all that rain they had recently in Marbella, and you know how she's had her eye on a cast iron one for ages now . . .'

Have I ever had a conversation with my mother regarding patio sets? Didn't even know she had a back garden. Last time I had a decent conversation with her was over a week ago and even then, she was only ringing up to talk to Lily.

Ahh, Lily. It seems that even a small child isn't immune to Helen and her Miss Congeniality charm offensive. I've never seen anything like it; Lily took one look at this shadowy figure who she vaguely remembered from Christmas dinners, not to mention all the birthday cards and gifts that had been posted up from Cork over the years, and instantly idolised her Auntie Helen, practically from the moment she walked through the front door. Turns out Helen is a born natural with kids, the way she's a born natural with everyone, and now on the rare occasions when I'm home, all I'll get from Lily is a rough shove followed by, 'NO! Not YOU, I want Auntie Helen to read me my storwy. Then Auntie Helen can gimme my bath and put me to bed.'

Don't get me wrong, of course I could kiss Helen's feet,

I'm that grateful to her, but that doesn't mean it's not killing me inside.

No words to describe it, when you suddenly feel unwanted at home. When you're superfluous under your own roof.

'No, please don't worry about rushing home, Eloise,' Helen's said to me time and again this week, 'you don't have to cancel your meeting and leave the office yet. Lily and I are having such a ball here! We've made cupcakes and I'm just teaching her how to ice them now. Stay in work, I know how important that is to you. And don't worry, we're all fine here, we're having great fun!'

So far, the pair of them have been to the park together, the movies, the Build-A-Bear factory at the Dundrum Town Centre; they've even had tea parties for all of Lily's dolls in the back garden and picnics at Sandymount Strand. Everything that I want to do with Lily but can't.

So if I'm being brutally honest . . . I'm in equal parts grateful to her, but not a little jealous of her too. Burning childhood memories resurface; the way everyone, absolutely everyone just prefers her to me, she's a bright light that people can't help be drawn towards, moth-like. My own daughter, it would seem, included.

'You know Eloise, I've been thinking,' Helen beams over the top of the sofa at me, turning down the volume of the TV.

'Umm?' I mutter distractedly, my head buried deep in the pile of post that I'm still wading through.

'Lily still hasn't stopped talking about her dad you know, it's become almost like an obsession with her.'

This, by the way, is delivered with a look that might as well say, 'if you were around more often, you'd know.'

'Oh come on, not this again . . .'

'Yes, this again. You have to listen to me, Eloise. It's the first thing she talks about when she wakes up every morning, last thing she asks me about before I put her to bed. When am I meeting him, where is he, have you found him yet, where are you looking . . . the poor little thing's not letting it drop. And to be honest, I don't think this is something that's just going to go quietly away all by itself, like you'd thought.'

Okay, so now she has my attention.

'So if you think about it,' Helen goes on, pausing to dump the now empty tub of ice cream on the coffee table in front of her, then licking every single last dribble of chocolate sauce off the back of the spoon. 'Would it be such a terrible thing if we did a bit of detective work and tracked him down? I mean, I'd be more than happy to make all the phone calls and do all the work for you. I know how busy you are, but trust me, you wouldn't have to lift a finger. I'd report back to you at every stage and I wouldn't do a thing without your say-so . . .'

I stand stone still and throw her a look so icy that it could freeze mercury. At least, that's what I hope it conveys. Lately Seth Coleman has been saying behind my back that my glacial stares, once so terrifying, are now starting to make me look a bit constipated.

'I mean . . . it absolutely goes without saying . . .' she hastily backpedals, realising how unimpressed I am by all of this shitetalk. 'Not that we'd want him to be a part of her life in any way at all. This is just so Lily can put a face to his name. That's all. To help her get closure on this and you know . . . put it all to bed. She's become unhealthily obsessed and I really think this is the best way to deal with the whole issue.'

90

Helen trails off, waiting on my response. Then for good measure tacks on,

'So, emm . . . What do you think then?'

'Helen,' I begin, arms folded, nearly swaying with tiredness by now, 'Are you completely insane? Why are you even raising this subject? Lily isn't quite three years old yet, she'll have forgotten all about it in a few days.'

'But she hasn't forgotten, that's the whole point that you're missing!' Helen insists, forcefully coming right back at me. 'You work twenty-four-seven; you haven't heard her asking about him morning, noon and night . . .'

'Oh here we go,' I sigh deeply, sinking exhaustedly down into the armchair opposite her and kicking off unforgiving high shoes which have been pinching me since I first put them on . . . at five this morning. 'Throw in the absentee mother jibe, why don't you. Go for it, play the low card.'

Then I remember my manners, remember just how much I owe her for being here when I'd no one else to turn to.

'Sorry, I really didn't mean to sound so grouchy,' I compose myself and apologise.

'That's okay. I think that after almost twenty-eight years, I'm well used to you by now,' she smiles benignly, then looks back at me expectantly, clearly waiting on a fuller discussion to follow.

'Thing is, I'm very, very tired, Helen. I've had the longest day in the longest week you can possibly imagine. Tracing Lily's father is completely out of the question and to be perfectly honest, I'm not a hundred percent certain that I appreciate you even bringing it up.'

'But I'm only doing it for Lily,' she says sweetly, refusing to get riled.

Which of course only riles me up even more.

'Because you know, this isn't a bullet that you can dodge that easily,' she chatters on easily, ignoring the waves of boxed fury emanating from my corner of the room. 'Sooner or later, the day will come when she's going to track him down for herself, you know.'

'Yeah, fine, maybe when she's eighteen, so why don't I just cross that bridge when I come to it? I've told you Helen, it's completely out of the question. I won't have some total stranger barging his way into my baby's life and maybe even letting her down and wanting nothing to do with her. Which he'd be perfectly entitled to do, you know. I'm only trying to protect her, that's all'.

'But you're completely missing the point,' says Helen calmly, reasonably. 'She's not a baby any more, she's a little girl. And all kids want is to be normal, to be the same as the others. If you won't do this for your own reasons, then at least do it for Lily. Let her just put a face to the word daddy, then let it go. She's already well able to understand that you're not with her dad, but just let her get this out of her little system. Then next time other kids in a playground ask her about her father, she can be one of them and answer truthfully about where he is and what he's like, instead of having to tell the world that she doesn't even know where he is or what his name is. It's this whole mystery surrounding him that's making her so obsessed.'

'You're completely exaggerating, she is not obsessed . . .'

'Oh no? Do you realise that every picture she's drawn with her new colouring set is of her dad? Then today we got the bus to the park and she waddled up and asked the driver was he her dad. Same thing to a guy serving on the till in Tesco. Then later on she was watching a DVD of *Shrek* while I was getting dinner and now she's got it into her head that her father is king of some faraway kingdom.'

'Well . . . This is just a phase and she'll soon grow out of it.'

'How do you know?'

'Because kids do.'

'I didn't.'

Which of course, suddenly stops me dead in my tracks.

'I'm sorry . . . What did you just say?'

'Eloise, do you honestly think that I spent my whole childhood and adulthood not wondering about my own natural parents? Who they were and where they were from? And what were the reasons why they'd given me up for adoption? Do you really think that's not something that obsessed me for just about as long as I can remember?'

'But, you never mentioned anything before . . .'

My voice gets increasingly smaller and smaller then trails off into nothing. Because the thought is unspoken between us. Why would Helen tell *me*, of all people? Why would anyone bother to tell me anything about their private life? Even if she had phoned me to talk, chances are all she would have got would have been my voicemail, or else a promise from my assistant to get the message to me. Which, I shamefacedly have to admit, the chances of my returning would have been slim to none.

Have to say I'm feeling very, very small right now. Something that's happening far too often lately.

Thankfully Helen is too humane to really hammer the point home though and I feel an even deeper surge of gratitude towards her for this small mercy.

'You see,' she goes on to explain, distractedly picking up

93

one of Lily's stuffed cats from the floor in front of her and thoughtfully playing with it, 'because our parents were fantastic to me and I loved them both so much, it seemed almost like ingratitude to want to know who my real family were. But that didn't stop me from always wondering, and in later life, becoming absolutely determined to find out the truth about my birth family. Who were they, why they gave me up, all of that.'

'But Helen,' I say, a bit softer now, 'Mum and Dad adored you, idolised you.' You were like their little treasure. I want to tack on, and we both know that I was the also-ran daughter, the difficult one, the one they always had to worry about, but somehow there's no need to. It's unspoken between us. She already knows.

'I know all that and believe me, I couldn't have been more grateful to either of them. Or, God knows, have had a happier childhood. But you're missing the point. Because no matter how loving a family you grow up in, knowing you're adopted still leaves a scar. You spend so much time wondering. Think about it. Your mother, the person who's supposed to love you and protect you more than anyone else in the world, gives you away. The first thing that happens to you in the first few days of life is that you're rejected. And I just had to find out why. And also to let her know that I was okay and thank God, that things had worked out well for me. So, it took me years to pluck up the courage, but eventually I decided to do a bit of detective work. I told our mum of course; I'd die if she thought I was doing anything behind her back. But she understood that this was something I absolutely needed to do and she was incredibly supportive. Came with me to the adoption agency and everything.'

'And . . .?' I manage to get out, overwhelmed by the tidal wave of guilt at not being there for her. At not even knowing about this before now.

'I was too late. My birth mother had passed away about two years previously. She'd had breast cancer and apparently died very young, in her early fifties. She was only sixteen when she had me and it turned out my biological father, her boyfriend, had been killed by a drunk driver in a car crash shortly before I was born, which was why I was put up for adoption in the first place. She was grieving, I imagine, and felt she couldn't cope with a new baby on top of everything else she was going through. I don't even blame her either – chances are I'd have done exactly the same thing in her shoes. She was only sixteen for God's sake, she was still a kid herself.

'But please listen to me on this Eloise,' Helen says gently, leaning forward and looking at me intently, 'I now have to spend the rest of my life living with the fact that I was too late. That if I'd gone about tracking down my birth mother years ago, I may have been able to meet her, might even struck up some kind of a relationship with her. Maybe I could even have seen her before she passed away. But I kept putting it off and now I have to live with the what-ifs. All I'm saying is, don't put Lily through what I've been through. She's obsessed about finding her real dad just like I was and it's not going to go away. So please, for her sake, deal with this now, while there's still time. She has a right to know, just like I did. And our mum supported me when I went digging for the truth, so why not do the same for Lily?'

Oh God, I think, looking sympathetically across at her. I feel so awful for Helen, for what the poor girl had to go through. And could she have a point? Is this whole thing turning into an obsession for Lily that won't go away until she finally finds out who her father is? Then one awful mental image after another starts to crowd in on me; of the child sitting on a bus today and asking the driver if he is her dad. Of her not even being able to enjoy a harmless TV movie without fantasising about who her real dad is . . . Drawing pictures of him . . .

Who knows what's going through her little mind?

Helen knows me well and must sense that I'm wavering, because next thing she's sitting cross-legged on the sofa in the Lotus position, looking serenely calm, fair hair neatly flicked over her shoulder.

'Aren't you in the least bit curious yourself,' she puts it to me, 'to know anything at all about him? I mean, he must come from good stock, he's got to be intelligent, because Lily couldn't just get it from you and you alone. Sure, just look at her. She's so alert and advanced for her age, don't you think so?'

I nod, tears of pride surprising me by stinging my eyes. Lily is incredibly bright; I've no doubt about that. She never even had baby-talk, she started speaking words clearly and distinctly at eighteen months and by aged two, she was talking in whole sentences, like a proper little lady. Already she's learning to read and can assemble all her own toys and even more impressive, can amuse and entertain herself for hours without getting bored. She even surprised me by being musical at a very young age and when I bought her a piano, she took to it like a duck to water. She's too young for proper lessons yet, but the second she is old enough, I've been intending to hire private tuition. To be perfectly honest, I'm only itching for her to turn three so I can get a proper IQ test done on her. Because I know she'll score high, just know it.

'I'll bet her father turns out to be . . . A senior consultant cardiologist in the Blackrock Clinic,' Helen chips in dreamily. 'Or because she's so musical, maybe a conductor. With the Philharmonic at the New York Met. Or maybe he's a physicist well on his way to winning the Nobel Prize by now. One thing's for certain though, he must be really good looking, because she's such a gorgeous little fairy.'

'Hmmm,' is all I can say, getting intrigued now in spite of myself.

'Either way,' she goes on, still in her fantasy world and I think barely even registering me now, 'if you were him, and if you had a little girl this special, wouldn't you want to know about it?'

The funny thing is that when it boils down to it, I actually know so little about Lily's father myself, it's ridiculous. And I'm surprising myself by wondering about it now, as it's something I rarely do. Once I had Lily, I banished all thoughts about whoever he might be completely out of my mind. She's mine, I thought. Mine and no one else's. One thing is for certain though, whoever he is and wherever he is, he's got to be someone very special – because isn't Lily the living walking proof of that?

Oh, sod this anyway. You know something? It's curiosity that'll be the death of mankind. Not all this crap about climate change.

No, it's curiosity, plain and simple.

The fertility clinic I attended went by the unlikely name of the Reilly Institute, which at the time, appealed. It sounded like a place where you do night classes, I remember thinking at the time, not somewhere you've to reveal all about your private life and your full medical history, get totally undressed, then undergo possibly the most mortifying medical procedure ever devised by man. I'll spare the details, but all I'll say is that it involves lying on a sheet of freezing metal naked from the waist down, while being prodded with a load of ice-cold spatulas, and I'll leave the rest to the imagination. Trust me though, no torture meted out to witches in medieval times could have been more excruciatingly painful or mortifying.

You know me by now; I did my homework and did it thoroughly. Firstly I found out from the concerned, mercifully sensitive nurse who was looking after me, whether or not the bank recruited, let's just say, a certain type of donor? Because I was fussy; I wanted someone intelligent, talented, from 'good stock', as Helen put it. I bombarded this poor, patient nurse with a thousand questions – on average how old were the donors? (Under age forty apparently is preferable, I knew from my own exhaustive research on the subject. Higher sperm motility.) How and when did donors sign away legal rights to any child conceived using their sperm? And most importantly of all, how exactly was confidentiality maintained?

I must have driven her nearly insane with my inquisition; I requested a full list of donor profiles, then asked for information about each donor's physical characteristics; ethnic background, educational background, occupation, general health, and hobbies and interests. Some banks will even provide photos, which I took a lightning-quick scan though, then dismissed. Somehow it made the whole mortifying process far simpler not to attach a face to a number on a donor profile.

Made me feel a bit more in control, if that makes any sense.

I'm not exaggerating when I say that the whole process

took weeks. I trawled through each and every profile on offer, knowing that this was probably the single biggest decision I was ever likely to make in my life. And finally, finally finally, I found The One. No name, just a number, but this one seemed to tick all the right boxes. Blue eyes, fair hair and fair skin, just how I imagined my little baby would look. Supermarket genetics come to life.

The Chosen One seemed sporty and athletic too: he'd won gold medals for the two hundred metres and was a member of the Trinity College rowing team. This appealed; if I had a boy, I reasoned, he'd have great biceps and would look like he rowed everywhere. And he'd grow up with shiny skin and cheekbones you could grate cheese on, like all athletes seem to have. His profile also claimed that he'd written a thesis on Ireland's economic meltdown and the subsequent road to recovery, which immediately gave me a mental picture that maybe he worked as a high-earning TV economist, one of those young preppy guys who look straight to camera and gravely tell us we're all doomed, but do it with such persuasive charm that you end up not really minding that much at all.

What swung it for me though, was that his profile claimed he was musical as well as everything else and played classical piano right up to concert grade. That alone made me almost able to picture him; tall, gifted, clean shaven, articulate and an all-rounder. A real renaissance man. The type that if I ever happened to meet him in a bar in real life, most likely wouldn't give someone like me a second glance, but would be surrounded by tall blonde modelly women with caramel skin and perfect Hollywood smiles.

But not here. Because in the Reilly Institute, it was me that was calling the shots. And I'd decided on him and that was all there was to it. He was good at sport, academically sound and cultured too – barring him having become a self-made billionaire by the age of twenty five, what more could I possibly ask for?

Then came the science bit. A Dr. Casement, with the cold clinical dispassion of someone who spends half their day looking down a microscope, advised that we needed to find out how many pregnancies this donor's sperm had previously produced. Ten is the recommended limit apparently, to lessen the chances of a single donor's offspring ever meeting and producing children of their own, instantly making me think of just about every Greek tragedy I'd ever yawned my way through. But my luck was in; astonishingly, I was the first woman through there to have chosen this grade A specimen. Massive sigh of relief.

Then as soon as the sample was fully medically assessed for family history, heritable conditions, any diseases that could be passed down – not to mention infectious diseases like chlamydia, HIV, hepatitis, syphilis and let's not forget the delightful gonorrhoea – the rest was plain sailing.

I was told it would take a few rounds of treatment before we'd have a successful outcome, so not to be too disappointed if it didn't take on my first go. But I was having absolutely none of it. Because under no circumstances was I going through all of this malarkey all over again, so I willed my uterus lining to thicken up and do what it was told and miraculously, astonished everyone at the clinic by getting lucky first time round.

Out came Lily, punctual to the dot nine months later and thus ended my involvement with the Reilly Institute.

Until now, that is.

Chapter Four

Initially, Helen gamely offered to do the detective work for me – the Jane Marple bit, as she put it – but I told her there was no need. Firstly, as any self-respecting control freak will tell you, either you do the thing properly yourself, or it doesn't get done. And secondly, whenever you're cold-calling and trying to find out, let's just say, information of a sensitive nature, you've no idea how much this magic phrase works. 'Hi there, I'm senior editor of the *Post* and I'm calling to inquire about . . .' Works like a charm every time. When people, and particularly Irish people, realise you're a journalist, they will open up and tell you absolutely anything, if they think it'll get their name into the paper. Or better yet, their photo. In colour. For all their mammies and pals to see.

The first part is astonishingly easy. Next day at work, I kick closed the inner door to my office and make the call, being careful to keep my voice discreet, calm and business like.

'Hello, you've reached the Reilly Institute, how may I direct your call?'

A woman's voice, curt and businesslike. So I explain that I was treated there four years ago and now need urgent access to my patient file. For, ahem, personal reasons. We're terribly sorry, comes the crisp answer, but I'm afraid we don't give out that information.

As it happens though, I anticipated this and am prepared for all of this red-tape crapology.

Yes, I fully appreciate that, I tell her, but this is a pretty unique situation. As it happens, I'm about to commission a piece about fertility clinics in the Dublin area and this is all part of the research I'm carrying out for the article, writing of course from the basis of my own personal experience, blah-di-blah. I even tack on, astonishing myself at the sheer brazenness of the fib, that I'd be attaching a full-colour photo of the Reilly Institute, with plugs galore.

Funny how lying through your teeth becomes kind of second nature to you when you've worked at the *Post* long enough. Bit worrying, really.

But it really was that easy. A slight, wavering pause, then a supervisor is called to the phone, so I repeat verbatim the conversation with the carrot attached and we're away.

My file is reopened and here it is.

Wait for it, his name is William Goldsmith. William Goldsmith. Of course he's a William, I think a bit smugly, sitting back in my swivel chair and gazing absent-mindedly out the window, in a rare moment of self-indulgence. I like the name William; always have. Sporty, athletic, cultured guys always have names like William I think, suddenly getting a sharp mental picture of Prince William on his wedding day, looking hot to trot in his scarlet army uniform with rows of medals hanging from his well-toned chest.

Best bit of all; he is, or was at least when he filled out all his details at the Reilly Institute, a post-grad student in Trinity College. Then some details I already knew and remembered well, that he's exactly the same age as me, six

102

foot two, blond, with blue eyes. No address of course, but that I look on as a minor challenge and nothing more.

Jesus, why didn't I do this years ago?

Never mind Lily wanting to meet him, now I do too.

Right then. Next stop, Trinity College.

I have to sit through another two editorial meetings before I can snatch a quiet bit of alone time to make my next move, itching to get out of there and back to the privacy of my office. Again, I slam the door shut, call Trinity and get put straight onto the registration office. I'm inquiring about a post-grad student by the name of William Goldsmith, I tell them with great confidence. Do you have any forwarding details, or maybe even an address?

I'm put on hold for ages, which allows me more time to drift back into my little fantasy balloon. I'll bet William is good-looking, the kind of guy you look at and think, yeah, that's natural selection at work. Bet he's the kind of guy that otherwise intelligent women lose their thought processes and speech patterns over. Bet he lives in a gorgeous city-centre apartment, conveniently close to college, with amazing panoramic views over the city, where he hosts elegant soirées with everyone talking about the shards of our economy and how exactly they'd go about fixing it. 'Hi, great to see you, how are your lectures going? Hey, I'm going to William's for a drink this evening. You know William, William Goldsmith? Of course you do, everyone knows William. He's just been elected most popular auditor of the Literary and Historical Debating Society ever, in history. Just wondered if you were coming? William's parties are always the best, you know . . .'

Could there be a girlfriend or wife in the picture? Hmmm. Possibly. Maybe even other kids too.

But somehow my gut instinct, honed from years of hard-nosed graft at the coalface of journalism, is telling me no. Because let's face it, leaving a deposit at a sperm bank is hardly the kind of thing guys in long-term relationships tend to do in their spare time, now is it? Unless my antennae are very much off-kilter, I don't think so. No, I'm thinking, someone as bright and undoubtedly gifted as William (love saying the name over and over, can't stop myself: William, William, William) probably figured it was an act of selfless humanitarianism on his part to share this tiny part of him with the world. Because don't genes as rare and special as William's deserve to be propagated?

'Sorry to keep you,' says the warm, friendly lady eventually coming back to the other end of the phone.

'Not at all,' I smile, supremely confident that William probably graduated with a first. And might even be lecturing or tutoring there by now, who knew?

'But I'm afraid there's a bit of a problem this end.'

'Oh?'

'Well, but it seems there was no William Goldsmith doing any of our post-grad courses here. Not at any stage in the past four years. It seems we've no record of anyone by that name at all.'

Shit, shit, shit. What is going on?

'Are you absolutely certain? Maybe there's some kind of mistake?'

'No mistake, I'm positive. I've been through our computer files twice for that period. Nor do we have any record of a William Goldsmith ever studying here. Sorry, but I'm afraid I can't help you any further.'

Odd. Why would they have no record of him on computer? But then I quickly snap out of it and think, okay, this is just a dead end, nothing more. A minor clerical error, a bump in the road, a hurdle to be got over, that's all. I thank her politely, she hangs up and I immediately ask the Trinity switchboard to put me through to security. Because not only is every student required to have a security pass, but I remember from my own college days that no matter who you are, even if you're working down in the bowels of catering, you can get neither in nor out of the place without one.

Same drill. I slip into my patter of, 'Hi there, I'm the editor of . . .' But if I'm expecting a magical door in the wall to be suddenly swung open, I'm wrong. Instead, it's slammed shut right in my face with a wallop so violent that it feels like a slap.

'Sorry love,' says a bored-sounding guy with a twenty-fags-a-day rasp.

'That's classified information, that is.'

'But, you don't understand,' I say, trying to keep the pleading note out of my voice. 'I'm ringing from the *Post*, we're doing a feature you see . . .'

'Listen love, I'm not bothered if you're ringing from the White House, I can't give out private information about anyone who studied here. More than me job's worth.'

Okaaaay. From my days as a humble hack, I know how to gamble in a situation like this. Bit below the belt, yes, but sometimes . . . just sometimes, if you hold your nerve and keep steady, you can hit the jackpot.

'You know,' I say, quickly scanning down through my desktop computer to see what shows, events, or film premieres are coming up in Dublin. Anything posh or glamorous that's considered a hot ticket, I need right now.

'I'd hate for you to do anything you were uncomfortable

with, of course,' I tell him in my most cajoling voice, 'but you know, if you were to do this massive favour for me, I'm quite sure I could do the same for you. *Quid pro quo* and all that.'

'*Quid pro* wha'?'

'Say for instance . . .' I scroll down the computer screen in front of me. Bingo. Just what I'm looking for. 'If you were a fan of U2? I'm just saying that here at the *Post* we get bombarded with all sorts of free tickets and if you happened to know any fans, I'm sure I could arrange two complimentary tickets for you.'

I'm a bit of a dirty player, I know, but there you go. That's what years of working at the coalface of journalism will do to you. I leave it hanging there, take a deep breath and wait it out.

Still no response.

'For the opening night, of course,' I throw in hopefully. 'VIP tickets, obviously. Where you'd get to meet the band afterwards, it goes without saying. Backstage.'

I'm almost about to tack on, 'and if you really want, I can probably fix it so you get to spend the rest of the night quaffing Chateau Rothschild with Bono and The Edge up in their dressing room, chatting about what the hell possessed them to try and make Spider-Man into a Broadway musical.' Because right now I'm prepared to say absolutely anything at all that might just swing it for me.

But instead a bored yawn comes from down the other end of the phone.

'Wouldn't go to see that shower of gobshites if they were playing out in me back garden.'

Oh for God's sake.

Now what?

Then, after yet another excruciating, long-drawn out pause, I'm suddenly thrown a lifeline.

'Tell you what though, love. If you could swing me two tickets for the *X Factor* live show in London, then I *might* just might be able to do something for you. Strictly confidential though, you know what I'm saying? I mean, if I was ever to be found out, it'd be more than me job's worth.'

'Of course, this is totally confidential; and yes, I'll make sure you get all the *X Factor* tickets you want.'

How in the name of God I don't know, but sure I'll worry about that later.

'Right so. Gimme your number and I'll get back to you.'

I do what he says, hang up gratefully and head into my next meeting.

Five o' clock comes and still no news. Half an hour later, still nothing. My phone's on silent but somehow I can't prevent my eye from wandering over to it every five minutes, just to check.

Why hasn't he got back to me yet? How can something this simple be taking so bloody long?

It's well past half six in the evening before eventually the call comes. I'm down in the depths of the print room going over the first draft of tomorrow's layout when my mobile rings and the Trinity number flashes up.

'Excuse me, I urgently need to take this,' I tell our duty manager, then skip out of there, desperately looking for somewhere I can take the call with some bit of privacy. Which ends up being at the bottom of a deserted stairwell.

'Well?' I hiss, like I'm suddenly in an espionage movie. 'What have you got for me?'

'You'll get a right laugh out of this love, I know I did.'

'Just tell me!'

'Oh yeah, turns out you were right. There was a William Goldsmith working here in Trinity, not for long mind, just for about six months or so.'

He *worked* there? I think, mind racing. Worked as what? A tutor?

'Now I've no phone number, but I do have an address for you.'

'Brilliant thanks, that's all I need.'

'But I'll tell you something love, if your man told you he was a student here, then I can tell you right now he was talking through his arse.'

'I'm sorry, what do you mean?'

'Because the William Goldsmith that's on record here was from the sanitation department. Over in the residential halls.'

'What?'

'He was working as one of the cleaners.'

This is fine, this is okay. Not by any means the end of the world. So William did a fairly menial job to support himself, what's so wrong with that? I mean, I waitressed my way through college and it didn't do me any harm. And so technically he never actually studied at Trinity per se, but clearly he was drawn towards academia and who knows? Maybe he just couldn't afford the fees?

Suddenly I feel a huge pang of sympathy for William, getting a sharp mental image of Matt Damon in *Good Will Hunting*; gifted guy, high IQ, no money for education, but desperately trying to haul himself up by his bootstraps and make something of himself in the world. And if I'm slightly peeved at him for lying on the Reilly Institute form, then I brush it aside. Because everyone tweaks the truth on those things, don't they? Let's face it, claiming to be a post-grad Trinity student on a sperm donor application form is always going to make you sound a far more tempting proposition than the fact you scrub down toilets for a living, isn't it?

So far, I forgive him. So far, I can even understand where he's coming from.

So far.

As luck would have it, the address I got for him is actually fairly close to our offices. Flat two, number twenty-four Pearce Square, right behind Trinity College and only a ten-minute walk from here.

An hour later, I'm back upstairs in my office, signing off on tomorrow's editorial and taking a call from Robbie in foreign affairs at the same time, but somehow I'm finding it impossible to concentrate on either. Or to multitask, like I normally would.

It's just gone half seven now. I've got a window of exactly thirty minutes before my next meeting.

I could, couldn't I? Just slip out of here for half an hour and race up to Pearce Square? I'd be back in plenty of time and sure no one would see me, I'm sure of it.

Feck it anyway. Don't think about it, don't overanalyse it, don't debate it, just GO. Think of Lily. Remember I'm doing it all for her.

Decision made, in a flash I grab my bag and coat and slip out the office door down to the lift. Everyone seems to have their head buried into a computer screen, so no one even looks up at me or as much as throws me a second glance. Anyway, it's not like I'll even be gone that long anyway. Because I only want the answer to a handful of simple questions. Who is he? Where does he come from? Why did he leave Trinity after such a short time, where did he go afterwards and most importantly, what is he at now?

Okay, so maybe more than a handful of questions, but there you go, old journalists' trick. Saying 'can I just ask you one thing?' then sneaking in another fifteen questions and hoping no one will notice.

One thing is for certain, the answer is only a stone's throw away from here and I know myself well enough to know that it'll consume me until I've completely laid the whole thing to rest. Mind racing, head pounding, I slip my raincoat on and have just made it through the security barrier inside the main door of the *Post,* one hand on the revolving doors all set to make my escape, when suddenly from behind a voice stops me.

'Eloise? Surely you can't be leaving this early, can you?'

Shit, shit, shit.

I don't even need to turn around to know who it is. There's only one person I know who speaks in that snivelly, nasal twang.

And there he is, right behind me, Seth Coleman. Looking me up and down like he always does, the unblinking, lizardy eyes taking everything in.

'Course I'm not leaving, Seth,' I force myself to half-smile. 'Just stepping out for . . . emm . . .'

'You're going OUT?' Seth says, deliberately stressing it that way. 'As in, OUTSIDE the building? What on earth for?'

Ahem, good question. Can't say for coffee, we already have Starbucks in here. If I say personal reasons, sure as eggs he'll start spreading it around that I'm in the throes of a breakdown and am sneaking off to see a psychiatrist on company time.

110

Think, think, think . . .

'Highly confidential,' I eventually say, trying to sound as brisk as possible. 'Can't possibly give you a name. And you know me, I wouldn't dream of revealing a source, not under waterboarding. But for safety and security reasons, we've got to meet on neutral ground.'

OK, now it sounds like I've suddenly morphed into Bob Woodward in *All The President's Men*, about to meet Deepthroat in some deserted underground car park.

'I'm afraid I don't quite understand,' Seth sniffs, whipping a monogrammed white hanky from his breast pocket and wiping his long, bony nose with a flourish, a mannerism of his that, quite irrationally, drives me up the walls. I mean who in this day and age still uses linen hankies anyway?

'Couldn't you simply have assigned this lead to one of the dozens of reporters still in the building, who'd only relish a new story?' he asks, eyebrows arching skywards. 'It's not as though the editor has time to run around chasing up every single lead that lands in here. Surely your skills would be put to far better use elsewhere?'

'Thanks for your concern,' I snap back at him, sounding rude and not even bothering to conceal my waspishness. 'But my source would meet me and only me, in person, and frankly I'm not prepared to discuss the matter any further.'

Nosey, slimy git . . . Who does he think he is anyway? Telling me how to do my job?

'Well, I'll see you back here for our next news conference in half an hour then,' he throws back at me, still sounding unconvinced, as I turn on my heel and stomp off.

Imagine Seth Coleman going to a sperm bank, I find

myself furiously thinking as I belt my raincoat tight around me and stomp down the street. Jesus, and some poor misguided woman unwittingly giving birth to his child?

Doesn't even bear thinking about.

It's freezing cold, wild and windy and takes me the guts of about ten minutes to get to Pearce Square, just off busy, bustling Pearce St, only finally clearing itself of rush hour traffic now. The address I have is for number twenty-four, and I find it easily enough. Small, corporation two-up, two-down redbrick, a nothing-special kind of house in an identical terrace of houses just like it, with no ornamentation of any kind to be seen, not a bedding plant or a window box in sight, nothing.

I press the doorbell and wait. And wait. Press again, still nothing. I wait a bit more, then glance anxiously at my watch and decide I'm only wasting my time and might as well get back to work before I'm missed. I'm just about to admit defeat and head back, when an elderly woman in a headscarf battling against the wind and pushing one of those tartan wheelie shopping trolleys that old ladies love so much shuffles by, notices me, then stops dead in her tracks.

'Are you looking for Michelle, love?' she asks, sounding genuinely concerned about me, looking as out of place as I do in my little black power suit and briefcase in the middle of a residential corporation estate.

I must look like I've come to foreclose on a mortgage.

'I'm sorry, did you say Michelle?' I ask. Michelle? Some girlfriend of William's, maybe?

'Yes, that's the owner of number twenty-four. She rents out rooms for a few extra quid, cash only, sure you know yourself.' Then suddenly, she clamps her hand over her mouth, like she's only just realised the full import of what she's said and is now desperately trying to claw the sentence back from out of thin air.

'Ah here . . . You're not by any chance from the Inland Revenue are you?'

'No, no I'm not . . .'

'Because when I said she only takes cash, I didn't really mean it the way it came out, honest to God I didn't . . .'

'It's absolutely fine,' I reassure her and she looks so petrified that I nearly want to smile. 'I promise you, I don't work for the tax office, but what I'm actually trying to do is trace someone who used to live here . . . who might even live here still . . .'

'Lot of tenants came through here, love.'

'Yes but you see, there's one in particular . . .'

'Michelle's the best person for you to ask then. But you'll never get her home at this time.'

'Do you know where I might find her?'

'Course love, she'll be in work by now. She always starts early, round this time. You should get her there.'

'And where's that exactly?'

'The Widow Maguire's pub. Only ten minutes down the road from here. Michelle does a lovely chicken and chips in a basket, you should give it a try if you haven't had your dinner yet.'

'Great, thanks so much, you've been really helpful.'

'Not at all love. They'll be delighted with the extra bit of business.'

'Why's that?'

'Oh, health and safety closed them down a few weeks back. Something about mouse droppings in the kitchen. But I'm sure it's all sorted out by now.'

Lovely.

113

As if on cue, the heavens start to open and of course I can't get a cab, so I'm like a bedraggled, drowned rat by the time I find the pub and burst in out of the lashing rain. It's a Thursday night so the place is fairly busy, though the clientele seems to be predominantly male and with an average age of about seventy-five. A real old-fashioned man's drinking bar.

Like in a Western, the minute I step through the door, soaking to the skin and clutching a soggy copy of today's *Post* as a makeshift umbrella, all eyes turn to me and unless I'm very much mistaken, the whole place gets that bit quieter. Gravelly voices drop to whispers as they all take me in, looking utterly out of place as I must.

Aware that time is ticking and that I need to get back to the office ASAP, I steel myself and approach a bosomy, middle-aged woman with a spiky, gelled-back haircut behind the bar, who's ostensibly wiping beer glasses as she takes me in from head to Prada heels, clearly wondering whether I'm from the Health Board and am now about to flash a scary looking ID badge in her face and demand to see the insides of her toilet cisterns.

'Excuse me, are you Michelle Hughes, by any chance?'

'Who wants to know?' she says guardedly, eyes slit, arms folded, fully prepared for trouble.

I give her the whole hi-there-I'm-from-the-*Post* spiel and tell her all I'm doing is trying to track down a tenant that was traced to her house, one William Goldsmith. My subtext of course being that I'm one hundred percent, absolutely nothing to do with either the Health Board or the Revenue Commissioners and have no comment or quibble whatsoever to make on whatever under-the-counter business dealings she has going on the side.

'William who? No, definitely not, never heard of him,' she snaps and just like that, it's conversation closed and back to wiping glasses.

'Oh come on, you must remember something; anything at all would help me. Tall guy? Probably fair-haired? Blue eyed? Working not far from here, in Trinity?' I plead with her. Then just in case there's some reason she's afraid to open up to me, I tack on, 'Look, I'm not any kind of official or anything and no one's in trouble here. I just need to find him, that's all. Please. Anything you can tell me would be a huge help.'

There's something in the half turn away she does that makes me think . . . Yes! I might, just might be onto something here.

'Well, now I come to think of it, I did have a fella who looked a bit like that lodging in the house about two or three years ago, yeah,' she says, a dim spark of recognition in her eyes as she turns back to me. 'He's long gone now but I do remember him; quiet fella, kept himself to himself, always with his nose stuck in some book.'

'Yes, yeah, I'm sure that's him,' I say excitedly. Don't even know why except that in my mind's eye William struck me as a bookworm. God knows, Lily certainly is and she can't even read properly yet.

'But that name you gave me, it's wrong.'

'Sorry?'

'William . . . whatever you said, whatsit.'

'Goldsmith?'

'No,' she says, flinging a tea towel over a broad shoulder and racking her brains. 'At least that wasn't what he called himself round here. The fella I'm thinking of had a different name . . . Billy, Billy something . . .'

'Billy O'Casey is who you mean, you eejit,' says the barman barging into our conversation, a moustachioed, improbably suntanned guy in his mid-fifties, who if not for the Dub accent I'd only swear was Italian.

'That's it! Thanks Tommo,' says Michelle, playfully pucking him with her tea towel. 'Billy O'Casey, God how could I forget that name? And I'll tell you something else too; that stupid fecker just upped and shagged off without paying me my last month's rent.'

'You think that's bad?' says the barman. 'Do I have to remind you about the size of the tab he ran up in here?'

Next thing, an overweight guy with what looks like two arses trailing behind him saunters in from having had a cigarette and pulls up his seat at the bar.

'You all talking about Billy O'Casey?' he butts in. ''Cos I'll tell you something. If I ever as much as set eyes on that fella again, I'll rip the bleedin' head off him.'

'So how much does he owe you then?' asks Michelle, suddenly all interested.

'Best part of two hundred euro, love. I won it in the darts tournament here and he was quick enough to ask me for a lend of it. Course that was around the same time he did his disappearing trick and I never saw or heard of him again.'

'Bastard.'

'Useless fecker.'

'Gobshite.'

'If he ever shows his face in here again, I'll kick his arse all the way back to Darndale . . .'

'You and me both.'

Right then, this could go on for quite some time, so I step in.

116

'Sorry about this, but I'm in a bit of a rush and was wondering if any of you knew where he went?'

'Are you mad?' says the overweight guy. 'Sure if I did, I'd be straight after him to get my money back, wouldn't I? Then I'd beat the crap out of him. In that order.'

Okay, I think on my feet as I race back through the rain to the office for my next meeting. So he's not a misunderstood, down-on-his-luck tortured genius who put up with a menial job in Trinity just so he could hover around the fringes of academia.

No, instead he's a fly-by-night who absconds without paying rent, runs up bar tabs he doesn't pay and borrows cash he never bothers to give back. With a highly annoying habit of changing his name to boot.

You know something? The more I hear about Lily's father, the less curious I am about him and the more urgent it becomes for me to somehow track him down. To see exactly what it is that I'm dealing with here, and – once a control freak, always a control freak – maybe even see if I can troubleshoot the problem in some way before it's too late.

Because there's no doubt about it; Helen's right. If I don't do it now, the day sure as hell will come when Lily will. And it would just stab me to the heart if she were ever to find out her dad was some drug addict strung out on methadone, who spent his time sleeping in doorways and park benches. Which frankly, is where my instincts tell me this modern day Greek tragedy is headed.

Darndale . . . the barman mentioned something about Darndale . . .

By Wednesday, I've run about fifteen searches on a Billy or Bill O'Casey from Darndale, and the database that we

117

use in the office – bit like the one police use – throws up no less than fifty-nine men with that name, all with a Darndale address. A thin lead, but hell, it'll just have to do me. I narrow down the search a bit by adding in his age, and that suddenly cuts it down to a more manageable three. One is a hairdresser who's been running his own business in Coolock for the past fifteen years, so I discount him immediately.

Which only leaves two.

By Thursday, with further shameless use of the office database, I have addresses. And by Friday, two full free hours to spare in my schedule – a minor miracle for me. (The result of further shuffling around of meetings and one out and out whopper of a lie to Rachel at reception; I told her there was 'someone I have to meet in person, back in an hour.') Please God, they'll all assume it's some super-shy source that I'm gently coaxing into going on the record in some top-secret, soon-to-be-released story that I think so worthy of my attention, it'll pay dividends by quadrupling our sales.

Even though the traffic is mercifully light, it still takes almost half an hour to get to Darndale which, be warned, ain't posh. The main street is full of pubs, bookies and chippers . . . The shops that don't have metal hoarding sprayed with graffiti pulled down over them, that is. Nor are there any cute neo-Victoria urns with bay trees flanking elegant doorways here, and not a four-wheel drive to be seen. No two ways about it; I'm not in Kansas any more, Toto.

The first address I have is for Primrose Grove, a vast, sprawling social housing estate which makes me feel like I'm driving straight onto the set of a Roddy Doyle novel come to life. Kids running round the place everywhere, playing soccer on the road, then screeching at me and thumping on the bonnet of my car while I gingerly try to drive through a gang of them without running over their ball. I even see a heavily pregnant women pushing a buggy while sucking on a fag at the same time.

Now it's not that I'm easily intimidated – I cut my teeth as a junior reporter trawling through far worse hellholes than this, let me tell you, and I lived to tell the tale. It's just that I'm suddenly aware of how much I stand out in my brand new car, wearing my uniform of black Reiss suit, black Gucci shoes, black glasses, black shirt, black tights, black everything – including a matching black soul, if you're to believe the vast majority of my work colleagues. But looking round me now, I realise the smart thing would have been to do what I used to on assignments like this years ago; gone undercover in a bra top, a pair of sprayed-on jeans and wheeling a buggy while sucking on a fag. If I'd really wanted to blend in, that is.

Takes me ages and a lot of U-turns to finally find the number I need, but finally I hit on the house I'm looking for and thank God, there's a car with a taxi plate on it parked right outside. Which means, with a bit of luck, that there's someone home. I hop out of my car and ring the doorbell. And wait. Sounds of the TV blaring from inside the front room window beside me; some daytime TV show, *Cash in the Attic* or similar.

I ring again. Wait. And again. Then suddenly start wondering about what in hell I'll say to him if he's home and opens the door to me.

Hi there, you don't know me, but I'm the mother of your child? Ehhh, no, don't think so. Hi there, approximately

119

four years ago, did you by any chance go to a sperm bank and leave a deposit? Because in that case, have I got news for you . . .

Have I really thought this through? I suddenly start to fret as beads of inconvenient worry sweat starting to leak right down to my ribcage. Because all I know about this particular Billy O'Casey is what I got on the office database. I know what his social security number is, I know that he's got four penalty points on his driving licence and I also know that he once got out of jury service on account of an elderly relative he had to take care of.

Me, who's famous for having plans and more plans and five year plans and plans within plans. Now here I am, standing on a total stranger's doorstep feeling like I'm carrying the third secret of Fatima and I haven't the first clue how I'm even going to phrase what I have to say to him.

All I know is that the conversation I'm about to have with him is bound to come as a shock. God almighty, he'll probably think I'm here to demand maintenance money and back payments on three years of child support. But on the principle that I've come this far and have precious little to lose, I give the door one last and final hammering. Still nothing, just the sound of some TV show going on about a vase from the nineteen fifties that's now worth a life-altering eighteen euro. I'm just about to turn on my heel and leave when an upstairs window is opened from right above me and I hear a man's voice yelling down.

'Ah here, what's all the bleedin' racket down there?'

I look up and see a guy about my own age with his head half stuck out a bedroom window, wearing just a vest and not much else.

'Ehhh, sorry to bother you,' I yell back up at him, 'but I was wondering if you could help me?'

'What, like now? This minute? Give us a bleedin' break, would you? I'm not long off my shift, I've been out in my taxi since two this morning, love . . .'

I know I've only got a moment before he snaps the window shut and heads back to bed, so I go for it.

'I'm looking for a Billy or Bill O'Casey. Any idea where I can find him?'

'You're talking to him.'

'I'm sorry, *you're* Bill O'Casey?'

'Yeah, what's it to you?'

Okay, in that case this is absolutely, definitely not him. No DNA test required here, this is one hundred per cent not Lily's Dad.

'Emm . . . Nothing. Absolutely nothing. No problem at all, my mistake entirely. I'm terribly sorry to disturb you, but I'm afraid I've got the wrong address. My own stupid fault, please forgive me, so sorry to have disturbed you . . .' I mumble up at him, backing out of there and inching towards my car.

'Does that mean I can go back to sleep now?' he growls back down at me sarcastically.

'Yes of course, and apologies again . . .'

I hope back into the car and reverse out of there, feeling deflated, but not defeated. Not yet. A text comes through from Helen, anxious to know how I'm getting on, so I call her.

'Well?' she says hopefully, having to raise her voice over the sound of Lily bashing away at the piano in the background. Then as soon as she realises Auntie Helen is on the phone to me, I can hear her asking in her little-angel

121

voice, 'has she found my daddy yet? Is he coming to see me soon?'

It would stab you right to the solar plexus, it really would. My heart aches with an indescribable pain just wondering what's going through the poor child's head right now.

'Shhh darling, let me talk to Mummy for a minute.' I can hear Helen soothing her and giving her big mwah, mwah kisses on her tiny head.

Ordinarily I'd get another stab just at hearing this, usually one of pure jealousy, to my shame. That someone else was mothering Lily right now, while I'm stuck like a gobshite on a housing estate in deepest Darndale, on a possible fool's errand.

But not now. Not when the person I'm doing all this for is Lily.

Besides, I'm now working to a clear-cut plan. Because who knows, maybe I can help this guy, whoever and wherever he is? Give him some kind of leg up in life, so that when the day inevitably comes when Lily does get to meet him, he can be someone she's actually proud of, with a job and a car and a mortgage and healthcare and a pension plan. Not some flake who changes his name and skips off without paying back money he owes. I haven't exactly done a huge amount of good for other people in my life, but there's no reason why that can't end here and now, is there?

And there's something else too, something that's really taken me by surprise. Because tedious as this is; rough, even scary as it is; somehow doing all the plodding footwork is reminding me of another lifetime ago, when I first started out as a rookie reporter and was constantly sent off on humble doorstepping jobs like this. Long, long before I started fast-tracking my way up to the glorified heights of the editorial suite on the executive floor, that is.

Most journalists look down their noses on and despise that kind of work, but it's seen as a sort of apprenticeship; necessary flames you've got to walk through before you get to sit behind a cushy desk and bash out stories from there. And in the weirdest way, I hadn't quite realised how much I missed those days, which almost seem carefree now when I think back. The sheer adrenaline rush of chasing down a story, of trying to coax people into going on the record, of racing back to pass your story by your editor before the deadline, then the thrill of seeing it in print with your name attached, up beside an 'additional reporting by' tagline.

Course back then, like just about every other hack in town, I'd gripe and whinge about the interminably long days and even longer freezing nights spent shivering outside housing estates where I was waiting on some suspected drug baron to either fall in the door drunk (whereupon I'd smile sweetly at him, shove a tape recorder under his nose and get whatever incriminating statements he slurred on record), or sometimes even better, an off-the-record interview with a wife or girlfriend, many of whom liked to say far more than their prayers and would happily jabber away to me, blissfully unaware that it would all appear in print the next morning.

But when I cast my mind back and compare it with the treadmill of stress that my life is now, I think, ahh, those were the days. Didn't know I was born. Sometimes it's not being at the top that's the truly joyous part of success, it's getting there.

'No sweetheart,' I hear Helen tell Lily soothingly down the phone, 'no chocolate fudge till after you've eaten up all your pasta, good girl. Eloise, are you still there? Sorry about that,' she says, her voice less muffled as she comes back to me. 'So what's happening where you are? Any sign?'

'No go,' I sigh, 'forget it, I'm out of here.'

'What do you mean? Were you not able to find Bill O'Casey?'

'No, I found him alright. But he's the wrong guy.'

'How do you know? Did you ask him? Was he the right age and height and eye colour and all that?'

'Oh yeah, he ticked some of the boxes alright, but trust me, he's definitely not Lily's father.'

'How come you're so sure?'

'Not that difficult to work out really. Because he's black.'

And now with the clock ticking against me, I'm down to my last and final lead. And if this doesn't work out . . . then that's it. I have no Plan B. Another address in a Darndale housing estate, all of which seem to be inappropriately named after flowers. Primrose Court, Tulip Drive, Rose Gardens . . . and the one I'm looking for is Daffodil Terrace.

By far the worst one yet. At least the other estates didn't have burnt-out cars abandoned on the side of the roads; I even have to inch the car past a mattress dumped right in the middle of the street. There's a green in the middle that all the houses centre around and I'm not joking when I tell you it looks like a fly-tipper's idea of a paradise dumping ground. No kids paying soccer in the streets here; they probably all reckon it's too dangerous, even for them.

I speed up a bit, anxious to do what I came for and get the hell out of here fast. All the houses are identical apart from the graffiti that's sprayed along most of them and with a sinking heart, I finally find the one I'm looking for.

I pull up, park, then trip up the driveway and knock at the door in the most non-threatening way I can.

Subtext; trust me! I am neither a debt collector nor someone who's come round to repossess your furniture. I Swear!

This particular Bill O'Casey I know least about of all. No social security number, which is odd, in fact no records of any kind whatsoever. Like he's just a vague shadow of a person, almost as if I'm chasing down a ghost. I mean, who doesn't have a social security number in this day and age?

Not a long wait, then Hallelujah be praised, I'm in luck. The door opens and an old, old lady, almost bent double with arthritis, is standing in front of me, with parchment-thin skin and hair the exact colour and texture of a Brillo pad. In fact she looks so frail that I immediately feel guilty for having dragged her all the way out to the front door and half want to steer her back inside, wrap her in a nice warm blanket and plonk her down in front of the daytime soap operas, then make her a big mug of Complan.

'Have you come to read the meter?' she asks in a feathery, wispy voice, as the smell of the house hits me in the face; Lily of the Valley perfume mixed in with something else, almost like a combination of damp and that antiseptic that you get in hospitals.

'No, I'm so sorry to disturb you . . .'

'Meals on Wheels?'

'I'm afraid not. I'm actually looking for a Billy O' Casey and I was told that he lives here. I don't suppose you'd have any idea where I could find him?'

'Speak up, will you?'

'Sorry . . . Do you know where I can find BILL O'CASEY, by any chance?'

'Who did you say?'

'BILL O'CASEY.'

There's a pause for a moment while she thinks and for a split second her pale grey eyes look sharply at me, while she weighs up whether or not I can be trusted.

And decides no. Slowly, she shakes her head.

'No, no, I'm sorry dear, you must have the wrong house.' She goes to close the door, but I move to stop her.

'Please, it's very important that I speak to him and I promise he's not in any kind of trouble. I just wanted to ask him a few . . .'

'No Bill O'Casey here love, and there never was.'

'If you had a forwarding address, or better yet, a phone number?'

'Have to go, *Emmerdale* is starting now and it's my favourite soap.'

Door slammed, end of interview.

It's at this point I start to get frustrated.

Given the sheer mentalness of the rest of my day, I have to abandon the search here and get back to the office, but throughout all my afternoon and night meetings, the same thought keeps buzzing round my head, playing over and over again on a loop.

That old lady definitely knew something and was covering up. But why?

One thing is for certain, I think as I sit at my desk bashing out a first draft of tomorrow's editorial: from this point on, I have nothing. Not one more shred to go on. Nothing. Helen calls to see if there's news and I fill her in.

'So that's it then?' she asks, deflated. 'We're at the end of the line, I suppose.'

'Are you kidding me?' I tell her firmly. 'Helen, let me

126

tell you something. Chasing down any lead is always a nightmare, with doors constantly slamming in your face while you hurtle your way from one dead end to another. Know what separates a good reporter from the herd?'

'No, what?' she answers automatically.

'They don't give up, don't take no for an answer and most importantly of all, they call in the big guns.'

I'm in too deep here to let this go. Call me an obsessive-compulsive (and believe me, plenty do) but if it's the last thing I do, I'm tracking down Lily's dad and I'm going to help him. Okay, so maybe right now he doesn't exactly sound like a desirable character who I'd ever want her to be around, but Helen is right. The day will surely come, years from now, when Lily will want to know more. And more than anything, I want her to be proud of him when she does meet him – and to stay proud of him. Sure, maybe this guy has a flaky, shady past, but just wait till I get my hands on him. I'll bring him up squeaky clean. I will be like a sort of female Henry Higgins to his Eliza Doolittle.

I'll make him respectable, if it bloody kills me.

Then, in years to come, he'll thank me and credit me with helping him live a normal ordinary life, not one where he faffs round from one address to another, changing names, changing jobs, the works. Whoever and wherever you are, I sent out a short, silent message to the Universe, you have no idea how over this part of your life is. Time for your Act Two, and this time mate, I'm the puppet-master pulling the strings.

As it happens, I do have one last, single ace in the pack. It's a long shot, but who knows, it might just be worth it. Years, years, years ago, when I was young and struggling with a story, I always had a Plan B. Namely, one Jim Kelly – a stringer who used to work as a freelance for a number of papers, but now that he's semi-retired you'll often see his name popping up as an 'additional source' on TV investigative documentaries and whistleblower shows.

Jim I know of old; everyone does. He's a wizened, senior hack of the Marlboro-smoking, vodka-drinking-during-working-hours school, who cut his teeth working undercover primarily on crime stories and was hugely instrumental in bringing down more than one underworld boss. Rumour has it that one high profile drug trafficker, now serving a stretch in a maximum security prison, has a price on Jim's head – to such a worrying extent that police have apparently offered Jim a place on the witness protection programme.

Stout heart that he is though, he told them where to shove it and continues on with his work regardless.

Soon as I get a spare minute, I call him and fill him in on what I need.

A long-drawn-out cough, then wheezily, he comes back to the phone.

'I'm not promising anything,' he says in his throaty voice, 'but I'll do what I can.'

Gratefully, I give him the thin scraps of information I have and I can hear the scratch of his pen off a notebook as he takes it all down. Jim's the best in the business. If he can't find this guy, then no one can.

'One thing,' he growls before hanging up.

'Yeah?'

Without him having to say another word, I know what's coming next and mentally steel myself.

'Why? Why this guy? What's he to you?'

I sigh and try to make my answer sound as flippant as possible.

'Jim, can we just say that it's for personal reasons?'

The week goes by in such a blur of meetings, deadlines and conferences, that I barely have time to give the whole thing another thought. The only time this impinges on my consciousness is whenever I call Lily for one of our little chats during the day and she'll say, sweet as you like, 'Mama, Mama! I'm having the best time EVER with Auntwie Helen and I never want another nanny ever again! I want her to live with us *forwever*!'

'That's wonderful, pet, but you know Auntie Helen will have to go back to Cork soon, and Mama's going to have to find another minder for you . . .'

'NO! NO other nanny! I only want Auntwie Helen FORWEVER!'

I sigh deeply and mark this under the mental file, 'to be dealt with later'.

'AND you know what else, Mama?'

'No bunny, tell me.'

'I know what I'm going to wear when I get to meet my daddy! And I leawned a new tune on the piano to play for him! AND I drawed a picture of me and him too!'

'Well you know sweetheart,' I tell her gently as I can, 'we're all doing out very best to find him, but maybe he doesn't live here any more. Maybe he's moved to another country,' I tell her, desperately trying to shield her from disappointment. But of course, she's not even three yet. She doesn't know the meaning of the word disappointment.

'You'll find him Mummy,' she tells me proudly. 'You can do anything! You're like Superwoman 'cept only better!'

Thursday afternoon and still no word back from Jim, not a progress report, nothing. I text him and get a curt message back saying, 'BACK OFF AND GIMME A CHANCE, WILL YOU?'

Fair enough. Tail between my legs, I meekly do as I'm told.

The weekend comes and goes, and still nothing. Then, just as I've abandoned all hope and am wondering how in hell I'll break it to Lily, Jim calls me out of the blue the following Monday afternoon.

'Where are you?' he asks gruffly, but then that's Jim for you. Never any kind of a preamble or a hello-how-are-you, none of the above.

'In the office.' Where else would I be?

'Can you get out of there for half an hour? I need to talk to you, face to face.'

I glance at my watch. Could I somehow find a window to get out of here? I tap on the computer screen to bring up today's schedule, but I'm totally chocka. I'm about to ask him if I can call him back later and see if I can squeeze something in then, but he's having none of it.

'I'll be in the underground car park off Abbey Street in ten minutes. Just be there.'

Oh Christ, if anyone sees me?

Somehow though, I manage to slip out of the office undetected, asking poor, puzzled Rachel to tell anyone who's looking for me that I'll be right back. Her stunned expression at something this unheard of says it all. Like I've just told her that I've handed in my notice and am now off to start selling copies of *The Big Issue* on the corner of Tara St.

Sweating and palpitating, heart pounding so that the sound of the blood pumping through my ears almost deafens me, I get into my car and weave my way through the heavy early evening rush hour traffic all the way to the Abbey St. car park.

He must have news for me, he must have . . .

My mobile is beeping the whole way there, but I ignore it and keep driving, just focusing on the road ahead.

Mouth dry, chest walloping, I eventually get to the car park and mercifully, there's no queue to get in. I slide the car down the ramp inside, take a ticket and then slowly drive round in circles. Next thing, the passenger door of my car is opened, nearly giving me a quadruple heart attack as Jim jumps in, looking even more wizened and gnarled than I remember him, a trail of cigarette smoke wafting after him.

'Park over there, in the right, then turn off the engine,' he barks at me and I obediently do as I'm told. But then, there aren't too many people who contradict Jim on a regular basis.

Next thing, he's fumbling round his jacket pocket then producing a battered notebook which he flips open and starts referring down to.

'Just out of curiosity Eloise,' is his opener, 'where in the name of arse did you come across this waster anyway? I mean, look at you. And look at your life. What I can't figure is, what's the guy to you? What can a tosser like him possibly have to do with you?'

I look pleadingly across at him.

'OK if I say "don't ask", and let's just leave it at that?'

He shakes his head, sending dandruff flakes flying every-where, and gets back to his notes.

'Well for starters, the fecker keeps changing his name. I traced him from Darndale where he was calling himself Bill or Billy O'Casey, to D.C.U. . . .'

'D.C.U.?' I interrupt. Dublin City University. What is it about this guy and universities?

Suddenly I start to feel an irrational hope. I knew it. I knew we were dealing with a rough diamond here, someone with a thirst for knowledge, wanting nothing more than to pull himself up in the world . . .

'– where he changed his name again. This time to James Archer.'

'Changed his name again?'

'Yeah, signed up for a creative writing course but then dropped out after only three weeks . . .'

'But why would he do that?'

'For Christ's sake, let me finish, will you? So that's about two years ago and then he resurfaces again, but this time he's calling himself Brown. Robert Brown. Got a job working in a Statoil garage on the Long Mile Road and was sharing a flat with two other guys, let's just say who are known to Gardai.'

Okay. 'Known to Gardai' is not a phrase that you want to hear when trying to trace the father of your child.

'. . . And from this point on the search starts to get interesting. So I fished around a bit, asked a few questions, talked to a couple of contacts that I have and it turns out this guy has fallen in with a right shower of messers.'

'How . . . Just how bad?' My voice sounds tiny, like it's coming from another room.

'All of them have criminal records the length of your arm, been in and out of remand homes since they were in nappies. Nothing major, not long stretches, but this gang your man is in with, they've done time for breaking and entering, shoplifting, car theft, you name it. So I make a few more inquiries . . .'

'. . . And?' I'm nearly hopping off the edge of my seat now, half-dreading what's coming next.

'. . . And surprise surprise, he's only gone and changed his name again, which doesn't make my job any easier. Calls himself Oscar Butler now . . .'

'Oscar Butler?' I can't help myself from repeating out loud. It sounds so makey-uppy, as Lily would say.

'I know,' Jim nods in agreement at me. 'Some of the places this guy hangs out and some of the gang he's in with, I'm surprised he didn't get his head kicked in for going round the place calling himself by a tosser's name like that. Anyway, he leaves the Statoil garage after only a few months, owing a lot of people he worked with money I might add, and then he goes all quiet. Takes me a full two days to track the fecker down after that, but I get a lead that a mate of this guy's was involved in a burglary case, and your guy was his driver. Only by then he's changed his name again . . .'

'Jesus,' I mutter under my breath, slumping my head over the steering wheel.

'So this time, I talk to a contact of mine who's in the Gardai. And suddenly I'm onto something. Things start hotting up. So I ask round a bit more and just about an hour ago, I nailed it.'

I look mutely across at him, half-dreading what's coming next.

'For starters, his real name is Jake Keane.'

'And do you know where he is?'

'Oh yeah, that was the easy part. As it happens, I can tell you *exactly* where he is, right this very minute.'

Oh God, I think I might need to breathe into a paper bag.

'Don't get a shock, OK?'

'Tell me,' I say hoarsely. 'I need to know.'

Next thing Jim's looking at me kindly, almost paternally.

'You just listen to me first though. Whatever's going on Eloise, just take my advice and drop it right here and now. Trust me, it's not worth it and if you go any further, you're going to get yourself into a whole lot of trouble.'

'Please . . . Please just tell me.'

'Jake Keane is in prison. Just coming to the end of a two year stretch. And I don't think you want to know what he's in for either. But it's not for having an expired TV licence; I can tell you that for nothing.'

I try to thank him, but for some reason, no words will come out of my mouth.

PART TWO

Chapter Five

The thing that no one ever told you about life on the inside, Jake Keane often thought, was that it was the little things that got you through each and every day. Small victories were what made all the difference between surviving, versus a day where you'd gladly hang yourself off a light fitting just to escape the place, just to experience some sort of freedom, before you completely forgot what it ever tasted like in the first place.

Yet just the tiniest little thing could help you sidetrack the black dog of depression that haunted everyone here and survive another interminable day, each one so long that sometimes even a single hour dragged by like a month. Jake had been reading a lot of Virginia Woolf lately, an author who really seemed to understand what incarceration felt like, and could fully understand what she meant when she wrote that lasting through a day was relatively easy: it was the hours in between that nearly killed you.

There were times when he'd look at the clock at eight in the evening, then congratulate himself on having survived a whole entire hour since seven. And the next challenge to himself would then be to last all the way up until nine. That was how you got by, he now knew, lasting like that, from minute to minute, then from hour to hour. Till dark, till lockdown, till blessed silence and the deep joy of being able to say to yourself, that's that then. Another day survived. Another one ticked off.

But no doubt about it, little things helped. Like landing a window seat in the canteen at mealtimes. Like a meal that you could actually eat, one that didn't look and taste like cat food and come swimming in congealed grease and fat. Getting a bit of sunshine during exercise breaks in the yard outside, the only time in the long, long day you ever got to breathe anything other then the foul, stale air inside that stank worse than twenty minging gym bags. Even on days when the heavens opened and it bucketed down, Jake still went out there for the single hour they were permitted, never caring that he was getting drenched through to the bone. Anything, just to taste proper clean air. Amazing himself at just how much he missed it, at how little he'd appreciated it back in the days when he was a free man.

A good day could be one where he'd successfully cadge a fag, then trade it in for a decent book that might keep him going for days. Not one from the library, they were worse than useless. Some of the lads ripped pages out of them, sometimes to use for rolling joints, sometimes just out of pure badness, so you'd come to a critical plot point and ten pages would be missing. Books the screws smuggled in from outside were miles better. Cost you in the long run, but it was worth it. Jake had learned that one early on.

And reading was getting him through this. Keeping his nose stuck in a book and well out of everyone else's way. Because if there was a survival manual in here, it was this; head down, mouth shut, make neither friends nor enemies, be as neutral as Switzerland, blend in to the background like wallpaper. Strive to be someone people neither like nor dislike, then just forget about the minute you're out of their sight. And the golden rule; above all, never get involved.

His long-term survival mechanism was to keep quiet, keep to himself and at all costs, steer clear of all trouble. He got on reasonably well with the screws too, who from time to time would do him the odd favour. One even enrolled him on an Open University course, English and Psychology, which he loved and worked hard at. In his first year here, he'd done a TEFL course too and had surprised himself not only by thoroughly enjoying learning all the endless intricacies of the English language, but by getting a first class honour in it too, graduating top of his class.

Studying was a wonderful and a welcome distraction, gave him that extra bit of privacy too. When the others were on at him to play soccer in the yard during exercise break, he'd roll his eyes and indicate the pile of books on his knee that he had to wade through. And they'd jokingly slag him off and call him the Professor and leave him alone, in peace. Which suited.

You lived for visiting day, everyone did. Got you out of your routine, shook things up a bit. Every Wednesday, between two and four; trouble was though, you only got to see your family for about half an hour of that. The rest of the time, they'd be on the outside queuing to get in, doing security checks that would put the one at the airport to shame. Jake always felt sorriest for the wives and girl-friends traipsing in through all weathers, wheeling buggies and strollers, waiting outside in the freezing cold for hours just to get thirty lousy minutes with a loved one. And not even alone time; you were stuck in the visitors' room with half the prison looking at you. But Christ, what that half hour meant to you, if you were on the inside.

His main visitor these days was his mam, Imelda. Sixty-five years old and yet she'd still battle her way on two buses, plus the mile-long uphill road from bus stop to prison gates, not to mention the hour-long wait she'd then have to get through security. And all so she could just to get to see her youngest son for half an hour, one day a week. But she never once missed coming, not even when her arthritis was at her, not even last winter when she had the flu. It was heartbreaking. Always there with a weak smile for him, always putting on a brave face, never letting on how deeply ashamed she must be. Wearing her good coat and the special perfume she only ever wore either to weddings or funerals. She knew he had no one else to visit him, so she never once let him down.

Tough love was his mam's thing, though from where Jake was sitting on the far side of the grille from her, it often felt more like soft hate. Bloody holiday camp in here, she'd gripe at him, though Jake knew her well enough to know this was her reverse psychology way of trying to cheer him up. Sure, what have you to do only lie around reading all your books all day, she'd tease him, though they both knew that was about as far from the truth as you could get. And would you just look at this place, she'd gesture around her, it's like a three-star hotel. You sleep in a room with its own telly, where the quilt covers match the curtains and you get three hot meals served up to you a day and what's more, you even get paid an allowance by the gobshite government for doing the time in here.

None of this was strictly true, but if it helped his mam get by imagining that he was living like a guest in the

Holiday Inn, then it suited Jake to let her continue on in the fantasy.

Then just as she was leaving at the end of each visit, she'd reluctantly pull her good coat and woolly hat back on, the ones she always saved for Sunday Mass. It was a small, insignificant thing, but one that always seemed to stab right at the bottom of Jake's heart. That his mother alone, out of everyone he knew and had ever known, had put herself out so much, that she'd even got herself all dressed up just to spend thirty short minutes with him.

Aside from her though, only solicitors had special visitors' privileges. If you'd a trial or an appeal coming up, your solicitor could arrange to see you at any time and the wardens had no choice but to let them. Not that this had ever once happened to Jake. His trial was nearly two years ago and even then he'd been on the free legal aid, which meant he got a well-intentioned but utterly inexperienced law graduate who looked about fifteen and who almost gave himself an anxiety stroke at the very sight of a judge and jury, then got red-eyed and trembly the minute the verdict was announced. To the extent that Jake felt so sorry for the poor kid, he ended up consoling him while in handcuffs waiting to be taken off to the Cloverhill Detention Centre, the first place they sent you before a bed could be found for you in prison proper.

Would have been comical, if it hadn't been so tragic.

So that sunny spring day not long after Easter, when Jake got a message to say there was someone to see him and that he was to head to the visitors' room immediately, he was completely at a loss. He was certain no lawyer would be coming out all this way to see him.

Jake knew the screw that lead him down to security well, name of Cagney, a likeable fella once you stayed on his right side. Had four small kids and worked all the overtime he could get, so he was well known in here.

'Any idea who this is?' Jake asked him, as he was searched and patted down, then put through a security X-ray device on his way out of Block C.

Cagney shrugged.

'Could be your parole officer?'

But Jake knew that was unlikely; for starters, his parole hearing wasn't coming up till the end of the month, way too early for someone to be talking to him about it now. Guys from parole didn't operate like that; they kept you sweating right up till the very last minute. Made you think you hadn't a snowball's chance of getting out, keep you on your toes, extract the very last drop of good behaviour out of you.

'Because you know,' Cagney went on in that chatty, likeable way he had, 'and on the QT, of course, you've every chance of getting out of here early. If every prisoner behaved as well as you have, I can tell you, it would make my job a helluva lot easier. Between ourselves, I'll certainly be giving you a glowing report when the time comes and that's a promise.'

The prospect of early parole hadn't occurred to Jake, good news rarely did. It was far safer to assume the worst in here, spared you the dull agony of disappointment when things didn't go your way. Which in his life, was most of the time.

But when he finally cleared security and got to the visitors' room, he saw no one he recognised and certainly no one that looked like they were from the parole board either.

He walked up and down the narrow passageway on the inmates' side and checked the far side of each metal grille a couple of times . . . Not a soul that could possibly be there to see him.

And just as he was about to give up and head back, a voice suddenly stopped him in his tracks.

A woman's voice, clipped, clear and direct.

'Excuse me, are you by any chance Jake Keane?'

It certainly wasn't anyone from the parole board. Instead he found a youngish woman, early thirties at a guess, whippet thin and pale as a ghost, which only made her coal-black eyes stand out even more. Fine, dark brown hair neatly tied back, wearing a smart black suit, black briefcase, black everything. Attractive, even if she did look like she hadn't slept in about the last three years. But if she put on half a stone and got a bit of sunshine, Jake thought, she'd be something to look at: pretty, even. A solicitor, Jake guessed. She definitely had that official, formal, tense look about her that lawyers visiting here always had. Like she'd just come to say her piece, get the hell out of here then quickly head back to the comforting warmth of the law library as soon as possible.

Jake sighed deeply, knowing the type all too well. Knowing right well that this would make an interesting anecdote for her to tell her other lawyer cronies in Doheny and Nesbitts or whatever trendy watering hole the legal set hung out in these days. 'Girlies, you won't *beeeeelieeeeeeeve* where I had to go to see a client today!' he could imagine this one shrieking to her other well-heeled professional pals. As if dispatching guys to rot out here was just a distasteful part of their job description, best treated as a joke in a pub. Unaware of the reality, what life in here was really like for her more unfortunate 'clients'. Made his blood boil to even think about it, and not for the first time, he wished he could force every lawyer he'd ever had the misfortune to come across to spend just one single night in here. See how they liked it then.

But if there was one thing that doing time taught you, it was the value of silence. So Jake said nothing, just sat down opposite the grille from her and waited for this woman to talk, to explain the extraordinary reason for her being here.

'Good morning,' she began, clearing her throat. 'Emm . . . Apologies for disturbing you, but I just wondered if I might have a moment of your time?'

'Well, in case you hadn't noticed,' Jake smiled wryly through the grille at her, 'I've got all the time in the world. I'm kind of what you might call a captive audience.'

Then he shoved his fair hair out of his face, folded his arms and sat back prepared to listen, taking her in from head to toe. A real hard nut, was his first outside guess about her. He could tell by the way she sat ramrod straight in front of him, like she was about to chair a meeting any second. Jake tended to classify people as either being tough or soft, and they certainly didn't look any tougher than this one.

Then he noticed her thin, bony fingers drumming off the narrow ledge in front of her and thought no, hard is the wrong word, she just has something on her mind, that's all: she's here on a clear mission. So he decided to make it easy for her.

'Look,' he told her, more gently, 'I've no idea who you are, but if you're from Legal Aid, then you've had a wasted journey. I'm up for parole in a few weeks . . .'

'I'm not a lawyer. My name's Eloise Elliot,' she explained

crisply and for some reason the name rang a bell with Jake.

'Eloise Elliot,' he repeated, racking his brains to remember where he had heard it before.

'Senior Editor at the *Daily Post*.'

And then it all slotted together in his head. Of course, he read the online edition every day in the prison library; he must have seen that name a thousand times on the editorial page. Okay, so now it was suddenly easier for him to get a proper handle on her. Someone married to her job, he guessed, one of those workaholics who was chained to her desk, a woman who didn't just live for work, but who ate, drank and slept it too.

'Anyway, here's the thing,' Eloise Elliot went on, in the brisk, business like way she had. 'I'm about to commission a series of stories on former inmates and how they readjust to life on the outside, as soon as they're released. And what I'm here to ask you, is whether you might have any interest in taking part? It would of course mean monitoring how you readjust to life outside over the next few months, how you coped, how things work out for you, that kind of thing. All done anonymously, of course, your name wouldn't appear in the paper or anything like that. You'd just be there for deep background info to the, emm . . . series, nothing more than that. So, what do you think?'

Jake said nothing at first, just sat back, taking her in. Had to give the girl this much, he thought, most people on their first visit here seemed shaken to hell at the conditions around them. Particularly the women, who'd barely be able to make eye contact with you, just wanted to say their piece and get the hell out of there.

But not Miss Eloise Elliot. Instead she sat opposite him waiting on his answer, cool and composed, not seeming in the least bit fazed by where she was, or the fact that she was talking to a convict. Clearly this woman wasn't just made of strong stuff, but had nerve endings lined with lead titanium.

For some reason, that impressed Jake.

But her coming to see him was still a mystery. What in the name of God could the editor of a huge paper like the *Post* possibly want with him? That was what he couldn't figure; made no sense to him on any level.

'Okay if I call you Eloise?' Jake eventually said, looking keenly at her.

'Of course.'

'You mean you don't insist on 'Madame Editor,' like on your letters page?' he threw in, grinning.

'Eloise is fine,' she said, looking impressed that not only did he read the national paper of record, but the letters page to boot.

'In that case Eloise, I have to tell you that what you just said sounds like the single greatest load of horse manure this side of the Grand National.'

'*Excuse* me?'

Right then, he thought. Here's a woman unused to being spoken to like that. But on the other hand, she'd got him all the way out here, and it sure as hell was an improvement on hanging around in his overcrowded cell. Might as well have a bit of fun while he was here, he figured.

'Well, for starters,' he said, lazily stretching his long legs out in front of him, like a man with all the time in the world.

'Why in the name of God would the *Post* have the slightest interest in writing about someone like me? I read your paper day in and day out and even I'm able to tell you this much. Your readers are predominantly ABC1, am I right?'

She nodded.

'Now if you were the editor of say, the *Chronicle* or the *Evening Tatler*, I might at least be able to understand where you were coming from, but your lot are about as far removed from tabloid readers as you could possibly get.'

'Well, yes . . . but, I don't understand what you're driving at.'

'Eloise, it makes damn-all sense to me why you think your average *Post* reader would possibly be interested in the likes of me. Never mind what'll become of me on the outside. With the exception of my mother, my own family barely even care. So who do you possibly think would ever give a shite about an ex-con, back on the outside?'

'Well for starters, I would,' she told him firmly, returning his gaze full on. Almost, the thought hit him from out of nowhere, like she'd rehearsed her speech on the way over.

'And you can be sure that if I would, then plenty of other people would too. Jake, it's precisely because this is not the kind of series that's ever been commissioned before that I want to do it. And you're absolutely perfect for us. I called the governor to ask if he could recommend someone who I might be able to talk to and he said you were far and away the best candidate. A model prisoner, in fact, is how he described you.'

Next thing, she was whipping a notepad out of her bag and referring to some neat notes she'd made earlier.

'Ah Jesus,' Jake groaned. 'Don't tell me you're starting now?'

'Just look at this,' she went on, ignoring him, and sounding far more animated. 'The governor also mentioned that you came top of your class when you took your TEFL qualification. Jake, that's amazing! And not only that, but apparently you're studying for your Open University exams too. He says your chances of making parole are excellent and that you're unlikely to re-offend . . .'

He sighed deeply while she talked on. Okay, so she knew all there was to know about him, presumably including what he was in for; she'd obviously done all her homework, and had somehow decided that he wasn't a threat. But that wasn't what bothered him – in here, the first thing you surrendered at the door was any right to privacy – he'd long since taken that for granted. But there was something else about Ms. Eloise Elliot, something a bit disconcerting. (Definitely a Ms., he decided the second he locked eyes on her. No way would this one going by the prefix Miss; he'd stake his parole on it.) Not so much what she was saying, but the utterly focused, intent way she was studying him while she said it. Like she was reading each and every one of his features, scanning his face, almost as though she recognised someone else in it.

And she wasn't aware of it, but she had a slight tell whenever she spoke about this so-called series she was commissioning, like she wasn't being entirely truthful. Every time she mentioned it, she'd colour a bit and glance shiftily to her left. It was tiny, she probably wasn't even aware she was doing it and it wouldn't have taken that much blinking to miss it, but Jake caught it alright. Two long years in here had left him expert when it came to reading 'tells'; he played a lot of poker with his cellmates and it got so you could read people as easily as one of his books.

But why would she come out all this way just to lie to him? Made no sense on any level, no matter what way he looked at it.

'So Jake, what do you think?'

I'll tell you exactly what I think, Ms. Eloise Elliot, he thought to himself. I think that there's a lot more to you than meets the eye. And that you're possibly the worst person at covering up a lie that I've ever seen and I've seen a few.

But then he caught the desperate, almost pleading look in her black eyes and softened. She'd come all this way. She'd gone to so much bother to find out about him. Go easy, he thought.

'Tell you what, can I sleep on it?' he said and she smiled, looking relieved that at least he hadn't turned her down flat.

'Of course, Jake. But before I go, would it be OK if I ask you just one or two more things? Just for, emm . . . deep background?'

'Fire away,' he said easily, thinking, 'deep background' my arse.

'Do you have family?'

'Are you kidding me? Yeah, too many.'

'How many of you are there?'

'Do you mean who are still speaking to me? That'd be just the one.'

'Are your parents alive?'

'Yeah, but my dad left when I was a baby so now there's just my mother. Who, just in case you want to write it down in your notebook, is the one person in my family still talking to me.'

'Oh, right,' she said, looking as if she was trying her level best not to ask why the others now had nothing to do with him.

'And where do you live?'

'When I get out? As they'd say in your paper, I'm currently of 'no fixed abode'. My mam's sofa, if I'm lucky.'

'What about grandparents? Any still living?'

He saw her suddenly bite her tongue, as if she knew she'd gone too far and was beginning to sound nosey.

'You really need to go into that much detail for your series?' Jake grinned cheekily across at her.

'Sorry, no of course not. But if you didn't mind, would you be able to tell me a little bit about yourself? You know, like how you pass the time in here? I know you study, so you must read a lot, but I wondered if you'd any other interest or hobbies, like sports? Maybe even . . . playing a musical instrument?'

And so he went along with it and humoured her, even though she kept using the word 'why' so much that it gave him a strange feeling in the pit of his stomach, not unlike when he was being interrogated by police. A memory he'd actively been trying to tune out for a long time.

'Oh and another thing, why do you keep changing your name?' she threw in suddenly. Like this was a particular niggle that really tried her patience.

'You know about that?'

'Well, yeah . . . From the governor.'

He nodded, not really believing her. That slight tell she had of looking to the left, again giving her away.

'Okay, then let me put it to you this way. If you ever had the kind of characters coming after you that I've had to put up with over the past few years, believe me, you'd start calling yourself Mary Smith and you'd emigrate to New Zealand on a one-way ticket, leaving a cloud of dust behind you.'

She gave a broad grin at that, which softened her whole face and knocked years off her, he thought distractedly.

'And I'm sorry, but I have to ask you this. Why William Goldsmith?'

'Easy. *She Stoops to Conquer* is one of my favourite plays,' he shrugged back at her. 'And when I saw the statue of Oliver Goldsmith outside Trinity College, I though it'd be a good idea to take Goldsmith as my surname and William after William Blake, another writer I love.'

She nodded, again looking impressed by the fact that he'd actually read the classics.

'But then what about Bill O'Casey? Where did that one come from?'

'Kind of people I used to hang round with would never call me William, it was always either Bill or Billy and O' Casey was after Sean O'Casey. I'd been reading *Shadow of a Gunman* at the time and loved it.'

Another half-smile.

'But then . . . James Archer?'

'Ah, now you mightn't like this one, but I was reading a fair bit of Jeffrey Archer at the time. A writer who gets slagged off mercilessly, but you can't deny he writes a great page-turner.'

'Okay, but what about Oscar Butler then? Hang on, let me hazard a wild guess; you'd been reading Oscar Wilde at the time,' she said dryly, but he noticed her mouth twisted down into a smile again.

He shrugged and nodded.

'So basically, every false identity you've ever had has been in homage to a writer, either living or dead?'

'Something like that,' he told her, armed folded, sitting well back, ostensibly taking her in, but his mind was miles away. What was it to her? Why did she even care? And what was really going on here?

On and on she went with all her questions, almost as though she was carrying some kind of image in her head of what he should be like, how he should behave, and was trying to make him fit that same identikit picture. And it certainly sounded like she'd already done her homework. Because this one was thorough. Seemed to know as much about him as his own mother did.

He was wrong there though, because just as she was wrapping up to leave, it looked like there was still one question she was burning up to ask him.

'So, emm,' she began, picking her words carefully. 'One last thing, if that's okay?'

'Fire ahead.'

'Well . . . Can I ask you what your plans are once you get back outside? Do you plan to finish the degree course you started, maybe even get a decent job out of it?'

The implication was there, hanging in the air between them. Jake had got very good at reading the unspoken.

Did he intend going straight after he got out?

But he couldn't give her a straight answer to that one.

Because at this particular point in time, it was a question there was just no answer to.

Chapter Six

One month later and to Jake's utter astonishment, Ms. Eloise Elliot had been as good as her word. Surprising absolutely no one but himself, he sailed through his parole hearing and following one kick-up-the-arse pep talk from his parole officer along the lines of I'll-be-watching-you-and-don't-think-I-won't, he found himself a free man for the first time in two long, long years.

He had nowhere to stay of course, only his mam's, but he didn't want to go there. At least not yet. It would be too easy for them to find him, too easy to get sucked back in. And if there was one thing he was certain of, it was this; there was no going back for him. Not now, not after everything he'd been through. And he knew of old that it could all happen so frighteningly easily, a phone call here, a recalled favour there and next thing he knew he'd end up right back where he'd started.

Not long before his release date, Eloise called to visit a second time, to ask him a few more questions, again under the pretext of commissioning a feature for her paper.

She couldn't stay for long she said, as she had to get back to work, even though it was a Sunday and he figured she'd take a day off, like anyone else. No, she told him, no such thing as a day off in her gig, the news didn't stop and so therefore neither could she. It struck him as funny that even though it was ostensibly the weekend (ostensibly was his new word for that day, he loved the sound of it, loved the way it rolled off his tongue), here was Eloise still dressed head to toe in black, in one of those interchangeable power suits she seemed so fond of. Neat, structured, minimalist cut, no frills or ornamentation of any kind; almost a bit like how a bloke would dress.

The apparel oft proclaimeth the man, Jake thought, looking through the grille at her. (He'd been reading Hamlet for his course at the time, and some of the quotes just stubbornly got into his head and stuck there.) She was still white as a sheet, still utterly exhausted looking; yet another mystery to Jake. What in the name of God did this woman do in her spare time anyway? Did she have any kind of private life, or even family? Or did she really just work, sleep and visit ex-cons whenever she could? Was her life really that empty, almost as empty as his own? Didn't make sense, but then none of this did. Why would someone this smart, successful and together be bothered with the likes of him?

'Guess what?' Eloise told him excitedly. 'I've got news. Well, more like an offer. That is, if you're interested.'

'Tell me more,' he said, smiling even as she uttered the words, *if* he was interested. Without even hearing what it was, he was just about ready to jump down her throat at whatever it might be and say yes. When did anyone ever offer him anything, bar trouble? And what other offers were there for him on the table at this point in time, only dangerous crap that would surely be a shortcut to him landing back inside in no time?

154

'Well,' she began, 'I've got a sister Helen, who rented out her flat in Dublin a few years ago when she moved down to Cork.'

'OK . . .'

'Now, I won't bore you with the details,' she explained in that enunciated, school ma'am way she had, 'but basically now my sister's staying somewhere else in Dublin. Emm . . . staying indefinitely. Anyway, her tenant moved out months ago and for the life of her, she can't get anyone else to take the place. You know what it's like renting in this market.'

Jake didn't, but nodded politely.

'Anyway, now Helen desperately needs someone to house-sit for her. She was about to put an ad in the paper, and then I thought of you. So basically, there's an empty flat that you're welcome to stay in until she's able to rent it out again properly. I thought that it might just suit you for a few weeks, at least until you find a proper place of your own. Plus it's on the other side of town, so at least you'd be out of harm's way there, none of your, well, let's just say no one from your past could possibly ever find you. You'd be doing her a favour too and all she asks is that you look after the place. It's been empty for seven months now, and needs someone to live in it.'

He sat back, digesting this.

'So . . . What do you think?'

'It's incredibly generous of you and your sister, but Eloise . . .'

Shit. It was no use. He couldn't contain himself any longer.

'I have to ask you something.'

'Go ahead.'

'Why are you doing this? I mean, why me? You're a busy

lady, you hardly have time for this. What are you anyway, like one of those Victorian philanthropists who spent their time visiting the prisons and helping the less fortunate? Like some kind of angel in disguise? Don't get me wrong, I'm hugely grateful to you for the offer, but none of this makes the slightest bit of sense to me.'

She blushed at this. And took her time before answering him, he noticed.

'Because . . . Well, I mean, just look at you Jake, you've got such potential. All your brilliant exam results? You could easily make something of yourself outside of here, build a whole new life, a better one. I just . . . I really believe in you and if there's any way I can help out, I'm here. That's all.'

He looked intently back at her.

'And that's the whole truth? Just look me in the eye, Eloise. If you're holding back, trust me, I'll know.'

'Well . . .' she said a bit shiftily. 'It's partly the truth.'

'Partly?'

'Look . . . Put it this way. I'm someone who's always getting accused of putting work ahead of everyone and everything. I constantly hear that I never do anything good for other people. So now, I figure, well maybe here's my chance.'

He nodded, but still couldn't shake the feeling there was more to all this than met the eye. Considerably more. *What* though? That was the million dollar question.

'Anyway,' she went on in her usual back-to-business way, 'what do you think about flatsitting?'

'It's an incredibly generous offer, but I'd only take it on one condition.'

'Which is?'

'I'd insist on paying your sister rent. Upfront and from day one. And that's not negotiable.'

Eloise nodded, and seemed happy enough with that. Then she started to probe around a bit more.

'And another thing Jake. I wanted to ask you if you'd thought about how you'd manage for money once you get out?' she asked directly.

'Jesus! Like if it's not too personal a question?'

'Sorry, I just wondered, that was all,' she said, biting her tongue and looking flushed that she'd maybe overstepped the mark.

Jake sat back and shook his head. Because even just being asked that made him feel about two inches tall. She didn't mean to humiliate, of that he was certain. It was just unfortunate that this was her manner. He'd learned by now that if there was a wrong way to get around people, Eloise would pretty soon light on it. You could see it in the way she spoke to the screws, snappily, brusquely, like someone who was used to barking orders while all around her jumped to.

A real shame, Jake thought. Because underneath all of that toughness, there was a good heart there, if you only took the trouble to furrow down deep for it. A genuine warmth and a caring side that for whatever reason, she took great pains to conceal from all around her. Not for the first time, it made him wonder why exactly she'd chosen him to be on the receiving end of all this altruism. (Another new word for the day.) Because why pick a soon-to-be ex-con when she could easily help those with far more need of it? It was a mystery, one that baffled him, but if it was the last thing he did, he'd somehow get to the bottom of it.

'Look, I didn't mean to be rude or nosey Jake,' she cut

across his thoughts, 'I just wondered if you were okay for money, that was all.'

And at that point, he'd have sworn on a stack of Bibles that no bank manager on earth could have done it quite as probingly, cutting straight to the heart of the matter in seconds flat. If this one had an animal image, he thought, looking evenly through the grille at her, it would have been a bird of prey; an eagle or a hawk. She was that alert, that keen and clued in; she'd sound out any tiny detail you were not one hundred per cent sure of. In fact, she'd not only sound it out, but be on top of it in a matter of seconds.

So he paused, waited for a bit, saw that she wasn't going anywhere till she got the answers she was looking for, then finally realised there was nothing for it but to open up to her. What the hell, she seemed to have found out everything else about him from the governor, what had he to lose?

'I'll be just fine, thanks for asking,' he told her, coughing and keeping his voice deliberately low, hoping she'd just drop the subject and move on.

'You're sure?'

'Positive. As it happens, I've a few quid put by, not much but enough to tide me over for a few weeks till I find work.'

'What do you think you'll work at?'

He sighed. Because he'd been giving that one a lot of thought lately and the options didn't exactly appeal.

'Thought I might hire out a taxi plate,' he told her, but she didn't exactly look impressed. But then neither was he, particularly.

'It's a gig plenty of the other lads in here do as a kind of stepping-stone when they first get out,' he went on to explain. 'You don't have the expense of running the car, tax or insurance or any of that, the guy who owns the taxi plate looks after all that. So as long as you pay him his cut out of whatever cash you make, he's happy. Means I can do the odd night shift for some overworked driver who only wants to work more sociable hours during the day.'

'Oh Jake,' she said sitting back, deflated. 'That's really what you want? To ferry home a load of drunks out of their head on alcopops at four a.m., after all the nightclubs close?'

'That wouldn't really particularly bother me at all,' he said, unconvincingly. 'To be honest, I'd just be glad of the cash and can put up with anything, as long as they don't puke in the back of the car.'

There was only one disadvantage to the plan and he knew it only too well, though he kept it to himself. If he went back to driving, his old gang would surely find him. Chances were they'd track him down in no time. Nothing could be easier. If they wanted to, they could get to anyone, but a taxi driver was a particularly useful animal to them. They'd get you working like a courier, and before you knew where you were, you were back in trouble, back in court, back inside, back to square one, back where you swore you'd never go back to.

Eloise didn't actually say as much, but seemed distinctly unimpressed with the plan. It was in the slightly disdainful sniff she gave when he mentioned taxi shift work and in the way she impatiently tapped the tips of her skinny fingers off the metal counter in front of her, when he talked about night shifts and soilage charges. But then, he'd noticed she was good at communicating disapproval without even having to open her mouth. For a split second he wondered what life was like for all the legions of reporters and editors who worked under her. Were they all afraid of her? He'd nearly put money on it.

Jake knew so little about her, but could already guess that in a work situation, her bark was as bad, if not fifty times worse, than her bite. Idly, he found himself sitting back, arms folded, wondering when the last time was someone had used the word 'no' in front of Eloise Elliot.

'But you have a TEFL qualification,' she reminded him insistently. 'You got first class honours, you did really well at it! Why are you throwing all that away so you can sit on some taxi rank for hours in the middle of the night? Why not put your qualification to good use? And you're studying for your English and psychology degree. Surely pursuing these goals would give you a far more promising future then schlepping round night clubs in some borrowed taxi at some ungodly hour in the morning? Course, I know that your future is in your own hands and that it's none of my business,' she added, 'but it seems to me that you've got a real chance to make something of yourself here. To really start over, turn a new leaf, not look back.'

At that, he sat forward, starting to listen more intently now. Because without her even realising it, that last sentence had chimed a deep chord. He wondered if Eloise knew that was exactly what he needed to hear at this point in time. Wondered if she knew that the very thought of making a fresh start, of even taking a step up in the world was like music to his ears . . . Who knew?

All he knew was that he found himself suddenly paying alert attention to what she was saying. She had a way of making everything sound so easy, so achievable. God, he thought, this one was far, far better than any parole officer at encouraging you, guiding you to haul yourself up by the bootstraps and make something out of what was left of your life.

'You know what you could do Jake?' she went on, really warming to her theme now, 'You could apply for a job teaching TEFL courses to overseas students, maybe at one of the language schools that are springing up all over town. After all, education is the one recession-proof business,' she went on enthusiastically. 'I'd put money on it that you'd be well able to get work, even part-time.'

So Jake let her chat on, finding himself listening interestedly at first, then intently. Because she just made it all sounds so easy, so doable.

'You could be a proper TEFL teacher,' she encouraged him. 'You could do it, easily, I know you could. I'll even be a referee on your references for you. We can gloss up your CV,' she said, like it was already a done deal. 'I'll help you, I'd be delighted to. And in your spare time, you could finish your degree. Who knows what wonderful prospects it might lead on to in time? Streets ahead of doing night shifts in a taxi. So come on, what do you say?'

Jake said nothing, but just listening to her filled him with an utterly unfamiliar sensation. Hard to put a name on, but when he analysed it later on back in his cell, he knew exactly what it was. It was hope, plain and simple. No two ways about it, she was offering him a lifeline.

And he'd have been a fool not to grab at it like a sinking man about to be saved.

So this was it then, this was freedom. For the first time in two years, Jake had no one to answer to only himself. And it was – no other word for it – intoxicating. Delirious enough to get high on, if he hadn't sworn off all that years ago. He felt invincible, like William Wallace at the end of the movie *Braveheart*, as played by Mel Gibson with a faceful of Avatar-blue paint all over him, where he just wanted to yell out at the top of his lungs over and over again, that one delicious word . . . *freedom*.

Astonishing the things you missed when you'd been away. Ask any of the lads inside, and they'd all tell a different tale: some missed their wives, girlfriends, kids, others the little things like being able to stroll into a pub on a Sunday afternoon, order a pint, read the paper, maybe watch a match on telly. But for Jake, what he'd missed most was that rare thing, privacy. Never for one second were you left alone inside, even in the showers you were supervised, always being watched. It was a thing he vowed never to take for granted again, not as long as he lived.

And now here he was, Jake Keane, living the life of a respectable man. It was like some kind of strange, surrealist dream come true and in his darker moments – of which there were many – he worried about the tap on his shoulder, the unwanted phone call, or the midnight hammering on his hall door that would land him right back at square one. But he tried his best to tune those thoughts out and instead to focus on the positives. God knows, for once in his life, there were an abundance of them to choose from.

He owed Eloise so much, and Jake was a proud man, unused to either being helped altruistically or being under a compliment. Particularly to someone who'd just brush all his badly articulated expressions of heartfelt thanks aside. But if it was the last thing he ever did, he swore that somehow he'd find a way to pay Eloise back.

For starters, there was this gorgeous flat he now had the run of, for a reasonable rent he could just about afford. It was tiny, admittedly, a one-bedroom apartment just off the main Sandymount Road, in one of those new developments that had shot up like mushrooms during the property boom. Course now half of the apartments in block after block were little more than negative equity millstones round the neck of owners who had taken a punt on them in better times, and now they just lay empty and deserted. Kind of like living in a ghost town, with very few neighbours and even fewer lights dotted round the block whenever it got dark.

But to Jake, it was like crashing out in the penthouse suite of the Ritz-Carlton hotel. Sheer, unimagined luxury. And here, in his own tiny little space, he was finally, finally free.

He could do as he pleased, when he pleased. Go out for long solitary walks down Sandymount Strand any time it suited him, with no one's permission to ask. No sirens blaring that heralded a fight breaking out in some far-away wing, meaning lockdown for one and all, no lights-out at a time when you could still hear small kids out playing on the still sunlit streets, no handcuffs, no iron security gates to pass through every five metres, no clinking of keys . . . There was just him and him alone and there were times he thought he was drunk on the sheer high of it.

He felt like a proper adult, with a normal life all ahead of him, something he'd scarcely dreamt of only a few weeks back.

And all he had to do was not f**k it up.

Eloise continued to astonish him with her random acts of kindness, all done in her usual brusque, businesslike manner. He'd actually never expected to see her again. As soon as he'd moved into the flat and given her a month's rent plus a deposit upfront for her sister, that technically should have heralded the end of all her dealings with him. And yet still she kept coming back. Just for friendly chats, just to see how he was doing. Lately she'd taken to dropping in on him at the oddest times, like very late at night when she'd just have finished up work for the day, or early on weekend mornings, when again, she was only about to start her day's work.

Initially, she never stayed for more than half an hour at a time, just long enough for her to check what work he'd done on his CV and which language schools he was applying off to. Like a teacher looking for progress reports, he thought. As if she hadn't done enough for him, she'd even helped him out there too. She'd glossed up his resumé for him and had added on loads of embellishments he'd never even thought of. All the skills that he'd learned in Wheatfield, she'd pounced on, made an asset of.

And so now, under 'outside interests and hobbies', he had listed a not-unimpressive array of accomplishments, from carpentry to cooking. She'd even thrown in metalwork. Fleshes it all out a bit, she'd told him, makes you sound more interesting, more three-dimensional. Spoken with all the authority of a woman who'd not only scanned through thousands of CVs in her time, but who could also freely quote – in some cases dating from years back – examples from the ones that had impressed her and horror stories from the ones that arrived on her desk stained with coffee mug rings all around them.

'Photographic memory?' he'd asked her at the time, wryly grinning at her from the corner of his mouth.

'Comes in very handy in my gig, believe me,' she grinned back and as ever, it astonished him how approximately ten years fell off her face when she allowed herself to crack even the tiniest smile.

Not only that, but she'd encouraged him to open up a library account too, so he could borrow all the English and psychology books he needed to study for his Open University exams, which were only round the corner. She'd even earmarked a couple of language schools in town that she'd heard on the grapevine were stuffed to the gills with students and suggested he apply off to those first. Chances were they could do with having a few substitute teachers on their roster.

Jake gladly took her advice and was astonished to find that in no time at all, his days had become far fuller and busier than he ever could have anticipated. He would get up early each morning, cook a proper breakfast (cooking came easily after a spell inside; everyone was required to spend at least three months of the year working in the prison kitchens and what you'd learned stayed with you), then start into the books, which he loved far more than he could ever hope to put into words.

For hour after hour, he'd sit at the tiny desk in the one-roomed studio flat and pore over his course texts, cup of coffee beside him, feeling like a real, proper student. Feeling so very deeply privileged; as though all the chances he'd never had as a kid, or as a teenager, all the opportunities that he'd missed out on, had by some boomerang of a miracle, come back to him.

As it happened, he was studying *Pygmalion* by one of his favourite writers, George Bernard Shaw, for his English exam. And he found it ironic and funny at the same time, that a guy like him, an ex-con, a criminal with a past who'd been in and out of correctional facilities all his youth, could relate so easily to a character like Eliza Doolittle, a flower girl with a rough background whose main problem in life was that she said 'cuppa tae' instead of cup of tea and yelled obscenities at racehorses on Ascot opening day.

And yet in spite of everything, he could all too easily identify with this character. He'd even written a bit about the subject in one of the essays he'd had to hand in to his course tutor. He and Eliza Dolittle both despised where they'd come from and didn't want to get sucked back. They both wanted more out of life, without being dragged back into the past any more. The past was another country, Jake had learned, one he never, ever intended revisiting.

Enter Eloise Elliot, like a female Henry Higgins in a black power suit and high heels, who was good enough to provide a halfway house for him, all the time encouraging him onwards and upwards. And education, she impressed on him time and again, was the key to the unlocked low door in the wall, the one that led to a better life.

His mam laughed at him when he took two buses on the long trek out to Darndale to see her one Sunday afternoon, as did his nana. 'You always had notions about yourself,' she'd said, though he liked to kid himself that he caught a flash of pride in her eyes as she said it. 'Always too good for the likes of us, always wanting better for yourself. With your fancy books by writers none of us ever heard of by Russian writers that aren't even alive any more, sure what's the point in that?'

Jake smiled to himself at this, knowing his mother would think that reading anything more challenging than *OK!*

magazine was akin to reading a treatise on sewage management in the fourteenth century.

'Sure I remember you as a teenager,' his nana reminded him, through her whistling teeth that she then whipped out and stuck on the dinner table in full view, like she always did whenever they were at her. 'You were always writing out fancy to-do lists for yourself: must learn to speak better, must try to dress better, must study harder. How you didn't get the shit kicked out of you more often round here was a minor miracle,' she cackled at him toothlessly, the breath whistling out of her.

'I remember,' he smiled his warm, slow smile at her. 'I was reading *The Great Gatsby* and I wanted to be just like Jay.' But his nana just looked blankly back at him, the reference utterly lost on her, then grinned gummily and told him she really believed he'd do well no matter what. 'I wouldn't worry a bit about anything love,' she'd told him kindly. 'Sure look at you, you've the same hands as me. Intelligent hands. You'll do well for yourself, you'll be OK. Just don't forget us when you land some big fancy job in town for yourself. And no running off with any tarty little gold-diggers when you're rich and successful either, do you hear me?'

She was gently teasing him and all his notions of getting on in the world, but deep down Jake knew that of all people in his family, Nana probably understood best.

Understood that he'd had enough of the life he'd been born into. That he wanted to kill it as fast as possible and start over. Quickly, before they got to him and dragged him back in, like they always seemed to, just when he'd stumbled on a chance of getting up and on and out. And the invisible noose they had around his neck was already beginning to tighten, he knew only too well. Already, his ma said a few of the old gang had phoned the house, faux-casually asking where he was staying since he got out. He could trust his ma not to give him away though. 'In town, that's as much as I know' she'd told them firmly, and that seemed to suffice.

At least, for the moment.

In his coursework, he was reading about the Sword of Damocles and in his darker moments, that was exactly how he felt these days. Like he was enjoying a rare and spectacular piece of undeserved good fortune right now, but the sky was surely about to fall in on his head.

Like it usually did.

And it was just a matter of time.

Chapter Seven

One night back at the flat in Sandymount, Jake had been studying till very late and suddenly found himself unexpectedly starving. He was just beginning to fry up some noodles with chicken and green vegetables when there was a buzz at the intercom – Eloise, dropping off the latest draft of his re-done, re-worked, proof-read, ready-to-go CV. Come on up, he'd told her, door's open. It was one of those miserable, filthy wet nights you sometimes get in the middle of springtime, when it feels more like November than May, so he'd lit a fire hours earlier, then stayed up late reading his course books by its flickering warmth.

In she came, dripping wet and looking even paler than he'd seen her in the longest time, which was really saying something. The girl always carried a kind of tense, jumpy energy around with her, but tonight her nerves were practically pinging off the walls. Something was seriously up, he knew by the look of her. No one this side of a correctional facility went around looking that fraught and strung out, and he should know.

'You OK?' he asked quietly.

'Fine,' she said tersely.

'You sure?' he asked gently.

'Cosy,' she nodded brusquely, avoiding his question, arms folded and face taut as she took in her surroundings in one of her lightning-quick, up-and-down appraising looks.

'Thanks,' he nodded, towering like a colossus over her, even in bare feet, making the room seem smaller just because he was in it. 'Here, sit down at the fire, dry yourself off a bit.'

'It's okay thanks, I'm not staying, I need to go . . .' she began edgily, but then seemed to waver a bit as the tantalising smell of garlic and onions hit her.

'Are you *cooking*? In the *kitchen*?'

If she'd asked him if he was in the kitchen shaving his head, she couldn't have sounded any more stunned.

'Ehhh . . . It's actually what people do in kitchens, wouldn't be all that uncommon,' he grinned down at her. 'You hungry, by any chance? Plenty of grub for both of us.'

'No,' she wavered, but unconvincingly. 'That is, yeah, but I have to get home, I've still got a pile of emails I need to answer and I've so much else to do tonight, just to stay on schedule . . .'

'Oh for feck's sake Eloise, just for once, do as I'm telling you. Don't leave just yet. Sit down, stay and have something to eat,' he told her, in a don't-mess-with-me tone.

So looking like all the fight had finally drained out of her, she slumped exhaustedly into the armchair by the roaring fire.

'Atta girl,' said Jake. 'Do you good to let someone else mind you for a change. You look wrecked.'

'Tell me something I don't know,' she said wryly, rolling her eyes up to heaven. 'After the day I've had, my spine feels like a ladder of lead pipes.'

'Just sit back and relax. Grub's on its way.'

He went back to the stir-fry in the tiny galley kitchen, while Eloise looked all around her, taking everything in, and as usual, missing absolutely nothing.

'You've been doing some work on the place,' she commented, nodding towards a load of pictures left strewn around the floor by the last tenant, now neatly framed and dotted tastefully around the walls.

'Ahh yeah, I've just been fixing a few things round here up a bit,' he shrugged from where he stood at the cooker, making modest light of the fact that since he'd moved in, he'd done everything he could to repair anything broken around the flat, jazz it up a bit and generally leave it in turnkey condition for Eloise's sister. Already he'd revarnished the wooden floor, fixed the leak in the sink and shower, repaired the kitchen cupboard door that was hanging off its hinges; the works. Least he could do, he felt.

'Looks far better than it ever did,' she said approvingly, stretching her legs out in front of the fire and finally starting to relax a bit. 'Have to hand it to you Jake, I never would have had you down as a metrosexual that would be good at knocking things into shape around the house.'

He laughed, unscrewing the lid off a bottle of wine and pouring her out a glass.

'You mean, by the size of me, you'd swear I was the type better suited to smashing up things, rather than putting them back together again?' he teased lightly.

'No, I didn't mean that. The place is just so spotless, that's all. Usually in an apartment with a single guy living in it, you'd nearly expect to see a kitchen sink fit for mice to throw a party in . . .'

'Don't tell me, with the stench of a three-day-old micro-waved dinner for one from Tesco hanging in the air . . .' He grinned.

'Gakky underpants strewn across the back of the sofa . . .'

'. . . All while an FA Premiership match blares away on TV. Yeah, I've lived in plenty of places that fit that description in my time alright. Here, have a glass of wine.'

'Can't. Driving.'

'You can have a mouthful, can't you? Go on, put a bit of colour back in your cheeks. I've seen healthier-looking ghosts.'

And even though she protested she was too tired and strung out to eat, five minutes later she was heartily tucking into a big bowl of chicken noodles with a glass of white wine at her elbow. A decent hot meal brought a flush to her face, as did the wine, Jake thought, studying her. Made her look that bit less pale, he was pleased to see, as he eased his giant frame into the tiny armchair opposite her.

There was a tense lull in the chat, and for no other reason than to fill the dead air, she politely asked him how his studying was coming on, but he interrupted.

'So, are you going to tell me what the hell is wrong with you tonight or not?' he asked her straight out, cloud-blue eyes unflinching.

She looked blankly back at him, he guessed – correctly as it happened – unused to directness. In her line of work, Jake figured, everyone freely talked about you behind your back, but few people probably had the guts to say things straight to your face.

'I don't know what you're taking about . . .'

'Oh for feck's sake, do I have to drag it out of you?'

'There's absolutely nothing wrong with me, I'm just a

bit tired that's all,' she went on to protest, rubbing her black eyes exhaustedly.

'Eloise, are you familiar with the phrase "don't kid a kidder?" You walk in here like the whole world around you is about to collapse on your shoulders. All I'm saying is if you need a friendly ear, then I'm here and I've all night to listen. The floor is yours.'

Then he shrugged as if to say, if you want to talk, talk. If you need quiet, that's fine too. No pressure, up to you.

And so, slowly, hesitatingly, she began to tell him. Really open up to him, in a way he guessed she hadn't done in the longest time and for some reason, didn't seem able to do with anyone else. Out it all came tumbling, uncut and uncensored.

'It's just . . . All this pressure I'm under in work,' she eventually told him, sighing almost painfully. 'Gargantuan pressure, so intense that most of the time I feel like I'm trying not to drown, but I know one day – and one day soon by the looks of things – I'll surely get dragged under. The way things are going, it's inevitable. And it didn't used to be like this, you know. Time was, I loved my job, adored it, hated being away from it. Couldn't understand colleagues wanting holidays and time off. I *lived* to get into work. Whereas now . . .'

'Go on,' he said quietly.

'Well, now there are days when I honestly think I'm coming to the end of my life expectancy as editor of the *Post*.' She patted her chest as she said it, like it was a physical relief just to articulate her greatest fear out loud.

'I swear I can almost feel it in my bones.'

And he nodded and listened and encouraged her to go on and so she did.

She told him about the next bout of staff culling and redundancies that were only round the corner, which she'd have to deal with because, as she explained, no one else would. All the shitty jobs ultimately fell to her. Which was why everyone in the whole place, to a man, seemed to despise her. Told him about the board of directors she'd nicknamed the T. Rexes and their old-fashioned gentlemen's club and the way they effortlessly expected her to turn around the online edition of the paper, with absolutely zero encouragement from anyone, just bucketloads of crap that kept getting thrown down on top of her for every financial target she failed to reach.

Then she told him with particular relish about a guy called Seth Coleman, the managing editor and her number two, who'd basically been champing at the bit to get his hands on her job and now seemed to feel that his hour had finally come.

Just hearing this alone made Jake immediately want to go into that shagging office and wallop the living shit out of him.

Then, saving the best for last, she went on to tell him about what was really troubling her.

'So anyway,' she said, gulping back a big mouthful of wine, 'at about five this evening, I'm tied up in a meeting with union reps, safely out of the way in other words. And what does Seth decide to do? In a spectacular '*et tu, Brute*?' blood rush to his greasy head, the insinuating little git decides to completely override me and goes up to the executive floor to meet with the T. Rexes alone.'

'Gobshite. I'd sort him out in two seconds if you ever wanted.'

'You haven't heard the worst of it. He goes in to tell them

that he strongly feels the paper's slow and steady decline in sales is now in danger of turning it into nothing more than a white elephant that'll end up facing extinction, just like the *Tribune* did not so long ago. And on the principle that if you're sinking fast, you need a new hand at the helm, then the editorial job at the *Post* should be handed over to someone new and fresh immediately. Him, in other words. He basically said it's been my hobby horse for way too long now, but I've had my shot and now need to graciously accept defeat and bugger off,' she went on, really getting into her stride now.

'All of that would be bad enough, but then the duplicitous little snake-arse even went as far as to insinuate – thus verbalising my single greatest fear, by the way – that with my contract up for renewal soon anyway, maybe it's best not to just sideline me somewhere else, but to actually get rid of me altogether. Which of course would mean my chance of ever getting any kind of decent job in the industry again would be out the window.'

Jake sat back, then whistled.

'Bloody hell. Makes all the backstabbing that went on in ancient Rome look restrained. How did all of that get back to you, by the way?'

'I have ways and means,' she said wryly. 'The news filtered back to me fast, but then I make it my business to know everything that's going on at the *Post*. In my job, you have to.'

'Sounds a bit like working for the KGB in pre-Gorbachev Russia,' he teased and for the first time since she got there, she cracked a smile.

'Anyway, here's the real question,' she went on, taking another big, nerve-calming glug of the wine beside her, kicking her shoes off and curling her legs up.

Took every ounce of resolve Jake had to take his eyes off her long, slim legs and focus on her eyes instead.

'What do I do now?' she went on. 'Seth's playing a dangerous game of brinkmanship here, so I'm going to have to plot my way through it as carefully as in a championship chess game. Oh sure, one fine day I'll gladly see the two-faced git bastard hang, head on a spike, burnt at the stake, the whole works. But for now at least, I've no choice but to bite my tongue, play a long game and choose my next move as cagily as a cat . . . Mind you, it still doesn't stop me from wondering what in God's name I ever did in a past life to deserve Seth bloody Coleman. A managing editor is supposed to be my consigliere, my right hand. Not someone who's only waiting on their chance to stab me in the back, then dance on my grave singing Hallelujah.'

He just let her talk on and on, quietly listening, correctly sensing that this was a woman who'd never in a million years lie on an psychoanalyst's sofa Woody Allen-like and spill out her innermost thoughts. So therefore, he instinctively knew she must really be at break point to even consider opening up to him. She left nothing out either; told him the awful things that were said behind her back at work, when all she was trying to do was keep the show on the road and keep everyone in a job. And how she tried not to let it get to her but how much it all hurt her deep down. That in spite of what everyone thought about her and in spite of all the bitching that was done about her, she was actually a human being underneath it all, with normal human emotions.

'If you prick us, do we not bleed?' he murmured under his breath.

'What?'

'Nothing,' he said quietly. 'From *The Merchant of Venice*. Go on. What other bitching are they doing about you? Say it aloud, we'll have a laugh at it and then it'll go away. Trust me, I know what I'm talking about.'

She was on the verge of tears now, he could tell by the tiny wobble in her voice. And by the cut of her, you could tell that this was someone totally unused to crying.

'Latest is, courtesy of Seth Coleman, that I spread unhappiness wherever I go.'

'I know I don't know the guy and have never met him and would never want to, but Jesus, give me five minutes with him down a dark alleyway with a golf club.'

In spite of herself she sniggered, in a laughter-through-tears kind of way.

'Not as bad as the time he said that I'd had all human emotion surgically removed from me, but, yeah, certainly right up there in his top ten insult hit list.'

'Where I come from, we have ways of sorting out a git like that very fast, let me tell you. Nothing terminal of course, just a bit of a going over . . . Say the word, and I can have it taken care of for you. That guy needs teaching a lesson and I know a few lads who'd gladly take care of it in a heartbeat. Seth Coleman would never walk straight again.'

For a split second, she looked up at him horrified, then caught the cheeky glint in his eye.

'You're messing,' she half smiled.

'Course I'm messing. You think I'm ever going back to you-know-where?'

She grinned even wider his time, as ever he thought, completely softening her whole face.

'Eloise, will you tell me something else?'

Feck it, it was bothering him and he might as well ask her now, when she seemed to be opening up a bit.

'What it is?'

'No offence, you know I'm happy to talk to you any time, but why are you telling *me* all this? Isn't there anyone at home waiting for you who'd want to know all about your day?'

And like that, she immediately clammed up again. Not for the first time either. Whenever he as much as broached the subject of her home life, she turned back to stone. As if the temperature in the room suddenly just dropped down about ten degrees.

'Jake,' she said, suddenly tuning out. 'I'll make you a deal. I won't ask you about your past or your personal life and you won't ask me about mine. Okay?'

He shrugged.

'If that's what you want.'

'You have to trust me. It's just better that way.'

She got up to leave then, looking shattered and probably aching for sleep.

'Look, it's nearly coming up to eleven,' she said, as he stood to help her pull her coat back on and looking gratefully up at him. 'And I've to be up and back into work for six tomorrow morning, so I better hit the road. But look . . . I just want to say thank you. Just being able to talk through such a shitty, awful, crappy day was a huge help. You've no idea.'

'Any time,' he said evenly, arms folded, towering over her by at least a foot. 'Least I can do. Look at all you've done for me.'

'You're more than welcome, you know that.'

'Doesn't mean I don't feel bad for accepting all this help from you. But I promise you this Eloise, the day will come when I'll pay you back. I mean it.'

178

'Just concentrate on getting a good job that uses you to your best ability. Seeing that happen would be payment enough for me,' she smiled.

He couldn't resist.

'Just let me know whenever you want to start work on the feature you were talking about.'

'The what?' she asked, and he guessed that exhaustion was momentarily clouding her normally perfect recall.

'The feature for your paper? About guys like me and how they fare on the outside?'

'Oh yeah, the feature, of course,' she said unconvincingly he thought, her involuntary glance down to the left giving her away again. 'Not now, but another time, okay?'

A minute later, she had gone back out into the rainy night and all Jake could do was stand there, utterly baffled, thinking . . . why? Why was someone like her putting herself out like this just for someone like him?

He'd meant what he said to her, he didn't feel one bit comfortable at all with the help she was so freely giving him. True, he was paying his own way in the flat, but then there was all that work she was putting into his CV.

And another thing. Was the girl really that lonely, that he was the only person she had to talk her in off the ledge after a bad day? Where were her friends, her family?

Or was he really the only person in the world she had to open up to?

Chapter Eight

His mam's magic novenas to St Michael and St Joseph were answered and not long after, Jake got a letter from one of the many language schools where he'd applied to teach English as a foreign language, requesting – he thought he was seeing things – an interview. An actual interview. For a decent, respectable job and not driving taxis or flipping burgers or selling the *Big Issue* outside late night supermarkets like most of the ex-cons he knew.

He called Eloise immediately and even though she was in her office and couldn't really react, he swore he could hear the delighted triumph in her voice. 'We'll plan this all out later,' she hissed down the phone.

Planning, scheming, devising, taking total control, he'd learned, were Eloise's favourite pastimes in the whole world. The woman was utterly wasted at the *Post*, he reckoned, she should have been head of the CIA – she'd have the place running effortlessly smoothly with one hand tied behind her back.

True to her word, she popped into the flat late that night, on her way home.

'Okay, we've just got one problem,' she told him decisively, whamming her briefcase down on the tiny coffee table, whipping off her too-tight jacket and gratefully taking the glass of white wine Jake offered her.

'You've only just got in the door! Would you ever relax and tell me a bit about your day first?'

'Can't Jake. This is too important for us . . . I mean, for you. Have you any idea the amount of prepping we're going to have to do to get you ready in time? And while we're on the subject, there's something that's been worrying me . . .'

'You mean what to say if they ask what I've been doing for the past two years?'

'No, no that's not it,' she interrupted. 'At least, that's not *just* it.'

They'd been over and over the subject of how best to gloss over his past and Eloise had stressed time and again that any potential employer was bound to run background checks, even for a part-time job. So with that in mind, she advised Jake he'd no choice but to openly and honestly tell them the whole truth and nothing but. It was a huge gamble and they both knew it, but somehow she believed in him and genuinely hoped that his personality and passion for the job would sway things his way. Not to mention the fact that his score on his final TEFL exam was one of the highest in the country. Besides, from sitting on the far side of an interviewer's desk, she claimed to know from bitter experience that an employer was always far more concerned about the potential future of the candidate sitting down in front of them, and considerably less about their past.

'What's up then?'

'There's no easy way to say this, and you're not to take offence, but – it's your appearance.'

'What about it?'

'Ehhhh . . . Jake, to date all I've ever seen you in is either

181

a black or a blue T-shirt and the same pair of jeans day in day out. Two T-shirts does not a well-dressed interviewee make. Not good enough. There's an awful lot riding on this, so you've got to give yourself the best shot possible.'

'Ahh Christ, don't say what I think you're going to say.'

'You need a suit. You need a whole new wardrobe, in fact.'

'No way.'

'Yes way.'

'Suits are for bankers, developers who've gone bust and gay magicians on TV. The one and only time I was ever in a suit in my whole life, I was up in front of a judge in Circuit Court number six.'

'Jake, I interview people all the time and first impressions count. You have to trust me.'

The following Saturday, Eloise called him to say that as it was a relatively quiet news day, she could grab a short window away from the office to take him shopping.

'What, don't you trust me?' he'd teased her down the phone. 'Afraid I'll come home with stonewash denims and a shiny shirt with *Megadeth* written on it?'

He swore he could hear the smile in her voice.

'Just meet me at the bottom of Grafton St. at half one.'

'Fine, there's a tattoo parlour close to there, you can help me pick out a new one that says, "done time and proud".'

'Please tell me you're messing . . .'

'You have to ask?'

'Just stop acting the eejit and don't be late!'

Strange, he thought, being made over by someone with actual taste when it came to labels he'd never heard of and designers he'd only been vaguely aware of from TV shows, where stick-thin models cavorted down Parisian runways wearing what looked like their knickers and not much else. The lads sometimes watched that stuff inside so they could salivate over the models, but more often than not, they'd take one look at the get-ups on them and crease themselves laughing.

And now here was Eloise taking him into shops he'd never set foot in before in his life, making him try on clothes that looked poncey and totally gak on the hanger, but when he put them on, somehow miraculously worked.

She insisted on his stepping out of the changing rooms so she could give him the once over after he'd tried anything on. When he stepped out in an elegant pair of charcoal-grey trousers teamed with a pale blue shirt the exact same colour as his eyes, he could read the approval on her face.

'You're sure I don't look like a gay hairdresser?' he asked uncertainly, hating the way the male sales assistants were eyeing him up. 'I feel like a gay hairdresser.'

'Definitely not. You look,' she paused, eyeing him up and down from head to toe, thought for a second, then added proudly, 'you look . . . like a teacher.'

Jake nearly passed out when they got to the till and he discovered that he'd just spent close to three hundred Euro. His worst nightmare. Palms sweating, he realised that ate into most of the little stash of cash he had to tide him over till he found work. And so, mortified, he stammered at the sales guy in the upmarket boutique that he'd made a mistake and would have to put something back.

But just as the sales guy was looking snottily down his bony nose at him, dismissing him for the time-waster he was, Eloise calmly slid up beside the till and smoothly handed over her own credit card.

'No,' Jake hissed firmly at her under his breath, purple in the face at this and mortified beyond belief. 'No way. Not a chance. I'll shop in Penneys or Dunne's rather than let you fork out for this. This is *not* happening.'

'I insist,' she said cool as a breeze. 'Besides, it's only a loan. These clothes are an investment in your future. Trust me, when you get the job, you can pay me back out of your first month's salary. Deal?'

It wasn't one bit okay with him, as it happened. He felt deeply uncomfortable and had to fight the urge to smack the sales assistant right square in his patronising gob when he caught him smirking snidely, but on the condition that it was to be a loan and nothing more, he eventually swallowed his pride and gave in. Besides, he'd pay her back, even if he never got the job and ended up driving taxis for the rest of this life. If it was the last thing he did, he'd pay her back every shagging penny.

But if he'd thought Eloise was finished with him there, he'd another thing coming. Next stop was the men's barber shop in Brown Thomas, and he nearly baulked like a kid when he saw how intimidatingly posh it was. Designed to terrify. Like a gentlemen's club with copies of the *Financial Times* dotted around the place, where all the sofas were green leather and where even the cushions had cushions. The type of place Supreme Court judges would meet to have a shave and pause to brag about how much their individual wine collections were worth. For a split second, he had a mental image of himself sitting in a swivel chair while the same judge he might have appeared in front of sat down beside him, peered out over the top of his *Irish Times* and said, 'Excuse me young man, your face is familiar, haven't I seen you somewhere before?'

'I'm out of here,' he muttered, turning on his heel.

But Eloise was having none of it. 'You'll thank me in the long run,' she whispered to him, then swooped in like she owned the place and made an on-the-spot appointment for him to have a haircut and then a shave, in that order.

'But I know a bloke on Liffey St. who'll cut hair for a fiver,' Jake protested, 'and for feck's sake, I'm able to shave myself, thanks all the same.'

He'd even made it back out as far as halfway to the door, but then he felt her ice-cool grip on his arm.

'First impressions count,' she told him firmly. 'And when you walk into that interview, I want their first impression of you to be that you're groomed, elegant, articulate and ready for the job. I've done my fair share of hiring in my time and trust me, I know what I'm on about.'

So, against his better judgement, he went along with it, while Eloise waited for him, tapping away at her mobile, firing off emails and having low, hissy conversations down the phone with someone called Marc, something about a review in that weekend's culture section. God only knew what the poor guy had written, but from what Jake could gather, Eloise was far from impressed.

'Absolutely not, it has to be rewritten and that's all there is to it,' he could hear her whispering urgently, phone clamped to her ear. Then he found himself smiling when she added, 'because a review that pretentiously bollocky is exactly the kind of thing that puts people off going to the theatre. And another thing, about your TV review of the Jane Austen drama series, it's way too harsh. What, may I ask, is wrong with a good, corsety, bonnety drama anyway? Rewritten and on my desk by four p.m., thanks.'

The barber caught Jake's eye and gave him a

conspiratorial wink that seemed to say, 'Glad I'm not on the receiving end of that call, mate.'

Half an hour later, and he was done and dusted, ready to see the final result. And Jake, who only ever looked in a mirror about once every six months, barely recognised himself by the time the barber was finished with him. He was, no other word for it, transformed. His longish fair hair was now neater, tighter, his skin looked shiny and glowing and healthy, the scruffiness was gone, the just-fell-out-of-bed- unkemptness vanished. In short, he looked, as his mam would have said, *cleaner.*

'Good work,' Eloise said to the barber approvingly as Jake fixed up, making sure to include a decent tip, as he figured you were expected to do in posh places like this.

'Better service than you get from the prison barber, I'll say that much,' he hissed to Eloise as they left. 'The last haircut I had was a number one.'

'A what?'

'Shaved head. Though some of the lads get corn circles cut in as well. All the rage inside. Prison chic, dontcha know.'

'Shhh, enough of that. All in the past and time to move on.'

She had to get back to the office, so he walked with her for company. Well, you never really walked with someone like Eloise, he'd learned, she power marched everywhere and you just kept pace as best you could. Even the way she walked was a battle. Jeez, didn't this one ever slow down? For anyone? Ever?

'What's your rush?' he asked her as she strode down College Green, like Apache Indians from an old black-and-white Western were chasing after her. 'It's Saturday. It's a gorgeous sunny day. It's lunchtime and for God's sake, you haven't even eaten.'

'Oh Jake, if you only knew how much I have to do this afternoon . . .' she panted back at him, expertly weaving her way round the shoppers laden down with bags who were blocking her path, delaying her.

'Ah get over yourself, I'm not listening to you any more,' he said, firmly gripping her by the arm and steering her into the Lemon Tree coffee shop on Dawson St., almost lifting her off her feet.

'No, would you stop it please? I told you, I don't have time for this,' she protested, but he'd learned by now that if you just firmly ignored her, she'd eventually give up.

'I can eat back at the office, you know.'

'Yeah right, eat what? By the look of you, I'd say you live off a couple of celery sticks and coffee. Now either you can shut up and eat, or else I can ram it down your bony throat, the choice is yours.'

'Okay, okay,' she sighed.

So Jake ordered her a large egg, cheese and bacon crêpe with two coffees to go, paid up, then handed hers over to her so she could at least eat walking down the street on her way back to work.

'Out of curiosity, do you ever take time off, ever?' he asked her as they headed towards the *Post* offices on Tara St.

'I mean, just look at you. It's the weekend. Normal people all over the world are relaxing and recharging their batteries, and here you are, racing back to the office so you can stay on schedule. On a Saturday. Jeez, what do you want for your next birthday anyway Eloise? A nervous breakdown?'

She was munching hungrily into her crêpe and had allowed her pace to slow down to a gentler stroll, he was pleased to see.

'Would take time off I could, but I can't,' she said, mouth

187

full. 'Believe me, you've no idea the pressure I'm under. Even though it's a Saturday, we still go to print tonight . . .'

'I know, I know, I've heard it all before, the *Post* holds up the sky and you're single-handedly holding up the *Post*, and the whole world will crumble if you work anything less than an eighteen- hour day. All I'm saying is that sometimes it's okay to stop and smell the roses for a bit. Graveyards are full of people just like you, who were indispensable to their jobs, you know. I'm only saying.'

It was almost painful to hear the deep, long-drawn-out sigh she gave.

'I hear you,' she nodded. 'But I keep telling myself that one day I'll have time to do all the things I want. One day.'

'Like what?'

'I couldn't say.'

'Yes you bloody well could. Go on, tell me. A day in the dream life of Eloise Elliot.'

'Well . . . I dunno . . . In my dream life, I'd like to actually be able to sleep for starters. And to eat actual meals. And to go a whole day without once using my mobile. And to read a book right the whole way through. And drink a glass of wine in the afternoons if I was in the humour. And go to the movies midweek because I feel like it. And . . . take an actual holiday to somewhere like EuroDisney. Where I could take my lit . . .'

She stopped herself from finishing that sentence, he noticed. Odd. He picked up on it, but said nothing.

'What I mean to say is,' she corrected herself, 'I feel I'm working this hard now because in a funny way, I'm storing up time that I can enjoy later on, down the line. Does that make any sense?'

He took a giant glug of his coffee and nodded.

'Does to me. I know all about storing up time alright.'

She smiled up at him. 'To be honest with you,' she added, 'I feel like I've spent the past couple of years just waiting on the storm to pass. But one day it will. Won't it?'

'Life isn't about waiting on the storm to pass. It's about learning to dance in the rain.'

They chatted easily and walked on as far as the *Post* offices on Tara St., when suddenly . . .

'Eloise? That really you? I thought I was seeing things.'

It was Ruth O'Connell, the *Post's* Northern editor, wiry and alert as ever, looking curiously at Jake, then at Eloise, then back to Jake, just waiting to be introduced.

'Ehh, oh, sorry,' said Eloise, mouth full of cheese crêpe, suddenly flushing like a wino in an off-licence. 'Emm . . . Ruth, meet Jake, Jake, Ruth. Well I'd better get going, busy afternoon. You heading back in Ruth?'

'Jake, was it?' said Ruth, taking everything about him in with beady-eyed curiosity, missing absolutely nothing.

'That's right,' he nodded amiably, going to shake hands. 'Friend of Eloise?'

A trick question. Ruth knew Eloise didn't have any friends, just people who didn't despise her.

'Yes,' Jake answered evenly, looking down at her. 'Yes I am, as a matter of fact.'

Eloise, for no reason, flushed even more at this. 'Okay, so that's that then,' she said in a panicky voice, several notes higher than usual. 'Come on Ruth, let's get going . . .'

'So, how exactly do you two know each other?' Ruth asked Jake in her deadpan Norn Iron accent, in absolutely no rush to go anywhere.

Eloise semaphored a flustered look across to Jake, but there was no need. He was expert at reading people, sensed

189

Eloise's discomfort and wasn't about to give anything away or let her down in public.

An awkward pause while they all stood around the busy street corner, waiting to see who'd blink first.

'Perfectly simple question,' said Ruth, breaking the now awkward silence, bony arms folded, giving Jake her best head-girl glare. 'I'm just curious to know where you two met, that's all.'

'Err, well . . . you see,' Eloise began to stammer, for once not quick enough on her feet to think up a fast answer. 'The thing is . . . I met Jake through . . . emm . . . '

'Very simple as a matter of fact,' said Jake smoothly taking over from her. 'I'm renting an apartment belonging to Eloise's sister.'

With that, she shot him a *thank you* look of deepest gratitude.

'I see,' Ruth nodded, sounding unconvinced. 'And how long have you known . . . ?'

'You know, much as I'd love to stay here and natter for the rest of the afternoon,' Eloise interrupted her briskly, sounding a bit more like herself now, 'we've got a news conference in exactly ten minutes Ruth. You haven't forgotten? Come on, better get going.'

'Oh, right then,' said Ruth, a bit wrongfooted.

'Nice to meet you,' Jake nodded casually at her.

'We'll be seeing lots more of you in future, I'm sure,' was Ruth's parting shot, accompanied by one last incredulous glance back at him.

He grinned his wide, happy grin, kissed Eloise lightly on the cheek, told her that he'd chat to her soon, and like that, was gone.

* * *

190

Eloise insisted on rehearsing, prepping and grooming him over and over again for the interview like they were training him for an Olympic hundred metres, and not just a half-hour chat in a language school on Camden St. Ever meticulous, the night before the interview she even called round to Jake's flat late one night after work, so she could role play the part of the interviewer and really put him through his paces this last and final time.

'Right then, so tell me what first made you want to teach English as a foreign language?' she asked, sitting opposite Jake at the tiny kitchen table, legs crossed, hands neatly on her lap, interrogation style.

'Funny you asked me that,' he replied lazily, legs stretched out, yawning. He'd been studying for his looming exams since early morning, his head was melted and frankly the last thing he was in the mood for was yet another game of interview charades with Eloise.

Didn't she ever give up? Or even, God forbid, clock off early from work? Ever?

'Come on Jake, answer me.'

'Ah well you see, I was doing a two-year stretch in Wheatfield and figured that doing a TEFL course would be a far jammier way of passing the time than working in the prison laundry, washing manky, cack-stained underpants.'

In one lightning, quick gesture, Eloise immediately whipped her briefcase up off the floor and stood up to go.

'If you're not going to take this seriously, then neither am I,' she all but snapped. 'Are you aware that interview coaches out there charge up to two hundred and fifty euro an hour for this? And here I am, wrecked after yet another endless day and you seem to think I'm doing all of this for the good of my health? Honest to God, sometimes I wonder why I even bother putting myself through all this for you, if you're not even prepared to make an effort . . .'

'Sit down for feck's sake, will you relax?' he said, arms folded, blue eyes teasing her. 'I was only messing. Come on, you've had a long day, can't we just chat normally like people do, instead of working the whole shagging time?'

'Now that's another thing I've been meaning to say to you. Your language. Talk like that in the interview and you'll be out the door so fast . . .'

'Eloise, will you calm down? You think I don't know all that? You think I'm going to go in there and tell them I'm looking forward to teaching Spanish students how to say feck off and call each other gobshites, so they can really blend in on the streets of Dublin? Just chill out for two seconds, will you? Everything's going to be fine. I haven't come this far to let you down now. Now come on, it's half ten at night,' he continued smoothly. 'You've had a killer of a day by the look of you and so have I. Just have a glass of wine and relax. The interview will be fine; sure I'm prepared upside down, inside out and sideways. I'll end up grilling the interviewer and not the other way around, you have me so primed for it.'

'Need I remind you the interview is *tomorrow morning*,' she answered curtly in her best don't-even-think-about-contradicting-me tone of voice. 'After that, you can relax and chat all you like, but don't think you're getting off any hooks for tonight.'

Jake did a fake Nazi salute at her and just shrugged when she glared furiously back at him. By now he'd learned that whenever she got up on her high horse like this, the best thing you could do was tease her out of it. Laughing at her

192

seemed to make her see how loony she was acting, far more so than taking up the cudgels with her.

'Jake,' she turned to ask him wearily, red behind the eyes by now. 'Have you any idea what it's like out there at the job-hunting coalface? I know you've been out of circulation for the past two years, but let me tell you something. We're in the throes of the worst economic slump since the Great Depression, there are virtually NO JOBS and you're going in there tomorrow up against the crème de la crème; candidates with diplomas and MBSs and masters degrees hanging out of their earlobes. And another thing, none of them will have, let's just say, the inkblot on their past that you're dealing with. So you take this seriously or else I'm out of here, I'm not coming back and you can go back to driving taxis, or working in an all-night garage, or wherever your ambition takes you. And you can spend your spare time daydreaming about getting a degree and having a better life, but that's all it'll ever amount to. Tuppenny-ha'penny daydreaming. And by the way, don't think my walking out of here is an idle threat on my part either, because, I don't make idle threats. My head is splitting and I no more want to run through interview questions than you do, but you're going to and so am I.'

'Okay, okay, you've made your point,' he said softly, arms in an 'I surrender' gesture. 'Right then, I'll run through the whole shagging thing if that'll make you happy, yet again . . .'

'What did I tell you about your LANGUAGE!'

'For the thousandth time, if you'll just have a glass of wine and chill out a bit first,' he brokered gently.

By now Jake understood this driven side of her character, the ruthless, stop-at-nothing side. He knew just where she

193

was coming from and could see that she only had his own best interests at heart. It still didn't mean he liked it particularly, but at least she did what he asked and sat back down again with an exasperated sigh. He took that as his cue to go to the fridge and pour her out a glass of that fancy white wine she drank.

'Out of curiosity,' he asked, passing the glass over to her and watching her take a big, nerve-calming gulp, 'do you ever, just once, switch off?'

'What are you talking about?' she asked him, genuinely puzzled by the question.

'The fact that it's late at night, you've probably been at your desk since first light and yet here you are, still on the go, go, go, still not clocked off for the night. We've already worked so hard to get me ready for tomorrow but, here's the thing. From here on in you just need to trust me. It's okay to surrender control every now and then Eloise. Now can't you for once just unwind for five minutes and tell me about your day?'

She gave him a tiny half-smile. But then, apart from Helen, who was usually sound asleep by the time she crawled in late from work, Jake was the only person who ever asked her about how she was feeling and coping and about the ten thousand minor skirmishes that made up a typical day at the *Post*. These days he was fast becoming the one person she could really open up to, someone who never judged her or automatically expected her to be on top of things, always. He just listened and let her talk her problems away.

'You really sure you want to hear this?' She sighed deeply.

'Yes,' he said looking at her thoughtfully and sitting down opposite her, 'as a matter of fact I do.'

'Oh God,' she sighed almost painfully, slumping forward

and covering her head with her long, thin, white fingers. 'Where do I start?'

At it turned out in retrospect, there was absolutely no need whatsoever for her to stress and fret about Jake's big interview. Because the interview hadn't just gone well – it had gone swimmingly. Far, far better than he himself ever would have thought. His past hadn't come up at all, but taking Eloise's advice, he'd raised the subject himself and told his interviewer everything, honestly and openly. Made it clear that he'd made one stupid mistake and paid the highest price imaginable, but now the past was firmly behind him and he wanted nothing more than a chance at a better life. He produced a wad of glowing references; everyone from Eloise herself to the prison governor, backing up exactly what he'd said. He talked about his commitment and passion for learning, and how he wanted nothing more than to be able to pass that on.

And somehow, a miracle happened, and his interviewer had seen what everyone else so clearly could; potential. The guy had taken a chance on him, purely on a trial basis of course, but that was all Jake asked for; one single shot.

No sooner was he back out on the street again, still reeling from how well it had all gone, than he fished out his phone to call Eloise.

'Well?' she hissed, voice low.

'Disaster,' he said, teasing her a bit.

'What happened?'

'They quizzed me inside out and upside down about the glaring gap on my CV for the past two years . . .'

'WHAT?'

'You should have been there, these guys were like worse

than anything you'd see on *C.S.I.* Real interrogative pros, shone a light in my eyes and everything. Kept repeating key phrases over and over, like all those field operatives are trained to do . . .'

'Jake, if you're messing with me . . .'

'Tell us your secret, they kept saying . . .'

'If this is your idea of a joke . . .'

'. . . You're an ex-con, aren't you? So what were you in for anyway? Mugging little old ladies? Armed robbery? Burglary? Arson? Worse?'

'Jake . . .'

'. . . So I cracked under questioning, confessed all, and, long story short, they called security, flung me out of there, tore up my TEFL cert and told me if I ever showed my face in any language school ever again, they'd make sure I'd get put away for another two years.'

'JAKE!' she hissed, really getting alarmed now. 'Please tell me you're kidding?'

'Course I am, you eejit. It went so well that they guy interviewing me asked me if I'd mind hanging on a bit so I could meet the school principal, who took one look at my grades, told me they were a bit short staffed for the summer months and basically asked me when I could start. Just a few hours a week at first, is all they could promise me, but am I complaining? Are you kidding me?'

Without even knowing she was doing it, Eloise let out a whoop of pure joy, causing Rachel, who'd been having a discreet earwig nearby, to nearly spill an Americano all over her keyboard.

'So I just have one question for you, Missy,' Jake asked down the phone.

'What?'

'Where do you want me to take you tonight to celebrate?'

Jake had bought her a bouquet of flowers for starters, to really start the night off in style. Lilies. For some reason, he'd remember her saying something about loving lilies and that single word – lily – had lodged in his mind. So earlier, he'd gone to a local florist and gone the whole hog, splashing out on the biggest bunch they had in the shop. And when he presented them to her, she actually blushed, like it had been years since anyone had spontaneously bought her flowers. Made her look so pretty and young and vulnerable, he thought, suddenly getting an impulse to hug her, but afraid she'd misinterpret it.

After all, ostensibly, the only reason she was even in his life in the first place was because of the feature piece she'd claimed she was about to run in the *Post*. Jake had tried raising it with her a few times lately, but all she'd do would be to swat his concerns away, saying that, for the moment at least, his job interview should be their sole focus. The feature, she'd crisply told him, could be shelved until he'd become an upstanding, tax-paying member of the community again. Will even make for better reading, she'd added. Because after all, who didn't love a happy ending?

'Oh . . . They're absolutely beautiful,' Eloise said, sounding utterly shocked as she played with the ribbon tied around the cellophane-wrapped bouquet and burying her face deep into the lilies, breathing in their gorgeous sweet smell.

'You deserve them. You should be given flowers more often. And while we're on the subject, you should be chloroformed, physically dragged out of that shagging office and taken out to dinner more often.'

'Me? Ha! That's a laugh.'

'Why not?'

'Oh, let's not even go there.'

'I don't get the kind of fellas you must hang around with, I really don't,' he said, shaking his head as he pulled on his jacket and got ready to leave his flat.

'You're a lovely, gorgeous person, intelligent and successful too. Any guy should be proud to have you on his arm, only delighted to take you out on a Friday night.'

She looked up at him, deeply touched.

'I mean that, by the way,' he said, simply.

'I know you do,' she said, an inconvenient lump suddenly appearing in her throat. 'And thank you. After the day I had, I needed . . . Well, let's just say I needed a bit of kindness.'

'So come on then, what are we waiting for? I said I'd take you out to spoil you rotten tonight and that's exactly what I'm going to do.'

He knew exactly where too. He'd walked past Raoul's, a gorgeous local French restaurant, nearly every day for the past few weeks and made an inner vow to himself; if he got the job, he'd treat Eloise to a celebration dinner there as a way of thanking her.

As usual, he could practically see the tension beginning to roll off Eloise after a few gulpfuls of wine. She'd begun to open up to him more and more, he'd noticed, every time they talked now. Told him more about Seth Coleman and his latest shenanigans and how he was insidiously going out of his way to get rid of her once and for all.

But there was something else too, something she'd skirted around before but never really got to the marrow of. Eloise knew only too well, she confided in him, how unpopular she was in work and all the horrible nicknames her colleagues had given her behind her back. No one really liked her and they never had. Not even the few, the very few who, even if she didn't count them as actual friends, were at least allies. If it came to a heave against her in favour of Seth, she stressed, and he swore he could hear the agony in her voice as she articulated the terrifying thought out loud; then who in their right minds would possibly choose her?

'But you've been there for years,' he counselled gently. 'Why is it that you feel so friendless? Tell me, because I honestly don't get it. The Eloise I know is nothing like the woman you describe.'

She took another sip of wine and gazed distractedly down at her napkin.

'Been like that all my whole life,' she eventually confessed and her honesty touched him more than he could say.

'Seriously?'

'Not a word of a lie. So you can't really miss what you never had, can you?' she added, musing aloud. 'I'll tell you this though, if I had my time over, I'd do things differently. Maybe not try to drive everyone around me in the office as hard as I do, maybe be a bit more human around co-workers, a little more lenient and understanding. Because it's bloody hard going in there day after day, trying to keep the show on the road and in return just being practically hate-vibed out of it, by people whose jobs I'm only trying to protect.'

'How do you mean?' he asked, listening intently.

Another deep-soul searching sigh from her.

'Well . . . it's like this. If people need a bit of time off, I tend to just jump down their throats and remind them that if they can't hack the job, there's scores behind them who could and who are only gagging to be given the chance. My catchphrase in work, is that I never ask anyone to do anything I'm not doing myself. And it's true, I don't. But instead of respecting me for driving myself and all around me so hard, they all seem to hate and despise me for it. No matter what I do. But if I don't, we won't reach our targets, and then even more people's jobs are on the line. So there you go; catch twenty-two. Damned if I do and damned if I don't. No matter what I do, they'll still all hate me.'

She didn't even tell him the worst of it; that was something to be kept locked deep into a secret file marked 'humiliation', never to be discussed. The dozens of petty slights she suffered on a daily basis; the way other women instantly stopped talking and left the room whenever she went into the ladies, how on the rare occasions when she would go into the staff canteen, anyone around her would instantly shuffle guiltily back to their desks, like she even begrudged them meal breaks. Hearing about all the birthday parties and weddings and nights out that she was never asked along to.

Not that she'd even have had the time to go, but sometimes she thought it would just be nice to be asked, that was all.

'Never too late to change,' he told her softly, instinctively reaching across the table to squeeze her hand. It felt right though and she didn't pull away.

'Never too late to go a bit easier on everyone around you, maybe even cut them a bit of slack every now and then,' he added. 'So maybe try being a bit more tolerant and social with people, give them the time of day a bit more. Go on, give it a chance,' he suggested, looking at her keenly. 'You might well be astonished at the turnaround. Remember the people around you are the greatest asset you have.'

He didn't think it appropriate to bring it up, but he remembered all too clearly overhearing the brusque, almost dismissive way she'd spoken to her culture editor on the phone that day while he was at the barber's a while back and knew how very little it would take on her part to tone it down a notch. Be less attritional, not be quite so demanding on all around her.

And she could do it, he knew she could. There was a soft, caring heart in there, just waiting to get out; he could see it, even if no one else could. She nodded gratefully as their starter arrived and Jake sensed she wanted to get off the subject, so, ever the gentleman, he obliged.

'Anyway, this isn't a night to talk about work' he reminded her. 'You know what I'd love to hear about instead?'

What?' she smiled.

'I'd love you to tell me all about your family instead.'

And for once, miraculously, she didn't clam up.

'Well, not much to tell you really. I told you my sister's in town at the moment . . .' she broke off though, not saying why, or for how long.

'What does she do?' Jake asked her innocently.

But Eloise neatly evaded the question and instead, started telling him a bit about her mother who lived in Marbella.

'And every time I see her, which isn't nearly often enough, I swear to God, the woman is blonder, more suntanned and even more glam than the time before. Don't get me wrong, life in the sun suits her down to a T, but . . . I just wish I could make more time in my life for her.'

'You must miss her.'

'Course I do.'

'So, then do something about it! Come on, you must have years of stored-up holidays due to you from work, so instead of just wondering about her, take time off and go and see her. Hop on a flight with that sister of yours and just go. You've only the one mammy in this world.'

But all she did was roll her eyes heavenwards.

'Jake,' she drily reminded him, 'need I point out that holidays are for retired people and not for the likes of me?'

'One day you'll change your mind,' he told her firmly. 'One day you'll have all the quality time you want to travel and see people you care about and – perish the thought – actually start to *enjoy* your life for a change.'

She looked wistfully out the window at that, as though miles away, that heart-shaped look she got in her black eyes whenever she was thinking about something, or someone, else.

She was holding something back on him, and something important too; Jake would have staked his life on it.

Another guy, maybe? Someone from her past who'd broken her heart to shards? No, somehow he didn't think so. It just didn't ring true for her. Eloise wasn't the 'crawl under a duvet with a large jar of Nutella and a bottle of Chardonnay to drown your troubles' kind of gal.

So what, he found himself dying to know, was she thinking right now? What was suddenly making her come over all wistful and far-away?

Jake would have been very surprised, if he'd only had the guts to ask. Because as it happened, she was thinking about him. About how long it was since she'd been taken out, wined and dined, treated like a proper lady. All day long, she was surrounded by upper-class college graduates, all from impeccable backgrounds, with degrees and masters hanging out of their earlobes and they were nothing but rude, bitchy, bullying and on several occasions per day, downright vicious behind her back. And yet here she was, sitting across a table from a convicted criminal from the roughest part of the city, a man who never behaved like anything other than a perfect gentleman towards her.

Could he even see how moved she'd been at the beautiful flowers he'd given her? Ridiculously expensive, she knew, and he could ill afford it, but somehow he felt she was worth it. Jake, she thought, taking another sip of wine, was lovely. That was the only word to describe him. Just lovely.

Then her phone rang and of course it was the *Post*. Who else?

'Let it go to voicemail,' he told her sternly. 'For God's sake, just give yourself an hour off to eat and then get back to whoever it is. You're surely allowed have a meal break? Jeez, even in prison we get those.'

She looked up at him, thought for a second as though weighing it up, then gave him a happy grin, clicked her phone off and began to eat hungrily.

PART THREE

ELOISE

Chapter Nine

Good news. Lily, thanks be to God, Allah, Buddha, Santa – anyone up there who listened to me – has ended her obsession with going up to total strangers in parks and on buses and asking them if they're her dad. Course the odd time she'll still crawl into my bed early in the morning for a cuddle and a little chat, then completely out of left field, in her early morning croaky voice she'll ask me, 'have you found my daddy yet, Mama? You'll find him weally soon, won't you?'

And I'll pull her in tight to me, kiss her, tell her that Mama never makes promises she can't keep and faithfully promise that one day she'll get to meet him. One day.

By the way, to great jubilation from every single one of my colleagues at work, I've now shifted our first editorial meeting of the morning to a far more civilised nine a.m. start, mainly so that Lily and I can get to share these precious mornings together. Sod the whole lot of them in work, I figure; I'm making more time for Lily and if they don't like it then as Jake says, they can feck right off. Helen gets to spend the rest of the day with her, but early mornings are mine, all mine. And it happens far, far less often than it used to, but Lily still sometimes stuns me by letting something slip that shows just how clearly the whole dad subject weighs on her little mind.

The other day being a case in point. Lily waddled into my bedroom just before seven, clambered up and snuggled into me, still warm and woozy from sleep and telling me all about a dream she had where she accidentally got locked into Smyths toy store for the night and had the best time of her life, till police came to rescue her the next morning and found her sleeping inside a Wendy house. Then, just as I was drowsily hauling myself out of bed and asking her if she'd like porridge or fresh fruit for brekkie while she was, as usual, demanding Coco Pops, suddenly she looked at me with those wise little eyes and out of nowhere said, 'Mama, how come some kids have two daddies and I don't have any?'

Well, that woke me up. And when I got to the bottom of it, it turned out that a little girl called Daisy she'd befriended in the park has not only a biological dad but now thanks to her mum's remarriage, a stepdad too. So I give Lily my first line of explanation about how all families are different then proudly tell her that yes, I can safely promise that someday we'll find her dad. That she'll get to meet him properly. Well her round blue eyes, eyes so like Jake's it would nearly astonish you, instantly brightened at this as she flashed me that gorgeous, gappy little smile, then happily scrambled down to the kitchen with me for breakfast.

You just wait, my little darling, I thought smugly to myself. You just wait till you see the rare gem that Mama is prepping for you. Because finally, finally, finally now my cunning masterplan is almost in place. Come the fine day, when I eventually think the time is right for Lily and Jake to meet, what'll she find waiting for her? A tall, handsome, fair-haired, well-spoken teacher, with her exact size and shape eyes, same fair, freckly skin, same crinkly, slightly crooked smile. Someone Lily can be proud of and look up to, like all little girls' dads should be.

Like I say though, the 'where's my dad' chats are happening with far less frequency now, mainly, giving credit where it's due, down to Helen and the unbelievable way that she's bonded with Lily ever since she first moved in here, all those weeks ago.

Ah Helen. I feel churlish and mortified beyond belief at myself when I think back to how jealous I felt back then, listening to Lily excitedly rattle off all the fabulous, fun excursions she was having with her 'new best fwiend, Auntie Helen'. Because now, with a hunk of burning humility in my gut, I have to admit, I was horrible to be so envious of her, and owe her nothing but the biggest debt of gratitude all round.

Most astonishing of all to report though, over the past few weeks, Jake and I have even become the unlikeliest of friends. Good friends too. I can tell him things that I can't tell anyone else, that no one else could even possibly begin to understand. And he listens patiently and can always find something in whatever I'm stressing or fretting about to make me laugh at.

I know; *me. Laugh.* Actually throw my head back and hold my sides till the giggles pass. Before I met him, I hadn't had a decent belly laugh in so long, I'd nearly forgotten what my teeth looked like.

Day after day, night after night, he'll patiently give me wise and measured advice that I may not like hearing at the time, but which always and inevitably turns out to be the right course of action to take. And he'll say absolutely nothing while I rant on and let off steam about whatever office politics happen to be in play, then calmly reduce all my stresses and worries to their proper proportions. A real friend, in other words.

That rare and precious jewel that I've never had before.

Not for the first time, another totally disconnected thought strikes me. Although I go around inwardly congratulating myself on changing him for the better, could it in fact possibly be the other way around? It is him that's having even more of an effect on me? Because I see how he is around people and slowly, I'm learning from him. I see how friendly and unfailingly polite he is to everyone that comes into his orbit, from waiters in restaurants to the guy who sells *The Big Issue* on the corner of the street. How warm and interested he is; the way he always has a few words for everyone. And bit by bit, I'm starting to do the same.

Another thing too; can't quite put my finger on it, but it's like ever since I met him, I'm a far more relaxed person to be around now. Not that I'm sure anyone's even noticed, but I'm eating better, sleeping better, getting far fewer ulcer cramps (my own personal barometric stress warning). I'm just more contented, more grateful for everything I have. Laughter lines are starting to appear on my face in the most unexpected places.

In the past few weeks, after the longest time, I've somehow found my smile again.

'So tell me this Eloise,' Helen asks me, 'what's your long-term plan here? With Jake, I mean.'

It's still relatively early but I've just managed to crawl home from a meeting with the night editor, so Helen and I can have a badly needed glass of wine and a catch-up chat about our respective days. Another new habit and one I'm really starting to enjoy.

Tonight though, she sounds a bit distant and stressed, which is unlike her. Throughout all this, she's been a staunch supporter of the leg-up in life that I've been giving Jake, on the principle that what's good for Lily is good for us all. So I grab the bull by the horns.

'Helen, I hope you don't mind my asking, but what's all this about? Is something bothering you? I mean, I don't get it. Why are you asking me about long-term plans all of a sudden?'

'Hmmm?' she says distractedly, focused on an episode of *Come Dine with Me* on TV.

'Are you listening?'

'What? Oh, emm, yeah, I mean no, it's nothing. I was just a bit . . . worried about where this is all heading, that's all.'

'Come on hon, if there's something you want to say to me, then I really wish you'd just come straight out with it. Besides, what exactly is there to worry about here? Haven't I for once in my life done someone a decent turn?'

One of the many, ahem, criticisms frequently levelled at my head in work is that not only do I never put myself out for anyone else, but that I've never done one single, disinterested nice thing for another human being ever in my life. And now, sod the lot of them, I have. So what in the name of God could be bothering Helen now?

I even reach out to grab the remote control and turn the TV onto mute, so there's no avoiding my question.

'Yes, yeah,' she nods, 'of course you have, it really sounds like you've worked wonders on the guy. I wasn't for a second suggesting otherwise.'

'So, what's up then?'

'Well,' she goes on, swirling her wine round the bottom of the glass, 'it's just that . . .'

'Just that *what*? Helen, please tell me. Because if I've done something I shouldn't, I'd be very curious to know exactly what it is.'

'No, no it's not that you've done anything wrong, it's just, well, you're such a great one for plans and more plans and plans within plans . . .'

'And?'

'. . . And you seem to be really pally with him now.'

'Oh come on, now what's so awful about that? It's . . . I can't describe it, but it's just comforting to have an actual friend. A buddy. Particularly a tough male one who makes me laugh whenever he threatens to sort out Seth Coleman,' I smile. 'Mainly because I know he's not messing. He really would if I asked.'

'No, no, that wasn't what I meant at all,' she muses, totally lost in thought and staring at the stressed hostess on *Come Dine with Me* getting her dinner guests steadily drunker and drunker to compensate for a curry that looks not unlike pig slop. Prison food, as Jake would say.

'What, then? Come on, you have to tell me.'

'Just thinking ahead really, I suppose,' Helen eventually says, not able to look me in the eye.

'Ahead to when exactly?' I say, exasperated now.

'Look,' she eventually says. 'I know I've never even met Jake . . .'

'We've already been over this, hon. You know it's impossible. For starters, who'd take care of Lily if I was to introduce the two of you?'

'I know, I know all this,' she says, stretching out to the

212

bottle of Pinot on the coffee table in front of her and generously topping up both our glasses.

'But the fact is, I can't stop myself from thinking ahead to whenever you decide the time is right for him and Lily to meet up. In a heartbeat, the minute she meets him is the minute Jake realises you've been holding back on him all that time. You don't think he'll wonder why you kept the fact that you had a daughter from him? A daughter that's his? Because how exactly do you think that'll make him feel? And how exactly do you suggest explaining that one away? Or is your plan right now to just disappear out of his life as quickly as you came into it, leave him to his own devices and just hope and pray that he's still on the right track, by the time Lily is old enough to track him down for herself? Because it seems to me that your work with him is done. You've woven your magic and trans-formed an ex-con into an upstanding middle-class teacher, who you probably make go around with a tweed jacket and matching leather elbow patches to prove it and who, knowing you, you'll have driving round in some teachery style Fiat Punto in no time . . .'

'I do not . . . !'

Though come to think of it, not a bad idea.

'Eloise, all I'm saying is this. You're dealing with a human being here, not another project that you've successfully managed. Yes, you and he are now the unlikeliest of friends and that's terrific, if it's what you want. You really like him; I sometimes think an awful lot more than you even know. But friends don't lie to each other or keep things from each other. And you're keeping so much from him, it makes my head spin. So just be honest with him. Because sooner or later, the day will come when he'll find out exactly how much you were holding back. And what I'd very much like to know is this; what'll your master plan be then?'

And as she's chatting, suddenly out of nowhere, a new and disconnected worry hits me square in the face. I sit bolt upright in the chair and just stare straight ahead, miles away.

'What is it?' Helen asks, sensing the shift in mood.

'Just thought of something else. Oh shit, I can't believe it never struck me before this.'

'Come on, spit it out.'

'Well . . . All along I've blithely assumed that I'd one day introduce Lily to Jake and that he'd automatically love and adore her the way everyone loves and adores her and would immediately want to be a part of her life. But supposing I'm wrong? Suppose I've read the whole thing arseways?'

'How do you mean?'

'There's something that neither of us has considered. Just say I come clean to Jake as you suggest and he baulks at the whole idea and wants absolutely nothing to do with Lily? Which, let's face it, the guy would be perfectly entitled to do. Not to mention legally entitled; you should have seen the amount of paperwork at the Reilly Institute they showed me, all of which has to be signed by prospective donors, clearly stating that they'll not pursue any rights of access to any offspring. The question is . . . What do I tell Lily then? That I *know* who her dad is, but that he wants absolutely nothing to do with her?'

She doesn't answer me. And all I can do is keep staring distractedly into space, mulling the whole thing over.

A long, long pause worthy of a Samuel Beckett play, before Helen eventually breaks the silence.

'You want my advice?' she eventually asks, distractedly swirling her wine round and round the glass.

'Please,' I say, sounding and feeling like a total dullard.

'Plan A, you come clean with him. Now, without delaying it any longer. You do what friends do, and you tell him the truth. It's a bit late in coming, but better late than never. And I mean everything – about why you tracked him down, about Lily, and most of all, why she's the real reason you wanted to give him a bit of a boost up in life. He may not take it well, may be shocked, even annoyed with you for not being straight with him after all this time, but in the long run, at least you'll have got it off your chest and done the right thing. And if he doesn't want to see Lily, then at the very least you've been honest with him and given him the choice.'

'And what's your plan B?' I ask Helen, in a tiny voice that I hardly recognise as my own.

'You're not going to like it.'

'Tell me.'

'Plan B is you cut all ties with him. Starting from now. Stop hanging round together. You've helped him all you can, so now call it a day. Because leaving aside the fact that he may not even choose to be a part of Lily's life, what you're doing is so grossly unfair. You've made friends with someone who at the end of the day, you're effectively leading up the garden path. You're deceiving him. Every bit of time you spend with him, you're more or less lying to him. So just think for a second; how would you like it if someone treated you like that? I know you say it's lovely to have a buddy, but trust me, this is not how friends treat each other. So I don't envy you either of your two options love, but that's the way it is. Come clean with him, or else

215

stop being deceptive. And the only way to do that is to step away from the vehicle.'

Then she looks keenly at me.

'So what's it to be?'

Still silence from me.

'Come on! Not like you to dither.'

I can't articulate this out loud, but, well, cutting ties with Jake just doesn't appeal. Not at all. I'd . . . I'd miss him. He's the only pal I have that I'm not related to and I can't even get my head around what life would be like without him.

'Eloise?'

I lace my fingers through my hair with sheer frustration.

'Okay then, but you won't like it. I honestly don't know what to do, is the answer. All I really want is for everything to stay just as it is. Until I decide what to do and more importantly, when the time is right to do it. Helen, for once in my life I'm happy just the way things are. Can't I for the moment at least, just continue in the bubble I've been living in? Please?'

If I thought that no one in work could tell that a subtle change has come over me lately, it seems I'm very much mistaken. Early the next morning, I'm at my desk, scanning down through the ad pages for next weekend's Culture section. Yet another God-awful task that falls to the senior editor; it seems the T. Rexes on the floor above me in their infinite wisdom have decreed that on top of everything else my job entails, I now have to comb through each and every single one of the ads we place in all editions, to make sure that they're 'fully in keeping with the tone, image, and content of the national paper of record.' Like they thought people would ring up the *Post* classifieds wanting to sell vibrators or second hand dildos. As if I hadn't quite enough apart from this shite-ology to be getting on with, but that's a whole other story.

(Shite-ology. New hyphenated word I've picked up from Jake. Not to self; stop using it in work.)

Anyway, it's barely eleven a.m. when there's a gentle tapping at my office door and in comes Rachel; lovely, cool, calm Rachel who in all the years we've been working together I've never seen act with anything other than Prussian efficiency and unfailing politeness to one and all around her. Rachel that would nearly put a debutante just out of a Swiss finishing school to shame.

And now she's in front of me, sobbing, actually sobbing, hot tears spouting out of her poor, bloodshot red eyes and trembling like a shock victim.

I'm instantly on my feet and over to the girl like a bullet, gently putting my arms around her and almost cradling her, the way I cradle Lily whenever she's heavy with sleep, into the chair opposite my desk.

'What? What is it, tell me what's wrong?' I ask her, rubbing my arms up and down her shoulders, the way you see coastguards doing with swimmers who've narrowly survived drowning.

'It's H-H-Harry,' is all I can get out of her, between gulps of tears. Harry, I remember is her boyfriend, and dad to her little girl, who's only about six months older than Lily.

'Tell me, pet. Tell me everything you can.'

God love the girl, but it takes roughly ten minutes to get the whole story out of her, she's that distraught she's having difficulty putting two sentences together. Meanwhile, I whirl efficiently all around her; getting Kleenex, fishing a bottle of Rescue Remedy from the bowels of my handbag and sticking my head out the door to grab a passing intern, telling her to run across the road to Slattery's Bar and not to come back without a good, decent shot of brandy.

Back to poor Rachel, who seems to be breathing that bit easier now.

'I know I sh-shouldn't even be taking up your time like this, Eloise,' she stammers, '. . . And I'm so sorry to do this to you, but it's just that, that . . .'

'Shhh, it's OK. You can tell me. That what, love?'

'I've . . . I've come to hand in my notice. I'm so sorry to let you down, but I can't go on like this any more. I just can't.'

'Don't be so daft,' I tell her softly, perching down on the ground beside her. 'You're going absolutely nowhere until you tell me exactly what's wrong with you, and with Harry too, for that matter. Tell me. Come on, we've known each other a long time and you can tell me anything. We can talk about your wanting to leave later. First fill me in on whatever's wrong with you, because that to me is far more important.'

My office phone and mobile ring simultaneously and keep ringing and I completely ignore both of them. Just keep looking at her, waiting on her, willing her to talk as soon as she's ready to. She looks at me in dull surprise at my not rushing off to deal with the calls, seemingly astonished at my even giving her the time of day. But something in my eyes must convince her that the tiger-blooded dragon boss of old has softened a bit because, when the shot of brandy arrives and when I've made her knock it back in a single gulp, the colour slowly starts to seep back into her cheeks and finally, she starts to tell me in broken sentences exactly what's wrong.

Harry's broken up with her, it seems. They're together nearly five years, have a gorgeous little girl called Molly, and the bastard announces to her just this morning that, quote, 'I can't do this any more, I need to be with someone more committed to me.' This, by the way, communicated – wait for it – via *email*.

And that's not all, it seems. Even though he was made redundant from his job in an IT firm about six months ago and has basically been financially dependent on poor Rachel ever since, he still had a go at her for putting in such long hours, claiming that not only was Molly growing up barely knowing her own mother but that it put unfair pressure on him being the only caregiver and having to run the whole house by himself.

An accusation that stung me like a bleeding viper, I've had it levelled at my own head so many times in the past, by the long string of nannies who've all walked out on me. Makes me sick to my stomach that any woman should be punished and accused of bad parenting, just for having no choice but to work hard to keep the show on the road.

'BASTARD!' I keep saying over and over again, as my hot little heart pumps into righteous overdrive and a searing fury floods through my veins. 'Cowardly, bloody, bastard!'

'I'm so sorry Eloise,' says Rachel, shakily getting up to leave. 'I shouldn't even be bothering you with all this when you're so busy, but now you can see why I've no choice but to hand in my notice. He's gone, he's really gone, so I'll have to work far fewer hours on account of Molly and that's no good in my job, is it? You need an assistant that's here all the hours that you are. It's not fair on you otherwise. So, so, you see, that's pretty much it for me . . . Isn't it? I'll have to leave. Won't I?'

Another fresh bout of sobs here, sending me flying off to find yet more Kleenex, and shoving them in front of her.

'Rachel,' I say, levelling with her. 'If I ask you a straight question, will you give me a straight answer?'

She nods weakly.

'Is that what you want? Do you really want to walk?'

Then I wryly throw in, 'Am I honestly that much of a troll queen to work for?'

'No! Not at all! And you know I've never listened to what everyone else . . .'

She stops herself just in time.

'Right then. Here's what we're going to do,' I tell her, all businesslike. 'If you want to stay on as my assistant, nothing would make me happier. But as of today we're drawing up a whole new contract for you. For starters, I'm cutting your hours right back . . .'

She looks at me in horror, but I cut her off '. . . with absolutely no corresponding cut in your salary whatsoever. For God's sake Rachel, you're here as long as I am, you're like my right hand and not once in all those long years, to my shame, have I ever given you a single pay rise or promotion. I'll designate one of our interns to deputise for you so you can work a normal forty-hour week. That way, at least you can be home by six every evening to be with Molly.'

She looks up at me, mouth open, the very cartoon picture caption of the word stunned.

'Eloise – really? I mean, are you being serious?'

'Never more serious in my life. And another thing. When's the last time you took a holiday?'

She has to rack her brains to think. And I know well that she works almost as hard as I do; if she manages to get two days together off at Christmas, it's a miracle.

'Emmm' she stammers. 'Well . . .'

I shake my head and scrunch my nose up.

'No, for the life of me, I can't remember the last bit of time you had off either. Right then. Come on, get your coat, I'm putting you in a taxi right now and you're taking the rest of the week off to sort out whatever's going on at home.'

She looks up at me like I've lost it, like I'm the one who's having a meltdown and not her. Like alien clones have taken over the body of Eloise Elliot and I'm some kind of avatar stand-in who looks like her and sounds like her, but who has a totally different personality. A far softer one for starters.

'Eloise,' she says, tears shining in her eyes, 'are you really sure?'

'Not taking no for an answer. Molly needs you now and you need to be with her. Far more important than any shagging job. Just promise me one thing. Don't come back till you feel ready to. Your job will always be here for you and that's a promise.'

By Friday of the same week, lovely, gentlemanly Robbie from Foreign, probably the only other living soul round here who puts in roughly the same kind of hours that I do myself, lets it slip that he's missing his daughter's Confirmation today on account of having to stay at the office to cover the election primaries live from the US.

Takes roughly an hour for this to filter back to me, but as soon as it does, I'm straight over to his desk, seeing him bent double over his computer, like he always is, working, working, working. So I tell him in no uncertain terms that he's taking the rest of the day off so he can make it to the Confirmation and that if his deputy editor can't cover for him, I'll personally do it myself.

221

Swear to God, the thick white shock of hair sticking up on his head turns even whiter at my even suggesting this. Not for the first time, Jake's wise words of advice come back to me: 'Get to know your colleagues and cut them a bit of slack. You might just be astonished at the results.'

And I *am* astonished, not just at how good it feels to treat people well for once, but at the change in atmosphere round the office. Sure we're all still stressed out of our heads and grinding towards the never-ending tsunami of deadlines that are part and parcel of life around here, but now there's a light-heartedness in the air that was never there before, and what's more, I'm pretty certain I'm not the only one who's noticed.

By the following Saturday, I decide, what the hell, I'm cutting everyone else around me loads of slack, why not do at least a bit of the same for myself? Helen calls me to say there's a summer festival happening in Stephen's Green this afternoon, including a teddy bears' picnic for under-fives, and as it's a gorgeous, rare sunny day, she and Lily are going to bring along her favourite teddy, the appropriately named Mr Fluffles. I wish them both a fab afternoon, put the phone down, and instead of feeling the usual lump of envy mixed with guilt that I'm not there and Helen is, an idea strikes me.

Impatiently glancing down at my watch, I see that it's just coming up to one o'clock though. Then, a flash of sudden inspiration. I could do it, I think, nothing easier. Stephen's Green is only a ten-minute walk away from me. What's to stop me from taking an actual lunch break for a change, instead of just shoving half a banana and an oatmeal bar into my mouth at the desk, like I do every other day? I could just surprise the two of them and turn up with a little picnic for the three of us, couldn't I? Where's the harm in that?

Like Jake is always telling me, the mighty pillars of the *Post* are hardly going to crumble down round my ears if I take a tiny break outside of here for a change, now are they? Feck it anyway, I think, Lily's not going to be this age forever and I'm sick to my back teeth of missing out on ever doing anything fun with her. I'm taking an hour for lunch and let the Seth Colemans of this world make of it what they will.

So I do, and it's the single most exhilarating thing I've done in weeks. I race into the Marks & Spencer food hall and stuff a cooler bag full of juices, sandwiches, choccie treats and an ice cream for each of us, then hot foot my way up Grafton St. through the meandering crowds of Saturday afternoon shoppers all the way up to the Green, texting Helen en route to find out exactly where they are. No messing, my heart actually swells to bursting point at the way Lily's little, freckly pink face lights up when she sees the unexpected sight of me making my way through the crowded park to find her. And when she clocks the strawberry Cornetto I hand over too, of course.

It's bliss like I haven't known in decades, just lying on a rug on a hot summery day, watching my grown-up baby make friends and swap teddies with another little girl about her own age. Meanwhile Helen and I loll back on a picnic rug she's brought from home, soaking up the sunshine, listening to a jazz band playing summery songs in the bandstand nearby. We natter on about pretty much anything and everything, but mainly all about her boyfriend Darren and how she hopes and prays her being away is finally starting to put manners on him, all while stuffing our faces with paninis and delicious, gooey strawberry cheesecake. Food, particularly from M&S, Helen always reckons, takes a huge amount of the sting out of being in an LDR. (her abbreviation for long distance relationship.)

There's even a dinky little food market nearby selling local organic produce, honeycombs from Bantry Bay for five euro, that kind of thing, and as soon as we've hungrily guzzled just about everything in sight, Helen says to hang on, that's she's got a great idea. She disappears and next thing, I see her half-stumbling in her too-high wedges across the uneven grass back to where I'm watching over Lily and her new little friend, carrying two glasses of Pimms and a punnet of strawberries for us to share. Like we're a pair of spectators at Wimbledon on a glorious sunny afternoon with not a care in the world and two Centre Court tickets to see Nadal play Federer.

'Ah come on Helen,' I tell her, 'You know I can't drink when I've to go back to work!'

'One won't kill you. It's a Saturday afternoon for God's sake, normal people do actually take a day off, you know.'

'You're beginning to sound like Jake now,' I laugh back at her.

'Shut up and drink.'

And I do as I'm told. Nothing like it, I think, lying back on the rug, kicking my shoes off, feeling more at peace and relaxed than I've done in years. Loving the hot sun on my face, hearing Lily's happy, girlish squeals and giggles as she plays with her new pal, while I lie gossiping and chatting with Helen, like real sisters.

Not for the first time I think with a massive pang of regret about all the years and years I invested as a child, and subsequently as a teenager, in being consumed with jealousy at the thought of my younger, prettier, more popular sister. Pathetic git that I was, I think now, lying back on the rug she's thoughtfully brought from home, sipping on a mouthful of the deliciously bittersweet Pimms and contemplating the clouds above.

What a total waste, I think. How did I even allow us to ever drift so far apart in the first place? We're not exactly a big family; there's just the pair of us and Mum, who I see so rarely it's a disgrace. Something else I'll have to rectify soon. We've no cousins, in-laws, extended family, nothing. Helen and I have only really got each other and yet I was perfectly prepared to let all of that slip quietly away. But the reason why is all too obvious. Because of the three essential downfalls in my character; stubbornness, snobbery and a complete blindness to what was staring me in the face the whole time, that's why.

All those long, lonely years when I could have been so much closer to Helen, had I only got over myself and realised in time what a genuinely fabulous, warm-hearted human being she really is. And okay, so she's not bookish like me, she may not do sudoku in bed to help her get to sleep or be a member of Mensa or have a high-powered, high-octane career with all the trappings and the stress ulcers to prove it.

But at the end of the day, so what? If there's one thing I'm determined to do now, it's to make up for all those decades of being a crap older sister to her. Because what we have in common far outweighs our surface differences and to be brutally honest, there are times when I think deep down that she's actually the smart one, not me. Her quality of life far outweighs mine any day; she's taught me just to enjoy each day and appreciate the wonderful people

225

that are around me. Just like Jake is slowly teaching me to loosen up a bit; that contrary to my whole belief system, I actually am not indispensable and that it's okay to skive off a bit, to take stock every now and then, to stop and smell the roses.

Jake. Funny how even at the most disconnected moments, he seems to have a way of inveigling himself into my subconscious. Helen is still animatedly chatting away in the background about Darren, mentally keeping tally of the number of text messages he's left for her so far today, versus the number she's left for him. Vastly improving, she reckons. Time was when it seemed to be a case of out of sight, out of mind, with her in Dublin and him in Cork, but slowly that seems to be shifting. The novelty of eating dinner in his mammy's night in and night out seems to be wearing off for him and it seems that time and distance is making him realise what a rare gem he let slip away with Helen.

Repeat guests in the tiny B&B he runs have been asking for her, wondering when she's coming back. Staff are saying that all kinds of problems are cropping up now that never did when she was around to smooth things over. Supplies not being ordered, wages not put through the bank in time for payday: the kind of infuriating crap that would drive anyone working there completely nuts.

On and on Helen happily chats, idly wondering if she should call Darren first this evening, or wait till he calls her, then act all surprised to hear from him, in the perpetual game of 'who'll blink first' she seems to play with him. Meanwhile, I fish through my overstuffed bag and produce some of Lily's high-factor sunscreen which I lash onto my face (more than likely rash red by now).

'Lily? Will you come over here pet, so I can put more

cream on you?' I discreetly change the subject, calling over to where the child is having the best laugh with another adorably cute little girl, with a mop of springy jet black jack-in-the-box curls that stretch all the way down to her bum.

'NO Mama! Me and Hannah are playing teddies picnic!! Hannah's my fwiend now!'

Now, normally Lily is a terrible little attention seeker whenever there are grown-ups around: 'Mama look at ME!' every two seconds, that kind of thing, but today she's so utterly absorbed in bonding with her new buddy, she's barely looking twice at me or Helen. And I smile, absolutely loving this newfound independence she's developing.

'Isn't this just the life, Eloise?' Helen eventually says, lying back down and stretching out on the rug again.

'The sun? Oh yeah, just bliss . . .'

'No, you eejit, I mean you and me. Being able to sit here and talk boys. Do you realise this is the first time I think we've ever done this?'

I smile at her and lie back on the rug again, luxuriating in the heat, happy to see Helen if not happy and in love then at least reasonably contented with her lot – for the moment at least – and Lily so elated, playing away with her new little pal.

God's in his Heaven, I think contentedly, all's right with the world.

This warm, blissed-out feeling lasts for approximately another two minutes . . . and that's when I see them.

Relaxed as you like, strolling through the Green, deep in chat.

Jake. But he's not alone. He's with a youngish woman, tall, tall, tall, so tall that when I look at her, all I see is long, suntanned legs all the way up to her earlobes, wearing skinny tight, tight, tight jeans that really only an eighteen-year-old can carry off. Looking like she's on her way to do a promotional gig for a sports car. Long, dark, swishy hair, bracelets that jangle with her as she walks and teeth so pearly white they'd nearly dazzle you. For some reason, just looking at her makes the song *The Girl from Ipanema* randomly drift through my head.

In a second, I'm sitting bolt upright and rooting though my bag for my sunglasses, which thank God are the approximate size of two dinner plates and effectively cover up most of my face.

He hasn't seen me, there's every chance he hasn't seem me, or Helen or . . .

Oh for f*ck's sake . . . Lily . . .

I scan around to check on her, but know right well that if I even try to drag her away from her new pal and all the fun she's having, she'll immediately scream the whole Green down, thereby attracting even more attention to us.

Best to leave her be and hope he just keeps on walking . . . *Please, for the love of God, don't let him look over this way . . .*

But it's too late. There's a fork in the path Jake and The Girl from Ipanema were on and of course, life being what it is, they take the path closest to us.

It's okay, I think, my vision dimming as a dull, sickening panic starts to set in. All is not lost. If I can just keep my head and quietly sneak out of here right now, all may yet be well.

He won't even know Helen or Lily, so as long as he doesn't see me, I may just come out of this and live to tell the tale . . .

Next thing, I'm surreptitiously glancing around for either a tree or some bushes that I can make a run for, like an extra in a Vietnam War movie diving for cover, when Helen suddenly sits bolt upright, seeming to sense the tense, nervous agitation practically pinging off me.

'You OK, love?' she asks me, all concerned.

'Got to go,' I hiss at her brusquely. 'I'll tell you why later. Gotta run, right now. Explain to Lily for me and I'll call you when I'm back at the . . .'

'Eloise? Is that you? Jeez, thought I was seeing things there for a minute.'

Shit and double shit.

Too late. He saw me, it's him. As ever, towering over me, eyes crinkling at the sides as his warm, trusting face breaks into a big, delighted smile.

'Oh . . . emm, . . . Jake! Hi!' I say, over-brightly, standing up and brushing some of the grass off my work skirt. 'Great to see you! I was, emm, just leaving! Now!'

He seems to sense the rising hysteria in my voice, and is straight onto me, the way he's always onto everything in a nanosecond flat.

'You OK?' he asks, face screwed up with concern.

'Oh, yes! Just great! I really do have to get going now though, right NOW. So we'll talk soon, byeeeee!'

'Sure you're alright?'

He and The Girl from Ipanema are looking uneasily at each other now, wondering why in hell I'm being quite this rude and anxious to get away from them. Meanwhile I'm furiously semaphoring to Helen to keep her mouth shut and at all costs not to mention Lily . . .

Lily. Happily playing just a few feet away from me, like a ticking time bomb.

'Eloise, this is Monique,' Jake eventually says, introducing her in that relaxed, easy way he has, while Monique smiles

229

her perfect smile and says, ''Allo,' very sexily in what I can only describe as a smokily throaty voice, if ever I heard one. Her face is totally untroubled either by worry or experience, I notice, which irritates me for absolutely no reason whatsoever. Like it's somehow her fault for only looking about twenty-one, tops.

'Monique is a student at the school,' Jake casually chats on. 'She's from Catalonia, but doing great at the aul' English, aren't you Monique? Improving in leaps and bounds.'

'Every day, me Engleeesh get better a leetle bit,' she says huskily, as Jake nudges her playfully and I catch a tiny, adoring glance as she grins back up at him.

And even in the throes of my panic, even though it's just the tiniest gesture, I feel I'm witnessing a burgeoning intimacy between them. Again, which shouldn't bother me, but does. Your English is improving? I think cattily. Yeah, right. You sound like you've just been translated by Google.

And now Jake is looking expectantly from me to Helen, patiently waiting to be introduced.

F**k. Which means it's my turn. And there's no getting out of this now.

'Emm . . . Well, this is Jake,' I say to Helen, hoping she'll correctly interpret the hot red panic in my eyes. That fraught, urgent look that I hope says, nod, smile, shut up and let's get us – and more importantly Lily – out of here.

'. . . And this is Helen,' I tack on, 'my sister.'

Helen's eyes light up with recognition as she shakes hands with him and Monique while Jake beams even wider, suddenly realising just who she is.

'Well, I think I owe you a massive thank you,' he tells her kindly, the big eyes twinkling warmly down at her, 'did you know that I'm lucky enough to be staying in that lovely flat of yours?'

A quick, panicky look from me, but there's absolutely no need. Helen doesn't let me down and chats away easily about how happy she is that he's settling in, stressing that if he ever has any trouble with the stopcock in the loo or the water pump under the sink, to call her immediately. Not for the first time, I find myself offering up a silent prayer of thanks at Helen's easy, natural way of bonding with total strangers over the tiniest thing, in this case immersion heaters and the lagging jacket on the boiler. On and on they chat about the flat, Jake filling her in on all the improvements he's done and is doing, while I surreptitiously swivel round to check on Lily.

It's okay. So far, I think I'm just about okay. She's playing happily away with her new little pal about six feet behind me, her back to us, totally oblivious, not noticing anything and not running over to me yelling, 'look at me, Mama!' every two seconds, like she normally would.

Which is good. Which is great. Which means I might just get out of this alive, look back and if not laugh, then at least be able to breathe normally again, oooh, in about a decade's time or so.

A moment later, I'm aware that all small talk has quietly petered out and everyone's looking at me, so I pre-empt yet another bowel-clenchingly awkward silence by starting to pack up my bag.

'Well, sorry about this everyone,' I laugh hysterically, my voice getting higher and higher in direct proportion to how anxious I am, 'but I've really, *really* got to get . . .'

'Back to the office, let me take a wild guess,' Jake smiles and I totally overreact by guffawing like a nutter.

'No worries at all,' he says, looking at me so keenly it makes me wonder just how he's interpreting my uneasiness. 'Monique and I have a class anyway, so we'd better make a move too.'

'Sure! Well, have a great class, don't let me keep you!'

Not a word out of Monique, just a curt nod and a toothy smile, so I'm guessing she's badly in need of a few English phrases to get her by. Mind you, I think cattily, to the Moniques of this world who go around the place looking like Brazilian underwear models, I'm guessing your body language does most of the talking for you, particularly around guys.

'Well lovely to meet you, goodbye now!' I call out gaily, bag in hand, all ready to rock and roll.

'I'll give you a call, Eloise,' Jake smiles kindly at me. 'Hey, maybe we can meet up this weekend? Have a drink or a bite to eat, if you'd like? Knowing you, you'll only eat a packet of birdseed and a banana to do you till Monday morning otherwise.'

'Emm, well . . . You see . . .'

Can't think straight, can't answer him, can't do a shagging thing.

'Don't worry,' he grins easily, 'I'll be in touch.'

Then he turns to Helen and warmly says how lovely it was to finally meet her. 'Heard a lot about you.'

Oh for Christ's sake, enough with the bloody social niceties, just go, for the love of God, GO . . .

'Likewise,' Helen smiles back, shooting a discreet, 'you don't know the half of it' look to me.

They've almost gone, almost, I'm nearly out of the woods, when next thing, out of nowhere – disaster.

Lily, seeing me with my bag strapped to me, immediately

232

cops on that I'm leaving and runs over to me as fast as her pudgy little legs will carry her.

No, no, no, no, no, no, nooooooooooooo . . .

'Don't go . . . PLEASE!' she yells at me, while I bend down to her, hysterically trying to signal to a toddler not to call me Mama, please not now, just not now, just this one time, just not for the next two minutes, just till they're gone.

'I have a new fwiend!' she grins toothlessly up at me, 'AN . . . you have to say hello! Her name is Hannah.'

'Well goodbye then!' I say to Jake and The Girl from Ipanema, wishing, willing them to get the hell out of here. Just for the love of God, LEAVE. PLEASE. NOW.

But I'm out of luck.

Next thing, Jake is kneeling down to talk to Lily, so he's on a level with her.

'Well hello there, little lady,' he grins at her while she looks up at him, mesmerised. 'What's your name?'

And suddenly it's as though no air moves.

All I can do is look on, utterly helpless and dumbstruck, imagining that I see a flicker of something in his face . . . recognition?

Oh Christ, now my knees are physically starting to buckle.

'Lily though weally it's Lily Lilibet Emily,' she tells him seriously, looking at him, totally fascinated.

Jesus, the resemblance between them is so strong it would almost knock your breath away.

Same eyes, skin, hair colour, build . . . It's astonishing.

Helen has copped it too; I know by the gobsmacked, shell-shocked look on her face.

Jake MUST notice it, he can't not. It's not possible that he doesn't see how alike they are . . .

Meanwhile I'm rooted to the spot, lantern-jawed,

horrified, unable to say or do anything except stand there mutely, wishing I had a paper bag handy to hyperventilate into. For once in Lily's life, I'm cursing the fact that she's not a bit shy around strangers.

Helen clocks my thunderstruck expression, seems to realise that I'm paralysed and useless, totally unable to stop this and calmly rescues me, scooping Lily up into her arms and taking total control of the situation.

'Come on pet, who'd like another ice cream? And maybe your new friend Hannah would like one too? You know, I think I heard an ice-cream van nearby, how about we go and find it?'

Oh thank Christ for you Helen, thank Christ at least one of us was able to think clearly, to act normally.

'Yay! Tank you!' Lily squeals delightedly, her little pink face lighting up. 'I wanna chocolate one with pink spwinkles on the top!'

'Come on then, let's go,' says Helen calmly, as Lily kicks to be let down again so she can waddle off and grab her pal.

'She's such a beautiful kid, a real little princess,' Jake says simply, looking fondly after her as she waddles off happily.

'Is she yours?' he asks Helen simply.

A half beat.

'I'm babysitting her,' Helen says.

'And she's how old? I'm guessing about three?'

'In a few weeks' time, yeah. How did you guess?'

'I've a nephew exactly that age. Not as much of a cutie as little Lily though.'

A tense moment, made worse by my mutely standing on the side lines, powerless to say or do anything in case I make this worse. That's Lily's cousin he's talking about, is all I can think. Lily that never stops harping on about how much she wishes she had little cousins to play with. And the tragedy is that she does, she just doesn't know it.

But thank you God; the torture, it seems, is finally over. Next thing, Jake nods and smiles, wishes us a lovely afternoon and a second later, he and The Girl from Ipanema have swished past us and on their way.

I slump exhaustedly back onto the rug again and knock back the dregs of not only the Pimms I was drinking, but Helen's as well. If I smoked, I'd be pulling on them two at a time right now.

'Oh my God, he is only bloody divine looking . . . You never said!' says Helen, still staring starry-eyed after him.

'I don't know about you,' is all I can mutter back, still shell-shocked and with beads of sweat slowly seeping their way from my armpits all the way down my ribcage. 'But I've just had about two years knocked off my life. Now, will you excuse me while I go and have a coronary?'

I'm running late by almost a full hour when I finally do get back to the office, with a sunburnt red nose and blades of grass stuck all over my black skirt, but for once in my career, I don't give a shite.

Can't. I'm too shaken and trembly and still not the better of what just happened. Maybe in about five years I'll have recovered, maybe, after some fairly intensive therapy and years spent lying on a psychiatrist's couch, at a cost of several hundred euro an hour, but sure as hell not now.

Helen is right. I'll have to confess all to Jake, I think, mind racing, as I step into the lift on the ground floor going up. I cannot and will not ever go through anything like what just happened. No chickening out of it or putting it on the long finger because I'm so busy having a lovely time with him, I'm just going to grab the bull by the horns and bloody well do it. No more arsing around or dithering; next time I see him, I'm telling him straight out. He said we'd chat this weekend, so when we do, I'll suggest meeting up and I'll just come out with it once and for all. Obviously, this will involve getting several large glasses of Pinot Grigiot into me to get up the courage, but hey, there you go.

And then suddenly I notice that the lift hasn't stopped on the fourth floor, where my office is. Instead, it's overshot and is now whizzing right the way up to the top floor. Where the executive suite, or the T. Rexes' den as I like to call it, is.

Shit. I wallop the button for my own floor again, still desperately trying to calm down, and try to just concentrate on breathing; in and out, out and in, all while checking my breath for a boozy smell and picking blades of grass off my bum. One massive slug of Rescue Remedy later and I'm starting to feel a little bit more like myself. By which I mean my hands have at least stopped shaking involuntarily and the dizziness is slowly but surely beginning to pass.

Next time you see him, I tell myself sternly. Get it over with. For better or for worse. Cannot risk a repeat performance of this afternoon or else I'll end up on a double dosage of Xanax every day of my life until Lily turns eighteen. It's okay, I try to calm myself. I'm at the office now. It's all over. I can breathe easy again.

Just like Tiffany's in New York, nothing bad can happen to me here.

Abruptly, the lift stops at the T. Rexes' floor. Another tiny panic, but I force myself to calm down a bit more. After all, it's a Saturday afternoon, and the chances of any of the directors hanging round the office when they could be on a golf course are slim to none, aren't they?

But then suddenly, with a heart-walloping thump, the doors glide slowly open and in gets . . . Oh sweet Jesus, no . . .

Yes. In steps none other than Sir Gavin Hume, our esteemed chairman, a sixty-something, portly, red-faced, slightly swollen about the gills figure: the Gorbachev of the print world as he's known, liked and trusted by all. Distinguished looking, which as we all know means ugly, with money. With a reputation for being what was once politely referred to as a 'bit of a ladies man'. In fact, you might say his default adjective is 'flirt', but to his credit, he's always treated me fairly and I know for a fact he has taken my side on numerous heaves against me in the past.

Out of the whole mighty pack of T. Rexes though, this is the one who trusts me and respects me and has stood by me, and now here I am, half trembling like I was just in a car crash, with straw practically coming out of my hair, grass all over my arse, an open half-drunk bottle of Rescue Remedy in one hand and more than likely looking like a candidate for care in the community.

Oh, and lest we forget, smelling of drink too.

Shit, could this day possibly get any worse? Beside, what the hell is he doing here anyway? The T. Rexes never, ever come in at weekends; it's practically carved in stone on the architrave above the boardroom: Thou Shalt Bugger Off Every Friday Afternoon To The Nearest Golf Course And Thou Shalt Stay on the Fairways till Monday At The Earliest.

'Ahh, Madame Editrix,' he smiles, seeing me.

This by the way, is what he always calls me, but then to Sir Gavin I think I'm a bit asexual, neither male nor female, so editrix covers all his options nicely. Plus it saves him the bother of having to flirt with a woman he clearly finds as unattractive as me.

'Everything okay?' is all he asks, a bit worriedly, taking in the hack of me.

'Hmm? Oh, yes, fine, just, emm . . . you know, busy as ever,' I smile over brightly, trying to sound cool and calm, brushing my skirt and frantically smoothing down the bushy state of my hair.

Jesus, what next? The sky opening up and a piano falling on my head?

'Good,' is all he says back at me a bit worriedly. 'Good.'

Okay, the first 'good' reassured me, the second one didn't.

By that evening, the Chinese whispers have all floated back to me, same as they always do.

Hot gossip. Either Eloise Elliot is having a nervous break-down or else she's in love. With that guy Ruth O'Connell saw her strolling down the street with a while back, eating crepes and drinking coffee, remember? Total hunk, Ruth says, real man's man, not at all the type you'd expect Madame Elliot to be dating. And apparently she bunked off this afternoon, God knows where, and came back drunk and covered in grass, shaking like a leaf. Not a word of a lie, didn't Gavin Hume himself meet her? Besides, there's no other explanation for the way she's been acting lately; did you hear what she said to Rachel before she sent her home? She said your family is far more important than any shagging job! I know, it sounds made-up, coming from her, but it's the God's honest truth.

And she told Robbie that we weren't an Asian sweatshop, then gave him the rest of the day off for no other reason than to go to a Confirmation . . . I know, she'd have snapped at him for even asking for time off only a few months ago. Mark my words, something's come over her and if you ask me, it's either a heavy-duty dose of Valium for her nerves that's making her act so weird, or else it's all down to this new guy she's supposedly seeing.

Just remember, you heard it here first!

And this time, I couldn't even brush it aside, as I normally would.

Mainly because most of it was true.

Chapter Ten

I'm wide awake at five in the morning, my brain alert and whirring, ready to go. Barely slept a wink all night, in fact. All I can think over and over again like a loop playing in my head is . . . I'm doing it. I'm coming clean to Jake. Before this day is out. For better or for worse. What Helen said to me the other night in her calm wisdom, is the right thing to do. She's absolutely on the money and what's more I know it. Every spare hour that I spend time with him, every phone call, every long, meandering gossipy chat is time that I'm effectively leading the guy up the garden path. Should I choose to continue being as pally with him as I have been up till now, then I'm deceiving him, simple as. Something friends do not do.

Not that I'd particularly know how friends behave or how they don't, but as I pointed out to Helen, I'm on a learning curve.

Anyway, ever since that toe-curlingly awkward meeting in the Green yesterday, I can't handle keeping the truth from him anymore. I swear it's physically giving me heartburn. And I know it's going to be awkward, and Jake will have every right to be furious with me, but for better or for worse, I'm telling him out straight. As we say in the

240

Post, welcome to the wonderful world of got-no-choice. Should he choose to meet Lily and be a part of her little life, then whoop-di-do, but if not, then at the very least, I hope we'll part company as friends.

I *hope*.

Christ alive, to say I nearly had a heart attack yesterday afternoon is an understatement and I still shudder to think of what might have happened. All it would have taken was for Lily to waddle over to me demanding some chocolatey treat and calling me Mama, like she always does. That's all, then the game would be up, it would be all over bar the shouting. And, I keep asking myself, would it have been in any way fair on poor Jake to find out like that?

But, somehow, miraculously, the angels took pity on me and let me get away with it, albeit leaving me a nervous, trembling wreck for the rest of the entire day. So by far the best thing all round is just to get it over with and just pray he doesn't want to do a runner or storm off in high dudgeon the minute he realises exactly how much I've been leading him on. As, I reluctantly have to admit, he'd be perfectly entitled to do.

Because in a rare moment of introspection I realise that, well, I'd miss chatting to him, wouldn't I? I'd miss being able to sound off against him, miss telling him all the thousand irritating little minutiae that make up my average day. I'm surprising myself at how much my heart physically twists at the very thought that after this day is out, there's a chance I might never get to see him again. I'd miss hearing him chat all about his day too and about how he is getting on at the language school. And I'd especially miss sniggering at all the devious tortures that he's always threatening to carry out on Seth Coleman as punishment for continuing

241

to bark up my bum day and night. Miss it all far more than I'd ever have thought possible.

With sudden realisation, I can clearly see now just how dependent I've become on him. The extent to which I lean on him. Me, of all people, whose proudest boast once was that no man was an island, but that I sure as hell was. Which is why today is D-Day. Endgame.

As it's Sunday, I'd planned to take Lily to a Disney movie she's been pestering me to see, then I dithered a bit about whether or not to invite Jake along, so he and Lily could spend a bit of time together. But on Helen's sage advice, I decided not to.

'I'm worried it might all be too much too soon, for Jake, not to mention Lily,' she wisely counselled. 'Better to meet him alone, just the two of you, and break it to him then.'

'Easier said than bleeding done. Then what?'

'Then just see how he feels about the whole thing and take it from there. If he agrees to see Lily, then and only then, I think would be the right time to tell her. At the very least, you're protecting her from being let down. Remember, we don't know if he's going to want to be a part of her life yet. Far better at this stage just to play it safe, don't you think?'

Four in the afternoon and Helen, Lily and I are just streaming with the crowds coming out of the multiplex cinema, with Lily singing at the top of her voice then, as usual, demanding ice cream, when my mobile rings. The office of course, screaming at me to get in, that there's an emergency with next week's Culture section that needs troubleshooting.

Rats, so much for precious Sunday afternoon Mummy-time.

Reluctantly, I drop Lily and Helen back home, then race on into work. And on the way, with my resolve still solid, I call Jake and arrange to see him for dinner later on tonight. He already left a few messages for me yesterday evening which to my shame I never got back to; couldn't. Needed time to plot and plan out what the hell to say to him.

'You know I'd love to,' he says. 'But I've got a night class at eight. Unless I pick you up at work beforehand and we have a quick bite to eat then? Would that work for you? I'm already starving.'

I tell him that's fine, thinking that it's not really; I'd far rather have the whole evening to talk to him when he didn't have to rush off, but it's at least better than nothing. He agrees to call into the office for me and that's that. The stage is set.

Three long hours later and I'm still with Marc from Culture, hammering out the final layout for the following week's magazine and having one of my bickering sessions with him over what gets the final cover. As usual, it goes along the following lines:

Him; has to be some band that have played fewer than twenty gigs in their whole life but who are now not only a massive YouTube phenomenon but who are about to play their debut gig at the Oxegen festival and need all the press promotion they can get. Otherwise they'll end up gigging in a remote field in County Meath, surrounded by a few indifferent cattle, while half a dozen mud-drenched revellers drunkenly look on. Assuming they're lucky and get even that much of a turn out, that is.

Me; over my dead body, no one's ever heard of that shower, barring they've spent the past two years on the lunatic fringes of the internet. They're way too obscure, and anyway, who wants to read a magazine cover story about a band that's largely unknown outside of their own living room? The cover needs to go to either a big Oscar-winning movie that's opening or else our national theatre's touring production that's about to open on the West End. Which, unlike Marc's bloody no-name band, chances are more than a handful of the cognoscenti might, perish the thought, actually want to see.

Next thing, Rachel's stand-in sticks her head round my door and curtly informs me that there's someone here to see me. (This one's name is Ursula by the way, and she's an honours journalism graduate whose style secret appears to be heavy black eyeliner and a complete and utter refusal to smile.)

The door is already half open and next thing, standing there, all six feet two of him, is Jake. Grinning cheekily and bless him, carrying a gorgeous bunch of Stargazer lilies, my favourites. Half of me lights up, genuinely delighted to see him, but the other half of me starts to get a bit shifty, knowing what's ahead. And dreading it.

But here he is, standing large as life in front of me. No getting out of it now.

'Hey,' he says, filling up the doorway with the sheer hulking size of him. Looking handsome, in a crumpled, laid-back way and wearing a light blue shirt the exact colour of his eyes.

'Sorry, didn't mean to interrupt . . .'

'Oh that's quite alright,' says Marc, taking him in from top to bottom and back up again, like he's sizing him up for a new suit. In fact he's staring at Jake so intently that an utterly disconnected thought flashes through my head;

244

bloody hell, never knew Jake would be Marc's type. Knew he was gay alright, (the hair being the key giveaway; no straight man would dream of wearing it quite that bouffy for starters) but I'd have sworn he was in a long-term relationship with Sean from Advertising on the QT. So anyway I introduce him to Jake, who's still standing patiently at the office door, bouquet of flowers in hand, and suddenly Marc's French architect-style glasses nearly steam up.

'Oh *right*,' he says, recognition lighting him up as he puts two and two together and gets four million. '*That's* who you are. Yes, of course, I've heard all about you, Jake.'

I shoot him a look that's primly intended to convey, 'Ahem, hello, wrong end of the stick here mate,' but it's no use. Received office wisdom round here is that Jake and I are an item and I know of old that the best way to let any story die down is purely to ignore it and let it just die a quiet death in its own good time. Adding useless denials is nothing more than fuel to the fire and tends to only prolong things round here.

'Right then,' says Marc, gathering up his manbag and laptop, 'well, that's me off then. See you in the morning Eloise. *Great* to finally meet you, Jake. Better get going, I've a movie screening to catch tonight.'

'Anything decent?'

'*Transformers 4*.' This, by the way, said in the exact same tone as someone in revolutionary France on their way to the guillotine.

'You have my sympathies,' I half smile at him, knowing that having to sit through a kids movie would be anathema to someone with Marc's more elitist cultural leanings.

He rolls his eyes up at me and on his way out throws back,

'I'll have the cover mock-ups for you by about ten tonight.'

'No rush. It's a Sunday night.'

A look so shocked from Marc that I have to resist the sudden urge to smile.

'I'm sorry . . . Did you just say "no rush"? Did I really hear that right?'

'Come on Marc, you've earned some breathing space. Enjoy a bit of time off after your movie and we can take this up again tomorrow.'

A stunned, dazed look from him and just like that, he's gone, leaving Jake and me alone.

'Hi.'

'Hi.'

'For you,' he says, thrusting the flowers over.

'Jake, they're lovely, thank you.'

'Come on then, I just got paid this week and I'm treating you to dinner at the poshest restaurant we can find.'

Twenty minutes later we're sitting at a cosy little table for two in Ciao Bella, a gorgeous Italian bistro only about a ten-minute stroll from the office. Popular with the T. Rexes, but as it's a Sunday, I reckon I'm safe enough from them. The place is quiet tonight, which couldn't suit me better. Privacy for what I'm about to say, I reckon = really good idea. We order and while we're waiting I think . . . Just bloody well do it now. Go for it. Get it over with.

But somehow, I just can't. Just silently sit looking at him, thinking how in hell do I ever begin?

A tension knot inconveniently forms in the pit of my stomach and suddenly I'm finding it difficult to breathe.

'Good to see you taking a bit of time out to eat a proper nosh,' he smiles across the table at me, eyes twinkling, giving me his big, open, trusting smile.

Silence from me. And now I'm aware of the background music playing; Marilyn Monroe singing *My Heart Belongs to Daddy*. A sign, surely?

'You know, I really worry about all the crappy food you eat? Sometimes I think you're on the John the Baptist diet – you'd live off grass shoots and the odd fistful of herbs if you could – the odd Big Mac meal, now Missy, would do you no harm at all.'

I nod absently. Still skirting around it, formulating in my head how best to approach this. Feeling like a child caught up in a complex lie.

Guess what Jake, you're a dad . . . And I never told you . . . And by the way, I've been lying to you basically since the first time I met you . . . Ehh . . . no, probably not.

'. . . Plus it's always lovely to have an actual dinner with you,' he grins across the candlelit table at me, 'not just try and get you to wolf down a sandwich in between meetings.'

Still no reaction from me. Our food has arrived by now and as Jake horses hungrily into a deluxe-size cannelloni chatting easily away, I play with a house salad, pretending to eat. Doesn't take long though for him to cop there's something up with me and, as ever, is straight in for the kill.

'Eloise?'

'Hmmm?'

'What have I just been talking about?'

'Emm . . .'

'I knew it. Knew you were miles away.'

'Sorry, I'm just a bit . . .'

'Here's me warbling on about my big exams next week and ordinarily by now you'd be messing round with your iPad and producing study timetables, but instead you're just staring into space, totally tuned out. Are you OK?'

'Sorry Jake,' I say, regrouping, snapping out of it. 'Didn't mean to be rude. Your exams, that's important. Sorry, tell me more.'

'Never mind the fecking exams for a minute.'

'No, go on, tell me.'

'Some other time,' he says, shoving his plate aside and looking at me keenly with his cloud-blue eyes unflinching. 'Right now, I'd really like to know what exactly is going on with you. You're not yourself at all tonight and you hardly said two words to me on the walk over here. So come on, what's bothering you?'

Still I can't answer him. Bloody hell, this is exactly how Lily acts when she's in trouble. Just stays stony silent so I have to try and drag it all out of her.

'Eloise, you're really starting to worry me now. Is there something going on?' He's looking directly at me now, worry clouding over him.

No avoiding this.

'Someone or something bothering you in work? Come on, you know you can tell me. You can always talk to me. Or let me guess, are the walls in here bugged by the T. Rexes at the *Post*?'

He's looking straight at me now in that unflinching way he has; oddly disconcerting when you're on the other end of it.

'Jake, I . . . Well the truth is, there *is* something I want to talk to you about.'

'Whatever it is, it's okay. You can tell me anything, you know that.'

'Can I, Jake?'

'Of course you can.'

Shit, what's keeping the bloody glass of wine I ordered? Need alcohol to get me through this. Very badly.

'Well . . . you know how you and I have an unspoken agreement never to talk about our private lives?'

'Well, yeah . . .'

'The thing is . . .' I break off again uselessly.

A silence and I swear I can physically feel his eyes burning into mine.

'Eloise? Were you . . . I mean, are you . . .?'

'What I'm trying to say is . . .'

'Eloise, are you married? Is that what you're trying to tell me?'

Now he looks bewildered and a bit hurt.

'No! Where'd you get that idea from?'

'Separated? Living with a guy that you don't want to know about me?'

'None of the above, you've totally got hold of the wrong end of the stick. It's just that . . .'

'Well, well, well. Look who we have here. Of all the gin joints in all the towns in all the world.'

Shit and double shit.

I do not buggery well believe this.

Like a lingering bad smell that just won't go away, Seth Coleman is standing right beside us, as ever, looking like a forty-year-old choirboy whose mammy continues to dress him for work. But that's not what makes a cold clutch of terror grab at my chest. Right behind him, smiling benignly in that patrician way he has and taking in the whole scene – me, Jake, the bunch of flowers, the candle-light, the works – is none other than Sir Gavin Hume.

'Ahh, Madame Editrix, there you are,' he smiles kindly as I leap to my feet and rush to shake his hand.

Oh holy fuck. What in the name of arse is Sir Gavin doing with Seth? And here of all places, when I so badly needed to be alone with Jake?, What the hell is going on between this pair that I don't know about?

'Hello there,' I try to say calmly, composing myself. 'Can't believe you're both meeting outside of work – and on a Sunday too! Everything okay?'

My intention is for that to sound innocuous and breezy but it comes out so strangulated, I'm practically singing soprano.

'Oh, Seth and I just had one or two bits and pieces to discuss,' he says lightly. 'Nothing whatsoever for you to worry about, Madame Editrix. You two seem to be, well, otherwise occupied as it is.'

Now, whenever anyone tells me not to worry, my shoulders will, on cue, instantly seize up and my heart will start palpitating. But when it's the chairman of the board saying that to me, then believe me, I'm *this* close to needing emergency services.

'We're just having a quiet dinner *à deux,* as it happens,' Seth smoothly informs me, just a hint of a gloat in his snively voice.

'Indeed,' says Sir Gavin, patting his portly, overhanging stomach. 'And in fact if we don't order soon by the way Seth, I'm in danger of passing out with hunger.'

Right, that's it, my mind shoots up a gear to overdrive now. *They're having a quiet dinner?* Just the two of them? Unheard of! So who asked who, is what I immediately want to know. I stand there with a frozen smile practically hard-wired onto my mouth, thinking all the while, Jaysus help Seth if he even thinks about writing this off as a company expense and if I find out, that's all I have to say.

'Emm . . . would you like to join us?' I ask desperately.

'Wouldn't dream of intruding on your romantic evening. No you enjoy your meal and we'll just have our little chat privately.'

'Well, enjoy,' I manage to say weakly, hoping it came out politely, but afraid my subtext is all too apparent. I hope you enjoy it, Sir Gavin, but may Seth Coleman choke on an asparagus tip and end up in an overcrowded emergency room surrounded by screeching kids with saucepans stuck on their heads. Serves him right for doing whatever he's doing behind my back. But mark my words, I'll find out precisely what's going on, even if it bloody kills me in the process.

'Tut, tut, Eloise. Now where are your manners?' says Sleazebag Seth, noticing Jake now and suddenly in no rush whatsoever to leave. 'Aren't you going to introduce us to you new friend?'

Jesus, I think, suddenly irrationally furious. How does he do that? Manage to make the word friend sound like 'gigolo'?

I mumble my way through the introductions, hot flushing like a menopausal matron.

'Heard a lot about you,' sniffs Seth, taking Jake in from head to toe, while Sir Gavin just shakes his hand then stands patiently by, saying nothing, just glancing up at a board with all the day's specials written on it every now and then.

'Likewise,' Jake smiles politely back.

'Right well, have a lovely meal,' I say, having to clear my throat a couple of times before it comes out right.

'Yes, we'll leave you to it.'

Then I think, feck it. Might as well throw this in.

'Emm . . . Sir Gavin, are you sure you don't need me to be aware of, well, whatever it is that you are discussing?'

'No need at all. Nothing for you to fret about, you've quite enough going on as it is. That's all too apparent. Well, nice to meet you Jake.'

'You too, Sir Gavin,' Jake smiles easily, utterly unfazed by all this, while I just stand there clutching and unclutching sweaty palms.

They're almost gone, it's almost over when Seth pauses for a split second before turning back to our table, *à la* Peter Falk in *Columbo*.

'Just one more thing, Jake, wasn't it?' the slimy git says as he whips out one of his monogrammed hankies and dabs his long, bony nose in a gesture a dowager countess circa 1910 would baulk at using. 'I'm assuming I'll see you next weekend? At the directors' corporate function?'

Jake doesn't answer, just shoots me an inquiring look, so I try to flummox my way out of it.

'You know, I don't actually think that's going to be possible.' I half stammer. 'Jake is teaching, you see and his hours are a bit . . .'

'Nonsense, of course you'll have to be there,' says Seth, clearly sensing my discomfort and revelling in it. 'Won't he, Sir Gavin?'

'Yes, yes, of course,' Sir Gavin chimes in. 'You must come Jake,' he nods politely, 'as a guest of Madam Editrix, you'd be more than welcome. I absolutely insist. Everyone will be delighted to meet you.'

'Wonderful!' I say in a strangulated high-pitched voice I hardly recognise as my own.

'So that's settled then,' is Seth's last, triumphant word. 'See you next weekend Jake. And by the way, I'm very much looking forward to playing a round or two of golf with you.'

Jake, I notice, says nothing to this, just stares back at him, arms folded, giving absolutely nothing away.

And finally, they're gone to the upstairs section of the restaurant, mercifully leaving us alone.

Oh bugger this to hell. It's as good as decreed now. If Sir Gavin himself has invited Jake, then short of the *Post* going into receivership before next weekend, that's it. He's got to come with me and that's final.

As soon as they're well out of sight and safely upstairs, Jake's sprung to his feet, gripping my arms as he gently eases me back into my chair. Then he sits me back down, as ever, making me feel tiny beside the sheer hulking size of him.

'You okay?' he asks me, looking straight into my eyes, all concerned. 'Jeez, you were tense enough before they came in, but look at the state of you now . . .'

'I'm so far from okay, I can't tell you.'

You just don't know why, that's all . . .

'Sir Gavin seems alright,' he says thoughtfully, 'but if you ever want me to sort out that Seth git for you, believe me, it would be my absolute pleasure. I feel very protective over you, and God help anyone who tries to have a go at you when I'm around, that's all I can say.'

'One day I'd like to have that man vaporised, but for the moment . . .'

'Now you're beginning to sound a bit more like yourself,' he smiles, the old twinkle coming back into his eyes. 'That's a lot more like the strange and troubled woman I know. So just listen carefully to what I'm telling you. Let. It. Go.'

I give him a wobbly smile, all while thinking, how do I get our conversation back on track? He sits back down and now we're back to pin-drop silence, which, for once, Jake misreads.

'Eloise,' he says softly, 'don't get stressed about why Sir Gavin is meeting with git-face Seth. It's not worth it. Whatever's going on, I'm sure it's nothing for you to worry about.'

No, nothing compared to what I'm about to land on you.

'Besides, if it had been anything concerning you, don't you think they'd have told you?'

I nod, though for the minute, I'm not even thinking about Seth and Gavin. Yeah, sure something's up between the two of them alright, I can practically smell it. Don't know what, but it'll only a matter of time before it all filters back to me. Sooner or later everything does. And I'll deal with it then, and only then.

I take a sip of the wine that's finally arrived and look over to him, worry now etched all over his fair, freckled face. Though he's not half as fecking worried as I am.

'Jake, just to get back to . . .'

'Please,' he says, leaning against the window now and looking intently back at me, 'I know what you're thinking and I don't want you to get all stressed about it. You don't have to. Because I won't go unless you want me to. I mean come on, me? At some corporate weekend do? Playing golf with gits like that Coleman wanker? Are you kidding me? I'd end up punching him in his smug self-satisfied gob if he as much as looked crossways at you.'

'It's not that, Jake,' I shift around uncomfortably in my chair.

'Wish you could tell him the only use we have for golf clubs where I come from . . . '

'You don't understand.'

'What? Tell me.'

Just then, the bill arrives, which Jake very generously insists on paying, then starts getting ready to leave.

'You have to go already?' I say, stunned. He can't go, not now, not yet.

'Yeah, sorry I have to rush, but remember I told you I was teaching an English class tonight? In fact I gotta run or I'm going to be late. So what was it you wanted to say to me anyway, before we were so rudely interrupted?'

Oh God, not now, not when he's running out the door. *Shit, shit, shit.*

'It was . . . emm . . . nothing that can't wait.'

'You're stressed out of your mind about this whole corporate weekend, aren't you? Isn't that why you've been so jumpy all night?'

'Well, partly . . .'

'What, is it like some kind of partners' thing, or something?'

'It is, actually . . .' But that's the least of my worries.

'I see,' he says, thoughtfully. Then after another pause and a good long look at me he adds, 'and for what it's worth, I think I do understand what you were trying to tell me. Or rather, what you weren't.'

More bloody silence, and for once I can't think of a single thing to prise out of my mouth that might fill it.

Next thing, he's on his feet, pulling his jacket on.

'Jake? You've got to leave right this minute?'

'Yeah, or I'll be late.'

'Oh,' I say, deflated. 'So maybe I'll talk to you afterwards?'

'Listen, Eloise,' he smiles down at me, 'if you need company at the corporate piss up, count me in. I'll be there for you and I won't let you down. Sure, I'd do anything for you, you know that, don't you?'

I give a weak, automatic smile, not wanting him to go, not yet.

'But as for the partners side of it . . .' He went on, not quite able to look me in the eye now. 'Eloise, you've been so good to me and I'll never forget you for that. You were a true pal when I needed one most. But . . .'

'Yeah?' Not sure where that 'but' could be headed.

'Well then maybe this might put your mind at rest a bit. I was going to tell you, but . . .'

But what, I think?

'That girl I met you with in the Green the other day?'

'Yes, I remember. Monique, wasn't it?'

Hard to forget the Girl from Ipanema, tall and tanned and young and lovely and the adoring way she batted her two-inch long Bambi eyelashes in Jake's direction.

'As a matter of fact . . .'

And I swear with a journalist's knife-edge instinct, that I already know what's coming next.

'She's been asking me out for a while, so we're just going out for drinks to celebrate my exams being over at the end of the week. Just as pals, you know.'

'Oh, I see.'

'You and I have always been straight with each other, so I just thought I'd let you know.'

Me? Straight with you? You don't know the half of it, sunshine, I think, barely able to meet his open, trusting, blue eyes. So exactly like Lily's that it would melt a heart of stone.

'Oh absolutely,' I manage to smile brightly, 'that's great news.'

256

'Yeah, she's a lovely girl, Monique. She's twenty-two.'

'Twenty-two?'

'Yup. Teaches Bikram yoga and as you probably gathered the other day, needs English lessons VERY badly.'

'Yoga?' I repeat stupidly.

'So just in case you were worried about me taking the partners thing seriously . . .'

'Oh no, no, not at all . . .'

'But if you want me to go with you as your buddy, you can count on me. You know that.'

'No worries. Have a lovely night and I'll see you during the week?'

'Sure, I'll call you once my exams are out of the way.'

'Best of luck!' I call after him brightly, and two seconds later, he's gone.

I knock back the dregs of my wine and speed dial Helen the minute he's gone, hissing everything that's just happened down the phone to her.

'You mean you didn't get to tell him?'

'Couldn't. I tried my best, I really did, then Sir Gavin and bloody Seth Coleman interrupted us.'

'I don't believe it!'

'I know, I nearly choked.'

'So tell him before you go away for the weekend then.'

'Can't.' I sigh helplessly. 'He's got five full days of exams ahead. How can I land this on him on this of all weeks? If he failed, it would be entirely my fault. And he's worked so hard.'

'The weekend then. You'll have to tell him then. You can't put it off any longer. You've waited this long, you can wait another six days, can't you? And until then, just stop all your worrying and put it out of your head.

Nothing else you can do. In fact, the weekend is probably an even better time, because it's down the country and you'll be able to snatch a bit of time alone together, won't you?'

I'm only half-listening to her though.

'And another thing, he's dating that slapper we saw him with in the Green yesterday.'

'Oh shit, you're kidding me.'

'When do I ever?'

'You know what?' she says to the soundtrack of Lily bashing out *Twinkle Twinkle Little Star* on the piano in the background. 'I'm quite psychic. Saw this coming a mile off.'

'Saw what exactly coming?'

'Well, you've gone and done all the heavy lifting on him, haven't you?'

'Explain?'

'You've gone and found this rough diamond and sanded him down and moulded a perfect gentleman out of clay: you've groomed him and prepped him and all for what? So some other girl can just step in and have all the benefit? I don't know what he was like when you first met him, but to look at him now, you'd think, that guy can have anyone he wants. He's perfect. Handsome, lovely, kind, polite, intelligent. And you're the one who made it all happen. I often think the same about me and Darren, you know. I've spent years honing and sanding down his rough edges and if we ever break up, what'll happen? The next girl that comes along will get all the benefit of all my long years of patiently grafting and nagging and he'll be married to her within a year. Seen it happen a thousand times.'

'Helen love, just so you know, men aren't always the answer.'

'Then why do we always end up talking about them?'

'And another thing; don't forget that Sir Gavin's wife insists on being addressed as Lady Hume.'

'Ah get off the stage, please tell me you're having a laugh.'

'When do you ever see me joking?'

'You're seriously telling me that I have to call her *your ladyship*?'

'Yup. Won't answer to anything else these days. Unless she happens to have a few drinks in her, in which case you may be invited to call her by her Christian name.'

'Where does she think she's living anyway? Versailles? Late eighteenth century?'

'Jake, just do as I ask, please.'

'Out of curiosity, what's her real name anyway?'

'You ready for this? Shania.'

Okay now I actually have to hold the phone away from my ear, he's guffawing that hard.

'Sorry,' he all but snorts, 'just getting a mental picture of the reaction Lady Shania Hume the Fourth, or whatever she calls herself, would get if she started giving herself airs and graces round where I come from.'

'Well, in that case, you'll love this. She's inner-city born and bred and if you're to believe the rumour mill, worked in Burdock's chipper there for years. Became a model, worked her way up, met Sir Gavin when he was just a humble hack, and never looked back. During the Celtic Tiger years, her proudest boast was that the highlights in her hair matched her car.'

'Piss off.'

'Jake! Language like that in front of the T. Rexes and I will personally murder you!'

'I know, I know. Will you chill out, for feck's sake?'

'Course now she's all in with the Kildare horsey set and to see her swanning around the place, you'd nearly swear she was reared in a stately home and related to the Middletons. She's even changed her accent too and now she sounds posher than one of the Mitford sisters, by way of the Queen.'

I can almost hear the sound of his eyes rolling.

'Well if she worked in a chipper, she and I'll have lots in common then. We can spend a happy afternoon sharing stories about queuing up for butter vouchers. Or better yet, I can tell her that she looks a bit familiar, then ask her does the phrase "Can I have two curry chips and a batter burger with a tin of Fanta to go?" mean anything to her.'

'Very droll. Oh and don't forget Ruth O'Connell, you remember Ruth? Pinched face, permanently disappointed look about her?'

'The Northern editor, yeah I remember her. Looks at men like she's either going to kiss them or kneecap them.'

I half smile. But then, Jake has this innate knack of immediately paring people right down to their basic, elemental truth.

'Anyway, the woman is capable of ferreting a juicy story out of a large lump of lard. So just be on your guard round her, that's all I'm saying.'

Course that's the least of my worries, but I say no more. And then my stomach does a flip worthy of the Cirque du Soleil even just thinking about how much else could go wrong. It's like a whole kaleidoscope of worries about this whole shagging weekend is now unfolding, almost sickening me.

Now you know me, I've planned out as much as it's possible to without actually handing out a scheduled time-table to Jake. The Saturday is an afternoon get-together, followed by a posh nosh-up that night with speeches, the whole works. But then the Sunday morning is 'free time'. Or decoded, four or five hours for the lads to arse around a golf course and talk shop. So, Sunday morning it is, then.

I've thought it all through; I have a plan. I'm going to take Jake out for a walk over the grounds after breakfast and when we find a nice, peaceful spot, miles from any distractions or unwanted interruptions, I'll tell him then. Everything, the whole works.

Sunday morning it is, for better or for worse.

'Eloise, listen,' Jake cuts across my stream of worrying, taking me out of my own head and back to our phone call. 'Stop your fretting, would you? We've been over this time and again. You've prepped me inside and out and we can do no more. I know who everyone is and I've enough titbits about the lot of them to last me if we were all going off on a luxury cruise liner for three long months, never mind just for one lousy weekend. I know what to say and more importantly, what not to say. So will you just relax, for Christ's sake? The point has come where you're going to have to relinquish control and learn to trust me.'

Relinquish, I think absently. Must be his new word for the day.

'I do trust you. You just have no idea what you're letting yourself in for, that's all. Oh and one more thing . . .'

'Ah here, what now?'

'Robbie Turner . . .'

'Yeah, yeah, political guy, I'll know him by the shock of white hair, you've already drilled it into me . . .'

'If I could just finish my sentence – I was going to say his wife is Adele and she's lovely, very warm and friendly.'

'Safe for me to be myself around, in other words. That what you mean?'

'Be warned though, she's no fan of mine. Blames me hugely for the fact that she and her kids rarely see Robbie, because the hours he has to work are so mental.'

'Ah, Eloise. You mean you never cut the guy a bit of slack?'

'Believe me, I've been trying to, but you don't realise what being a foreign editor involves. The sheer number of man hours you've got to put in and then you've got to factor in the time difference if you're covering a breaking story from Washington.'

'Don't worry, I get it. Because the whole world will come to an end if you're not all chained to your desks for at least eighteen hours a day.'

'I'm just saying, Adele's no fan of mine, so be warned.'

'Eloise, short of you sending me mailshots of everyone with their CV attached, we can't prepare for this weekend any more thoroughly that we already have done. Now would you ever just relax and switch off, for God's sake? Isn't it supposed to be an enjoyable two-day break? Isn't it all meant to be a bit of fun? Can't tell you how much I'm looking forward to it after a week of exams.'

'Fun? Did you just use the word *fun* in connection with the directors' weekend? Because let me tell you, this is all about stress and tears and sweat and hair loss. Fun doesn't even *begin* to come into it.'

'All I'm saying is, will you just for once chill out a bit?'

'I am. I mean I'm trying to. I mean, yes, I will.'

'And another thing.'

'What?'

'Given that it's supposed to be a casual country house get-together . . .'

'Casual? There are internent camps out there more casual than one of these bloody weekends, let me tell you.'

'I wasn't finished,' he says, calmly overriding me, the way he always seems to be able to. 'As a matter of fact, it's about you.'

'What about me?'

'Remember when I was going for my job interview and you took me out shopping? Made me buy clothes I'd never buy in a million years? And I hated wearing them, but then they got me the job and now I'm so used to going around in non-sports-related gear . . .'

'. . . And not wearing trainers all day every day, thank God.'

'By now it's almost become second nature to me to dress all, you know, middle-class. Whereas you, on the other hand . . .'

'You have a problem with how I dress?' I splutter, as the sudden bile of indignation surges through me. 'Excuse me, my suits are all either from Reiss or else Karen Millen and I do actually own a pair of Louboutins, I'll have you know.'

'Ehh, let me hazard a wild guess. All in black?'

'Well, yeah.' I mean the soles of my fancy shoes may be scarlet red, but sure enough, okay, everything else is black.

'Thought so,' he teases. 'Sounds like you alright.'

'What's wrong with black? It's for the office and it's practical. Editorial.'

'Nothing wrong with it. I'm just sick looking at you dressed like you're going to the funeral of an elderly relative that you didn't particularly like and who left you next to nothing in their will. For god's sake, this is supposed to be a relaxed weekend in the country, that's all I'm saying,' Jake goes on, reasonably. 'So would it kill you just this once to wear a pair of jeans and a few casual tops instead? In actual colours too? You'd look good in colours.'

Jeans, I think, miles away. Haven't shoehorned myself into a pair of jeans since I was in college.

'Look,' he goes on, undeterred by my silence. 'You took me shopping with you once, and now it's my turn to repay the favour. You free now?'

'Jake, you're meant to be studying! I was only calling you to see how the exams are going so far.'

'I've been at the books cramming since dawn and my brain is just about melted. I could really do with getting out of here for an hour and taking a break. Tell you what, I could you meet at the top of Grafton St. in twenty minutes? Come on, it's a Thursday evening, everything's open till late, you could easily manage it.'

Suddenly the sound of loud shrieking comes from the kitchen as Lily and Helen, who are baking cupcakes, start having what sounds like a particularly messy flour fight. I cover the phone with my hand and stick my head round the door, nearly guffawing with laughter at the sight of their twin ghostly white faces, four big surprised eyes looking back at me.

'NO, Mama, NO,' Lily squeals excitedly, eyes full of mischief and energy, shoving me away and getting little floury paw-shaped handprints all over my neat black skirt. 'You're not 'llowed be in here! Me and Auntie Helen are making a supriwse for you!'

'Give us an hour and come back then?' Helen asks me hopefully. 'Lily really wants to bake cupcakes for you.'

'What's all that racket in the background?' says Jake. 'You still in the office?'

'Nothing. Nothing at all,' I say, instinctively keeping my hand well clamped over the phone. 'Ehh, look, I have to go now. But yeah sure, why not? I'll meet you in ten minutes.'

I hang up, dust the flour off myself, then tell Helen that I'll be home in an hour or so and head outside to the car. And okay, so my head may be whirring like a Vegas slot machine with everything I have to stress about. But seeing Jake even just for an hour or so will calm me down a bit, I think.

Somehow it always does.

Besides, what's wrong with enjoying these last few days of normality with him while I still can?

Chapter Eleven

The weekend is taking place not at the usual, intimidatingly posh five-star Adare Manor, but in slightly less salubrious surroundings, in deference to the fact that we're in economic meltdown and the *Post* just isn't pulling in the numbers in the way it used to. So for this year's annual tension-fest, we're in Davenport Hall, a stately pile now renovated to budget-friendly three-star standards, but crucially, with a massive golf course attached, so the T. Rexes can do what they all pretty much came here to do. That is, arse around the fairways talking shop and deciding who's next for the chop. And although the thought of two full days away from Lily is killing me, all I can think is maybe, just maybe, if the Gods smile down on me, by the time it's all over, I might be bringing her home a dad that's chomping at the bit to meet her. Her dream come true, in other words.

Anyway, the hotel is only about an hour's drive from Dublin and I have to say, I'm sincerely and genuinely glad of Jake's company on the way. Whatever tomorrow brings, I think, I'm just going to enjoy today.

Can't describe how lovely it is to arrive here with someone. Even if they're most emphatically *not* your partner, it's still completely wonderful and a huge novelty for such a perennial loner like me. Lovely to have a guy who insists on carrying my bags, lovely not to have to trip up the huge hulking stone steps to the hotel reception all alone and loveliest of all to face into the awful melee of the Saturday afternoon 'meet and greet' with an actual pal beside me. And okay, so I may not have actually chosen to invite him here, but now that he is, I have to admit I'm bloody glad of it.

What can I say? After all my years of facing into crowded gatherings all alone with no one beside me, it's beyond comforting to have a friend with me, supporting me. Someone who I've painstakingly prepped with all the ins and outs involved in the social and political minefield we're about to step into and who's somehow, miraculously, still okay with it all. Still hovering by my side, checking that I'm alright, making sure I've got a drink, every now and then glancing over in my direction, even when we're separated, throwing me a surreptitious wink as much as to say, 'you're doing fine.'

Must be really magical to be in a proper relationship with someone genuinely caring and supportive, is all I can think.

Not that I'd know, but I mean, I'm guessing.

And I have to hand it to Jake, he's playing a blinder. Didn't turn a hair when we were only allocated one room between us, and when I asked for a second one, was told the hotel was totally overbooked, so it was a case of share and get on with it. Turns out it's a double room, so after a flushed and mortified silence from me, Jake just laughed his easy, relaxed laugh and gallantly offered to sleep on the sofa.

It was on the tip of my tongue to ask what his bendy, Bikram-loving, Malboro-voiced 'friend' from Catalonia might have to say about this whole arrangement, but decided for once in my life to keep my trap shut. He hasn't mentioned her once, so why would I? Even if I've a mental picture of bendy, supple Monique or whatever her name is, with both legs wrapped round her neck, going 'Tell me more about zee present indicative, Jake baby.'

Have to hand it to him, he looks terrific too. Absurdly gorgeous, as just about every woman here is at pains to point out to me. At the afternoon meet and greet in the hotel's drawing room, he's dressed in jeans and a simple white cashmere jumper that really brings out the light suntan he's picked up. My eye keeps subconsciously wandering over to him, only dying to ogle him, every time I think he's not looking. He really is that good looking, tall and broad and classically handsome, casually leaning against a wall, towering over all around him. And every time I do sneak an admiring peek in his direction, he must feel my eyes on him because next thing, he'll be looking back at me, smiling at me, winking at me, mouthing at me that everything is fine.

And for now, he's right. For today at least, everything really is fine; for once in my life, I can physically feel it.

You should see him though, chatting away to everyone, mingling easily, shaking hands with strangers then nodding with easy recognition as they introduce themselves. Broad and imposing, by a mile the tallest guy here, with some fruity-looking, summery cocktail clamped to his hand that I know he'd rather die than drink (he reckons cocktails are only for straight women on hen nights, or else gays). Honest to God, I think proudly, the guy really looks to the manner born.

Like he's been moving in these circles all his life.

If you didn't know for sure, you'd swear he was a multi-millionaire businessman who'd miraculously survived the recession, or else maybe a wealthy and secure hedge fund manager here to relax and chill out for a well deserved weekend's rest. But never would you even randomly guess this guy was barely a few months out of a high security prison and currently on parole. Not a chance.

I actually lose count of the number of people who come up to me in the crush specifically to tell me how lovely Jake is, then politely ask how long we've been an item. All my 'Oh, well, we're really just good friends,' lines are brushed aside as the rumour mill takes over, reaching me, as it somehow always does, with the usual approximately thirty-minute time delay.

They're such a lovely couple, and the effect he's having on Eloise Elliot is quite extraordinary . . . She's a completely different person these days. So much more relaxed and softer than Madam Tiger Blood of old. For God's sake, just take a look at her! She's actually wearing a pair of jeans and for once in her life isn't trailing around in one of her terrifying black power suits! Just wish she'd met that Jake guy years ago, that's all I can say, life might have been a helluva lot easier in work for the rest of us . . .

And there's another thing too, another reason why I find myself glowing this afternoon. Now, I'm someone who has never in my whole life known popularity. My place was perennially to accept that while my younger sister was the pretty, likeable one who everyone instantly warned to, I was her scowling termagant sidekick that any sane person would rather open up one of their own veins than spend time with. In fact, for years and years, I used to consider any social event with my work colleagues a success if I managed to get home alive and still in one piece.

But not now. There's a sea change in the air, I can practically feel it. It starts with Adele Turner, Robbie's wife, normally so stand-offish and cool with me, who comes up and actually physically hugs me, nearly knocking the air out of my lungs, it's that tight and heartfelt. She thanks me over and over for letting Robbie off to get to their daughter's Confirmation, says it made the whole day for them and that she was so grateful to me. Asks if it's true that I personally covered for Robbie that day, which I brush aside and instead deflect the chat onto how the Confirmation went instead.

Then Jenny Wilson from accounts – again, no fan of mine ever since I had to cut her back to a three-day week during the last staff culling – comes over, all full of smiles and chat. Warm and friendly as you like, she tells me that she'd heard what I'd done for poor Rachel, who also happens to be her best friend; that she'd been to visit her at home only recently, and that she's doing a whole lot better now.

'That was really considerate of you, Eloise,' she tells me, her eyes shining with sincerity. 'You didn't have to, and not many other bosses would have been so compassionate. Rachel was very touched, I can tell you. As we all were when the news got out.'

I of course modestly brush it aside.

But deep down I am secretly chuffed beyond words.

Ordinarily at these mind-bendingly boring functions, I'm either shoehorned into a corner with one of the T. Rexes who'll bore me to sobs about his golf handicap, or else I'm left standing all alone on the sidelines with no one to talk to, cradling a drink, watching everyone else having a good time and feeling nothing but hate-vibes pulsating towards me. Oh, and checking my iPhone every few minutes, to at least make it look like I'm not particularly bothered that no one's bothered with me.

Not now though. Somehow, for the first time in my life, I find myself right at the very epicentre of a big group of co-workers, all chatting and yabbering away to me, including me in their in-jokes, making me feel like I really do belong. And I love it, it's intoxicating and wonderful and to my great shame, I'd never really realised before just how great my colleagues really are. Never got to really know them, as people.

Out of the corner of my eye, I see Seth Coleman's skeletal outline, with a tall, beautiful modely one on his arm. So out-of-his league stunning in fact, Sarah from advertising whispers to me that she must be a hired high-class escort paid to be with him for the weekend. And we both giggle into our drinks, enjoying a genuine moment of girlie bonding, something completely new and utterly lovely for me.

Can't tell you the warm, comforting feeling that genuinely belonging gives to me. I've missed out on so much these past few years, I think. Missed all the camaraderie, the messing, joshing each other along in the office, anything to make the long days go that bit faster. How much more pleasant would my life have been, I wonder, had I only taken the time and trouble to get to really know these people sooner?

Dave, the night editor, almost brings a tear to my eye when he muscles down into a seat beside me, and warmly says, 'You know something? I never really knew how sound

271

you were before. And I want to say sorry if I've ever misjudged you, Eloise. I used to think that everything you ever said or did was calculated to intimidate. But what can I say? I completely and totally had the wrong idea of you, couldn't have been more wrong about you, in fact. And I'm not the only one round here either.'

I shoot him a look of deep gratitude, then as much as to say, 'you're one of us now', he lightens up a bit and says, 'right then, it's your round Elliot, now up off your lazy arse and mine's a gin and tonic.'

'Sure, I was on my way to the bar anyway,' I smile back at him, touched that he thought enough of me to give me a gentle slagging. Because no one's ever done that at work before, *ever*. 'But can I just say one thing before I go? Thing is Dave, I really think that I'm the one who should be apologising to you.'

'How do you mean?' he asks, looking me straight in the eye.

'All those late nights with me nearly sweating blood down in the print room? Come on, Dave, how you managed to not shove one of my bare limbs into the presses is a shining testament to your eternal good nature.'

And he rolls his eyes jokingly and grins at me and just like that, years of tension, angst, blood, sweat and tears just melt away.

Best of all, I see Jake out of the corner of my eye, stuck in a conversation with, ahem, Lady Hume, but every now and then throwing sideways glances over at me, just checking on me. And I meet his warm, soft gaze and he gives me a wink and I think, for the moment at least, it doesn't get any better than this.

Turns out I'm dead right. It doesn't.

It gets worse. Far, far worse.

Initially my warm glow of newfound popularity lasts the whole way through afternoon tea and right up to when we all merrily and a bit drunkenly head up the massive stone staircase to our respective rooms, to get dressed for dinner. I've only had two and a bit glasses of champagne, but barely got to eat a single scrap, I was that busy chatting and laughing. The net result of which is that I'm now a bit tipsy and giddy, on a total high from how unbelievably well the whole shindig is going so far.

Ever the gentleman, Jake allocates me full bathroom rights first while I get changed and liberally apply yet more slap to my sunburnt face as we natter away through the half-open door.

'You're playing a complete blinder, you do know that,' I shout out to him proudly, shoehorning myself out of my jeans and into a long, bugle-beaded, slinky, silver cocktail dress that Jake insisted on buying me the other night. I naturally baulked at this, as it was a Louise Kennedy that even on sale still cost a bleeding packet, but he insisted. Said it looked well on me and besides, it was payback for the suit I bought him, what seems like another lifetime ago now. I tentatively step into it, clinging to the towel rack with one hand for support, I'm that tipsy, then yank up the gossamer-fine straps, zip it up my back as far as I can by myself and step back to check it out in a full-length mirror conveniently placed by the bathtub.

Not half bad, I can't help thinking, twirling this way and that, straining to get a better view. Now believe me, I'm no Cameron Diaz, but there's just something sexy and magical about the way the dress clings and shimmers, even in awful bathroom flourescent light. If I don't exactly look a million dollars, then for tonight at least, I certainly feel it.

The dark circles under my eyes, I notice, have slowly started to fade a bit from being out in the sun with Lily so much lately, and there's a colour in my cheeks now that was never there before. Most likely down to the fact that Jake's getting pretty good at ramming food down my throat, combined with the fact that I'm sleeping a lot more soundly these days. Normally I go around looking not unlike Morticia Addams I'm that white and pasty, but not now. There's an unmistakable glow there that was absent before and there's only one thing I can put it down to. It's feeling like I'm not alone any more.

It's not me *contra mundum* any more and it doesn't need to be, ever again. Because I've got buddies now, real pals. Some of whom, to my shame, have been under my nose for the longest time, including practically everyone that I work with.

'What about that Shania one, Lady Up-Your-Arse or whatever she calls herself though?' Jake chats away through the bathroom door. 'I don't think I've ever come across anyone quite like her.'

'Explain?' I call back at him, while practically screwed up against the vanity mirror above the sink trying to lash on actual make-up. Harder than it sounds when you're someone who rarely bothers with the stuff. No time, I always think, not to mention very little point. No sooner do I put it on than it's sweated off me after approximately one hour of being even near the vicinity of the *Post*.

'Well, it's weird. While she's talking away to you and seemingly interested in pursuing a half-normal conversation,

274

the whole time she's got her mobile out and is on Twitter. Non-stop.'

I roll my eyes to heaven.

'Yeah, sounds right. Seen her do it a thousand times. She tweets like she's running a director's commentary on her own life. TMI syndrome I call it.'

'Which is?'

'Too Much Information. People who feel the need to tweet what they had for breakfast, lunch and dinner. Very annoying I'd imagine, if you happen to be following her.'

'Bit of a fake, isn't she?'

I smile to myself, while picking up wet towels and hanging them out to dry. Funny thing about Jake, he has the innate knack of being able to spot a phoney faster than Kim or Aggie can spot mildew.

'And another thing, what's the story with that guy Marc, your culture editor?' Jake chats on companionably through the bathroom door. 'Has to be gay, doesn't he?'

'Getting married at the end of the month,' I shout back, lashing on more bronzing powder than you'd normally see on an X-Factor finalist, just to be on the safe side. 'A civil partnership with a guy who works in advertising at the *Post*. And what's more, not only did he tell me all about it this afternoon, but he actually invited me to the wedding too, I couldn't believe it.'

'Why wouldn't he?'

'Well, I've known him years and in all that time, I just automatically assumed he never really liked me. He and I do nothing only snipe at each other.'

'Why wouldn't he like you? Jeez, did you see yourself this afternoon? You were totally surrounded by people everywhere you went. And they didn't seem to just be rubbernecking you or sucking up to you because you're their boss, they genuinely seemed to be having a laugh with you.'

'You think? Really?'

I mean, I think so too, but it's great to be able to get a second opinion from someone who was there, observing from the sidelines.

'Are you kidding me? You were like Miss Congeniality downstairs, they were buzzing round you like wasps round a jam jar. Everyone wanted to chat to you, myself included. Only trying to get away from your woman I was stuck with, was next to impossible. Jeez, she's something else isn't she? Shania – Lady Up-Your-Bum, I mean. Kinda reminded me of Cruella de Vil's granny.'

'Oh Jake,' I say guiltily, 'I'm so sorry for not rescuing you . . . I was just so busy chatting, I kept on trying to get to you, but then someone always seemed to waylay me.'

'No worries at all,' he says kindly. 'It was great to see you having such a good time.'

'Well, thank you. I only hope you weren't bored stupid.'

'Not a bit of it. Have to say though Eloise,' he chats on easily, 'the whole shindig was a helluva lot better than you'd let me to expect. From what you'd told me, I was dreading the whole thing, kept thinking that I'd been in correctional facilities that sounded more relaxed. But I have to say it was – well, I haven't seen you look as alive as you did down there, not once, in all the time I've known you. It was great to see, it really was.'

I stop in my tracks, deeply touched at this. What a total sweetheart, I find myself thinking, pausing for a second and pulling back from the mirror, where I'd been trying to put on eyeliner straight. Not many guys who'd have the patience to put up with a work do like this. Not *any*, as far as I know.

A random thought; should I go ahead and tell him right now? I'm certainly drunk enough and it sort of feels like the right time . . . But I swat it aside. Not before the big dinner tonight. Stick with the plan, Eloise. Tomorrow. After breakfast. Outside, in the gardens, where there's no distractions. Just be patient, wait till then. You're about to tell him potentially life-altering news, so it's worth picking the right moment, isn't it? Besides, I've already waited this long and we're having such a lovely time . . .

Then I step out of the bathroom in all my silvery finery, to an appreciative wolf-whistle from Jake, which I immediately swat away, red-faced. He's lying up against a mound of pillows on the bed now, shoes kicked off, stretched out like a sunbather, the picture of chilled-out relaxation.

Looking decidedly sexy too, I find myself thinking, right out of left field.

Jeez, where'd that come from?

Oh who am I kidding, I've been thinking it all afternoon. Just like every other straight, single woman at this do.

Still though, note to self; no more booze, strictly water for me from here on in.

Must be a hell of a lot drunker than I thought.

'You look gorgeous,' he says softly, eyeing me up and down in a way that I haven't been looked at in years. Decades, even.

'Come off it,' I giggle back at him, I'm sure blushing hotly. 'It's not me, it's the dress. Besides, you're used to seeing me going around in my black widow's weeds.'

'No, you look really terrific,' he repeats slowly, stretching his arms behind his head and looking at me so admiringly that now it's starting to disconcert me a bit. I'm not used to it. Men either see me as asexual or else just treat me exactly as they would another guy.

'Have to hand it to you,' Jake goes on lazily, 'I never realised you'd such a great body going on under all those identical black power suits.'

'Jake?!'

'Look at yourself, would you? You've a fantastic figure. It's just that no one ever tells you. I've always thought that you don't get complimented enough, all you ever seem to get is bucketloads of shite thrown all over you. So take it from me, tonight you're any man's fantasy come true, just a pity that the only person who can't see it is you. And to me, you're the sexiest, loveliest, most gorgeous woman here.'

I'm flushing right to the back of my molars now and suddenly after all of our messing and chat and banter, there's an awkward silence, where we both look at each other, sensing that our friendship is about to cross a major line here.

But onto what?

There's a silence now, all our easy chitchat has suddenly stopped. And now it's like even the air in the room isn't moving.

'Your dress is unzipped,' he eventually murmurs, pointing to the back of it.

'Oh rats, yeah, I couldn't reach,' I mumble, staring at him stupidly.

'Come here. Allow me.'

'Oh, emmm, thanks.'

I go over to where he's sitting up against the pillows and sit down gingerly on the edge of the bed, with my back to him. Next thing, I feel his warm hands lightly lifting my hair off the back of my neck as he zips the dress all the way up. For just a millisecond longer than necessary, his hands linger on my bare shoulders and now there's a tingling thrill shooting down my arms, bringing my whole body out in goose pimples.

Hadn't counted on this . . . Hadn't even considered the deep, swell that starts inside my chest then slowly starts to spread over my whole body, until my fingers tingle, and each and every one of my nerve endings feels like it's physically starting to ache.

Christ, I think randomly, have I really been withering for the want of a human touch this badly? And for this long?

His giant hands linger on the nape of my neck, then gently start to play with a loose strand of my hair as my stomach contracts with longing . . . Whatever else happens, I don't want him to stop . . .

Okay, I'm starting to feel dizzy now, loose and watery and find my head slowly turning round to face him as he cups my face in his huge hand, massaging it with his long, slow fingers.

'This alright?' he whispers so softly, I can barely hear him.

The rational part of my mind says, stop this lunacy right now, get up while I still can, say something smart and get back downstairs to the party proper. Because the thing is, I *like* being Jake's friend. Surely the superior and permanent position of friends is a pretty good place to be. Isn't it? Not to mention the bombshell I'll be landing on him tomorrow . . . So why am I in danger of blowing everything right now by turning back to him, mumbling 'Mmmmm,' softly under my breath, wanting nothing more now than

279

for him to hold me, to lie down beside him, to feel his lips on mine . . . He must be able to hear my heart hammering, I think, he must . . .

'You're amazing, you know that?' he murmurs into my hair, and now I can feel his tongue lightly grazing off my ear. Oh God, he smells so delicious too, musky and gorgeous. And suddenly it's like a furnace in here and even just looking at him is making me break out in a clammy sweat.

'Most incredible person I think I've ever met.'

Another flush from me and now he's smiling down at me.

'I love watching you blush. It's so against your nature and you're so pretty when you do.'

I inch back a tiny bit, to look him full in the face.

'Jake . . .'

'Mmmmm . . . ' he says, pulling me back towards him, his grip like iron now.

'What are we doing here? Are we both sure about this?'

'Never been surer of anything in my life.'

'But what about your woman? The Girl from Ipanema, sorry, I mean, what's her name, Monique?'

'Nothing.' He just smiles that wry crooked smile I love and looks at me the way he always does whenever he thinks I'm acting like a complete mental case. 'No story whatsoever. We're friends, that's all. Went to a movie together once and that was it. I already told you that.'

'Yeah, but, I just wondered . . .'

'Come on love,' he smiles, lazily tracing a line of light kisses along the path of my collarbone, 'the only reason I even mentioned her was because you seemed so edgy with me when we were out to dinner last week. I honestly thought you were about to tell me you were married or in a long-term relationship or something. So I just thought it might put your mind at rest a bit, take some pressure off you if I told you about Monique, that's all. If you'll remember though, I did make it clear to you we were only going out as friends . . .'

Now. This is it. The perfect moment.

'Jake . . . there was something I wanted to tell you that night, but I never got a chance . . .'

'Shhh, can't you see I'm trying to kiss you here?'

With that, he grabs me by the waist and pulls me towards him so that now we're face to face, inches from each other and all I can do is forget what I was about to say and look deep into his beautiful, wide blue eyes, just wishing he'd lean down and kiss me properly . . . And when he eventually does, it's an endless kiss, strong and deep and so, so sexy and I can't help myself from moaning softly as he strokes down the whole length of my body . . . it's hot and getting hotter and I don't want him to stop, don't want this moment to be over, want nothing more then to commit this to memory, so I can relive it later . . .

It takes every gram of strength I have to pull away, but somehow I manage to.

'No, please Jake, not until I've talked to you . . .'

'What's up love?'

Next thing, the bedroom phone rings.

And now I'm startled, almost shocked back to sobriety.

'Let it ring and tell me what's bothering you,' he says thickly, arms clamped tight around me.

But I can't, in case it's Helen or Lily or some problem at home. I detangle myself, slide away from him towards the bedside table and pick it up.

'Hello?'

'Eloise, where in the name of god are you?'

Ruth O'Connell, sounding even tipsier than I feel right now.

'Hi Ruth, you OK?'

'Come on, the party's started and you're late! We're all down here waiting for you, so hurry up! And get that gorgeous slab of a man of yours down here too! Steve from accounts is making serious moves on me again and I need to talk boys with you!'

I smile, hang up, then turn back to Jake.

'Party's started,' I tell him. 'Time for us to go.'

Can't tell him now. But for the first time all week, I think maybe, just maybe, everything will be fine when I do.

'Party hasn't even begun to start,' he grins broadly. 'You just wait till I get you back up here later on. Now that'll be the real party.'

Five minutes later and arm in arm together we both trip down the massive stone staircase into the large, looming and slightly terrifying library, where aperitifs are being served before dinner. Jake holds open the door for me, winks at me, then brushes his hand lightly up and down my bare back as I waft past him. And it's thrilling and sexy all at once and as I smile coyly up at him all I can think is – later.

Just wait until later. That's all we have to do. In a few hours, all this work malarkey will be done and dusted and then it'll just me and him . . . *alone.* And I'll come clean to him and with luck we'll just pick up exactly where we left off on that gorgeous, conveniently oversized big double bed . . .

Jesus, I'm acting and feeling like a teenager, I think, totally assaulted by a mixture of relief and happiness as a dizziness comes over me just at the memory of him touching me. Nor does Jake show any signs of regretting what just happened either. Every chance he gets, he's brushing up against me, slipping an arm round my shoulders, making it clear to one and all that we're together. Which they all automatically assumed anyway, but still.

And each time he lightly grazes my bare back, it sends a thrill through me that I have neither felt nor experienced in such a mortifyingly long time – I'm guessing sometime during the Clinton administration. And it's all just so sexy and so beyond fabulous; like that feeling you get when you hear the opening bars of *Avalon*, only better.

Anyway, Jake heads to the crowded bar to get us some drinks while I slip into a quiet corner to call home and say nightie-night to Lily. I mwah-mwah her over and over again while she giggles, sing her two verses of *The Bing Bong Song* from Peppa Pig at her insistence and faithfully promise her I'll be home in time to make popcorn and watch a movie of her choice with her on TV, tomorrow evening. Then have to resist the urge to physically kiss the phone as she happily waddles off and Helen takes over.

'So, can you talk?' she asks me excitedly, dying to know all. 'How's it all going?'

'So, so well,' I hiss. 'LOADS to tell you, but just relax. I really think that somehow it's all going to work out, that he won't mind a bit when I tell him. Look, I can't talk now, but for once in my life I really, honestly feel that everything will be just fine . . .'

With that, I spot Jake on his way back with drinks.

'Gotta go, talk later!' I tell her, hanging up.

Later, later, later. And all Jake and I have to do is wait till later.

To be continued . . .

Anyway, the pre-dinner drinks party is packed to the gills, with everyone deep in chat and of course knocking back the freebie champagne and cocktails to beat the band. The vast majority from the *Post*, I can't help noticing, all executing perfect one hundred and eighty-degree head turns, so as to check that there's never anyone close by more important that they should be rubbernecking with instead.

But not me, not this weekend. Not on your life. Tonight to me is about having the one thing I rarely allow myself . . . fun. And possibly sex into the bargain, but I won't count my chickens. Everything is going so incredibly well so far, why shouldn't my glorious good fortune hold out? I think, more than a bit smugly, floating around with a beam on my face like someone who just won the Lotto, but doesn't like to gloat. But even besides Jake, aside from what just happened, tonight is a well-earned celebration with people I wish I'd got to know before and who I'd really like to get to know a whole lot better.

For feck's sake, I think, we do shop talk 24/7 in the office, can't we all just allow ourselves one night off to let our collective hair down? Christ knows, we've earned it.

Next thing I feel a warm hand slip through mine as Jake leans down to whisper reassuringly in my ear.

'Once more into the breach, dear friend.'

'Let me guess, your O.U. English course?'

'Henry the Fifth, the man himself.'

Photos are being taken all round us on camera phones as I beam back up at him, feeling light, lighter than air. He

284

leans down and lightly kisses me just as our picture is taken. I feel the flash in my face, startling me, then I pull back and we both suddenly burst out laughing.

And it's hard to believe it, but this is actually the last time that anything is ever normal between us again.

True to form, it's Seth Coleman who gets the ball rolling. Probably the only person here who's relatively sober, with the lardy-looking head of hair so slicked back tonight, that he bears more than a passing resemblance to Wolverine from X-Men. A galaxy-class schmoozer, the minute his gimlet eye spots us, he oils his way over to Jake then surreptitiously steers him away from me, out of earshot.

It's beautifully done: they're just far enough away that even while straining, I'm still only able to pick up annoying snippets of their conversation. All of which are enough to make my blood chill as a long shadow suddenly stretches itself across this near-perfect day. Because he's grilling Jake, sounding him out, doing a real number on him, almost worthy of a five-and-dime, gumshoe private investigator, circa nineteen-forty-five, by way of Raymond Chandler.

Even worse, I'm stuck with Lady Hume, who's already far more than three sheets to the wind. I can tell by the way she keeps pressing me to call her Shania, but then she only ever abandons the social pecking order when she's totally pissed as a fart. For once, she's abandoned her mobile phone and it's hard to say which is worse; trying to sustain a half-arsed conversation with her while she's rudely tweeting away in front of you, or else having to have a full-blown conversation with her, now that she's phoneless and Twitterless.

She's wearing a dress a good twenty years too young for her, exposing far more flesh than even a gap year student with a perfect body ever should, with her too-blonde hair and too-fake nails that I'm certain she must have spent an absolute packet on. But then Shania's one of those women the Celtic Tiger years really suited, but now that we're all broke, she just comes over as being grossly OTT and faintly embarrassing. There's always one at these things, that one person that you just dread ending up with and sure enough, it's my bad luck to have been collared by her.

'No one here likes me,' she slurs, standing way too uncomfortably close to me and breathing boozy fumes that nearly make me cough. Christ alive, has this one been on the booze for the whole afternoon?

'Even,' she says, starting to sway dangerously now, 'I might say . . . *especially* him.' She practically spits this out and when I politely follow her eye line, I realise she's referring to none other than her husband, Sir Gavin.

'I'm pretty certain he's having an affair, you know. And she's only bloody thirty. Some bitch journalist. Thinks I know nothing about it, but . . .' then her voice drops down to an exaggerated stage whisper, 'I make a point of checking his mobile phone bills every month AND his credit card statements . . . How about that?'

I nod as sympathetically as I can, all the while casting around for someone, anyone, to come and rescue me. But before I can even make eye contact with Jake, she nudges me sharply and sloshes a good half of the margarita she's been milling into all over the carpet. Jesus.

A second later, she's leaning in closer, grabbing onto the straps of my dress and locking her lolling head with mine.

'Wanna know what the useless fecker bought for her on Valentine's Day?' she asks me, and somehow it sounds like a threat.

I want to say no, not particularly, but find I can't. I shoot another worried glance over at Jake, but Seth's still monopolising him and he's too far away to dig me out of this.

'Diamond earrings,' Shania goes on, her posh affectation of an accent now almost completely evaporated. 'And you know what the bastard got me? A Magimix blender. A sodding Magimix buggery blender! Bitch he's shagging gets diamonds, I get kitchen appliances.' Then even more scarily, she starts laughing like a nutter.

'You take my advice Eloise, you stay away from all men. Even Mr Rock of a Hunk you've got on your arm tonight. Use him, then dump him and move on. Do you hear me?'

I nod placatingly and make the right noises, while Shania slurs a word that might or might not be 'miserable'. I'm straining to catch snippets of whatever Seth's probing Jake about. And the little I can hear is enough to bring on an out-and-out panic attack.

'So what school did you go to?' Seth is grilling him. 'And where exactly are you originally from? I'm finding that accent of yours particularly hard to place, and I'm normally good with accents. And who are your parents and family, might I know any of them? Do you have brothers and sisters? And what do they all do? And what did you work at before you got a teaching job? And where exactly did you go to study? Which college? And how did you support yourself before then? And where?'

Seth's stone cold sober too, I know by the way he's probably the only person in the whole room not flushed with the heat and with too much champagne. I strain my ears and lean as far back as I can to try and pick up Jake's replies, or even try to catch his eye, but every time I do, Shania, with that drunken sixth sense people get when someone's trying to extricate themselves from them, keeps gripping my arm so tightly she's nearly bruising it, pulling me right back to her.

Christ knows what deep probing Seth is doing on poor Jake. All I know is that there's a cold clutch on my heart that wasn't there before and tiny beads of worry sweat are inconveniently starting to pump down my temples.

Turns out I've every reason to fret.

Shania has strong-armed me down into the place beside her, with Jake on her other side, while Seth sits opposite leaving his date, who it turns out is called Vogue, on my left. Now having been exposed to Vogue for approximately five minutes, not only am I now convinced she is in fact a hired escort, but also that Seth is paying her an hourly rate. The giveaway being the subtle way she keeps checking her watch again and again. I'm sorry, but there's just no way on earth Seth could ever land a stunnah like Vogue, short of paying her two hundred euro an hour, minimum. She's one of those 'look no carbs!' thin women, with a glossy mane of Pippa Middletonesque, high-maintenance wavy hair, caramel skin and a mouthful of pretty white teeth so perfect, I'm thinking veneers. Spends twice as long as anyone else perusing the menu, and when it comes to ordering, it's like an assault course of, 'Oh no, I'm lactose intolerant, coeliac, allergic to fish and only eat red meat once a week.'

God love the poor harassed waiter, is all I can think, looking at him pityingly.

If I didn't have other things on my mind and for nothing

more than pure bloody-mindedness, it wouldn't have been easier for me to start grilling her about Seth, just as he grilled Jake out in the bar. Just a handful of questions, I correctly suspect, along the lines of, 'So tell me, how exactly did you two meet?' would be enough to flush out an escort from a genuine girlfriend before you could say, 'Dial 1-800-*hotsexydates*'.

But I don't get a chance to. Because Shania, having drained the champagne flute in front of her, then picks up mine and says, 'You're not finishing that, are you?' before downing it in one. I flash Jake a look that says, 'fasten your seatbelts, it's going to get bumpy', but Shania's bypassed drunkenness and has now moved onto obnoxiousness and once she's on a roll, there's absolutely no stopping her.

'Now pleeeeashe don't get me wrong Eloise,' she slurs into my face, 'this guy that you're with . . . Jack? Jock?'

'Jake,' I answer her absently, my thoughts miles away.

And, just so you know, he's not deaf and is sitting just one person away from you, I want to hiss at her, but she's now at that stage of pure stociousness that it wouldn't make the slightest bit of difference.

'Yeah, him. Thatsh's the one. Jock. He's a good-looking guy Eloise. Have you noticed? And he's completely changing your whole pershonality, everyone is saying so. You're the talk of the whooooole party . . .'

Oh would you shut up, please for the love of God, just shut up now. Do you know how much you're embarrassing both of us?

'He's sexy too. Jusht the kind of strong, silent type I'd happily go for myself if my bollocking hushhhhband wasn't staring over at me,' she says cattily.

'Here, have some lovely, cool, iced water,' I say artificially brightly, anything to get off this most mortifying of subjects and get back to all my silent stressing and fretting.

'Oh sod the sodding water!' she says, roughly pushing my arm away, so I slosh a bit of it over my own dress.

'Now you just lishen to me, Eloise. I alwaysh liked you. Alwaysh did. Even though all the other corporate wives said you were just this inhuman, ice-maiden bitch-queen, who terrified grown men and who had nothing else going on in her life apart from her job . . .'

'Here, have a bread roll, please, go on, just one little bread roll . . .' I say to her in the same coaxing tone I use to get Lily to eat her broccoli. Bit of food to soak up the alcohol, I reason, might just keep her quiet and sober her up a bit at the same time.

'But all that time, I shtood up for you. Said absolutely not! That you weren't just the overambitious saddo everyone said you were.'

I say nothing to this, just pick at the corner of a bread roll myself in silent fury, mind racing ahead, wondering what exactly it'll take to get her to shut the feck up once and for all.

And on she still goes.

'You wanna know what I shaid about you?' Shania nudges me so roughly she almost knocks me off my chair. 'Said to hell with what the lot of you think of Eloise Elliot, I admire a driven woman with a bit of determina-tion . . .'

'Oh look, isn't that Gemma Ingram over there, talking to Marc Robinson? Haven't seen her in years, let me just slip over to her to say hello . . .'

'Shtop changing the shagging subject!'

She senses I want to escape and is gripping onto my arm

now. Short of the fire alarm going off, there's just no way out.

'But you just lishten to me Eloise, and lishten good. Don't let any fecking man take over your life. Because that's what all men will eventually do. I don't want you to end up like me. I don't want to see you five years from now, having sacrificed your whole career for some man who'll then shhtart chasing after thirty-year-olds while you sit at home night after night thinking he's at a board meeting. At shagging *ten o' clock* on a Saturday night, for fuck's sake. Mark my words Eloise, let a man into your life and you'll loshe so much more than you have to gain. You have to trusht me . . . I've been round the block and I know exactshly what I'm talking about.'

'Oh look, here's the menu,' I interrupt her, brightly. 'Mmmmm, I'm starving, what are you going to order? I think I might start with the monkfish . . .'

'Sex,' she nods sadly into her now empty glass, her teeth already well-blackened from all the red wine. 'That's all they're good for. Sex. Even that big hunk of yours on your other side here . . .'

Jake, who's in turn being bored to death by Seth beside him, shoots me a quick 'you okay?' look and I feel him squeezing my hand under the table, but right now I'm beyond rescuing.

'Wanna know what I think the best FECKING thing you ever did in your whooole life was, Eloishe?'

'Why not tell me later? Come on, let's order . . .'

But I'm too late.

'Beshhht thing you ever did was deciding that you wanted to have a baby and not hanging around for any man to make it happen for you.'

Okay, now my stomach actually physically clenches. I shoot her a dangerous, shut-up-now-or-I'll-physically-throttle-you-with-my-bare-hands look, but it's no use.

Maybe Jake didn't hear that. Maybe not – there's a good chance he didn't. Every chance in fact . . .

Next thing, Shania is clapping her hands together, loudly applauding me, just in case we weren't attracting enough attention.

'Fair play to you Eloise, tshat's what I shay! You took control and did what you wanted to do! Who needs a fecking man anyway to have a baby with these days anyway?'

'Shania, shhh, please!' I'm almost snarling at her now, heat rushing to my face.

'Don't you dare shush me! I'm throwing you my pearls of wishdom here, you know!'

To make matters worse, by now the speeches have started and Jimmy Doorley, our CFO, is droning through a microphone with so much reverb that it nearly whistles, about last year's fiscal returns and how this year, our projected profits will be down five per cent and blah-di-blah-di-blah.

Meanwhile I'm telegraphing furious 'we need to listen to this!' looks at Shania, but she's on a drunken roll now and no power on earth is about to shut her up.

'In 2011, our net profit after tax was regrettably down almost five per cent on a lik-for-like basis, compared with the previous financial year,' Jimmy's monotonous voice is whistling into the gammy microphone, boring for Ireland, whining on and on and on.

Polar icecaps will melt and seabeds will rise before he ever shuts up, I think, willing him to get on with it as quickly as possible so we can get onto the meal and then get the hell out of here. But even though the room has gone quiet and everyone is at least feigning interest in his speech, no such concerns about politeness are troubling Shania.

'Courshe I remember all too well the gosship going round about you at the time,' she nudges me roughly. 'When you were pregnant I mean.'

'Shhh . . . we really need to keep quiet for this speech,' I hiss at her, nearly ready to stuff a napkin into her mouth if I thought it would do the trick.

'Oh don't be so ridiculoush!' Shania's voice is vinegary by now. 'Who in their right minds would wanna listen to boring old Jimmy Doorley anyway?'

A few filthy looks from the tables beside us, but they don't even register with her.

'Oh people shaid all kinds of things about you at the time. Who's Eloise Elliot's baby daddy was like a partshy game we all played – but you wanna know what I said? I said "to hell with the lot of you anyway!" I shaid that I admired any woman with the balls to do what you did. Because being a shingle parent is bloody hard. And didn't you have the lasht laugh? You've got a lovely little child now . . . Boy or a girl? I forget – but they'd be about three years old now, ishn't that right?'

'Shhh, please!' I shoot her a scalding stare and furiously grip her arm, but it's a waste of time.

I offer up a silent, panicky prayer to anyone up above who'll listen that Jake hasn't overheard any of this, but it's impossible to tell. He's sitting stone still beside me, looking straight ahead of him, fixing the podium with a borehole stare. All the gentle hand squeezing that went on under the table just a minute ago has suddenly stopped.

'Then when the truth leaked out, no one could believe

293

it! Artifishal insemination – genius! But I said, for Christ's shake why does any modern women need a partner to get pregnant with these days? Who wants some man in their life telling you how to be a bloody parent anyway? You were dead right Eloise. Are you lishenting to me? Look at me when I'm talking to you! I want to tell you that I think going to a sperm bank was the BESHT idea you ever had! Beshides, I think I might even be able to guess the name of the clinic you musht have gone to; the Reilly something, the Reilly Institute out somewhere in Shandyford, is that where you went? The name shtuck in my mind 'cos a friend of mine goes there for H.R.T. and she shays it's THE place in town to go to for artificial . . . artificial . . . whatdoyoucall it, anyway, you know what I mean. So, am I right? Eloise, anshwer me, for God's shake!'

She's actually thumping the table, infuriated now at being ignored and airbrushed away.

Please, please, please don't let Jake have heard, please God, Santa, Buddha, anyone who's listening, please . . .

But I'm wasting my breath. And it's the way Jake is staring straight ahead, glassy-eyed, that's worrying me.

He knows, I can just feel it. Knows everything now, Shania's lovely, tactful reference to the Reilly Institute surely put paid to that.

Plus, judging by the looks we're getting, not only our table, but half the room just heard Shania's last remark. I'm sweating worse than Robert de Niro ever did in *Raging Bull* and all I know is that I have to get her out of here. Right now. I don't care how rude it looks, I'll worry about damage limitation later.

'Right, that's it Shania, I think the best thing is if I take you outside for a bit of air, right now. Come on . . .'

I cast around our table, desperately needing someone to help me, but no one will. Not Seth, not his Dial-A-Date and not even Jake, who won't as much as make eye contact with me. So I try to arm-lift her out of her chair, but she's a lead weight and won't as much as budge for me.

'Get your handsh off me, I'm not going ANYWHERE!' Shania is almost yelling at me now, viciously swatting me aside. 'I wanna another drink!'

'Excuse me, is there some kind of problem at that table?' Jimmy politely asks into the microphone.

'No, emm . . . There's no problem here! Everything's fine!' I answer over-brightly, my mouth stretched into a smile so wide that my muscles start to twitch with the effort.

I'm now sickeningly aware that even though four hundred other pairs of eyes in the room seem to be solely focused on Shania and me, Jake alone just stares straight ahead, saying nothing, doing nothing, like he's wilfully ignoring me.

Jake, who's spent the whole evening so far looking over at me, checking on me, mouthing me little silent words of acknowledgement, slipping his arm round me when he thought no one was looking. It feels like the mysterious tele-pathic bridge that was always between us has just been broken in two. He knows, is all I can think. Knows everything.

'For feck's sake Eloise, will you let me go!' Shania yells, if not quite savagely, then in that general area. 'I was only trying to give you a shagging compliment, you moron!'

I nearly burst with relief when I see the white head of Robbie from Foreign leaping to his feet to help me lead her out. He mutters something to me about finding Sir Gavin, but he's up at the top table, rustling through a pile of notes and getting primed to make his own speech next, generally acting like his wife's carry-on is a relatively normal occurrence that he doesn't particularly want anything to do with.

'I was only trying to tell you,' Shania spits furiously at me as we eventually haul her out of her chair, 'that if I had my time over, I'd do exaxtshly what you did! Not bother with a man, jusht go to a sperm bank and have done with it! Now, will you fecking well let me go!'

Meanwhile Seth sits back opposite, fingers latticed thoughtfully, mouth pursed in a cat's-bum shape, looking from me to Jake and from Jake to me with just one expression hardened onto his face. 'Tonight just got interesting.'

'You know what they say, *in vino veritas*,' is the last thing I hear him tell the entire table, as Robbie and I gently steer Shania out of the room and to safety.

Takes every last gram of strength I have not to go back there, pick up an empty wine bottle, smash it up against his greasy, slimy head and pray that it causes lasting damage.

I would have infinitely preferred a full-frontal, blazing row with insults being flung, lampshades smashed and voices loud enough to raise the dead. *That* I could have handled. Rage and passion and temper and angst, I'd deal with. Wouldn't be much different from your average working day at the *Post*, to be honest.

But not this. Anything but this.

Jake and I are back in our room, having somehow limped through the dregs of the evening without managing to say two words, but now we can avoid each other no longer. And it's beyond awful. Like the lovely, warm-hearted, considerate, concerned Jake, my pal Jake, my buddy, has left the building and in his place is some kind of avatar who looks and sounds like him, but who's glacially cold towards me and who'll only talk to me in curt, clipped yes-or-no monosyllables.

No more than a few hours ago, is all I can randomly think, everything I wanted either for me or for Lily was in this room. And now look at us, moving coldly round each other like strangers, the attraction and desire that had been in his eyes all evening now completely ebbed away. I try to read him but I can't, so I look at him, waiting on the blow to fall, but it never does. He's furious, though you'd never know it if you didn't know Jake; he's very still.

As soon as we shut the bedroom door and are safely in private, he begins to pack.

Bollocks.

So I open with the obvious.

'Jake, leaving now is ridiculous. It's past midnight for God's sake; you'll never get a taxi from here all the way home.'

'Fine, I'll walk if I have to.'

'Well, now you're just being childish.'

I want to claw the line back the minute it comes out.

A long, cold look is all I get back from him.

'I think the days of you telling me what to do and how to live my life are long over,' he says, the words enveloped in bitterness.

'Can I just explain? After everything I've done for you, can you at least hear me out?'

'Nothing to hear,' he says, neatly packing a shirt and jacket in his suitcase. How can he be so fastidiously tidy at a time like this? I think, my twin, default emotions of anger and frustration now starting to bubble through my hot little veins.

'And as far as I'm concerned Eloise, all you need to know is that I can't be around you right now.'

'Jake, you have to believe me. I was planning on telling you this weekend . . . Tomorrow in fact, I had it all worked out. I've tried to tell you before – remember when we went to dinner last week? I was determined to tell you then, but . . .'

'Not determined enough, it would seem.'

'Would you stop bloody packing and just listen!'

Another icy look from him.

'Go on then.'

'Jake, you have no idea how much this has been weighing on me. But you have to understand the only reason I didn't tell you sooner was I was terrified you might not want anything to do with us if you knew. Believe me, I did try, but there was always something, like your exams last week. So then I thought . . .'

'You're honestly telling me you thought some shagging exams were more important than knowing that I'm a father, and we have a child and that you've basically been deceiving me since the day we met? Jesus, Eloise, do you ever stop to listen to yourself?'

'Look I know I should have come clean to you sooner–'

'A LOT sooner . . .'

'But that aside,' I begin to say, deliberately keeping my tone low and even, 'the only thing I'm guilty of is of wanting to help you–'

'You've lied to me practically from day one, lied to me about everything, and this is your idea of an excuse?'

'Well, you lied to me first!'

Typical editorial reaction, turn the tables round, draw first blood then await subsequent fallout.

'Lied how, exactly?'

'Excuse me, you'll recall the application form you were required to fill in at the Reilly Institute? Jesus, practically everything you wrote on it was a total lie! You said your name was William Goldsmith!'

'I already explained that to you a long time ago . . .'

'And that you'd written a thesis on the country's economic meltdown?'

'Oh here we go, you and your photographic memory.'

'. . . That you played piano up to concert grade?'

'What did you expect me to say? That I played the tin whistle?'

'May I remind you that you also claimed you'd won gold medals for the Trinity College two hundred metres and you rowed for the college team?'

'Will you let it go? What did you think I was going to put down anyway? That I played darts?'

'Jake, I BELIEVED all that! I fell for every line of it and it was all a complete lie!'

'I needed the money, I'd have said or done anything,' he says coolly. 'So I lied on some poxy form to a medical clinic three years ago. You think they'd have taken me on and paid me, if they'd known what I really was? Besides, what about you? That's chickenfeed beside what you've done. Practically every word out of your mouth since we met has been an out-and-out whopper. Tracking me down to Wheatfield with this completely mental cock-and-bull story about researching a feature on ex-cons and what they do when they get out?'

'I was trying to help you!' I insist, my voice getting screechier and screechier in direct proportion to how anxious I'm getting. 'That's all I ever wanted to do. You have to believe me.'

'Just one question before I go,' he says, bags packed by now, one hand on the door, ready to walk out. Christ, I think, this is like a Terrence Rattigan melodrama, and I'm the 1940s housewife about to fling herself round his knees and beg forgiveness.

'Why, Eloise? Why did you do it in the first place? Why even bother with someone like me?'

I try to compose myself, which is difficult, considering I'm on the verge of a full-blown panic attack; heart palpitation, ice-cold sweat pumping, blurry vision, the works. Even breathing is something I have to concentrate on as the air is only coming to me in sharp, jagged bursts. I can't even feel pain yet, instead there's just an empty space inside me with the expectation of pain to come.

'You want the truth?'

'For probably the first time since I've known you Eloise, yes, I do.'

I slump on the edge of the bed. I've no choice, the dizziness is that nauseating. And suddenly the bedpost is at the oddest angle.

A throbbing moment and I know I'll have to answer him.

'I didn't do it for you. I did it for my little girl.'

'A . . . It's . . . You have a daughter?' he says, voice breaking just the tiniest bit.

My stomach clenches just at him saying that. Beyond weird. *His* daughter he's talking about with such cold indifference, such clinical dismissiveness. His as well as mine.

Just for two seconds, I wish the old Jake would come back: he'd understand. He'd listen and realise where I'd been coming from all along, he'd instinctively know how I was feeling; he'd ask me if I was okay and put all this into its proper perspective. I could talk to the old Jake, tell him all about Lily, show him the photos of her I carry everywhere with me, tell him how much she takes after him, from her strawberry-blonde mop of hair to her huge blue pools-for-eyes. I want to tell him how smart she is, how eaten up with pride I am by her. No one has a cleverer, smarter, more beautiful, more precious little girl than I have – correction, than *we* have.

I could explain to the old Jake how I went on a wild goose chase all those weeks ago that took me on what felt like a trawl through every housing estate in the whole of the greater North County Dublin area. And more importantly, *why*. Because I never wanted my precious little girl to grow up and decide to track her biological father down, then realise that he was some deadbeat dad with a prison record. Someone who flittered from address to address, changing his identity to avoid trouble. And anyway, where would Jake have ended up had I not stepped in? That's what I'd like to know, I think, sudden self-righteous fury flooding through me.

Most of all though, I could tell the old Jake that, as usual, when it comes to human relations, I got it all arseways. Because at the end of the day, far from my being the one to change him, if anything, it's been the other way around. I try to remember back to the person I was before we met and find I barely can.

Because the battle-hardened harridan of old has long since left the building; in her place is a more rounded, relaxed human being and I've got Jake and only Jake to thank for that. I want to tell him all this and more, I want him to hold me like he did just a few short hours ago, so I can fill the hollow of his neck with tears, but when I bring my gaze up to his, something in his eyes freezes me in my tracks.

'What's her name?' he asks, giving me a scalding look. 'And don't lie or I'll know.'

'Lily,' I say weakly, but starting to gain a bit of strength, though my voice still sounds like it's coming from another room half a mile away. 'Her name is Lily.'

'Oh Jesus . . . The little girl I met you with in the Green that afternoon?'

'Yes.'

'And *still* you said nothing to me? Out of curiosity Eloise, is everything that comes out of your mouth a complete deception?'

'Stop it – will you just stop it please? If you want the truth . . .'

'You and truth are two words that seem at variance with each other in the same sentence.'

'Insult me all you want, but the truth is that all of this was for Lily, she wanted to know who her father was; you don't understand what it was like, she'd become obsessed with it . . .'

'And you never wanted her to grow up knowing that her father was an ex-con,' he says flatly.

I nod, eyes fixed on the floor. I can't meet Jake's stare, don't know if I can stomach that cold, flinty look he's giving me.

'And in all this time, you couldn't have told me? Couldn't have trusted me with this? We were friends for christ's sake, best friends – and could have been so much more. But friends don't treat each other like this. Do you know how difficult it is for someone like me to ever trust anyone? And I trusted you, worse eejit me . . .'

Exactly what Helen had prophesied he'd say. To the letter.

'What did you imagine I'd do anyway, Eloise?' he goes on, face white with ice-cold fury now. 'Drag you though the family law courts? Demand access rights? Teach a young child how to smash and grab and rob cars and not get caught? Is that really what you thought of me? "Once a con, always a con, this guy can't be trusted, particularly not around a little kid". . .?'

'No, that wasn't it!' I tell him firmly. Because if I don't get the chance to say this before he leaves, chances are I never will. 'All I wanted was for Lily to have a father she'd one day be proud of, that's all! And look at you Jake, look how far you've come! A few months ago, you didn't even think you'd make parole and now look! You're . . . Well, you're . . .'

I can't even begin to finish that sentence. I want to tell him how much he's grown on me, how much I've come to depend on him, but the words stick in my throat. So instead, I find myself doing one of those ridiculously over-dramatic gestures you only ever see in old black and white movies; walk to the fireplace and cling to the top of it, almost as though it's steadying me.

'I already know all this,' Jake goes on dispassionately. 'You don't need to remind me. You've made me respectable. A working-class father wasn't good enough for you, didn't fit in with your notions of respectability. So instead, you moulded me into your idea of what the perfect dad should be. Jesus Eloise, do you even realise just what a snob that makes you?'

Now suddenly out of nowhere, in the middle of all these accusations and insults, a rage of energy starts pumping through me.

'It wasn't just what I wanted,' I tell him, wishing my voice didn't wobble as I say it, 'you wanted it too. Come on, admit it Jake, you wanted respectability and a middle-class life just as much as I wanted it for you. You're a grown man for God's sake, why else would you have gone along with it like you did? So just don't accuse me of snobbery, because it's not fair. A lot of what I did was wrong and I'm truly sorry for that, but please understand I did it all for the right reasons. I wanted you to realise your potential. That's all, I swear to you, that's all I ever wanted . . .'

'And you've lied to me every single step of the way.'

For a split second we look at each other like two actors in a play who've forgotten their lines.

It's an aching moment, but in no time it's all over.

'Don't ever try to find me again, because you won't,' are his final words to me and I swear it feels exactly like a knife being plunged directly into my heart.

Then one quick, efficient door slam and it's all over.

For a long time after he'd left I stood statue-still, unable to move, the blood singing in my ears.

Took a long, long time to realise that he'd really gone.

Gone for good.

PART FOUR

Chapter Twelve

There was no doubt about it, Seth Coleman hadn't enjoyed one of those cursed directors' weekends as much in a long, long time; years, in fact. Back in the days when he'd first been headhunted onto the *Post*, he'd look forward to a directors' weekend in pretty much the same way he'd look forward to root canal work. Back then, certainly as far as the board were concerned, it used to be one excruciatingly long Eloise Elliot love-fest. And what concerned the board was pretty much all that concerned Seth ninety-nine per cent of the time.

Course that was in Madame Elliot's glory days, when no one at the top could see as much as a chink in the Iron Lady's armour; everyone from Sir Gavin down kowtowed to her, responding to each and every valid concern about the paper Seth had with a dismissive, 'well you know, Eloise has worked wonders for us in the past, so let's just see how this one pans out, shall we?'

And so Seth had stayed on the sidelines, biding his time, waiting to pick his moment, watching the paper's online edition haemorrhage cash as sales continued on a sharp downward trajectory. Easy enough to blame the recession for that, people just weren't spending in the way that they used to. Which was all the more reason why the online edition was now even more critical than ever. And it was Madam Elliot's weak spot, that was all too obvious. Her strategy was at best flawed, and at worst, not working. Which clearly meant it was time for Seth to step in.

But something had shifted lately and now Seth, with his fondness for littering conversation with foreign phrases wrongly calculated to impress women, found himself thinking *tout ça change*. At the directors' weekend she'd somehow morphed from the Ice Maiden into Miss Popularity. That was blatantly obvious to anyone with an eye in their head. Everyone had seen it, everyone from the top down had commented on it within his hearing at one time or another.

It had been quite an extraordinary phenomenon to witness first hand; editors like Robbie Turner, who'd regularly said he'd rather pan fry his own liver than spend more than two minutes in Eloise's company socially, now were literally fighting to get a seat next to her, laughing with her, joshing with her, treating her, well, like an old buddy. Had Seth not witnessed it for himself first hand, he'd never have thought it possible.

This astonishing, about-turn change in Madam Elliot had all begun several weeks back, when she kept mysteriously disappearing from the office, and no one could figure out why. Then the unthinkable began to happen, she started treating those around her like actual human beings for a change and not desk-chained automatons like she was herself. Or rather, like she *used* to be. Letting people slip off for family events, giving them early holidays on full pay, unexpectedly and thoughtfully bringing everyone Starbucks coffees to their editorial meetings, that kind of thing.

She's met someone, the rumour mill chanted. And he was softening her, slowly but most definitely, to the extent that the Queen Bee now finally seemed to be putting her own personal life ahead of her career. Which of course was around the same time that Seth finally made sure he got to meet this mysterious guy and made bloody certain that he was included in the directors' weekend. So he could grill him up close and personal.

Best decision he'd made in a long time, as it had turned out. Because the past weekend really was one for the annals; Sir Gavin's wife drunkenly making a show of herself at their table, then bringing up the unmentionable subject that Eloise had her child by artificial insemination . . . All *fabulous* stuff. You couldn't buy it. Seth had almost wished he'd had a video camera to tape the look on her horrified face. Clearly hadn't come clean to her boyfriend about that particular gem; that was all too obvious.

Not that there was anything incriminating about that, regrettably far from it. But you still couldn't get away from one thing; there was just something about that Jake guy, something Seth couldn't quite put his finger on. At least, not yet.

Oh make no mistake, he'd interrogated him every chance he got at the pre-dinner drinks, but came up against a virtual blank wall. Fired every question under the sun at him about his background and still came away with next to nothing. Still though, no harm in digging a little deeper, was there? Because Seth too had started out his career as an investigative journalist and knew that no one, absolutely no on, just landed on the scene without some kind of a history behind them.

But with this guy? *Nada*, not a thing. Went to a school

that Seth had never heard of, dodged a lot of his questions, knew absolutely no one that Seth knew, didn't even work with anyone he could use to get the low-down on him. Which was unusual to say the least, particularly in a glorified village like Dublin, where everyone not only knew everyone else, but had every last scrap of inside information on them, their next-door neighbour and their next-door neighbour's cat into the bargain.

Then there was that accent. It wasn't one he could place and Seth was usually good at automatically divining where you stood on the social pecking order by the way you spoke. It was a worked-on accent though, one that had been sanded down and polished, that was blatantly clear.

If there was one thing Seth was certain of in his bones, it was this. There was far more to Jake Keane than met the eye. Otherwise why would he have been at such pains not to chat a bit about his background, where he'd come from, who his family were, all the normal stuff that people tended to do socially? Made no sense.

With that barracuda instinct that he was fast becoming famous for, Seth had even taken the precaution of having a word with Sir Gavin over a round of golf, the morning after that excruciating dinner at Davenport Hall. Idly let it slip that Eloise Elliot's date seemed like a man with, let's just say, friends in low places. Sir Gavin had shrugged indifferently and kept on striding towards the fairways, but Seth's curiousity was well and truly piqued now. He was like a dog with a bone, determined to get the bottom of – what exactly?

He wasn't quite sure yet, but one thing was for definite. The editor of a paper of record like the *Post* was a public figure, and as such, like Caesar's wife, his or her personal life was expected to be above reproach. So on the off-chance that there was something shady about Eloise's new man, surely it was in the board's interest to be made aware of it? Course it was. Certainly if Seth had anything to do with it. And if, let's just say, any unsavoury associations should reflect badly on Eloise, then that was hardly his fault, now was it?

Which was why he now found himself heading into Finnegans bar on Poolbeg St., just before eleven p.m. on one of those summer nights when it's pitch dark, lashing rain and feels more like October. A real hardcore journos' pub this, one where pub closing hours were regularly ignored and old men spat on the floor and no one batted an eyelid.

Bloody typical of Jim Kelly to pick some dive like this for their rendezvous, Seth thought disdainfully, seeking him out, then immediately spotting him nursing a pint of Guinness in a corner snug. But then Jim Kelly was an old-school hack, someone everyone at the *Post* automatically turned to if they needed information, let's just say, of a more *sensitive* nature.

'There you are. Late,' growled Jim, seeing Seth sit gingerly down on the wooden bar stool opposite him, fingers twitching to whip out his hanky and give the seat a good dusting down first, before perching uncomfortably on the edge of it. Looking for all the world like the head butler at *Downton Abbey* conducting an interview with a new chimney sweep.

Seth made no apology for his tardiness, just offered Jim another drink, was relieved when he said no and came straight to the point. The sooner he got out of this filthy kip the better.

'Need a favour,' he told Jim, who nodded.

'Why else would you have called me?'

'Can you run a check on Eloise Elliot's new boyfriend? Guy by the name of–'

'Let me hazard a wild guess,' said Jim, sitting right back in his chair, arms folded, flashing his shark-like grin, teeth long-since yellowed from the fags.

'A certain Jake Keane. Would that be right?'

Seth nodded.

'How did you know?' he asked, a bit puzzled at how Jim had second-guessed him so fast.

'Make it my business to know a lot of things,' Jim answered vaguely.

'So what can you tell me?'

'If it's deep background you're looking for on that guy,' said Jim, knocking back the dregs of a Powers whiskey that had been sitting in front of him, 'I think I can save us both a considerable amount of time and trouble. Be warned, this information will cost you though.'

Half an hour later Seth was on the pavement again, relieved to be out of that stinking hellhole and feeling more exhilarated than he'd done in months.

Because right now he felt like a footballer with just one, precious shot to an open goal.

Eloise Elliot's whole career was sitting precariously on a time bomb. And now he knew precisely how to detonate it.

Chapter Thirteen

Same crapology, different day, Eloise thought distractedly as she shuffled her way through everyone else and into the *Post's* conference room, all set for the first news briefing of the day.

Ahh; crapology. Yet another one of Jake's, mash-up contributions to the English language.

Jake. Funny how, even at the most unexpected times, he still had the power to inveigle his way into her subconscious. And try as she might to banish him from her mind, somehow he kept intruding.

'Not that I've time to listen to the answer,' Ruth O' Connell said to her on the way in, 'but are you OK?'

'Ehh . . . yeah, why wouldn't I be?'

Eloise answered, puzzled at her even asking the question in the first place. Ruth never inquired after anyone, at any time, ever. As far as she was concerned, once you were alive, showing a resting pulse rate and continuing to turn up for work, you were assumed to be perfectly fine, unless subsequently stretchered off by a team of paramedics with paddles affixed to your heart, end of story.

In other words, just like Eloise herself used to carry on, not all that long ago.

'Oh, nothing,' Ruth backpedalled, instantly realising she'd said The Wrong Thing.

'I suppose I'm . . . just a bit tired, you know yourself,' Eloise tried her best to smile weakly back at her, as the momentary flush of irritation passed. Hardly Ruth's fault that she'd picked up on the low-level depression that had been hanging like a fog over her ever since . . . Well, ever since.

And in all this time, she thought, drifting back up into her cloud of anxiety, not so much as a single word from Jake; nothing. Like he'd just completely vanished right back to where he came from; thin air. He'd moved lock, stock and barrel out of Helen's flat and wasn't returning phone calls, not to mention any of the countless messages she'd left for him at the language school. During her darker moments in the rare bit of time that Eloise got to herself, she oscillated between bouts of fist-rattling, white-hot anger, then lately – even more worryingly – a deep unease about what in the name of God had actually happened to him.

Frankly, it was getting harder by the day to tell which was worse.

Yes, she'd messed up royally, yes what she did was wrong on so many levels, she knew that and God knows, she'd beaten herself up about it enough times. But still, she could be so annoyed at him, livid at how he could just stalk off Homer Simpsonlike in high dudgeon without even giving her the courtesy of a second chance. Hadn't he been given just that himself? But no, instead of putting what she'd done behind them and starting over, as far as she was concerned, he was sulking, letting her sweat while he hid out God alone knew where. Punishing her, torturing her, acting like a complete child.

This white-fury, of course, would quickly boomerang into annoyance directed squarely back at herself. For Christ's sake, she'd think in her stronger moments, wasn't dealing with almighty crap like this the very reason why she electively didn't ever do relationships? Or even friendships? Because this was what inevitably happened; you invested so much time and all of your considerable energies in one other person, only to have the door firmly slammed right in your face. So why did she even bother in the first place?

Then there was Lily, pretty much the only person in her life that could put a smile on her face these days. Every night when she rushed home to her, Eloise would play with her, sing to her, bathe her and put her to bed while the same thought ran round her head. The one good thing to come out of this whole mess was that she'd never introduced him to Lily. Because if he'd met her and then chose to bugger off on her, Eloise swore she'd have strangled him with her bare hands, gladly done time for it, and very likely ended up behind bars in Wheatfield Prison herself.

At least Lily was okay and oblivious to the backstage drama that had gone on. And now these mornings when she'd snuggle into her bed at the crack of dawn and ask, 'Mama? Have you found my daddy yet?' Eloise would just pull her tightly to her and gloss over the subject, telling her how loved she was, that she was the best little girl in the whole world and how lucky they both were to have Auntie Helen living with them. And Lily would smile her gap- toothed little smile at that and let it go.

Another thing though; now that Jake was officially gone from her life, why couldn't she seem to just do what she always did? Bury herself in work and get on with her career? The one thing that had never in her whole life let her down before?

Because somehow she just wasn't able to focus anymore. Found herself barely able to concentrate these days; she whose proudest boast once was that she could multitask for Ireland, keeping tabs on about ten different conversations all at once and still stay fully abreast of all of them. Normally, even on the bad days, and there were certainly plenty enough of them, work filled her, gave her a buzz that got her through the interminable hours until she could get home to Lily.

She thought habit and routine would save her, but for some reason, not now. All she knew for certain was that when you stripped away every fluctuating emotion she was feeling, here's what she was left with. Wherever Jake was, whatever he was doing, whoever he was with now . . . She just missed her friend. Missed him far more than she'd ever have thought possible. And night-times were worst. Because nights were when they used to talk. Not about anything life-alteringly huge; they wouldn't take the world apart then put it back together again; they'd just have long, meandering chats to each other about their respective days and if she ever dared stray into moaning or stressing territory, he'd gently bring her round, tease her out of it, make her laugh, make her feel like she wasn't battling the world alone all the time.

All over now, she sighed restlessly to herself. It was over and she'd never see him again. Her mind had already accepted this.

She just wished someone would explain it to her heart.

'Course, know what you need to cheer you up a wee bit?' Ruth playfully nudged her, as they took their seats round the already packed conference room, everyone laden down with briefcases, notebooks, iPhones, iPads, Starbucks takeouts, the whole works. All ready to hit the ground running.

'What's that?'

'A night of passion with that ride of a lover boy of yours. That'd sure as hell put the colour back in your cheeks, lassie.'

Half an hour later, and the rough cut of tomorrow's front page was finally beginning to take shape. The lead story, after much aggressive canvassing from Robbie, was the Republican primary in Washington, followed up by yet another interest rate rise pitched by finance editor Jack Dundon, the only calm, measured voice in a roomful of journos all yelling over each other like kids in a disorderly classroom, each desperately wanting to get their stories maximum prominence.

Eloise was working fast and furious today though, and in the space of twenty minutes, had already covered both foreign and political; a developing story of a government minister accused of planning corruption during the property boom . . . One to watch and monitor closely, she told the room to much nodding and grunting, as she briskly dealt with the story and moved on.

Wish some random outsider would step in and edit my life, she found herself suddenly thinking from out of nowhere as she stretched across the table to get her next set of briefing notes. Wish some higher being would decree from some heavenly conference table exactly what I need do to solve my own personal drama, and bark instructions at me as to how best I could move on from here.

Some bleeding chance, she sighed, suddenly realising that the room had gone scarily quiet as everyone just looked at her in a semi-trance, totally unused to her drifting off into space like this.

And so, picking up the pace, she moved onto domestic. As it happened it was pretty quiet, the lead story being the justice minister issuing an outright condemnation of the scenes of violence that had accompanied an Apprentice Boys parade up in Derry the previous day. Which they'd already covered in glorious technicolour and which, in spite of Ruth's table-thumping hissy-fit about giving it a full half page, Eloise was anxious to move on from.

'So what's happening in the courts today?' she asked the table.

'Not much, but the next few days should get a lot more newsworthy, as it happens,' replied Joe McHugh, courts correspondent; by a mile the elder statesman of the room.

'No hot, leggy models suing any of our rivals for defamation this week, then?' Kian from sports joshed to sniggers round the table. 'Pity, we need a few shots of a former Miss Ireland with mascara dribbling down her face after being cross-examined. I see the photo caption now: *Not All The Fake Tan In The World Can Help Her Now . . .*'

'Shhh, give it a rest Kian. Sorry, go on Joe,' said Eloise, scribbling furiously on the sheaf of notes in front of her.

'Okay then, here's my lead . . . Name Michael Courtney ring a bell?' Joe casually threw across the table at her.

Everyone else in the room continued on as normal, the low hum of conversation still buzzed, the world kept turning round on its axis.

Only Eloise looked up sharply from her notes.

'What about him?'

'He's finally standing trial early next week. Should be

juicy. He's been in a holding prison in Portlaoise for almost three months now while they've been trying to gather enough witnesses to testify against him. Which of course, is easier said than done. Might be worth a page six though or even in time, a page three. I'll see what I can do. But for now, I can at least get you five hundred words on what's he's up for and what the likely sentence is. Plus, just to remind readers exactly the kind of hardcase this guy is, maybe I could do a short profile of what it was he allegedly did, that eventually landed him behind bars. What would you say to maybe four thousand words?'

Again the low background drone of chat continued. Only Eloise stayed totally focused on Joe, her face growing whiter by the minute.

'No,' she said firmly. 'We're not covering it. And no mention of what he is or isn't allegedly up for.'

'Now hang on Eloise, the Michael Courtney trial will be a good one, well worth . . .'

'I said no,' she almost barked back at him, then instantly wished she could claw back how irrationally snappy she'd sounded, the minute the words were out of her mouth.

'I'm just saying, people will want reminding of what happened, for God's sake it was well over three years ago now. I just think we should bring them back up to speed, that's all. It was a huge page one at the time, you'll remember. Big story.'

'I remember perfectly well thanks, I just don't think it's news right now. Sorry Joe, it's a no.'

'Well, if we don't, you do know that the *Chronicle* will be sure to splash it . . .'

'So let them. Gimme something else instead. Right then,

319

who's next? Okay Kian, seeing as how you won't shut up, let's hear from sports.'

And the meeting moved on and almost no one appeared to notice. After all, the *Post* frequently dropped stories deemed beneath it, that were too tabloidy, not worth the attention of the paper of record. This was a fairly small story in the grand scheme of things; what could possibly have made it any different?

But directly across the table from Eloise, Seth had been quietly drinking it all in.

Scarcely able to believe his luck.

Just another few days max, he thought. That's all he had to wait.

And then everything would be in place.

Chapter Fourteen

Funny, but in years to come, Eloise would look back on this surreal moment as though it hadn't really happened to her at all, but to some other being that had stepped inside her skin for the day. It took a long, long time for her to be able to even recall, let alone process the exact sequence of events, but she was fairly sure the nightmare had all started in the early hours of the morning as she sat in her office, bashing out the following day's editorial.

A knock on the door. Sir Gavin himself, dressed casually in a golfing jumper and trousers, like he'd unexpectedly been hauled off a golf course and reluctantly had to be dragged back into the office to deal with some emergency. Immediately an alarm bell rang in her head. What the hell was he doing here? He was rarely around in the mornings, was in fact famous for keeping as far from the building as possible until lunchtime at the earliest. Even more worrying; the T. Rexes had already had their weekly meeting/grilling/ hauling over the coals with her the previous day, so why would he need to see her again so soon? And if he did want an emergency meeting with her, why not just call her and summon her up to the T. Rexes' floor, like he normally would?

He very pointedly didn't call her Madame Editrix either. Very Bad Sign.

Come in, sit down, she'd managed to say calmly enough, only the slight tremble in her hands betraying just how nervous she was. Janus-like, her head was normally focused in two directions so she'd always know exactly what any unexpected meeting was about, but for once she was completely stumped.

'We need to talk,' he'd said, easing his considerable girth down into the chair opposite her. He had a newspaper tucked under his arm, which he faux-casually spread out across his lap. Annoyingly, he laid it out face down, so she couldn't read what was on it, but she was pretty certain it was their rival paper, *The Chronicle*. One she made it a point of principle never to buy, read or even glance at, on the grounds that she begrudged that shower of bastards the extra business.

So what was Sir Gavin doing with the rival paper?

'Just a little chat, one on one, you and me privately Eloise, before the board will want to see you. I felt it was the very least I could do for you.'

Oh Christ, she'd thought, this is worse than I thought. Far worse.

'Name of Michael Courtney ring a bell with you?'

She nodded mutely, suddenly sick to her stomach. Years of instinct instantly telling her exactly where this would lead. She immediately felt like someone who knew for certain they were about to be murdered, but just couldn't guess how. Hung, drawn or quartered.

'It's come to my attention . . .'

Via Seth Coleman of course, she thought, her quick mind jumping ahead. Who else would bring this on her?

'. . . That for whatever personal reasons you may have had, you buried a story about him, Eloise. Care to comment?'

She bit her tongue, not sure where to start. He knew the truth, she was certain of that. He'd been told. And now there was nothing for it but to face the music.

'Because,' she stammered awkwardly, 'I felt at this point, the story wasn't sufficiently newsworthy.'

Weak, stupid, lame. She knew it as soon as the words tripped out of her mouth. She knew it and what's more, so did he.

'Not newsworthy?' he replied, eyeballing her coolly. 'The crime boss single-handedly responsible for most of the heroin trade in the city? Whose reign of terror takes in a spate of tiger kidnappings, bank raids, art theft, you name it . . . And you, as editor, decide this somehow isn't newsworthy?'

Eloise couldn't ever remember a time in her life when she'd felt so small. She had to at least try to defend herself, but what to say?

'As I say, Sir Gavin,' she said weakly, her voice sounding so faint it was as if it was coming from another room, 'I had every intention of monitoring it in a few weeks' time, as the trial progressed, but at this point, felt that there was little to be gained from covering it.'

'So, no connection at all with the fact that Michael Courtney just happens to be the same boss your close friend Jake Keane worked for? And even more disturbingly I now hear, actually served a prison sentence for?'

Oh Christ, she thought, physically starting to get nauseous, he *really* knows. Knows everything. But if Seth had been the one to rat her out, then who told him in the first place? Her mind raced, working backwards at the speed of light.

And then suddenly it all fitted. Jim Kelly, the bloody Snoop Dog himself, that's how. Who else could possibly have that information? Wasn't that how she'd found out about Jake in the first place for herself? And what could have been easier for Seth Coleman than to prise it out of him behind her back?

Now she suddenly felt weak at the enormity of what hit her. Because she hadn't a leg to stand on here. She knew it, Sir Gavin knew it; it was official. Game over. She'd fucked up, royally fucked up. And all for what? For a man who wouldn't return her calls, who'd effectively vanished into thin air and who it was doubtful she'd ever even see again.

But if she thought she'd heard the worst of it, she was very much mistaken.

'And then, as if things weren't looking bad enough for you,' said Sir Gavin, picking up *The Chronicle* from his lap and tossing it across the desk to her, 'this was brought to my attention at my golf club this morning by a colleague, who, let's just say, happened to recognise a familiar face from the directors' weekend.'

Christ, what now? Eloise thought, greedily taking the paper from him and doing a lightning-quick scan of the front page. But there was nothing there. She speed-read through the headlines again, in case she'd missed something, but no, nothing. Basically just a rehash of what the *Post* had already run with, lazy shower of unimaginative hacks, she found herself angrily cursing them.

'Turn to page five,' said Sir Gavin calmly, almost passively, fully aware that he held whatever career still lay ahead for her in the palm of his hand, but chose to wear this power lightly.

Eloise did as he asked, and there it was.

Her worst nightmare come to light. Exactly what she'd tried to bury in the first place. In black and white, for all the world to see.

As usual, Joe McHugh, her court correspondent, had been on the money. She hadn't run with it, so therefore her rivals had.

Beside a half page photo of Michael Courtney and a full exposé on the charges police were levelling against him, was a two-inch banner headline that screamed, '*AND MEET THE COHORTS WHO LOYALLY SERVED HIM*'.

Five names were listed below, but it was only when she saw the very last one that her heart physically twisted in her ribcage.

'. . . the youngest of his henchmen, convicted of driving the getaway van during the 2010 raid on a post office in Arklow, Jake Keane. Keane, 31, however, operates under many aliases and was recently released on parole from Wheatfield prison . . .'

It got worse.

There was a photo of Jake too, albeit a bad one. Clearly a police mugshot taken under fluorescent strip lights, one of those incriminating photos that could manage to make anyone look like they'd just massacred a roomful of orphans.

'So Eloise, my obvious question to you is,' said Sir Gavin, his round, florid face puffed scarlet with . . . what exactly? Mortification? Embarrassment? Hard to tell. 'is exactly how long do you think it will take for the connection between Jake Keane and you to be traced? And what then? You do understand, it's the reputation of this paper that I have a sacred duty to uphold.'

She couldn't meet his gaze, but felt his eyes burning into

her and knew she'd have to come out with something, however pitiful. Suddenly she was aware of her mouth moving but without necessarily finding the sound to come out of it. Pointless for her to protest that Jake had been guilty of nothing more than weakness and being unable to say no to a bad crowd he'd got in with when he was barely a teenager. Pointless to try and explain that he'd done the crime, done the time and had paid his debts to society.

She wasn't stupid; all those long months ago, when she first discovered he was serving time in Wheatfield, she'd made precisely the same assumptions that everyone else was probably making right now. Initially she'd been petrified, determined never to allow Lily within ten feet of a convicted criminal. She'd had him down as a hardened serial offender, an unreformed bad boy who'd more than likely nick the credit cards and car keys out of her handbag if she ever was reckless enough to come into contact with him.

But all that had changed in a single phone call. She'd spoken to the prison governor who'd put her completely straight about Jake. He'd patiently gone through Jake's file with her and explained that this guy wasn't like any of the others. Yes, he'd got himself involved in one job for Michael Courtney, but as a driver, nothing more sinister. He was an accessory, a first-time offender who'd been tried and found guilty and was now deeply repentant for what he'd done and highly unlikely ever to reoffend. He'd made a stupid mistake, had fallen in with a dodgy crowd who he'd borrowed money from, and their way for holding him to that debt was to coerce him into acting as their driver for that one job. If you were ever to meet with him, the governor patiently explained to Eloise, you'd see what I mean. This wasn't your usual low-rent

326

criminal; Jake genuinely had been in the wrong place at the wrong time and had now most definitely learned his lesson, the hard way.

And so Eloise had braced herself, remembering that this was all for Lily and Lily alone, and had gone to see him. And the rest was history.

But somehow she couldn't find the words to even try explaining this now. As far as Sir Gavin was concerned, she herself was tainted by association and now this was it; endgame. She'd effectively buried a story to protect Jake and now it was just a waiting game till she herself became part of the story.

'How do you want to proceed on this?' she asked him, surprising herself by sounding that bit calmer now. The worst, the absolute worst had happened and there was nothing for her to do now but to roll with the punches.

Sir Gavin sat right back, patting his portly stomach as though his ulcers were at him and exhaling deeply.

'I'm very fond of you Eloise, you know that.'

She didn't as it happened; in all her years working for him he'd never treated her with anything other than a cool, businesslike detachment. But she managed to nod her head politely enough.

'But when your number's up, I'm afraid it's up. You don't need me to tell you that this will be seen upstairs as a massive error of professional judgement on your part. You are, after all, a public figure with a profile and I'm afraid our rival papers will have a field day with this if it leaks. The editor of the paper of record must at all times be above reproach and unfortunately . . .'

She was, if nothing else, oddly grateful to him for not finishing that sentence.

'Look Eloise,' he went on, surprising her by sounding more kindly now. 'You're a smart woman. In your position, you must hear things. And your contract expires in a few months anyway. All I'm saying is if you happened to hear of any senior positions coming up, say at a rival newspaper, then you'd do well to pay close attention. Maybe speak to a few headhunting agencies while you're at it. You know I'll do my best for you upstairs to make your exit as dignified as possible and would even be happy to write glowing references for you. You will, of course, have to come upstairs to see all of us together; so we can discuss this, let's just say further and more fully. The sooner the better too. I'll make the necessary calls and set something up ASAP.'

She couldn't speak, couldn't move, could barely even acknowledge what he was indirectly telling her.

'But I need hardly tell you, I'm afraid it's not looking good for you. Not looking good at all.'

'I know,' she half-whispered. Had known all along in fact, with all the linear certainty of a Greek tragedy, that it would ultimately boil down to this. How could she not have known? She just never thought the whole house of cards would come crashing down on her so spectacularly fast.

'And if I may, just add on a personal note,' Sir Gavin said, hauling himself up to go, 'Eloise, really. An ex-convict? Some random jailbird? And you, of all people? You do know that this is complete madness, don't you?'

All she could do was nod mutely. Course she knew, she thought about little else these days.

'Must admit though,' were his final words to her, 'when I was first told, I was surprised. I thought Jake was quite the gentleman when we met.'

'He is,' she managed to say, a bit stronger now. 'He may

328

not have been born a gentleman but take it from me, he's one by nature.'

Which was more than ninety per cent of the people I work with, she thought, as he closed the door on her with a decisive and very final thud.

And virus-like, the story spread. Eloise had numbly spent the morning closeted up in her office, outwardly trying to act like she always did, while inwardly panicking. Heart walloping away like it was outside of her ribcage.

Please don't let it leak, please dear God, she found herself praying to a God she didn't particularly believe in. *Please let the story just end here, don't let it get any worse . . . I need this job, because, well, without this job, what am I?*

Sometimes brief clutches of hope would break in; after all, she did her best to reason with herself, very few people had actually seen her with Jake. Their friendship had always been so private, so personal. And really when it boiled down to it, out of all the people she dealt with on a daily basis, who really was in a position to link the two of them? Apart from Helen, only the colleagues who'd been at the directors' weekend, that was it.

Admittedly, to her shame, she reckoned that up to a few short months ago, any one of them would most likely only have been too delighted to shop her to the media along with a pull-out colour supplement on what an out-and-out bitch she was to work for, in an effort to prise her arse out of the editor's chair that bit faster. But surely it was all change round here now? Or was she completely misled in thinking that? She was, after all, getting on well with everyone now, so would anyone really want to rat her out?

And that's when all her stressing and fretting would come round to one thing and one person only. The devious, behind-the-scenes machinations of Seth Coleman. She could never prove it of course, never even hope to, but knew in her waters that he was the only mole in the building with enough of a grudge against her to leak everything he knew. Christ alone only knew what else he'd done behind her back; gone through her bins maybe, rooting for dirt on her? Given the bloody chance, she wouldn't have put it past him to sell tickets to her public execution and distribute free T-shirts with her picture on them bearing the slogan, *Ding Dong the Witch is Dead.*

Every three minutes, she was online ego-Googling, checking that the story hadn't spread to her. Typing 'Eloise Elliot' with trembling fingers into the search bar, yielded literally thousands of finds, but as she quickly scrolled down through them, she could see that they were all professional, articles she'd written in the past, or maybe editorials, or the odd photo of her, ghostly pale in a black suit standing alongside the T. Rexes, all looking florid and half-pissed in their suits of grey.

So then . . . nothing to worry about. At least, not yet.

Her luck held out till lunchtime and in the end, it was Robbie Turner, lovely, caring Robbie with a heart the size of the Port Tunnel who told her. Who had the manners, not to mention the compassion, to alert her to what had just broken. Funny thing was, that even though what he showed her put her into shock, deep shock on an almost cellular level, later on she could still recall each and every moment with perfect clarity. Could remember ever tiny detail, as though she might have to take a test on it later on.

Robbie discreetly knocking on the door. Sticking his white shock of hair round the door, politely asking her if he might have a quick word. Hours later she could still vividly recall his gently closing the office door behind him, then coming round to her side of the desk to tell her.

The story had finally broken. He'd just seen it on Twitter. About her and Jake. From a made-up-sounding user name, but then, weren't most of them? Worst of all, there was even a link conveniently posted to a photo of her and Jake that Robbie reluctantly showed her.

Shaking, she clicked on the link and there they were, looking every inch a devoted couple. Eloise in the silver shimmering slinky dress she'd worn to the directors' dinner that miserable night, Jake with his arm around her. She had to physically fight to stop hot, stinging tears from springing to her eyes; they both just looked so – no other word for it – happy.

'EDITOR AND EX-CON, TAKEN ON A RECENT ROMANTIC GETAWAY, AT A LUXURIOUS FIVE-STAR COUNTRY RETREAT', screamed the caption.

Numbly, Eloise slumped back against her chair, staring straight ahead of her. The shagging directors' weekend. Someone had photographed them and now had leaked it onto Twitter. Not too difficult to guess who, of course, but she knew only too well she'd never be able to pin it to anyone, or more correctly, on the one person she'd have liked to, given half a chance. But no, Seth would have been far too careful for that; even this Twitter account was under an anonymous name, '@concerned_onlooker'. Jaysus, what kind of a user name was that, anyway? And what hope could she possibly have of ever confronting him?

Besides she had to remind herself, at the end of the day,

apart from the 'recent romantic getaway' bit, the story was one hundred per cent true, wasn't it? There was nothing for her to deny or contradict or even try to wriggle her way out of, politician-style; best she could hope for was that it would all blow over and fast.

Yeah right, she thought. Like that was ever going to happen. Not a chance. Not after what she'd done, and worse, in suppressing the story, what she'd tried to do. Automatically, she grabbed for her phone, feeling an over-powering need to call Jake, to tell him, warn him, if needs be to sob down the phone to him. And then she stopped herself in time, remembering all the countless late-night phone messages she'd already left for him in the past days and weeks that had gone unanswered.

Okay, so now she felt sick. And just looking into Robbie's concerned eyes confirmed her very worst fears and pretty much told her everything she needed to know. What in fact everyone working in this building knew only too well.

That of course once a story hit Twitter, the papers were bound to pick it up at the speed of light. Twitter was if nothing else a godsend for lazy hacks; all they had to do was pick up a story there and half their work was done for them.

And it was all over bar the shouting.

But where would it all end? She knew all too well, knew from years of bitter experience exactly what investigative reporters were like and just how far they'd be prepared to dig even at the hint of a juicy story. And they didn't come much juicier than this, did they? The work-obsessive, high-flying, alpha female Eloise Elliot . . . and an ex-con?

And suddenly she thought about Lily. Could she possibly

be dragged in too? Would anyone make the connection between Lily and Jake? An ice-cold panic seized her at that very thought; she had to get hold of Helen, warn her to stay indoors and to keep Lily well out of sight till she could get home herself . . .

'Eloise? You OK?' poor Robbie asked her, eyes brimming over with concern. Eloise half jumped, but then she'd been so wrapped up in panic and trauma, she'd almost forgotten she wasn't alone. 'Because you know I'm here for you. We all are. And if there's anything I can do?'

Somehow, she managed to hear what he was saying to her, even managed a weak, watery smile back up at him.

'I know Robbie, and thank you,' was all she could get out though and even that was a big effort without bursting into tears. 'You've been so kind, always. But if you'll excuse me . . . There's someone I just need to talk to.'

Chapter Fifteen

Never in her whole life had Helen Elliot worried about her sister. Never had to. Worry? About Eloise? The woman who could run the country with one hand tied behind her back? Miss Independence? Pointless exercise; if you did, she'd just brush aside any well-intentioned concerns and tell you to stop acting like such an idiot for stressing over her, when she was so clearly and outwardly fine.

Not now though. Now Helen was well and truly sick with worry over her.

Ever since that bloody weekend away, she thought distractedly, as she picked up Lily's toys from the family room floor and put them all tidily away. Helen had carefully been navigating Eloise's moods and could see all too clearly that she hadn't been herself since then, not once. Right up until that point, she'd been so warm and friendly, chatty, full of banter, fun to be around, whereas now it was like she'd just retreated back into herself, and went around the place silent and morose most of the time.

It was like a film had descended over her, so all you could see was a lonelier, sadder woman with a chip taken from her heart, coping admirably the way she always did, but without that wonderful lightness of spirit there'd been about her for so long.

Of course, Eloise still rushed home every evening from the *Post* to get to see Lily, still got to read stories to her and have a bit of playtime with her before bed, which these days was the only time Helen saw even a tiny hint of a sparkle back in her coal-black, tired eyes. But otherwise, chats with her were now virtually monosyllabic. Helen would ask her if she was OK, and be told, 'Oh, you know, fine. Same old, same old. Just might slip into the study to catch up on some emails.'

Nothing more. She was like a closed book.

Helen knew only too well it was all because of Jake, but the million-dollar question was, what should she do next? Eloise had told her everything that had happened between them and for once Helen, usually so good at automatically knowing how best to deal with blow-out rows – after all, she'd had a lot of experience with Darren – didn't know what to say. She couldn't begin to understand what Jake must have felt at realising the truth and part of her couldn't really blame him for needing a bit of time out.

Providing of course that's all this was; time out.

But it had been close to two weeks now and still no word from him, nothing. No answer to any of Eloise's calls to his mobile either, not a thing. And now the ever-patient, even-tempered Helen was starting to feel a bubbling up of anger at him; yes, so Eloise lied and deceived him and had been uncharacteristically stupid, but wasn't there even a tiny part of him that wanted to get to know his gorgeous daughter? What about Lily in all of this? It seemed crystal clear to Helen, that if ever two people needed their heads bashed together, it was Eloise and Jake.

You could always contact him at the language school on Camden St., she'd suggested hopefully to Eloise one night, and had been immediately brushed aside, but then brute stubbornness was the one quality in her sister that Jake hadn't miraculously managed to sand down a bit.

So much for that, then.

And now, even worse, it seemed that Jake had walked away too. He'd even moved out of Helen's flat, lock, stock and barrel and neither of them had a clue where he'd gone.

It was Helen who'd discovered this, slipping round there one evening unknown to Eloise, when she was upstairs putting Lily to bed and reading her a story. Because she just couldn't stand this any more. Couldn't take one more day of her sister's black-eyed melancholy that seemed to seep into the very walls of the house, affecting all of them, dragging everyone down with her. If she and Jake needed a catalyst to at least get the pair of them talking again, then Helen was more than happy to oblige. Because anything was better then watching Eloise slowly sink deeper and deeper into the walking depression she'd been streeling round the place with lately.

And Eloise really did care about Jake. Helen, who was expert at reading and understanding deeper human emotions, could tell. Up until recently, it had all been 'Jake says this' and 'Jake was telling me that', or 'wait till I tell Jake, he'll laugh himself into a coma at this'. Helen would listen to her, smiling quietly to herself, wondering if Eloise even admitted to herself the extent to which she liked him. *Really* liked him that is, as opposed to the way she used to just battle her way through life, emotionally unavailable to everyone around her. And he sounded so perfect for her too, she who didn't need a boyfriend so much as a champion. But then, as Helen knew only too well, since childhood her sister had always been a maestro at concealing her own feelings, so it was like second nature to her. Concealing them even from herself.

Then, she had a brainwave. If neither of the two principals involved was prepared to make the first move, then why the hell shouldn't she?

Taking advantage of the quiet in the house now that Lily was playing out in the garden, Helen whipped out her mobile, rang directory inquiries and asked to be put through to the language school where Jake worked on Camden St. To hell with this anyway, she thought, I for one have had enough and want to at least try to do something about it.

Checking her watch, she saw it was only half three in the afternoon. Surely someone there would at the very least know when he was due to teach his next class?

'English Language School, how can I help you?' came a bored, indifferently-sounding voice.

'Emm . . . Yes, hi. I'm looking for one of your teachers, a Jake Keane, if he's there?'

'Jake Keane? Yeah, rings a bell alright. I think he might work here part-time.'

I know, Helen thought rattily, teeth gritted. That's why I'm phoning, you eejit.

'Could you check and see if he's in for me? I just needed to have a quick word with him, if that's OK?' she managed to force out, politely enough. Then to speed things up, threw in, 'I know he's probably in a class, but this is actually a bit of an emergency.'

'Hmm, gimme a minute and I'll check for you,' said

Bored Girl, in absolutely no rush whatsoever. Next thing Helen heard the tapping of nails on a computer keyboard.

Please be here, please, please, please be there, be there already . . .

'Nope, sorry, he's not in yet. But he's due in at four. Suppose you could leave a message if you like?'

'No, no, that's OK thanks,' Helen said, her mind racing.

Four this afternoon. If nothing else would work then at least she knew exactly where he'd be in just half an hour's time.

Twenty minutes later and she was having a nightmare even trying to get Lily out the door, but then NO! was most definitely turning into her newest and most favourite word these days. Particularly on a hot summer's afternoon like this, when she was having such fun playing doll's tea party out the back garden, with water in the teapot and a fresh batch of cupcakes they'd baked earlier.

Only the bribe/indirect threat of a trip to Smyths toy store so she could pick out her birthday present did the trick, but then Lily was looking forward to her birthday party as pretty much the highlight of her entire little life so far. And this year Eloise was throwing her not just a regular party, but the P.T. Barnum's of all birthday parties, with even the promise of a chocolate fountain thrown in for good measure.

Of course the magic words, 'birthday present' used in the same sentence as 'Smyths toy store', did the trick and Lily obediently pulled on her little pink fleece cardigan and clambered up into her stroller, all set for the bus journey into town. As far as Lily was concerned, her birthday was going to be even better than Santa Claus arriving, not only because of all the new little friends who'd all been invited, but because now she was actually getting to pick out her own birthday present in Smyths toy store? At that exact moment in time, Lily would happily have followed Helen through six-foot high flames if she'd thought there was the chance of a glittery new pink toy waiting for her at the end of it all.

Which was why Helen got no resistance whatsoever when she gingerly suggested to Lily that they just needed to take a veeery slight detour via Camden St., where the language school was that Jake worked in.

'But soon we'll be at the toy store, won't we, Auntie Helen?' was all the worried little voice from the stroller in front of her called back. 'To buy my pwesent?'

'Very soon honey, and you can pick out whatever you like from me, now won't that be fun?'

A huge squeal of delight and Helen figured she might, *might* just be able to chance her arm with this. Because if she was certain of one thing it was this; she needed to see Jake. Face to face if at all possible; over the phone it would be too easy for him to rush off, saying he was in work and had to go. She wasn't saying a word to Lily about who they were meeting or why, and instinctively felt that Jake wouldn't let the cat of the bag in front of the child either. But she absolutely needed to sort this out once and for all. To bang his head off a brick wall if necessary and urge him to at least try and sort things out with Eloise, no matter what she'd done. One thing was for certain, Eloise most definitely couldn't continue living her life like this. No one could, and that was final.

She'd managed to manoeuvre the stroller out the front door and was just facing into her daily battle of trying to gently ease the weight of it down the half-dozen uneven stone steps outside the house without the usual chorus of 'Aunwtie Helen, you're BUMPING me!' from Lily, when out of nowhere, a short, chunky guy with a camera slung round his neck strode authoritatively up the garden path.

With a definite purpose to him, like he was here on business.

'Here, let me give you a hand,' he said, immediately grabbing the end of the stroller and helping her guide it gently down onto the gravelled driveway.

'Thanks,' she instinctively replied, then added, 'emm, can I help you?'

'Looking for Eloise Elliot, if she's home. I just wanted a quick photo.'

An alarm bell immediately sounded off in Helen's head. Why would anyone need Eloise's photo? And wouldn't they just call the *Post* if they did? Why bother coming all the way out to her house?

And that's when her mobile rang.

'Excuse me,' Helen stammered, fishing round in the bottom of her overstuffed, oversized bag to find it.

Eloise. Sounding, well, weird. Not like herself at all.

'Helen, are you at home?' she asked urgently.

'Actually, no, Lily and I are just on our way out . . .'

'Go back into the house and stay there,' she said, calmly enough, but Helen knew her well enough to pick up on the underscored panic in her voice.

'Eloise, is everything OK? You sound like something's seriously wrong.'

'Just listen to me. Under no circumstances open the door or let Lily out in into the front garden. Go back inside, close the door and stay there till I get home. *Please* Helen. Just do as I ask. I'll explain later, trust me.'

'Well actually, there already *is* someone here now, looking for your picture . . .'

'Oh Jesus . . .' came Eloise's voice, weak as a kitten from down the phone. So this was it, then. The nightmare had started.

Just so, so much sooner than she'd ever have thought.

'Don't worry, we'll go back inside and stay there,' Helen told her as soothingly as she could.

'Now, Helen, fast as you can. And whatever you do, ignore the phone and the front door till I sort all this out.'

'Hon, what is going on? Are you okay?' Helen asked her, momentarily distracted, but that millisecond that she'd taken her eye off the ball was all it took. First she felt the flash of a digital camera going off in her own face, then in Lily's.

'Can you stop it, please?' she half yelled at the photographer, struggling to shield Lily's face as best she could.

'I really don't want my picture taken . . .'

'Helen?' Eloise urgently demanded down the phone. 'Is someone snapping you? And Lily?'

'Just a quick one love,' said the photographer, correctly sensing that the hounds of hell would be unleashed on him any minute. 'That Eloise Elliot's daughter then, is it?'

'Please! I said NO!'

Two minutes later, struggling for all she was worth, somehow Helen had managed to haul the stroller back inside the front door, glaring as furiously as she could bring herself to at the photographer and taking care to lock and bolt the hall door as loudly as she could behind her. So the bastard would hear.

'Eloise, are you still there?' she panted into the phone. 'You have to tell me what's going on. That guy just went

341

ahead and photographed me and Lily, even though I told him no . . . Why would anyone want our photo? What in the name of God is going on?'

'Okay, I need you to stay nice and calm,' said Eloise, wishing she could heed her own advice. Because if she was certain of one thing, it was this; if one photographer had already doorstepped her, others would surely follow at the shagging speed of light. And if any one of them as much as dared to drag Lily into this . . .

Thinking on her feet, she went back to the phone.

'Helen, listen to me. That little pal that Lily's always talking about? Rose? The one who she's having over for a playdate tomorrow?'

'Yeah . . . what about her?'

'You're really pally with her mum aren't you?'

'Ellen, yes, but why do you ask? Can you just please tell me what's the matter! You're really freaking me out here!'

'Can you call her and ask if Lily could come to her house for a sleepover tonight? Don't tell her any more, just trust me. I have to get Lily safely out of the house tonight. Please, just do as I ask. And don't worry, I'll explain everything as soon as I get home.'

Totally shocked, Helen agreed and put the phone down. Unheard of for Eloise to ever allow Lily to go on a sleepover, no matter how much the child begged her. Not, knowing her sister, without at least doing a full floor plan check of the house she'd be staying in first, and more than likely spending the whole night in her own car parked at the front gate, with binoculars trained on at the house. At all times.

Helen hadn't the first inkling what was going on; some huge scandal the paper were about to run with? Maybe some pissed-off politician was suing her for libel or defamation . . . who knew? She'd find out soon enough, that was for sure, but for now she'd an even more urgent matter on her hands to deal with.

To the soundtrack of Lily wailing at her in the background, she fished her phone out again and pressed the redial button for the English Language School.

'Auntie Helen,' whinged Lily, still in her stroller, 'why did we come back home? PLEASE can we go out again? This is weally, weally, borwing! I wanna GO!'

Helen tousled her little head of curls, shhh'd her down a bit and even managed to fish round in the bottom of her handbag for a packet of Cadbury Buttons to appease her.

'Shh Lily, there's a good girl. You know, I might have an even nicer surprise for you tonight, if you just stay quiet as a little mouse and let me make a phone call?'

'What supwise?' said Lily eyeing her suspiciously, her wails temporarily dying down while she weighed this up.

'In a minute pet,' said Helen as the phone was answered.

'English Language School?' said the same bored-sounding voice as before.

'Hi, I was onto you a few minutes ago, looking for Jake Keane? Can you tell me if he's arrived in yet? I really need to speak to him urgently.'

'Nope, sorry, not yet. And he's late for his class now. I couldn't tell you where he is, but I suppose you could leave a message if you like?'

'Come on, Auntie Helen . . . I wanna know what my supwise is NOW!' screeched Lily from her stroller and Helen knew this was utterly pointless. Politely as she could, she left her name and number and hung up the phone so she could tend to Lily, not having the first clue what was going on.

And if Jake wasn't in work, where he was supposed to be, then where the hell was he?

As it happened, at that exact moment, Jake was slumped in front of a computer screen, head in his hands, looking and feeling utterly defeated. Because the worst, the absolute worst had happened. What he'd dreaded more than anything. Courtney was coming to trial and somehow his name had been dragged into it.

Ben Casey, Jake's parole officer, who'd been good enough to take him in when he'd left Helen's flat, was absolutely right to have alerted him. Just over an hour ago, Ben had been in his study enjoying a rare day off and idly scanning the day's papers online, when he'd first seen the name Jake Keane appearing alongside his photo in one of the morning papers. But then, Ben didn't know the half of it. Poor old Ben's concern had been Jake's reputation at the Language School and the very probable chance he might end up losing his job over this. And initially, so had been Jake's too.

But as of a few moments ago, that was now the least of his worries. He'd been following the story like a hawk as it developed and now it seemed Eloise had been dragged into it as well. And now there it was, clear as you like, on the breaking news section of the *Evening Echo* online edition. A photo of the two of them, taken the night of the dinner and a full page article too, though with hardly a single fact in it.

'*Eloise Elliot, well-known editor at the* Post, *was today linked with the trial of Michael Courtney, due to be heard at the High Court next week. It seems Ms. Elliot's long term partner, Jake Keane, works as a driver for Courtney and had recently been released from Wheatfield prison where he served a two year sentence . . .*'

Jake could hardly bring himself to read another line. With more than a guilty conscience, he tried to call Eloise's mobile, but it rang out. No answer. Tried her again, still no answer. Tried her work number, nothing. Left a message, but she didn't get back.

Which meant this must be bad for her, far worse than he ever would have thought.

Shit, he thought frantically, his mind racing ahead. Why hadn't he even tried to see her since that miserable weekend? Because he'd been bloody well wallowing, that was why; lying low, licking his wounds after the shock of what had happened. Selfishly, he realised now, he hadn't wanted to see or hear from anyone till he got his head straightened out, unable to feel anything other than deep gratitude to Ben for taking him in when his back was up against a wall.

And now this. God alone knew what the girl had been going through since this first broke earlier . . . and still no bloody answer from her phone.

Answer, answer, for Christ's sake answer . . .

Was she okay, he frantically wondered, as another even more sickening worry came fast on the heels of the last one.

Her daughter. *His* daughter. Jesus Christ, if the papers managed to drag that little girl into all this mess . . . Lily . . .

Two minutes later, Jake was in the kitchen having one of the most panicky conversations he ever could remember having in his life.

'Ben?' he said hoarsely, 'Emergency. I need a favour.'

'Stay calm,' Ben wisely cautioned, 'and just tell me what I can do to help.'

'Emergency. I need to borrow your car.'

'You're not driving anywhere in the state you're in,' said Ben firmly. 'Just tell me wherever it is you need to go. And don't worry, I'll drive you there myself.'

Chapter Sixteen

Eloise had spent the past thirty minutes sitting alone in her office, numb. Catatonic. Just sat there letting the phone ring, not even attempting to answer. Hearing the urgent ping of one email after another landing into her inbox and not even bothering to glance at one of them. Her mobile was on silent, and every now and then a missed call would flash up, which she'd steadfastly ignore. Instead, all she could do was stare mutely out the window behind her desk and down onto the street below, watching the world go by, busy people swarming up and down Tara St. with things to do and places to be. Just like she herself used to have.

How can they just go on with their lives as normal, she found herself idly wondering, when her whole existence had just gone into freefall? Didn't they know the turmoil she was in? Seven long years of her life she'd given to this job, and now in a nanosecond it was all about to be snatched from her. Just like that. One slip-up, one 'error of judgement' as Sir Gavin put it, and all her years of blood, sweat and tears were just as though they'd never been.

A knock at the door and next thing Ursula, Rachel's stand-in, was in front of her. Looking unusually pale and rattled for someone normally so brimming over with swaggering confidence.

'Emm . . . really sorry to bother you, Eloise,' she said sounding genuinely apologetic. 'But I've been sent to tell you that they've been waiting for you up in the boardroom for about ten minutes now. It's an emergency meeting they've convened. They've been phoning and phoning you, but you're just not picking up.'

Eloise nodded back at her and even managed to give her a watery smile on her way back out. Wonder if Ursula already knows, she found herself thinking, then realised, of course she bloody does. You could be guaranteed the entire office knew by now. This would have been all over the building like wildfire in a matter of a few short minutes. And here she was, hiding out like a coward in the sanctuary of her office, terrified to her bone marrow at the thoughts of having to do the walk of shame out the door, towards the lifts and upstairs to face the music. All those eyes on her, everyone knowing just how royally she'd fucked up.

Dead Girl Walking.

But it couldn't be put off any longer. If there was one thing she'd never been in her life it was a coward, and she certainly wasn't going to start now. If it killed her, she'd be as brave as she could about it, hold her head high and somehow, someway, get the hell out of there and home to lick her wounds as soon as humanly possible. Home to Lily, home to Helen. Home to where she belonged.

Another knocking on the door, except more insistent this time.

'Jesus Christ, I already told you, I'm coming!' she found herself snapping, then immediately bit her tongue and turned around to apologise to Ursula. But when she looked up, it wasn't her at all. For a split second, her vision dimmed and she wasn't certain that she could completely trust what she was seeing.

Because there standing in front of her was Jake, all six feet two of him, looking exactly as ghostly and washed out as she felt.

Next thing, her instincts just took over, and before she'd time to think, even to react, she flung herself headlong into his arms, sobbing now, heaving arid, dry tears; the kind she never allowed herself, ever.

'You're here,' was all she kept saying over and over again. 'You're really here. You came back . . . Oh Jake, I can't begin to tell you how sorry I am . . .'

'Shhh, shhh honey,' he said soothingly, clinging tightly to her and wrapping his arms protectively around her. 'I've been so worried about you, I had to come . . .'

'But Jake, I've been over and over the whole thing in my mind and what I did to do, what I put you through, deceiving you the way I did, it was so wrong . . .' She broke off, wiping away tears that now they'd finally started, wouldn't stop.

'Come on, none of this now, not when it's all my fault,' he said softly, 'if you'd never met me, you'd be safe. Your good name would never have been dragged into all this.'

'Don't say that,' she half whispered, clinging onto him, feeling comforted beyond belief just at the warm, familiar smell of him, just at being able to snuggle deep into the small of his chest. Feeling small, fragile, broken, utterly vulnerable.

'Shhh love, later,' he told her and she swore it was the first calm, friendly voice she'd heard all day. 'We'll talk later. Right now, I just want to take you out of here, get you away from here till this whole bloody story dies a death.'

'I . . . I can't,' she told him in a tiny voice she hardly recognised as her own. 'It's not that simple. They're waiting for me, upstairs, now. The whole board of directors, the lot of them. Like some kind of public crucifixion.'

'Come on Eloise, whatever about the press attention, surely they can't fire you because of your association with me? And even if they did, wouldn't you have grounds for unfair dismissal?'

'Course they couldn't. But that's not what they're firing me for.'

'What then?'

'Because . . . You see, I . . . A few days ago, oh shit.' Her voice broke here and suddenly she felt weak, had to sit down or else she was certain her knees would buckle under her own weight.

Gently, like he was handling a baby, Jake led her to her a chair and sat her down, crouching beside her and massaging her hand.

'Tell me,' he said simply, looking directly at her.

She took a deep breath.

'I knew the story about Courtney would break days ago. We all did. And the *Post* wanted to run a feature about him, which would have named you, so I buried it. Stone dead. Then of course, our rivals picked up on it, made the link between you and me and now . . .'

She broke off here. Couldn't bring herself to go on. The rest was all too obvious anyway. And there was only one way this story was going to end, she now knew. Like the Greek tragedy it had already become.

'You did all that – for me?'

She looked up at him, watery-eyed, and nodded mutely.

Next thing, Jake was cradling her and the heavy, musky

350

smell of him was the only time all day she'd felt calm. Safe. Comforted.

Then the office phone rang insistently, for about the two hundredth time.

'That'll be them,' she said, instinctively pulling away. 'I'll have to do this Jake. Go up there and face them and take it on the chin. I don't exactly have much of a choice, do I?'

'As a matter of fact, you do.'

She looked at him blankly.

'Come on Eloise, look at you. You're a walking wreck. You're in absolutely no state to face anyone.'

'I know, I know . . .' she stammered numbly, like someone who'd taken so many body blows that they didn't know if another one could be fatal. 'And I'm so worried about Helen and Lily . . . There was a photographer outside my house just now, hassling them both. I just . . . Oh Jake, you have to help me – I can't think straight.'

'Then that settles it,' he said decisively. 'Call the board and tell them you're taking sick leave, or time out to re-assess your options or whatever the hell you want to call it. But I'm getting you out of here right now and I'm not taking no for an answer.'

She looked up at him, utterly bewildered, not having the first clue what he was on about. Leave? Just walk out the door and to hell with the lot of them?

And then an astonishing thought struck her. When it boiled down to it . . . why did she even care so much? Jake was right, she could barely stand up right now, never mind face into the dragon's den and somehow try to defend herself.

'Do you have any holiday time due to you or time off that you haven't taken?' he asked her, gripping her shoulders urgently.

For the first time in all that nightmarish day, she surprised herself by actually smiling.

'Only about seven years' worth.'

'That settles it then. Grab your coat. I'm taking you home.'

He's right, she thought, suddenly feeling like a load had been lifted. Let the board give her a stay of execution. They cared nothing at all about her, why should she bother returning the courtesy? All they were doing was hauling her upstairs to fire her arse anyway, that much was for certain. Let them wait. Besides, what was the difference if they fired her today or tomorrow?

By whatever miracle, she was with Jake now and finally, for the first time since that miserable weekend, she felt secure. Protected.

'Take me home,' was all she could bring herself to say.

PART FIVE

ELOISE

Chapter Seventeen

Now, I've had my fair share of bizarre experiences in my time; I've covered stories from war zones, followed breaking political stories until my eyes were ready to bleed, was even, at a far earlier stage in my career, forced to stake out various B-list celebs having rendezvous at various girlfriends' flats that their wives knew absolutely nothing about. (And by the way, give me Afghanistan any day.)

But never, in all my years, have I ever experienced anything like this.

Having spent my whole entire life either chasing stories or else editing them, it is by far the single weirdest experience of my life to now find *myself* the actual story.

Everyone around me keeps telling me it'll die down, that this is a flash in the pan, that all this newsprint is bound to be wrapping up fish and chips by tomorrow night, repeating it over and over as though repetition could somehow make it true.

But there's no sign of it dying. If anything, it's escalated.

So far, I've been the page two story on no fewer than four evening papers, the third lead item on three drive time radio talk shows and the second-last item on the six o'clock news bulletin, thank you to the shower of bastards that run Channel Six. Made me wonder what could possibly have been the last item: *Ants Cross Street in Straight line,* perhaps? The bad luck for me though, is that it's a particularly slow news day and this is exactly the kind of salacious juicy story that fills in a good three minutes of airtime.

And by the way, just for added humiliation, I'm the joke item; the nugget of 'news' that people take a moment to snigger at, then gossip about the next day. 'Did you hear about your woman who edits the *Post* covering up for her jailbird boyfriend?' That kind of thing. Need I say any more? Plus another photo of us at the weekend away has 'mysteriously' surfaced and been emblazoned across every tacky website going; Jake with his arm round me, both of us roaring laughing at some private joke right before that awful dinner . . . back when all was well between us and when I was so hopeful for what lay ahead.

So now there's no doubt about it, my name – my good name – and my reputation that I worked so long and hard to build from the ground up, have now become the punch line to a bad joke. Once I was held up as a poster girl for glass ceiling-smashing single women everywhere, and now all I'm waiting for is some smart-arsed comedian to do a 'Did you hear the one about Eloise Elliot?' skit on some late night news review show.

One thing's for certain though; the story has an inside leak. I swear I can almost smell Seth Coleman behind it all; the way titbits are being drip fed, usually originating via Twitter and getting picked up from there. He's way too clever to release this any other way; like this, he has full anonymity and all the licence to libel that only a made-up username can give you.

'*Exclusive! Read here about Eloise Elliot sneaking off during work hours to meet her jailbird lover*' went one story, which Jake gamely tried to make me laugh at, but somehow I couldn't bring myself to. What am I supposed to do anyway, sue them because technically Jake and I aren't, never were and never will be lovers? Pointless; I know it and so do they. The fact is, I still covered up for a friend. I did the crime, as they say, so now I'm doing the time. And let's face it, photos of Jake and me practically hanging off each other at the directors' weekend away are hardly helping matters, are they?

Then there's all the dozens and dozens of vague, unreferenced, indirect quotes, not one of which I'd ever allow to be printed; but it seems my rival papers have fewer scruples than me. '*An undisclosed source at the* Post *tells us*' that kind of shite. Jake tries his best to poke fun at some of the nuttier stuff, like '*Colleagues at the* Post *tell us that ever since meeting her ex-con lover, Eloise Elliot underwent what could only be described as a total personality change, mutating from a cold, work-obsessed slave driver to a far warmer, more considerate employer . . .*'

I wasn't laughing though. Mainly because that much at least was actually true.

'*How She Kept her Illicit Love Life Secret from Top Brass at the* Post' almost made me choke, until Jake physically switched off my computer and dragged me kicking and screaming away from it.

And every few minutes, to the accompaniment of a wave of nausea sweeping over me, the same old panic attack will hit me. Jake and Lily. How long before they find out? Is it a just matter of time before that hits the newsstands too? Because in spite of the living hell this whole thing has become, the one single thing I'm only too pathetically grateful for is that they still haven't managed to unearth Jake's connection to Lily yet.

Just this thought alone sends me off into another spiral of worry. Jesus Christ, is it possible? Can this nightmare really be happening to me? Where there was one single photographer outside my house earlier, now it seems there's a posse of the bastards at the gate outside, all weighed down with telescopic lenses the approximate width of my thigh. This, in spite of the fact that we've closed every curtain in the entire house, so none of the bastards can get a long shot of me lying prostrate on the kitchen sofa downstairs. Like Elizabeth Barrett Browning, minus the T.B.

For God's sake, I think, suddenly furious, I live in a nice, safe house with an alarm system and a front door with deadbolts on it and matching bay trees beside it, on a road with Neighbourhood Watch; surely this is somebody else's life and not mine? I'm not a drug baron, or a bankrupt property developer who owes billions. Just a newspaper editor who messed up, that's all.

But as I sit mutely on the sofa in the family room at home, with a warm blanket wrapped around me like a car crash survivor, a hot mug of tea in front of me that the very sight of is making me sick, the tiny part of my brain that can still function through the haze is telling me loud and clear that yes, this is real. This is actually happening. To you. Right now. And by the looks of things, it's not going to go away anytime soon.

Jake is by my side, hadn't left my side, never leaves, and his warm, protective arm around my shoulders is probably the one single thing I'm capable of feeling now, given the state I'm in. Helen's here too, of course, as well as a lovely,

358

concerned guy called Ben Casey. He seems as sick with worry as I am myself and in the useless, inert state I'm in, I'm genuinely grateful to have him here. He'd introduced himself earlier as Jake's parole officer and has been hugely helpful all day; even drove Jake and me back here from the office, as God knows, I'd have been a danger to anyone behind a wheel.

And Lily is safe and happy in her little friend Rose's house, playing in her Wendy house and having great fun and games putting make-up on each other. I called her earlier to wish her goodnight and to tell her I'd be picking her up first thing tomorrow, forcing my voice into its highest and happiest register, so she wouldn't suspect that Mama was on the brink of tears. One good thing to report though, as ever, her little voice acted like a soothing tonic on me and I knew she was having a ball for herself when she said, 'Not too early in the morning Mama, me and Wose want to have pancakes for bweakfast!'

And now hours must have passed and I'm still sitting on the kitchen sofa, with a hot drink in my hand courtesy of Helen. Everyone around me is being utterly fabulous. Jake especially, who's almost like a human anaesthetic, numbing me, holding me, telling me over and over that everything will work out for the best and that this will all blow over. Funny, but in my detached state, I'm deeply touched at how concerned they all are and feel surrounded with care and attention that's comforting beyond belief.

'After all, it was only a job . . .' Helen is saying, and I do my best to smile back at her, and look like I actually mean it.

'And with all your experience and sterling record, you're bound to pick up something else . . .' nice-guy Ben chips in kindly.

'Plus,' Jake adds wisely, 'remember how fast these stories all blow over. It flared up in no time, so let everyone just have their gossip about it, be done with it. And in a few days no one will even be able to remember what the fuss was about.'

He squeezes my hand and I squeeze his right back. Lovely thought, and even though I don't quite believe it, it's calming, reassuring to hear. For the first time all day, I allow myself the luxury of a deep breath.

Maybe they're all right and I'm wrong. Maybe this is just a minor embarrassment, a tiny inkblot on an otherwise spotless copybook that will soon be forgotten about. Something I'll look back on in years to come and have a good giggle at. Maybe it will all be done and dusted in a day or two. Maybe the board will overlook this mess and give me another chance. Maybe.

This sensation lasts all of about two minutes until the upstairs doorbell goes. Helen rushes upstairs to check it's not a journo, then comes back down to the kitchen a few moments later, white-faced.

'Eloise, you've got a visitor in the drawing room,' she tells me, sounding shakier than she has done all evening.

'Come on, she can't see anyone, she's not in any fit state . . .' Jake says on my behalf, but Helen interrupts him.

'It's Sir Gavin,' she tells me. 'And he's waiting for you.'

Takes approximately ten minutes for my seven-year career to come crashing down in flames and the weirdest thing of all is that somehow I can't bring myself to feel a single thing. Sir Gavin is cool, courteous, but ruthless; as you'd expect. Won't even sit down, or have a drink, just stands close to the door, impatient to get this over with.

Probably dreading that I'll start to cry and therefore ready for a fast exit.

His theme is unchanged since we spoke early this morning, or rather, since he lectured me; I made a massive error of judgement, I messed up royally, I had the appalling rudeness to stand up the board this afternoon and now it seems the editor of the paper of record has become a salacious news story herself.

In my detached, almost composed state of mind, I could almost count the number of times he repeats the same tired old clichés. 'We gave you every chance to explain yourself . . .' was one particular beaut. 'You have a duty to be impartial and to uphold the standards and good name of the *Post* and have failed in that most spectacularly,' another gem. This must be what it feels like to be expelled from school, I think. In fact, I'm half-expecting him to come out with a line like, 'I've already phoned your parents . . .'

But the punchline is the same. I'm out, and Seth is in, simple as. Funny thing is though, if Sir Gavin expected pleading, tears and handkerchief-twisting from me, he was disappointed. All I can do is look at him as though I'm having some kind of out-of-body experience and think, I gave you blood, sweat and tears all those years. I barely even got to see my little girl, who means more to me than any shagging job. Sacrificed all that, and for what? At the end of the day, for nothing, that's what.

I even surprise myself by smiling at him as I show him out. He of course, moaning and groaning at suffering the indignity of being papped on the way in and out of my house, me not much caring either way. Thinking, you were quick enough to shove me to the lions, now see how you like it.

'I must say Eloise,' are his parting words to me, 'you're taking this extremely well.'

'Why wouldn't I?' I tell him evenly. 'I think you've possibly done me the biggest favour of my whole life.'

And now it's well past ten at night, I'm still tucked up on the sofa, not quite able to believe what's just happened. I got fired – and somehow, it's all okay. The sky didn't fall in. The world continues to turn on its axis. It's weird, I actually feel physically lighter than I've done in years, not to mention deliciously woozy from the wine that the others have been practically ladling down my throat. Relieved in the same way that a crash survivor does when an out-of-control car finally stops spinning. Your whole life flashes before your eyes, but then you think, you know what? It's over and I'm going to be okay. I've survived the worst. And if it's one thing I've learned, it's this. With the people that I'm lucky enough to have around me, I know I'll pull through, start over.

Ben, by the way, has been invaluable all evening, and I can't help noticing with a smile, is paying more than partic- ular attention to Helen. Making her eat plenty of sandwiches and constantly topping up her wine glass, engaging her in chat and asking her loads of questions about herself. Attentive, caring, interested, not conventionally handsome, but certainly attractive in a scruffy, fell-out-of-bed way . . . I already like this guy.

He's over at the kitchen table making her laugh now, telling her some yarn about a guy he's working with on parole at the moment, who Ben had really gone out on a limb for, eventually managing to find him a job working on a forklift truck in a machinery plant out on the Westgate Industrial Estate.

362

'So I told him the good news, thinking he'd be delighted with the work,' Ben smiles at Helen, 'and that he was all set to start Monday and you know what this kid said back to me?'

'Tell me,' says Helen.

'He said, "You want me to work in Westgate? Two buses? Feck right off with yourself!"'

The pair of them guffaw as I look on silently.

Oh Christ, I think, immediately dismissing the thought with a smile; I got fired today, am facing into a dole queue without any visible means of being able to support my daughter and now I'm trying to play matchmaker?

Must be even more in shock than I thought.

Though now that I come to think of it, she hasn't once even mentioned the awful Darren's name, not even to drop his name into the conversation, or checked her mobile to see if he's rung, like she does a dozen times a day on average. Which is so not like her.

I'm not passing any comments, I'm just saying, that's all.

'You must be tired as well by now,' Ben says to her, looking gently across the table at her.

'Hmmm, I think all this wine is doing the trick,' Helen smiles warmly back at him, then stifles a yawn.

'Been a long day for you, as well as Eloise,' he says. 'Maybe it's time you tried to get some sleep?'

'Not a bad plan,' Helen nods, stretching her arms out tiredly.

'I'd better make a move too,' Ben says to me and Jake, as we sit side by side on the sofa, him nursing a beer and me I think already on my fourth glass of wine. It's doing the trick nicely though. After the horrors of today, I'm now beginning to feel more relaxed, calmer and, well, a bit floaty, like I'm on drugs.

'I arranged for Josh to have a playdate and sleepover after school, with his best buddy,' Ben explains, 'so I need to get back so I can pick him up first thing in the morning.'

'Josh?' says Helen. 'Is that your son?'

'Yup,' says Ben, pulling his jacket on and getting ready to hit the road. 'Six years of age and the light of my life.'

'That's, well, that's pretty much how I feel about Lily,' she smiles very prettily back at him.

'If it wasn't for Josh,' he goes on, 'I honestly don't know how I'd have coped these last few years since his mum . . . Since she left us.'

'Oh. You're divorced, then?'

He didn't answer immediately, which catches my attention.

'Separated?'

'Widowed.'

'I'm so sorry to hear that.'

Funny, I couldn't help thinking through my slightly woozy haze, Helen didn't look the tiniest little bit sorry. Not at all.

'Well, let me show you out on my way upstairs to bed,' she says, coming over to hug me and Jake goodnight.

'Do you want a lift home with me, Jake?' Ben offers.

Say no, please say no, I need you here tonight . . .

'I think I'll hang around for a bit longer,' Jake tells him, then turns back to me. 'If that's okay with you?'

I don't answer; just grin stupidly, drunkenly back at him. Marvelling that such a shitty day could have ended so miraculously. A minute later, Helen and Ben are clattering their way upstairs and finally, it's just us, just me and Jake, alone.

Next thing, his arm is tight round my shoulders and he's gently caressing my hair.

'You've had a rough day,' he says.

And although it's true, I haven't the heart or the energy to even start delving into work stuff, not to mention the fact that I'm officially on the brink of a dole queue. Besides, compared with the fact that he's here, actually here beside me, it all seems so unimportant right now. And at the end of the day, like I keep telling myself over and over, wasn't it only a job?

'But Jake, if you hadn't been around . . . I don't know what I would have done without you today. You've been amazing, a rock.'

'Eloise,' he sighs deeply, 'There's no way you would have had to suffer through what you did if it wasn't for your link to me. And I don't know if I can ever forgive myself for that. Jesus, do you know how much the very thought of it is killing me? Everything you worked so hard for?'

Now my arm is around him, and I'm stroking his cheek. My turn to comfort him, after everything he's done for me today.

'I know, of course I know how you must feel,' I tell him softly, 'but none of this was your fault, how could it have been? The only person responsible for what I did, is me.'

He's looking down though and for once I'm finding it impossible to gauge what he's thinking.

'Jake, look at me,' I tell him firmly.

He does, his eyes misty, bloodshot, exhausted looking.

'The past is behind us now,' I tell him insistently. 'Everything's out in the open. No one can ever throw an accusation at me or anyone connected with you again. It's OVER. Really and truly over.'

I want to throw in every other cliché I've even heard from 'tomorrow is another day,' to 'the sun will come out tomorrow,' but manage to shut myself up in time. Jake's smart. He already knows.

'Then my next question is this,' he says, leaning in closer to me now.

'Go ahead, ask me anything.'

'Can you forgive me? For taking off the way I did? For walking away from you? I was so angry, and a bit shocked, if I'm being honest . . .'

I slump back against his chest, relief flooding through me.

'Jake, it's the other way round. I'm the one who should be thanking you for even talking to me again after what I put you through. All that deceit, all those lies – that bloody weekend . . .'

'Seems like it happened another lifetime ago, doesn't it?' he says, arms locked around me now. 'And I felt like such a heel for leaving you there, for deserting you the way I did.'

'Stop, really there's no need . . .' I try to say exhaustedly into his shirt, but the sound comes out all muffled.

'Looking back, I think I was just completely knocked for six,' he goes on, lifting my legs up so I'm sitting on his knee now, lifting me like I weigh almost nothing. Making me love how big he is and how tiny I feel next to him.

'I mean I'd absolutely no idea . . . about Lily I mean, and although I was furious with you back then for keeping the truth from me, by the time I got to Ben's and cooled the head a bit, I realised – well, that everything you'd done, you'd only done for her.'

I nod, tearing up for about the fortieth time that day.

'And . . . well, what I'm really trying to say in a ham-fisted way is this; you've put yourself out so much for me already and I'll completely respect any decision you make about her, but . . .'

'But?'

'But if it was okay with you and with Lily of course, I'd love to be a part of her life. Meet her properly, not just bump into her in the park. Really be a proper dad to her, that is. I'd love to take her to the movies and teach her how to ride a bike and buy her ice cream whenever you're not looking and spoil her rotten. She seems like an amazing kid and it would be a privilege to be her father figure, it really would.'

I don't even need to think about it. Though I do smile, thinking back to the days when I'd proudly boast that single parenthood was the only possible way for an Alpha female like me to go.

All changed now though, changed unrecognisably.

'Jake, that would be wonderful,' I tell him simply. 'And I know you'll never just be her father figure, you'll be more than that. You'll be her dad.'

He smiles at me then pulls me in closer to him, lightly kissing my forehead now, his eyes burning. And in the woozy, drowsy state I'm in, it's sexy and lovely and comforting and suddenly, in spite of deep exhaustion, I want more.

Next thing, his hands are cupping my face, his kiss growing deeper and more intense now as I slip my arms tighter round him and feel his whole body tensing under me. Then he traces a soft line of kisses all along my cheeks before I can't take anymore, I'm like a hormonal teenager burning up for him, so I slide gently on top of him, loving the feel of his tongue lightly flicking mine, suddenly wishing I'd had the foresight to dot a few scented candles around the place to make it all the more romantic. He's slowly unbuttoning my blouse now, tracing a path of kisses all

367

along my collar bone as I lean back, mmmmm-ing and breathing heavier, and trying to calculate exactly how long it would take the two of us to get upstairs to my bedroom.

Chapter Eighteen

Next morning, I pick Lily up at her friend's and tell her I've got a very special surprise waiting for her back at home. Well her still-sleepy little eyes instantly light up at this and she plays a guessing game with me the whole way home. Barely even notices the straggled, now seriously depleted group of photographers still outside the house, far fewer of them than yesterday, now that the story's already reached a natural climax and started to abate, thank God. She doesn't even ask me why we're using the garden gate at the back to get in today, to avoid the bastards.

Just before we head inside through the patio door, I bend down to her.

'Sweetheart?' I whisper in her little ear.

'Remember I promised you I'd go to the ends of the earth to find your daddy for you?'

Suddenly, she looks brightly, expectantly up at me, shoving a fistful of her curls out of her forehead.

'Well, he's here darling and he can't wait to meet you.' Then scooping her up into my arms, I lead her inside to the kitchen, where Jake is standing nervously, waiting for us.

'This is him, Lily. I'd like you to meet your dad.'

Jake beams and instinctively reaches out to take her from me, with a half-fearful look on his face, as though wondering if she will really want to come to him. But he needn't have worried. Lily's beaming now and practically leaps into his huge arms, clapping happily, overjoyed to hear that one magic word. 'Daddy'.

'I KNEW it!' she squeals delightedly at him as he cradles her tightly. 'I KNEW that one day you'd come for me! I always said! Wemember Mama?'

It's beyond doubt one of the happiest days that I can ever remember. Not once do I even bother looking at a single paper, ego-Googling or checking out what shite is being said behind my back online, but for whole minutes at a time, I astonish myself by temporarily blanking out everything that's going on in my life outside of these four walls. Just like that. Block out all the pathetic, sneering 'sure, didn't that one have it coming to her all along' articles in the tabloids, even though my story has by now lost a lot of its heat. I'm not quite sure how it's happening, but I somehow even manage to block out the fact that I've effectively mortgaged my whole future. Not to mention the very real possibility that my career is over and from here on in I'll be lucky to end up covering the Charleville Community annual egg and spoon race for their local newsletter.

Because to see Jake and Lily together really would bring a lump to your throat. Even Helen keeps alternating between beaming at the pair of them, then dabbing a Kleenex at the corner of her eyes, unable to believe what she's seeing. Lily basically hasn't and won't let Jake out of her sight, constantly clambering all over him, insisting on parading all her toys out to him, then later on in the afternoon, even showing him how to bake cupcakes. This of course, involves Lily running and squealing all round the kitchen like an overexcited little puppy, managing to get just about every pot and saucepan in the whole place covered in thick, gloopy sugary-pink food dye. At one stage, I look up to see her and Jake both covered from head to foot in flour and with big pink splodges all over the pair of them. Then Lily hugs his leg, leaving flour all over his jeans, Jake scoops her up for a kiss and I look on with the stupidest, happiest, most idiotic beam plastered all over my face.

I can scarcely believe it, but for the first time in years, I'm actually happy. We eat, we laugh, we tell stories, we watch a movie, we do all the little things that make up the best parts of family life together. And it's beyond wonderful.

Much later that evening, I leave Jake and Lily sprawled out on the sofa together as Lily introduces him to the delights of 'Swek and Pwincess Fiona . . . my favouwite movie EVER!' Helen's tidying the mess that's in the kitchen and Lily is way too absorbed in explaining what the Kingdom of Far Far Away is to her new best friend to even notice me slip out the door and quietly head upstairs. I can only feel Jake's eyes burning into the back of my head as I leave, but otherwise, I'm all clear.

I head into the study and with trembling fingers switch on the computer. And there it is, waiting for me; today's online issue of the *Post*, the first one I haven't edited or had any hand in or part in years. There's a very discreet announcement on the front page, saying as simply as possible that, *'Owing to unforeseen circumstances, the* Post *will now be edited by Seth Coleman, former Managing Editor.'*

Short, succinct, to the point – and at least for that small mercy, I'm grateful.

Then, like some kind of masochist, I can't resist delving deeper. A bit like a Pot Noodle, I know this'll kill me, I know it's bad for me, but I just have to. Two seconds later, I Google my own name to see what else is being said, and am just about to start scrolling down the first page, the first of about twenty by the looks of it, when next thing there's a firm knock on the study door, making me almost jump out of my seat.

Jake, arms folded, shaking his head at me. Smiling that gorgeous half-crooked smile I love so much.

'Thought I might find you here,' he says, coming up behind me, putting his arms round me and gently massaging my neck. 'Come on then, switch it off, love. None of that matters now.'

'But I just wanted to . . .'

'No, and I'm not even listening to you,' he says firmly.

'Please, if I could just read what *The Chronicle* is running with today . . .'

'I'm turning it off. Now.'

'It would set my mind at rest to know how bad . . .'

'No, it wouldn't. I know you, it would keep you up till five in the morning pacing the floorboards with worry. Come back downstairs, Eloise. You don't need this. None of it.'

With that, he leans a long arm over me, switches off the computer and gently steers me out the door.

I give a long drawn-out sigh, then gratefully look back up at him, smiling.

Hours and hours later, when Lily's safely tucked up in bed – after Jake patiently read her a minimum of about six stories – Helen very tactfully slips out to meet a pal of hers, leaving just me and Jake alone, curled up together in front of the TV.

Wordlessly, he pulls me towards him before I've even got time to react; he's gently caressing the tip of my ear, his kisses light as air. Then he moves down, expertly kissing my lips and neck, his skin so soft and tender and now his huge, warm body is slowly stretching out on top of mine, but what's completely knocked me for six is the huge swell of desire that's sweeping over me . . . Next thing I can feel his chest hot against mine, as his hands run through my hair, neck, and then slowly, teasingly onto my breasts, opening my shirt and cupping them in his warm, rock-hard grip.

It's as though he's tantalising me like a maestro now and without wanting to, without even meaning to, I find myself responding, craving for nothing more than his lips on mine, wanting him to press me even closer to him . . .

Next thing, the gentle sound of footsteps on the back stairs, the patter of little-girl feet.

'Mama? Are you in the kitchen? Are you awake?'

In a second, Jake and I have leapt apart, and detangling ourselves like a pair of courting teenagers caught making out when they were supposed to be babysitting. I'm just hastily rebuttoning my blouse when a second later, Lily waddles into the kitchen, in her adorable little pink pyjamas, trailing her blankie behind her, hair like a bird's nest and rubbing her sleepy eyes. Then she sees that Jake is still here and instantly lights up.

'Daddy! Daddy's still here too! Yay!'

'Sweetheart,' I say, clambering up to scoop her into my arms, my whole face flushing like a forest fire. 'What are you doing out of bed? Aren't you tired?'

'No Mama, I was having dweams about all the places I want my daddy to bwing me. Happy dweams.' Next thing, she's wriggled out of my arms and is straight over to Jake, clambering up to cuddle into him.

'Where would you like me to take you, honey?' he grins at her and the heart almost stops in my chest at the sight of how astonishingly alike they are. Same hair colour, same eyes, same broad build, same everything. There is absolutely nothing of me in this child, it's quite astonishing. She's one hundred per cent Jake.

'The park, Daddy!' she tells him, snuggling up against him as he wraps his arms protectively around her. 'Tomorrow! I want you to meet my all my new fwiends. And you have to come to my birthday party too . . . There's gonna be a chocolate fountain!'

'Only if you tell me what you'd like for your birthday present first,' he tells her seriously. 'Birthday presents are very important, you know.'

She screws up her nose for a minute, thinking, then lights up.

'Okay, I know 'sactly what I want. Mama, come and sit here now!'

Smiling, I obediently do as I'm told and sit on the other side of her, while she grips my finger in one of her chubby little hands and Jake's in the other.

'This is what I want,' she beams and it strikes me that I don't think I've ever seen my little girl so happy.

'I made a wish for a pwoper family and now look! My wish came twue!'

Epilogue

Six Months Later . . .

. . . And Jake and I are still together. I know – no one can believe it, not even me. My longest relationship in . . . Well, ever. And I have to say, it's utterly and totally beyond wonderful.

Astonishingly, he and I are still in that loved-up first flush and nothing I seem to say or do is driving him mental. Well, as of yet. Mind you, I've always said that Jake is so laid-back, you could wallop the back of his head with a frying pan and still not provoke a row with him. He really, genuinely is that easy to be with, to live with, to love. The perfect guy for someone like me, in other words.

But am I for him? I'm always asking him teasingly in more playful moments and his answer is always the same. 'Eloise, I love you because of most of your qualities and in spite of some of the others.'

So like I said then, pretty much an ideal man for *anyone*, never mind me.

He adores the ground Lily walks on and she idolises him too, though like all little girls, still somehow manages to keep him securely wrapped around her little finger. Her big birthday party went ahead in spite of Mama's being jobless – not only that, but we went all out and gave her a huge party with full honours attached, including a clown and magician, a chocolate fountain, the whole shebang.

My mother surprised me by flying home from Spain for it and even asked me if she could stay on with me for a bit longer. Said she was having such a ball reconnecting with Helen and me, spoiling Lily rotten and getting to just chill out with her family, she wasn't ready to leave, not just yet. So of course I delightedly said yes, thrilled to have her back.

Funny but although I speak to her on the phone and see her fleetingly at Christmas, to my deep shame it's been years since I really spent any kind of quality time with her. I always left that to Helen and see now, not for the first time, just how much I was missing out on. Mum's mellowed a lot over the years too; far less the perma-tanned, cruise-ship blonde I so cruelly had her stereotyped as. Don't get me wrong, she's still very much a lady who lunches, immaculately groomed, gel-nailed and impeccably turned out at all times, but to see her playing dress-up with Lily and whirling her off to posh shops that I'd never dream of crossing the threshold of, then buying her the cutest outfits you ever saw, is beyond touching.

Helen and I gently asked her if she'd ever reconsider moving back to Ireland but it's still a firm no from her. Well, it's a no, but with a promise from me that my spare room is forever available to her whenever she fancies a good, long visit. And far more regularly from now on, I stress to her. Her friends and her life are all in Spain now, she tells us, but at the same time, I think she appreciates that there's always a welcome here in Dublin, whenever she wants. And each one of us hopes she'll be back a lot more regularly than just jetting in once a year for a few days at Christmas.

I think she genuinely enjoyed Lily's big birthday party too. Have to admit, it really was good to see her after so long and feeling like a daughter again. I honestly couldn't say which Mum was more shocked at; how big and bold Lily's grown or what a totally different person I am these days. She more than approves of Jake too, easy to tell. I knew the minute she told him with a sassy twinkle to drop the whole 'another cup of tea, Mrs. Elliot?' thing, and to just get her an ashtray and a large G and T in that order. And, her classic line with anyone she really does like, 'Mrs. Elliot was my mother-in-law, for Chrissakes, my name is Vera.'

Anyway, the birthday party itself was a total triumph and now, six months on, Lily is still talking about it. Basically more little girls than you'd see backstage at auditions for *Annie* descended on the house and Lily had the best afternoon of her life, Bozo the Clown scoring particularly high in the popularity stakes. But then little did the sugar-rushed three-year-olds know that Bozo was actually someone Jake knew from Wheatfield who'd just been released for good behaviour after six months, and who Jake now reckoned needed a bit of a leg up in life. So clowning became his thing, and after much pleading on Jake's behalf to stop swearing like a docker with Tourette's, now he's a full-time party clown-for-hire and from what I can see, making far more than plenty of junior reporters I knew back at the *Post*.

Ahh, the *Post*. Most astonishing news of all to come. After everything that had happened all those months ago, I took a full month off work at Jake's insistence, something I've never

377

done EVER, in spite of phone call after phone call from the T. Rexes requesting a meeting with me, 'at my earliest possible convenience, to discuss some options that have arisen.'

Initially it puzzled me, 'Options?' They've already fired me, I figured; they'd done their worst, so why the hell would they want to see me again? Then I thought . . . Maybe they're worried that I'll sue for unfair dismissal? Which I never would or could, but it was the only possible reason I could come up with as to why I was being summoned in. And I took great pleasure in not returning a single one of their phone messages. Let 'em sweat, I figured; God knows I'd sweated buckets enough for them over the years.

Instead, I spent the most fabulous time at home, doing something I'd never allowed myself to do before; being a full-time, stay-at-home mum and loving every second of it. Taking Lily to the park with Jake, or to an afternoon kids' movie or even just doing all the normal stuff, like cooking for the three of us, chatting, messing about, laughing, then vegging out in front of the TV.

Being a 'pwroper' family, as Lily loves to tell us, over and over again.

Then when I was good and ready but not a day before, I sauntered back into work to meet the board, dressed in my mummy uniform of jeans, T-shirt and flip flops. Subliminally telling the lot of them, 'Ehh, excuse me, just so you know, I had to leave my daughter at home so I could make this meeting, so you'd better keep it quick because frankly, I've better things to do.'

Before I left the house, Jake hugged me tight, his warm, solid heart in his big round eyes.

'Whatever it is they want you for, honey,' he told me, 'I know you'll do the right thing. And you know I'll stand by you whatever this is about – as long as you know what you're doing.'

'Oh don't you worry,' I smiled at him, leaning up on tip toe to kiss him. 'I know exactly what I'm doing.'

And as it turned out, I did. As soon as I stepped out of the lift onto the executive floor, Sir Gavin himself let the posse out to meet me and suddenly I was surrounded by elderly men in suits, all shaking me by the hand and heartily congratulating me on surviving 'such a trial by media'. (Sir Gavin's phrase, not mine). Anyway, I was led into the board-room and bluntly told that although I had utterly messed up by failing to cover the Courtney case to protect my own personal interests, it seems the goalposts had shifted signifi-cantly since then.

Seth Coleman, it seemed, hadn't turned out to be quite the hotshot in my old job he'd automatically presumed he would be. 'Needs a steady right hand behind him to ease him in a little more and to keep things running as efficiently as they've always done,' seemed to be the general gist of what they were all saying about him. And seeing as how the landscape had changed considerably, their key question to me was this. Would I possibly consider returning?

As Seth had now taken control of the editor's chair and was contractually obliged to stay there, basically the board are now offering me his old job as managing editor, on a considerably reduced salary, reporting directly to him. So in a nutshell, given that the managing editor is expected to put in even longer hours than the exec editor, it boiled down to this; more work for even less dosh.

'I would urge you to think long and hard about it, Eloise,' Sir Gavin pressed me. 'Because in no way can this be seen as a demotion. We're prepared to overlook the recent blot on your copybook in light of the fact that you were only protecting your family and also taking into account your sterling record to date. It's a generous offer, and we need you back.'

'It's an incredibly generous offer,' I tell him back, 'but I'm afraid it's a no.'

And it really was that easy. Didn't even have to think about it.

Well, put it this way; if I gave it a second thought, I certainly didn't need to give it a third one.

'Eloise, I would strongly recommend you to take some time out to reconsider. It's bad business to make rash decisions based on your emotions, you of all people surely are aware of that . . .'

But the truth was I didn't even need to. Image after image flashed through my mind; of poor white-haired Robbie Turner, old before his time and still at his desk bashing out stories well past midnight most nights, of Ruth from domestic politics, never, ever daring to take as much as a Sunday afternoon off work, of my long-suffering assistant Rachel almost being driven to a nervous collapse on account of the schedule she'd been expected to put in.

So as generous and all as the offer was, it wasn't just a 'no', it was a 'no, not on your life'. I'd been there, done all that, and was now ready to leave it all behind and move on.

Except this time, with my family.

I paused for a moment, looked around me and was just about to reassure them my answer was final, when out of left field, Jimmy Doorley the CFO piped up. 'Just out of curiosity,' he queried from the far end of the table, 'if it's not too personal a question, may I ask what exactly is the present nature of your relationship with Jake Keane? After all, he was at one stage a driver for Courtney with the prison record to prove it. What was it, two years for being accessory to a crime? It's purely your safety and that of your daughter I'm concerned about, you understand Eloise. Not to mention our reputation as the paper of record, should he continue to be a fixture in your life.'

I distinctly remember taking the deepest breath, eyeballing him and really taking my time to answer. Half of me appalled at the sheer rudeness of him daring to even ask me such a thing, the other half thinking, well, I am dealing with the T. Rexes now. What did I expect anyway? Respect? Sensitivity?

Yeah right, some chance. Thing is though, by then I knew exactly how to handle a comment like that with all the disdain it deserved.

'Certainly you may ask, Jimmy,' I eventually told him, as witheringly as I could. 'But it doesn't necessarily mean I'll choose to answer you. Jake Keane, as it happens, *is* my partner, and I hope will remain so for a long time to come. Yes, he once was a courier for Courtney when he shouldn't have been, and was caught and paid the price, but we're all allowed one mistake in life, aren't we? I certainly made mine.'

I neglect to mention that my one mistake was staying here for approximately six years longer than I should have done. I'm just hoping the subtlety won't be lost on them.

'It's an astonishing story, whatever way you look at it,' came another voice from the back of the table. 'Hope for your sake the tabloids don't drag it all up all over again.'

'If they do, in the words of the Duke of Wellington,' I smile as sweetly as I can, 'publish and be damned.'

Course, news of my turning them down spread like wild-fire the way the tom tom's always went into overdrive at the *Post* whenever there was hot news afoot and sure enough the next day I got a call from Rachel asking if I'd mind swinging by, 'to collect some stuff and so we can all say goodbye properly.'

So I did, and was puzzled to find the vast, cavernous, football pitch of an office totally deserted. Not a sinner. Then, just as I was about to turn on my heel and call back later, wondering why the hell the place was like the *Marie Celeste,* my mobile rang. Ruth from Domestic, screeching at me that they were all waiting for me in the conference room and to 'hurry the feck up and get my arse in there right away.'

So in I went and it was a party. An actual, proper, surprise farewell party. Just for me. With a giant cake that read, 'We'll really miss you Eloise!' banners, streamers, champagne, the whole works. They'd even clubbed together and bought me a stunning silver Tiffany charm bracelet, with a beautiful disc hanging from it engraved, *'From all your friends at the* Post. *We'll always love you.'* The gang was there in force, every single one of them, and they reduced me to tears more than once with their warm, heartfelt speeches about how much they'd miss me and telling me under pain of death that I was to stay in touch.

Out of nowhere, I had an instant memory flashback to that dreary, dismal night of my thirtieth birthday party, all those years ago, when no one bothered to turn up and I was left to celebrate my birthday utterly alone and totally friendless. And I can't help beaming at just how miracu-lously everything has turned around since that nightmarish night. Having Lily, meeting Jake . . . Who would ever have thought?

Now, every single day of my life, when I think deep and hard about it, I work out that I'm happy. Something that would have been completely inconceivable to me all that time ago. And when I try to remember the person I was back then, I find I can't.

'You're much missed, Eloise,' Marc from culture told me, sincerity shining out of him.

'Come off it Marc,' I teased him, 'may I remind you that you and I did nothing but bicker the whole time?'

'Doesn't matter. You were a boss and a friend. A boss-friend, if you like. You didn't used to be, but you are now. Well, you were until you told the board to go and shag themselves. Which subsequently made you my personal heroine. If I could only get you to change your hair a bit, that is . . .'

'Marc! I get it!' I laugh at him. 'Now, would you ever quit while you're ahead?!'

Anyway, hours and hours and waaaay too much champagne later, as I fall tipsily out the door, with Rachel on one side of me and Kian from sports supporting me on the other I notice one noticeable exception who didn't even bother coming to say goodbye. From the far corner of the room, I can just make out Seth Coleman's bony silhouette standing up against the closed blinds of my old office. Looking like some kind of ghoulish spectre at the feast.

And would I go back and trade places with him? Not on your bleeding life.

So now it's six months on, almost Christmas and so much in my life has already changed. Jake is still working at the language school, except he's been made full-time now and has effectively been supporting me and Lily with his salary, paying the mortgage, the whole works. Meanwhile, I took my own good time finding another job, sticking at all times to the one set of criteria I refused to stray from.

I will no longer work weekends.

I will not work later than five in the evening.

I will take six week's holiday every year and that's final.

Anyway, I was headhunted for several jobs at first, basically all a repeat performance of what I'd been doing at the *Post* for so long, and I turned each and every one down.

'Think about what you love to do more than anything else in the whole world,' Jake advised me late one night, when Lily was tucked up in bed and it was just him and me alone. One of my favourite times of the day, basically.

'And then see if you can get paid for it.'

And that's when it came to me; an epiphany. I thought back to how much I used to really love reporting way back in my early days and the huge kick I got out of being out on the road tracking down Jake, all those months and months ago. So I asked *The Daily Echo* if they'd be interested in hiring me as a freelance journalist and they snapped at it. Kept offering me editorial jobs higher up the food chain, senior editor in charge of this, executive editor in charge of that, all of which I've since turned down.

And for the first time in years, I'm really, genuinely loving what I do. I've lived side by side with anxiety for so long, now that it's gone, I almost don't recognise the new lightness of spirit I feel, skipping into work late mornings, or even better, working from home. Whole days go by when I completely forget to worry, then realise; I've nothing to worry about. Best of all, I can carry it off and yet still prioritise mummy-time. Because believe me, nothing on earth will ever change that ever again.

Helen, meanwhile, has still more good news to report. In a stunning development and to much silent whooping from me, she finally dumped the useless, worthless Darren and told him where to shove his B&B in Cobh. Then she reapplied for her old job in telesales and moved lock, stock and barrel back into her old flat in Sandymount. And the minute she was newly single and back in town, the lovely Ben didn't take too long to ask her out on a proper date. I'm delighted to say that they're still seeing each other, more and more seriously now it would seem. At least according to Jake, who reckons Helen is the first woman who's actually made him smile again since he lost his wife. She gets on brilliantly with his little boy Josh too, and he and Lily have become the best of buddies.

Lily now has a far more active social life than any adult I know, bar none. Since Jake came into her life, she's now acquired the one thing she wanted more than anything, but aside from a dad, she now has a shedload of cousins plus a brand new grandma too. Jake has a grand total of seven nieces and nephews and Lily adores all of them, constantly badgering me for playdates with them, anything to get to spend more time with them. And it's wonderful to see her playing with them, so happy. Surrounded by her family.

So now it's Christmas Eve and just as Jake promised us, as a special surprise present, he's whisked Lily and me off to EuroDisney in Paris for a few days' break. The child, I think will burst with the sheer happiness of actually being here, and to be perfectly honest, her mother's not all that far behind her.

As the three of us sit side by side in one of those giant cup and saucer waltzers, being swirled this way and that, screeching and laughing our heads off, loving every second of being together, I look up at Jake and there's a moment where the two of us grin broadly at each other, unable to believe our story could have ended so happily. But it has; I can scarcely believe it, but it really has.

Happiness I want to last for a delicious eternity.

And suddenly the future stretches out in front of us, like a rolling red carpet, as far as the eye can see.

Read on for an exclusive
Daily Echo feature
by Eloise Elliot

The Daily Echo

February 14th

LOVE, WHERE YOU LAST LOOK.
A Valentine's Day Special.
By Eloise Elliot.

How many times have we all been told, 'you know, the very minute you stop searching, that's precisely when the man of your dreams will find you'. Now I'd have dismissed that as a pile of total and utter horse dung, if you'd said it to me not all that long ago. But lately, let's just say from recent personal experience, I suddenly got to wondering all over again.

Could there possibly be any truth in it? Can it sometimes be the case that we invest so much time, trouble and energy into finding a life partner/soulmate, that sometimes all our good intentions have exactly the opposite effect, and send otherwise perfectly decent guys running for the hills? After all, we all know that men come with inbuilt radars for women who aren't so much looking for a boyfriend, as auditioning for a husband. Don't they?

And so, I decided to ask around a bit.

One: Laura's Story: 'You sometimes just have to bend the rules a bit to get a result'

So let me introduce you to my first interviewee, who has begged me on pain of death not to reveal her name on account of, as she put it, the holy mortifying shame of her story. So instead let's just call her Laura for now, and leave it at that.

Now Laura is a lovely, bright, successful women who tells me she's always had many wonderful things in life, fabulous blessings, all going in her favour. A job she loved and a great place to live in, for starters. She had family, great friends, disposable income; this was a woman who had it together. But, you guessed it: for years and years . . . utterly and totally manless.

And Laura had tried. God knows, this girl had seriously put herself out there. Speed dating, read dating (exactly the same thing, except you do it in Waterstones), she's even tried a new craze, 'eye-gazing dating'. Which apparently is a bit like speed dating, except you don't talk to the guy sitting opposite you, to see if there's any 'non-verbal chemistry'. (I know, I know, but apparently it's all the go in the States.) As it happened though, Laura just got a fit of giggles when some fella started to stare earnestly at her and that put paid to that. Brave soul that she is, she'd even badgered just about every pal she had to set her up on blind dates, and had gamely gone along on all of them. There she'd be, blow-dried, manicured, made-up, dressed-up, setting out with high hopes in her heart. And all with zero percent success.

'It was the ridiculous hours I worked,' she confided in me over coffee and a sticky bun. . .

I'm an investment analyst you see, and the hours nearly kill you. I've got to be at my desk from when the markets first open at the crack of dawn, right through till well after eight or nine in the evening, more often than not. So of course, by the time the weekend comes round, I'm usually just too bone-tired to even think about going out at night; all I want to do is catch up on sleep. And my pals. And it goes without saying, food.

Strange thing though; even though on paper, I ostensibly had it all – good job, a nice place to live, great buddies– the fact that I was perennially single somehow made me feel like I wasn't living my life to its full potential. I often think the feminist movement did so much for my generation, and yet if you're alone, you're still made to feel it. I sometimes imagine the ghost of Jane Austen rising from her grave, pointing a bony finger at us and saying, 'Ha! You lot thought the last two hundred years changed anything!

Anyway, flash forward to one Saturday a while ago, when I was meeting a girlfriend for brunch in this restaurant we both loved. Best eggs Benedict in town, and don't even get me going on their garlic fries. The perfect kick-start to anyone's weekend, trust me. So there we were, patiently queuing for a table, both of us starving and needing a) caffeine; b) eggs, bacon, anything; and in my case c) a very large and chocolatey dessert to follow. And we were both starving. Ravenous. So hungry, we were nearly getting ratty with each other.

Now I'm someone who normally does a lot of preventative eating before going outside the door. (And if you don't believe me, you'd want to see my handbag; whereas colleagues all take their ipads and iphones everywhere they go, I take Hobnobs and KitKats.) But as it happened, that particular morning, I'd absolutely nothing in the flat to eat, bar a few stale Cheerios and an out-of-date Innocent banana fruit smoothie.

'Ahh,' the hostess at the restaurant told us, 'bit of a seating problem, I'm afraid. We're completely full as you can see, so there'll be a bit of a wait.'

A bit of a wait? Not on your bloody life, not with me almost violent with hunger by now and ready to start gnawing at chair legs or else turning to cannibalism.

'But there's a free table for two right there!' I spluttered, pointing wildly at a cordoned-off section. 'Why can't we have that one?'

'Private party,' we were curtly told.

Now I'm not proud of what followed, but trust me, the delicious smell of fries and eggs was starting to waft our way and take it from me, I was powerless. Homer Simpson-style drool was starting to dribble out of my mouth and I knew I either had to be eating in the next few minutes, or there'd be a riot.

'Erm . . . yes,' I answered back. 'We're . . . actually with the private group. Both of us. Ok if we're seated now? Sorry that we're a bit late . . .'

My pal flashed me a 'you filthy, shameless liar' look, but as I told her later, the end more than justified the means. And so two minutes later, we're seated, we've ordered, coffee is on its way and I'm slowly starting to feel that bit more human.

Which was pretty much when we first took notice of the private party surrounding us. Now there must have been at least fifty of them, predominantly youngish, all incredibly well dressed and I distinctly remember almost all wearing black. Some chic, fashionista party, we wondered?

At midday on a Saturday though? Unlikely.

Then just as our food arrives, a guy approaches us. Friendly, warm open smile, shaking hands with us both and introducing himself as Adam.

'So how did you both know Harry, then?' he asked politely.

Harry? I thought. Who the hell was Harry?

'It's just I thought I knew most of Harry's friends and I haven't seen either of you girls before.'

Now I'm starting to get embarrassed, but my pal works in PR and is therefore that bit quicker off the mark than me.

'Do you know, I was just about to ask you exactly the same thing,' she smiled pleasantly back at him.

'Oh, I knew Harry from work,' Adam nodded. 'Although I've only been at the company for the past three years, but we'd grown close in that time. I'm going to miss him like hell.'

OK, so now an alarm bell is starting to ring in my head. He knew him? What's with the past tense? He's going to miss this Harry guy? Have we walked into an emigration party by accident, where the host has just headed off to the airport with a backpack and a one way ticket to Sydney?

'Tragic, wasn't it?' Adam went on.

Tragic? So now I'm starting to shoot my pal panicky looks across the table.

Have we just gatecrashed . . . a funeral?

Yes, was the short answer. Harry apparently had passed away in his early forties, a sudden coronary. Awful. Terrible. Just heartbreaking.

And now here we were. Trying to pass ourselves off as lifelong buddies to someone who actually knew him. And all for a plate of eggs Benedict with a side of garlic fries.

Now admittedly, yes, of course we could have 'fessed up there and then. We could have got out of there and still lived to tell the tale, but my pal is made of stronger stuff than that and decided to go down the 'sod it anyway, let's brazen it out, we've come this far,' route.

'And it's not like we'll ever see any of these people ever again, is it?' she hissed to me in the loo, a while after. So we did, and somehow, someway, got away with it. Lovely, friendly Adam seemed to buy the pair of us as childhood pals of the deceased who just hadn't seen him in years. So we chatted and we nattered and a few hours later, just as people were starting to leave, he shyly took me aside and asked for my phone number.

Well, I have to tell him, I thought. Simple as that. And the sooner, the better. Easier said than done though, because date one was just so perfect and lovely (dinner and a George Clooney movie and oh, the bliss of finding a straight guy who'd happily sit through it!)

So . . . what could I do? Ruin an otherwise gorgeous night with the first genuinely lovely guy I'd met in years?

Anyway, date one turns into dates two, three and four and still I haven't told him. Weeks pass, months pass, I'm falling for him deeper and deeper all the time, and eventually the nagging alarm in my head can be silenced no longer.

So, over a quiet plate of pasta and a bottle of wine back at his flat late one night, I eventually pluck up the guts to come clean.

'Adam? Remember the, emm . . . funeral we met at?'

'Course I do. Vividly.'

'Well, there's something about it you need to know.'

And out it all comes. How starving we were, how

394

desperate for grub, how my buddy and I would have happily wrestled old ladies to the ground, just to get a table for brunch that morning.

Then there was silence.

Awkward, bum-clenching, tense silence.

And then he suddenly threw his head back and guffawed laughing.

'I know,' he smiled. 'I've known for ages. Since that day, in fact. Before I ever spoke to you, I'd asked poor old Harry's family if they'd any idea who you were and they said no. Funny, I was wondering how long it would take for you to get around to telling me.'

Now that was three years ago and amazingly, we're still together. We got engaged last Christmas during a magical skiing holiday and are planning a September wedding later this year. It's all worked out magically.

But when people ask how we met, I just smile and change the subject.'

Lizzie's story: 'You haven't the first clue who I am, have you?'

'Men? Don't get me started,' Lizzie all but snorts down the phone, as I gently start to coax her tale out of her.

Because I had just about reached break point. Believe me, I'd had enough. I mean, come one, there are only so many bad dates one girl can go on, aren't there?

'Back in the day, I was a great one for internet dating; you know, all those sites like Match.com that faithfully promise you that five out of every ten couples that met via the site are now happily together, years later. And, like the moron that I am, I believed the hype.

Well, this is the way forward for me, I figured. I was between jobs and broke at the time, so I though this would be a fantastic way to socialise and meet like-minded guys, all without having to leave the comfort of my own cosy sofa. Plus, at least this way, I can interact with men sitting in front of my computer screen in comfy fleece pyjamas, with no make-up on and three-day old manky hair. Perfect!

But was I in for a right land, or what? Firstly, the lies people tell online, oh dear God, the outrageous, blatant whoppers. You couldn't make some of it up, but here's a rough guideline. For starters, if a guy describes himself in his profile as 'cuddly', it actually means 'obese.' Similarly, 'enjoys a drink', means 'would basically suck the alcohol out of a deodorant bottle'. And, as I found out the hard way, 'enjoys the company of women', means, 'ha! I'm actually going out with five other girls at the same time as you'.

And don't get me started on the sheer number of openly married men all trawling dating sites just looking for a bit of fun with no commitment or intention of every being anything other than married. No kidding, I even found one who told me that, and I quote, "I'm not free to meet at weekends, because my wife would find out." But weekdays between nine and five, when the wife was off at work, were OK by him. He'd even used his wedding picture as his profile shot . . . with his new bride conveniently cut out of it.

Needless to say, after a few months of this malarkey, I threw in the towel. Total waste of time and effort, I decided. So I started going out a bit more with friends, but none of us ever seemed to meet anyone interesting, date-wise. They were all either married, in long-term steady relationships or else gay. Demoralising, to say the least. I was well into my mid-thirties. Had I left it too late to find a significant other, and now had all the good ones been snapped up?

And that's when it happened. I was at the movies one night with a gang of friends, and we were all having a drink at the bar afterwards. It was mad busy, the usual packed Saturday night, and next thing I knew, some random guy bumped into me, as I was on the way up to the bar to get in another round.

'Sorry,' he apologised, then looked at me a bit more closely. 'Oh, hi! It's you!'

I looked up hopefully, but no, it was no one I recognised. A tall, gangly looking guy, with long reddish hair all the way down to his bum, hippie-era-circa-Woodstock style. Who the hell was this?

'You haven't the first clue who I am, have you?' he smiled down at me, and it was only then I began to see something vaguely familiar about him . . . but from where? My old job? No. The gym? Definitely not, sure I hadn't shown my face in there in months.

'Nice to see you with your clothes on for a change.'

Course by then, I was in a complete flop-sweat. Please for the love to God, don't let this be someone I had a fling with years ago, and I was too drunk at the time to even remember?

'Emm,' I gulped, 'I'm really sorry about this, but where exactly did we meet?'

'Give you a clue,' he teased, blue eyes dancing. 'I see you every weekend, at about the same time every morning, except more often than not you're wearing pyjamas under a raincoat. Oh, and you sort of pretend to drink low-fat milk; at least, you take it down from the shelves and have a good stare at it, but then you always seem to replace it with a full-fat carton. You've a big thing about chocolate croissants, which in a weird way I kind of admire. I mean any woman who eats chocolate for breakfast must be OK, I figure. Oh and although you buy *The Independent* every week, you spend a helluva lot of time flicking through *Hello!* And *OK!* which by the way, you never actually buy.'

He was having a great laugh at this, and then suddenly it came to me.

Petrol station guy. From my local Texaco garage. The same one I saw behind the till there every single weekend, when I'd stagger in there bleary-eyed and looking like a complete mong-head in my PJs with a coat flung over them, no make-up and still stinking of whatever I was drinking the previous night.

So I apologised profusely for not recognising him, but he gamely brushed it aside, then asked if he could buy me a drink. So we chatted and talked and it was amazing how much we had in common. A lifelong love of movies for starters. Turns out his name was Greg and he was putting himself through film school, so working at the garage helped pay his tuition fees.

Anyway, the following weekend you can bet I went into that Texaco garage fully prepared to stock up on my Saturday papers; no pyjamas for starters, decently dressed from head to toe and looking, for once, semi-presentable. And as Greg and I got to chatting again, he casually mentioned he had tickets that night for a movie screening and asked me if I'd like to go.

That was over a year ago, and neither of us have ever looked back. So I suppose the moral of my story is, don't just look to the left and right . . . look everywhere. There are thousands of great, single guys out there, and they're not necessarily trawling websites telling massive lies about themselves and doctoring their profile pictures. They're in coffee shops and standing at bus stops and sitting beside you on trains.

Just trust me. They're out there.'

Becky's story: 'Always the Bridesmaid . . .'

'So Dave, my BGF (best gay friend) was finally getting married to his long-term partner and he'd asked me to be the bridesmaid, or 'best woman' as he insisted on calling me. Now at the time, civil partnership was a whole new thing, and I hadn't the first clue what to expect from the day. Would it be all stiff and formal like a regular wedding? Because frankly, I wasn't sure my stress ulcers could take it. You see, my younger sister had got married the previous summer and I'm not joking, my mum and Auntie Sheila still weren't back on speaking terms after the blazing howler of a row they'd had over whether the bridal bouquet had exactly matched the toilet roll in the hotel bathroom. Or something of an equally similar magnitude, but then as we all know, the first casualty in any wedding is all sense of proportion.

'I'm delighted to be best woman,' I'd told Dave, proud groom-to-be, 'but please promise me three things. No stress, no rows and above all, you're not putting me in a stupid-looking pastel outfit that makes me look like a thirty-two-year-old trying to pass herself off as Bo-Peep. At my sister's wedding, I'm not joking, you could have easily fitted three midgets under my dress.'

Dave had just laughed away all my stressing and fretting. Relax, he told me. Because gay weddings were all about style over substance and totally OTT glitter balls on the dance floor and prancing down the aisle to Liza Minnelli. And therefore the total opposite of straight ones, he swore blind.

But of course, the big downside; there'd be next to no straight guys there for harmless flirtations with. I could get that right out of my head from the get-go. So, not such great news, if you happened to be a single gal hoping to get lucky on the night. (Although now that I think of it, that wasn't strictly true; there were one or two only straight men there aside from each groom's dad. Trouble was they all happened to be elderly uncles and pals of the parents, all without exception in the sixty-plus age category and all grandparents by now. But there you go. That's a single girl's lot, isn't it?)

And so, in the full knowledge that the whole day would be a manhunt-free zone, I gamely pitched up at Dave's house on the morning of the wedding, bottle of champagne tucked under my arm, in a simple black dress that at least I felt comfy in. Who'll be looking at me, anyway? I asked myself. Gay men spend their time eying up other gay men and refer to their women buddies as 'beards'. Known fact.

So of course, by the time I get to Dave's house for the pre-wedding boozy brekkie, it's like the party was already in full swing. His family were all buzzing round getting hair and make-up done while Dave posed for one photo after another, wearing a tiara and veil from the Pound Shop, in between him wolfing down mouthfuls of champagne and yelling at the top of his voice, 'Look at meeeeee, everyone! I'm a BRIDE!'

'You never told me you were getting a proper make-up artist,' I'd laughed at him. 'Oh yeah, that's Brien, I found him through a friend of a friend. Though it would be fun for the girlies. Go on, get him to lash a decent bit of war paint on you! At gay weddings, the best woman is absolutely allowed to look more fabulous than either of the grooms!'

So I sauntered over to this guy at the kitchen table, where he'd just about every Mac product known to man laid out neatly beside him, like a surgeon about to perform an operation. Turns out Brien was a complete dote too, tall and tanned with tight, gelled hair and a gym-toned body, but then as we all know, gay men go to the gym with the same level of devotion as religious people who do Mass every day. And he very kindly did a fantastic make-up job on me, really and truly transforming my usual pasty-face into someone glowing that I barely recognised in the mirror. I'd had professional make-up jobs done before, but somehow my face always ended up looking like a half-dissolved Rubex tablet, with the ridiculous amounts of bronzer and blusher they'd lash on. But this was really amazing work; Brien had somehow made me look like the best possible version of myself, the one that managed to get eight hours sleep a night and occasionally remembered to use night cream.

And all the time, he and I were giggling and messing and all I could do was look at him and think, why oh why are all the good ones gay? I always found any of Dave's buddies miles easier to chat to than any of the straight guys I knew; for starters, you were completely relaxed and at ease with them. You knew from the off that sexual chemistry was right out the window, so you could just totally be yourself around them.

So Brien joined us all for the big day and I have to say, it was by the mile the best wedding I'd ever been to in my life, bar none. Kind of like a straight wedding, but with all the boring, crappy bits cut out. For starters, both grooms came down the aisle together to Nat King Cole's 'Let's Face the Music and Dance' . . . none of your boring old wedding march here! Then another pal of Dave's got up to do a reading. Solemn-voiced and sombre, he began, 'A reading from the book of Beyoncé.' There were weird looks all around but then of course, two seconds later, we're all clapping and laughing and singing along too; amazing. The whole ceremony bit was all over in around ten minutes – which, by the way, is the perfect length for any wedding service – and before we knew it, Dave was married to the love of his life and dancing back down the aisle again to, what else? Abba's 'Dancing Queen', of course. You had to ask?

Anyway, at the knees-up afterwards, lovely Brien kept on asking me to dance time and again. We had an absolute ball and really got on like a house on fire so when he asked for my phone number at the end of the party, I was delighted.

My flatmate that bit less so, when I told her. 'You already have so many gay men friends in your life,' she warned me, 'do you really need another one? They're only filling up your time and preventing you from meeting someone straight. Someone that you might actually have a shot at a relationship with.'

Now OK, admittedly the girl did have a point. I seemed to spend far more time around gay men than straight ones, and I certainly spent way more time talking about their relationships than I ever did talking about my own. Or rather my own lack of them. In fact there was next to nothing I couldn't have told you about gay-land.

Somehow though, I couldn't bring myself to take my flatmate's advice; Brien was just way much fun to be around. Plus every time we went out, he gave me the most fabulous goodie bag samples from Mac and Clinique, not to mention stunning nail polishes from Chanel . . . Come on, what girl in her right mind wouldn't love having a new pal who came bearing freebie make-up samples? He and I became really close in a short space of time and pretty soon, we were inseparable. Then one night, after a plate of pasta at his flat when he'd asked me round to watch Strictly Come Dancing and slag off the judges, he tried to kiss me.

Well I nearly leapt off the sofa with the sheer shock of it. 'Brien?' I spluttered at him, 'may I remind you that you're a gay man!'

'What?' he looked at me, stunned.

'Well . . . I mean, you are, aren't you?'

And it turned out, like so much else in my life, that I'd got it completely arseways. He was straight! Really genuinely straight! Proper boyfriend material! Course he was well used to people thinking he wasn't, the whole make-up artist thing for starters, and as I told him afterwards, the sheer amount of time he spent in the gym alone would make any women seriously think twice about his orientation. But once I'd got over the shock of it, I started thinking . . . you know, this is really lovely. The two of us got on brilliantly and chances are, if I'd suspected he was straight right from the get-go, I'd have been all tongue-tied and on edge with him, almost with an invisible sign over my head saying, 'like me! Please like me, I want a boyfriend!'

Because of course, that was my whole trouble, wasn't it? The very minute I knew a guy was available, I started acting like a compete desperado in front of him. Wow,

403

what a turn-on. Was it any wonder I was well into my thirties and alone?

All that was about two years ago and I'm delighted to tell you that Brien and I are now happily and very compatibly living together. Funny though; to this day, when I tell people what he does for a living, I can practically see them doing a double take and wondering, does this one realise her boyfriend is gay? Just look at the biceps on him for starters!

Just as prejudiced as I was. But whenever it does happen, I'll just laugh it off and say yes, I know what you're thinking, because that's what I first thought too. But guess what? I was well wrong and so are you.'

I suppose the moral of my tale is this; don't judge anything by its cover . . . you might just be very surprised.'

So there you have it, girlfriends everywhere.

You might well think that Valentine's Day is complete rubbish and I wouldn't necessarily disagree with you there. 'A Hallmark holiday,' my mother dismissively sniffs, claiming that back in her day, it just didn't exist. Then of course, some bright spark sitting in a skyscraper on Madison Avenue, who I'd say scores of women would now want to disembowel if they ever met him, decreed that the gap between Christmas and Easter was just too long, and card companies needed something in between to keep their quarterly revenues looking rosy. And now here the rest of us all are, stuck with it, whether we like it or not.

Single people despise it, and with good reason; I mean, come on, who actually enjoys going to the newsagents only to have to battle your way through gakky heart shaped helium balloons and piles stacked high of garish pink and red overpriced chocolates? And you wonder; are these just 'grab something at the last minute to keep herself happy', type impulse buys for fellas, who know they'll be murdered for daring to come home on the big day empty-handed?

Nor is it a barrel of laughs for couples either. The pressure of trying to be romantic, just because the card companies and newsagents decree it. And you just try getting a last-minute restaurant reservation on the big night, so you can pay hyper-inflated prices just to sit there looking at other stressed-out-looking couples all doing exactly the same thing.

But all I'm saying, is let's try to get beyond this and see the bigger picture. Believe me I know from long and bitter experience all about being alone.

But I also know that romance is out there, and for all of us. After all, if I can meet someone, I know anyone can.

So if you're reading this and you're single, please let me leave you with this one final message.

Do not, I repeat, do NOT despair. Because trust me, he is out there. Somewhere.

And he's just waiting for you . . .

Happy Valentine's Day, keep the faith and much love,
From,
Eloise Elliot
xxxxxxx

Personally I Blame My Fairy Godmother

Where's a magic wand when you need one . . .

Jessie Woods absolutely believes in fairytale endings. So would you if you had a high flying career as a daredevil TV host, a palatial pink mansion, and the dream boyfriend.

But, quicker than you can say 'Cinderella', her life falls to pieces and suddenly her prince isn't quite so charming, her party-loving friends disappear and even her faithful friend Visa no longer loves her . . .

Utterly heartbroken and jobless, Jessie is forced back home, to live with her stepmum and two evil stepsisters.

Is it time for her to give up on the dream – or will Jessie learn that happy endings can come in the strangest of places?

Claudia Carroll presents a tale of princes who turn out to be frogs, Manolo Blahnik glass slippers and not-so-happily-ever-afters . . .

'It bubbles and sparkles like pink champagne.' Patricia Scanlan

ISBN: 978-1-84756-208-1
£6.99

A V O N

Will You Still Love Me Tomorrow?

What happens when two people decide to give themselves the year off...from each other?

Annie and Dan were the perfect couple. But now the not-so-newly weds feel more like flatmates than soul mates and wonder where all the fun and fireworks went . . .

When Annie lands her big break in a smash-hit show that's heading for Broadway, she's over the moon. Goodbye remote Irish village, hello fabulous Big Apple! But with their relationship already on the rocks, how will Annie and Dan survive the distance?

They're hitting the pause button on their marriage. One year off from each other – no strings attached, except a date to meet in twelve months at the Rockefeller Centre to decide their fate.

Will they both turn up? Or is it too late for love?

Lose yourself in a fabulously entertaining and poignant love story – perfect for fans of Sophie Kinsella and Marian Keyes.

'Hilarious, effervescent, heart-warming.' *Irish Independent*

ISBN: 978-1-84756-210-4
£6.99

A V O N